Blood on the Trailhead
A Lost Grove Mystery

Charlotte Zang and Alex Knudsen

Copyright © 2025 Charlotte Zang & Alex Knudsen

Printed in the United States of America
First Printing, 2025

ISBN 979-8-9897962-6-7 (paperback)
ISBN 979-8-9897962-5-0 (e-book)

Praise for *Blood on the Trailhead*

"This grim series maintains a compelling undertone and evocative world-building, weaving through the indigenous lore of the Wiyot, which adds carefully drawn authenticity to the story and grounds the supernatural elements in established traditions and belief...an original supernatural thriller, which skillfully crosses the genres of small-town procedural, mystery, and horror."
— *Self Publishing Review*

"A central theme involves the culture and heritage of indigenous peoples existing in today's world. These topics are handled with respect and care, adding layers of emotional depth to a story that is already rich in atmosphere, character nuance, and moral complexity."
— *Indies Today* (five stars)

"When the horror hits, it lands hard, not with cheap shocks but with creeping inevitability. I found myself both enchanted and unsettled by how human the story felt, even when it slipped into the supernatural. The grief, guilt, and obsession in these characters are raw. What really struck me was how the story handles belief, scientific, spiritual, and everything in between. It doesn't force explanations. It lets mystery exist, and that takes confidence."
— *Literary Titan* (five stars)

"The feeling of a small town, connected deeply, but plagued by the very land it's built on is incredibly powerful, and at no point does the story lose any of its intensity. It's a world that is deeply familiar with enough dark corners that you never quite feel safe."
— *Independent Book Review*

"The authors handle Indigenous history with care, grounding the story's supernatural elements in cultural authenticity rather than sensationalism. Terrifying and profound in equal measure, this gripping exploration of what happens when history refuses to stay buried makes for a riveting read."
— *The Prairies Book Review*

"Alex Knudsen and Charlotte Zang masterfully blend science, the supernatural, and the rhythms of everyday life in a way that feels entirely natural. It is a remarkable read, thrilling, engaging, and completely enjoyable."

— *Alma Boucher, Reader's Favorite* (five stars)

"This is a stunning addition to the series, building on the character and world-building from the first two books."

— *Anne-Marie Reynolds, Reader's Favorite* (five stars)

Praise for *Lost Grove: Part One*

"Thriller, mystery, and gothic horror combine in Charlotte Zang and Alex Knudsen's LOST GROVE: Part One. It is a page-turning novel about a missing-person investigation in a small coastal town that offers depth, surprise, eeriness, and great characters."

— *IndieReader*

"A dark dream for fans of contemporary horror...the sinister storyline laced with vicious cults, mental illness, amateur sleuthing, and divine forces makes for a multilayered and gripping read that will satisfy readers of both psychological thrillers and horror fiction."

— *Self Publishing Review* (four stars)

"Lost Grove is what would have happened if the TV show Twin Peaks (1990) had taken a more supernatural path...Because of the unraveling threads, this book can get addictive quickly. The city's lore will grip any reader's attention, and there is so much alluring strangeness going on...A paranormal mystery well worth reading, Lost Grove (Part 1) will have you questioning constantly why this creepy town is the way it is."

— *Independent Book Review*

"It is a testament to the authors' ability to craft a story that is as haunting as it is enthralling. This book is highly recommended for readers seeking a narrative that seamlessly blends mystery, thriller, and horror with a dash of the supernatural, creating a unique and memorable experience."

— *Literary Titan*

Praise for *The Orbriallis Institute*

"As in the first novel, the authors are skilled at blending horror, fantasy, science-fiction and crime story elements, ensuring the unsettling atmosphere developed in the previous book permeates this narrative throughout....The novel's pace builds to a revelatory and satisfying climax...this is a thoroughly entertaining novel. Fans of Part One will find plenty to enthrall them here."

— *Blue Ink Review*

"With fictional foundations in supernatural suspense and sci-fi horror, the novel's carefully crafted premise makes it easy to get hooked. The themes floating beneath the narrative are also timely and thought-provoking – ethical responsibilities within scientific research, privacy, and parental authority, alternative treatments for mental illness, and irrational reactions to things deemed either strange or unknown."

— *Self Publishing Review*

"Part One of the Lost Grove series merely tantalized with its mystical elements and unsolved crime, but this ethereal second act fully embraces all things supernatural. Thrills and chills swirl into a freaky collage of depravity and camaraderie in the nail-biting mystery, The Orbriallis Institute. "

— *Indies Today* (five stars)

"The authors manage to maintain the intense tension and eerie atmosphere created in the first book...There's much to enjoy about this conclusion. What a memorable plot and cast they're leaving behind! I know I won't be alone in thinking about this series months from now, daydreaming about the shady city and which mysteries were left behind beyond the established lore."

— *Independent Book Review*

Also by Charlotte Zang

See all of Charlotte's books and where to get them on her website at:
https://www.charlottezang.com/

Lost Grove
Part One

Blooding

Consuming Beauty

Lysander O'Connor
Satan's in Your Kitchen

Also by Alex J. Knudsen

See all of Alex's books and where to get them on his website at
https://www.alexjknudsen.com

Lost Grove
Part One

The Nawie

This book is dedicated to my mother, always my greatest champion in my ongoing creative efforts dating back to making short films in junior high. You will be missed every minute of every day.

Author's Note

This book is a work of fiction. While the story and characters are products of our imagination, we recognize and honor the real people whose lands provide the setting for much of this series.

The Wiyot Tribe are the original people of the Humboldt Bay region in Northern California. Too often, the history of the Wiyot is told only through tragedy, but it is vital to understand that the Wiyot people are not just part of history; they are alive, thriving, and continuing their cultural traditions today.

We encourage readers to learn more about the Wiyot Tribe by visiting their official website: www.wiyot.us.

Any errors or fictionalization are our own, and we extend deep respect to the Wiyot community for their ongoing presence, resilience, and contributions.

Prologue

The bell above the door jingled with a sharpness that cut through the hazy hush of morning. Hannah Albrecht blinked as she stepped inside Grouse Ridge Market, the last stop for hikers and park visitors heading out to the nearby trailheads for their day hikes. The place still smelled like old wood and brewed coffee, sugar-glazed muffins behind the case, and hand lotion from the basket of travel-size toiletries by the door. Morning light fanned through the front windows, pale and low and angled just right to catch the dust hanging in the air.

Her boots scuffed over the checkerboard tile, still damp from a mop. She barely glanced up from her notes as she headed to the coffee station. Her pen scratched out a rough glyph shape along the page's margin, one she'd first seen described in an eighteenth-century text with a third-hand account of Captain William Fellmore's failed rescue in what later became known as Devil's Cradle State Park. She still hadn't found the glyph he described, but she had confirmed that he had been here and he'd had a Yakama guide with him too.

Hannah blinked, dragging herself from the thought, just as a familiar voice said, "You on autopilot this early?"

Her eyes flicked up.

Cal Hensley stood at the coffee station, one hand on the creamer, his body half turned toward her with a smile on his lips, tugging at the corners of his eyes. His forest-green uniform looked somehow too crisp for someone who'd already hiked miles this morning. His braid hung neatly down his back, a few strands of wind-blown hair tucked behind his ears. "Morning, Professor," he said in a formal greeting.

Hannah grinned, tucking her braid behind one shoulder. She shut her book, slipping it under her arm. "Morning, Officer Hensley." She nudged her way beside him and reached for a biodegradable cup.

Cal stirred in the drop of creamer he'd added. "Are you heading out along North Grouse Bend still?" he asked, knowing that had been her most recent area of study.

"For a minute, I thought I might," she replied, pouring her coffee. "The glyph patterns and pictographs out there have been incredibly well preserved—especially along the southern rock face near the streambeds. There's some overlap in the layering of symbols, like the land's been revisited and marked repeatedly over time, and that's rare. Especially for petroglyphs this far north."

She added a small packet of raw sugar, stirring as she went. "But after cross-referencing some of the motifs with older Wiyot oral histories, I think I've been circling around the real site instead of standing on it. The orientation's all wrong for what I'm seeing. There's too much runoff, and some of the symbols feel out of sequence."

Cal tilted his head, listening closely, the way he always did when she talked glyphs and soil layers and symbology.

"So," she continued, "after going over it all with Paddy, I'm switching gears."

Cal sipped his coffee, eyeing her sidelong. "Switching to where?"

"Well," she said, warming to her explanation, "Paddy mentioned two possible spots. One's southeast, but I'm not convinced it's the right context. Then he mentioned a lesser-used trail farther north. He thinks there's a shelf of stone out there with etchings people don't usually spot—mostly because it's hard to access without knowing the old ranger roads."

Cal raised an eyebrow. "Paddy said that?"

She nodded. "Apparently he used to clear the trail years ago. Said it's not on most maps now. Overgrown. But he described it like it might be exactly what I've been looking for—glyphs at elevation, with exposure to both sun and fog line."

"Which trail?"

Hannah smiled, lifting her coffee in mock toast. "That's the best part. He called it 'Where the asphalt gives up.' You know the one?"

Cal exhaled slowly, his lips pressing into a line. "Yeah. I know it. The

Old Timber Spur."

"That's the one," she said, smiling.

"You're going alone?"

"Cal." She turned toward him fully, coffee cradled in her hands. "I've got my GPS, my radio, my topo maps, two flares, and bear spray. I promise not to chase any floating will-o'-the-wisps."

He didn't smile. "Just...be cautious, alright? That trailhead hasn't been maintained in a while. You lose signal quickly out there."

"I appreciate the concern," she said, and meant it. "But it's exactly the kind of place I'm supposed to be looking for. That's what makes this so exciting."

"Uh-huh," he replied, with a small upward tilt at the edges of his lips. He looked at her a moment too long. "You find anything lately that makes all this worth it?"

"Actually, I think I'm close to something...big. I don't want to jinx it. But yeah. Career-big." She'd begun to suspect the glyphs were part of a larger, organized system of an ancient Wiyot language of symbols lost to time that denoted boundaries leading back to a massive settlement or even an important ceremonial site.

Her hypothesis was simple but bold: If she followed the glyphs inward, tracing the way they seemed to cluster and align across certain old growth corridors, they would eventually lead her to the heart of it, the place all the markings had been protecting. She hesitated, then added with a breathless sort of bravery: "Tenure-big."

Cal chuckled and nodded, glancing down at her cup. "Then I won't keep you." He hesitated, then shifted his weight and gave her a crooked, uncertain smile. "Hey—listen—I was wondering if...maybe you'd want to have dinner tonight? Not one of those question-heavy family meals. Just you and me."

She blinked, surprised not by the offer but by the nervousness behind it. This wasn't the same Cal who'd offered stories from his uncles and parents over pot roast at the family house. This was different. There was weight behind the ask.

Her smile spread slowly, almost shy. "Yeah. I'd like that."

Relief flickered across his face, softened by something quieter, warmer. "Good. Then it's a date. You can finish telling me how you traced all this from a crusty old journal some aristocrat's nephew wrote about a retired soldier's ghost stories."

Hannah smiled. "It wasn't a ghost story. Fellmore may have been many things, but the way he described those glyphs... He remembered them. Carried them. That kind of memory means something."

Cal's expression softened, the usual glint of humor in his eyes dimmed to kind admiration for her drive. He looked down at his coffee, then back at her. "Still...it's a hell of a thing to follow a dead man's nightmares into the woods," he said, stepping back, thermos in hand. "Just promise me you'll radio me if you get lost or twist an ankle or something."

She laughed, brushing past him as she turned toward the register. "Deal."

He paused at the door, looking back once, long enough that she felt it in her spine. "Be safe, Hannah."

"I always am."

He didn't argue, but the subtle lift of his eyebrow told her he didn't quite believe that. He gave her a wink and turned for the door, leaving her grinning, clutching her cup, still warm from his nearness.

Outside, the sun filtered through the last threads of marine fog, the early chill already giving way to the burnished gold of late morning. Hannah drove with one hand lightly on the wheel, the other nursing a thermos nestled in the center console. Her journal lay open on the passenger seat, scrawled with notes and margin stars, breadcrumbs leading her deeper into the mystery. One of those stars marked a passage she'd reread a dozen times: Fellmore's account of the spiraled symbol. He'd described it with the kind of clarity reserved for fever dreams and deathbed confessions. She hadn't been able to forget it either.

The road narrowed as she left the main highway, the pavement pocked and splintered with age. Cracks spidered beneath her tires, filled with lichen and windblown pine needles. Then, true to Paddy's warning, the asphalt gave up entirely. Her tires rolled onto gravel, then packed dirt, the car dipping and rattling with each rise and rut of the old access path. Tree limbs reached low like arching ribs over a spine of road. She slowed to a crawl.

At last, a weathered wooden placard, half covered in moss, leaning slightly to one side told her she'd arrived at the Old Timber Spur. She eased into the narrow pullout beside it and parked. The trailhead was barely visible from the lot, swallowed in ferns and goldenrod.

She cut the engine, and silence reclaimed the woods. Hannah

stepped onto the narrow trail, her boots crunching softly against a carpet of needles and moss. The first stretch wound through coastal scrub and elder ferns, overgrown and unkempt, as though no one had walked this way in months. Morning sunlight slanted through the branches, but already the redwoods conspired to block the day. Shafts of gold cut between shadows like the last threads of a dream unraveling.

She walked slowly, carefully, her fingers trailing the rough bark of a cedar. In her pack, along with her water, sample vials, and a weatherproof notebook, nestled a tiny blacklight wand and a small UV-capable camera. Most wouldn't need such tools for ancient rock art. But then again, most petroglyphs didn't glow.

She wasn't looking for simple ochre patterns anymore. Not since the glyphs began showing up—etched too deep, too clean, too wrong to be naturally aged. She'd found them weeks ago, carved high into trees or notched into shale walls with a kind of intention that unsettled her. What struck her wasn't their design, but their placement. Their arrangement too precise to not have meaning.

Or what she thought might be meaning. *Protection. Warning. Sanctuary. Prey.*

She'd tracked them across ridges and gulches, drawn a rough map in her journal, and when she'd overlaid it on the topography of the park, a strange pattern had begun to emerge: a kind of radius. Like a perimeter drawn in sigils. She suspected she'd find something at the center.

She ducked beneath a fallen limb, brushing wet leaves from her braid. Farther in, the trail narrowed and darkened. Where the redwoods thickened, the air grew wet and close, full of the clean rot of living things dying. Hannah pulled out her camera and scanned the trunks one by one, finally spotting a faint curve, almost hidden by creeping moss. She cleared it gently with her sleeve.

The glyph was deep. Fresher than it should have been. Fungal threads, pearlescent and faintly green, ran through the groove like veins. She stepped back and flicked on the blacklight.

The symbol flared cool blue, like moonlit lichen. She took a photograph, crouched, and traced her finger carefully along the outline. A small spore puffed loose, caught the light, and drifted upward like dust in a cathedral.

Hannah rubbed her temple. A dull ache pulsed behind her eyes. She made a note.

North bend trail—Old Timber Spur vicinity. Third glyph. Pattern resembles earlier "protective" sigil, but with added curvature at base. Similar fungal bloom as others. Possible spore release response to proximity/light? Need to ask Dr. Raines.

She packed the camera and pressed on.

The hours slid past her, as time often did in the woods. Sunlight dimmed and changed angles, the gold giving way to the steely hush of approaching dusk. A fog bank moved inland again, low and ethereal between the trunks.

If her theory was correct, there would be one more glyph before the center. She could feel the closeness of her discovery. It made her heart thud against her rib cage. She had been right. They were leading her somewhere. And there it was, cut into the base of an outcropping, partially shielded by a fallen log. The pattern was more elaborate than the rest: spirals nested into spoked curves, like a sun collapsing into a whirlpool. The fungus here was heavy. It almost pulsed in the low light.

She crouched low and followed its curve with her eyes. This one was different. The lines were deeper and wider, etched with a hand that pressed harder. She reached into her pack for her flashlight and angled the beam just right. The glyph spread out across the shale like an unfolding sentence. Concentric spirals nested in a triangular cradle, fine offshoots like tree roots branching beneath.

It was similar to the other symbols she'd catalogued as "Sanctuary," but this one felt...more. More complete. More articulate. There was harmony in its proportions, a precision that made her breath catch.

"This is it," she said aloud, pulling her pack off and grabbing her camera. This had to be the glyph Fellmore had described in the old text—a winding knot of angles and curls that bent back on itself like a noose. He'd said it never stopped spinning in his mind.

She scribbled a note in the margin of her notebook:

Sanctuary-class glyph (Spiral Type IV). Exceptionally complex. May indicate higher-tier site. Possible marker of central node or ceremonial origin. Matches Fellmore's. May confirm hypothesis: glyphs forming perimeter around a lost ceremonial site or settlement center.

Her fingers lingered on the spiral. A whispering hum filled her ears. It prickled beneath her skin, like the air had shifted behind her eyes. She looked up and the woods changed.

It wasn't dramatic. The forest didn't bend or twist. But it tilted, subtly. Perspective collapsed into itself. The brush ahead parted in a way she couldn't remember seeing before. A subtle rearrangement, like nature had exhaled and opened something hidden. The hillside dipped differently now. The rocks were more exposed. Beyond the brush, thinner and framed between two leaning redwoods slick with dew, was a cave.

Except it wasn't just a cave. It reached toward her. The shadows inside pulsed with a waiting stillness. It felt less like she'd stumbled across it, and more like it had been presented to her. Like the forest, in some conscious, half-sleeping way, had said *'Finally.'*

Her feet moved on instinct. Scattered just before the entrance, she saw the impressions of fire. Charred marks in a ring, centuries-old soot melted into stone. Beyond that, blackened bones in the dirt. Elk, perhaps, or deer, scavenged by time.

She blinked, and for a heartbeat, the forest changed again. She saw it as it was. Not decayed or grown over, but alive.

Tents—no, woven huts—stood among the trees. Smoke coiled into the sky from a central firepit. Bundled herbs dried on lines of sinew. Women with painted faces stirred heavy pots. Men sharpened spears. Children watched her with solemn eyes from under painted brows, and beyond them all, the mouth of the cave. A hollow mouth in the stone. Painted, carved, alive with marks that shimmered like breath.

The moment snapped like a dry twig. The vision was gone. The silence returned, heavy and warm and wet. She was alone again, standing on the edge of discovery.

Her breath hitched as she pulled out her notebook.

Ritual site confirmed? Glyph proximity + vision/fugue-like episode suggests possibility of ongoing resonance. Markings around cave and fire pit ring appear original. Preservation level = extraordinary. Confirm material later. Don't forget to thank Paddy. This might be it.

She clicked her pen shut, then ducked into the cave.

The smell changed. No longer pine needles and moss, but a blend of damp stone and turned soil. Her boots scuffed against the cave floor, the walls crowding tighter around her shoulders, the light from the entrance dimming behind her until it barely touched the edges of her shadow. She didn't notice. Her eyes had already locked onto the mural.

It sprawled across the interior curve of the rock, impossibly vast for a cave so modest in scale. Lines of ochre, coal-black, and faded crimson curled and sprawled in a style that didn't belong to any tradition she knew.

At the center stood a massive tree, stylized but unmistakable—its roots snaked deep into the earth, too deep, deeper than gravity should allow. The branches lifted skyward, gnarled and tangled, where a blackened sun—eclipsed or dying—hung low in a bruised, painted sky.

Around the tree, the human figures writhed. Some bowed in reverence. Others seemed to be collapsing or crawling. Their arms reached upward or away, stylized agony captured in minimal brushstrokes. At the mural's base, dark ripple patterns surged from the earth, pulling the tiny humans under, swallowing them whole in waves of black.

Hannah's breath caught. Her eyes stung. This was it. This was *beyond* it.

It was older than she'd thought. More than a ceremonial site. This was a glyphic language so complete it nearly sang. She stepped closer. Deeper into the hollow, deeper into the dark.

She angled her flashlight to the far wall where older, more weather-worn paintings waited. Spirals that twisted like whirlpools. Stick figures with arms thrown wide in some silent scream. Geometric sigils that bent the eye if she stared too long. Angles that didn't make sense, that shouldn't have been able to close into shape.

"This is impossible," she whispered.

She took another step forward. The light from her flashlight stuttered in her hand. She felt pulled the same way a tide claims a swimmer too far from shore. Not fast, just inevitable. As if the cave wasn't a space she was entering but a mouth that had already begun to close behind her. The temperature dropped. She registered it as a factual note: colder in the interior. She should put on her fleece soon. Instead, she wiped condensation from her notebook and moved deeper.

More glyphs were etched into the curve of the inner wall half buried in dust and vine. The fungus bloomed here in fine threads. Filaments so delicate they looked like spider silk, glowing a faint sea-glass green. They pulsed gently as she passed, like veins responding to her presence.

She didn't notice that, either. She scribbled something in the margin. A loose translation of a new glyph. One she thought might mean *threshold* or *mouth*. A gust of warm air exhaled from deeper in the cave. It brushed her cheek like breath or a sigh. She shivered and turned. A dark passage twisted off the main hollow, curling downward into a tighter, slicker throat of rock. Her beam barely touched its back wall.

She should have stopped. Should have marked the wall and backed out, made notes to return with a full team. Instead, she stepped forward.

Just one quiet woman walking down into the stone with a journal in one hand and a light that wasn't quite enough anymore.

The forest outside held its breath.

And then a giant shadow swallowed her whole.

Chapter One
A Perfect Day, Broken

The mid-July sun barely penetrated the dense canopy of Devil's Cradle State Park. Towering redwoods stretched skyward, their trunks etched with centuries of secrets, their roots burrowed deep into the soil as if holding the Earth together. The air hummed with life—chirping birds, rustling leaves, and the distant babble of a creek. Families and adventurers meandered through the park, their laughter and chatter blending into nature's symphony. Devil's Cradle was alive with visitors for the summer season.

Grant Marlow, a man who wished he was more rugged than his job at a bank allowed, led the way down one of the well-trodden trails from the site of their parked camper. His wife, Claire, a fragile frame hiding a robust well of energy, followed behind while their nine-year-old daughter, Lily, skipped ahead, her braided hair bouncing as she hummed a nonsensical tune. Claire thought it sounded like one of Lily's favorite cartoons. She looked over her shoulder to her seven-year-old son, Kevin. He clutched a small branch as if it were a medieval sword, his eyes glimmering with curiosity and imagination as he swung it at imaginary foes.

"How far are we going?" Lily asked.

"We'll set up by the creek," Claire said. "Just a little further on. You can't miss it."

Lily nodded. Her skip turned into a jog as she raced to find the creek.

"Wait for me!" Kevin called, chasing after his sister.

"This is perfect," Grant said, falling back to be near his wife, wrapping an arm over her shoulders.

The warmth in his tone made Claire grin. "Stole the words right out of my mouth. We should come here next year. It should be our family vacation spot."

"The road trip wasn't bad," Grant said agreeably.

"The kids certainly wouldn't agree," Claire said with a chuckle, glancing ahead at Lily and Kevin, who were now just specks darting between the trees. "I swear, they had more fun at gas stations than they did at some of the stops we planned."

Grant laughed. "Kevin made it his personal mission to try every weird snack he could find. I don't know how he didn't get sick."

"His stomach's made of steel. Unlike yours," Claire teased, nudging him playfully.

"Hey, that gas station sushi *looked* fresh," Grant defended, though his grimace betrayed the regret he still harbored from that particular decision.

Claire rolled her eyes. "Next time, we're sticking to pretzels and bottled water."

Grant gave her a mock salute. "Yes, ma'am."

They walked in companionable silence for a few moments, the sounds of the forest filling the space between them. The babbling of the creek was getting louder, and the earthy scent of damp moss and pine surrounded them.

Grant gave her shoulder a squeeze. "I have to say, you were right about this trip."

Claire arched a brow. "I like the sound of that. Say it again, maybe a little louder?"

Grant chuckled. "I said, *you were right.*" He smirked as she grinned triumphantly. "I wasn't sure about the whole 'let's go off-grid' thing, but…this is nice. No emails, no work calls. Just the fam."

Claire sighed, content. "That was the goal. I feel like we've barely had a moment to breathe the past few months. This—" She gestured to the towering trees, the golden sunlight filtering through the canopy. "This is exactly what we needed."

Grant nodded. "And the kids seem happy."

"For now." Claire smirked. "Give it a few hours, and one of them will be whining about bugs or getting bored."

Grant groaned. "Let's hope they stay distracted for at least one afternoon."

Claire laughed. "Fingers crossed. I think I packed enough snacks to fend them off for at least the day."

"Thinking ahead, as always."

They rounded a bend in the path, and the creek came into view—a sparkling ribbon of water cutting through the landscape, its banks shaded by a thick canopy of trees. Lily and Kevin were already there, skipping stones and giggling as the water splashed.

"See?" Claire murmured, leaning into her husband's side. "Perfect."

Grant pressed a kiss to her temple. "Yeah," he said softly. "It really is."

They caught up with their kids investigating the creek. The sound was like a lullaby, bubbling water and dappled sunlight casting a dreamscape over their luncheon. Grant removed the pack, and Claire began unpacking, handing him the blanket to unfurl.

It didn't take long for Kevin to wander over. Growth spurts took a lot of energy, and this summer, he had grown a lot. His stomach was a bottomless pit. Claire often teased that he would eat them out of house and home. He tore into a sandwich, chips, and grapes, drowning it all in orange juice. The others ate at a more leisurely pace, finishing one sandwich by the time Kevin had eaten two.

"Can I explore?" he asked, already leaping from foot to foot.

"Yes, but stay close," Claire said, yelling the last of her instructions as he fled into the nearby tree line.

Lily stayed with her parents until they decided to take off their shoes and dip their feet in the water of the stream. They were acting silly. What her parents called "flirting" and what she called gross.

She ventured away in the direction her brother had gone and found a clover patch at the base of a giant rock so thick it was like walking on cushions. She sat among them and began a hunt for the lucky four-leafed variety.

"Catch!" Kevin yelled.

Lily looked up in time to dodge a stick from poking her eye out. Instead, it got caught in her hair. "God, Kevin," she screeched. As she yanked it out, the branch pulled a chunk of hair with it. Only when she had it in her hands did she realize it wasn't a stick but a bone. "Gross, Kevin. You're dead!" she shrieked, threw it to the ground, and chased after him.

Kevin laughed and darted into the trees, weaving around the massive bases of ancient redwoods and cedars, another larger bone in hand.

"I'm gonna tell Mom," Lily threatened as her little brother played keep-away by reversing direction around a tree. She almost got a hold of him, but he swept out of reach at the last minute and charged up a small embankment, where he stood, laughing at her. Taunting her.

"You can't get me," he teased.

"You're an idiot," she snarled.

"Whatever," he snorted. Kevin's attention shifted as a sharp trill echoed from somewhere deeper in the woods—a bird call, unfamiliar and beckoning. He turned. "Hey, did you hear that?" he asked.

Lily wasn't paying attention. "…tell Dad that you threw a bone at my head," she said, already walking away to tell on her little brother. "Like, honestly, where did you even find a bone?" Her voice faded away.

The sound came again, closer. It sounded like laughter. Curiosity tugged at him. Kevin tilted his head, listening intently. The trill echoed through the trees again, playful and strange, almost like a voice—but not quite. It was layered, like wind catching on hollow reeds, and it sent a shiver down his spine that he couldn't explain.

He glanced over his shoulder, watching Lily's retreating figure. She was already halfway down the path, her ponytail swinging furiously as she marched back toward their parents. For a moment, Kevin thought about calling her back. But then the sound came again—closer still—and his curiosity surged like a tide, pulling him deeper into the woods.

The boy's sneakers crunched softly on the leaf-strewn ground as he stepped off the trail and into the trees. His heart raced—not with fear but with that wild excitement of discovering something new. He didn't notice how the light dimmed under the thick canopy of branches or how the birdsong seemed to quiet around him. All he could focus on was that strange, lilting call.

"Hello?" he called out hesitantly, his voice barely above a whisper. The sound answered, shifting into a soft, warbling mimicry of its own greeting. Kevin's stomach twisted, but he pushed the unease aside. Maybe it was just a weird bird. Or someone playing a trick. Either way, he had to know.

The trees seemed to grow taller and denser as he moved farther from the trail, his grip on the bone tightening. One had some strange carvings in it that he didn't stop to investigate. The air was cooler here, damp with the scent of moss and earth. Kevin stepped over a tangle of roots, barely noticing the way the shadows seemed to stretch and shift around him.

Another trill came, this time so close it could've been just beyond the next cluster of trees. It was followed by something else—a soft, high-pitched giggle, like the sound of a child laughing. Kevin froze, his breath catching in his throat.

"Who's there?" he called out, his voice trembling now.

The response was immediate: a faint rustling in the underbrush, as if someone—or something—was moving just out of sight. Kevin squinted, his pulse pounding in his ears. For a moment, he thought he saw movement—a pale, feathered shape slipping between the trees.

"Wait!" he shouted, hurrying after it. His sneakers skidded on the soft forest floor as he ran forward, ducking under low-hanging branches and pushing through clumps of ferns. The pale figure flitted ahead of him, always just out of reach, like a shadow dancing on the edge of his vision.

Then, suddenly, the forest opened into a small clearing bathed in weak sunlight. Kevin stumbled to a halt, his chest heaving. His body wavered back and forth, his head feeling dizzy all of a sudden. The sound was gone now—no bird calls, no laughter, just an eerie, heavy silence that pressed down on him like a boulder.

The pale figure was gone, too. But in the center of the clearing, something glinted—a small, polished stone resting atop a flat, mossy rock. It was shaped like an egg, smooth and almost translucent, with faint patterns etched into its surface. Kevin took a hesitant step forward, holding out his arms to keep balance, his curiosity outweighing his lingering fear.

As he reached out to touch it, a shadow fell over him. The air turned icy, and Kevin felt a prickling sensation at the back of his neck like he was being watched. Slowly, he looked up.

Kevin's breath hitched, and he stumbled backward. Fear racing through his insides, he reeled his arm back and threw the bone toward a presence he only felt. An angry screech pierced his eardrums. The last thing he saw was a shadow engulfing him, and the last thing he heard was that strange, lilting laughter echoing through the trees.

Lily burst through the tree line, cheeks aflame with righteous indignation. "Mom, Dad! Kevin threw a bone or something at me! It almost hit my eye!"

Her parents, in the midst of folding a checkered blanket, paused, their hands deftly continuing their task as they exchanged a glance. The corners of Grant's mouth twitched, betraying his amusement before his expression fell.

"Did you say a bone?" he asked.

Lily shrugged. "It looked like one."

"Are you sure it wasn't a branch or something?"

Lily shrugged again and mumbled something incoherent.

"I'm sure it wasn't a bone, honey," Claire murmured, smoothing down Lily's hair with a practiced hand. "We'll have him apologize, sweetheart. You know how your brother gets carried away."

"Promise?" Lily sniffed, her voice quivering with the weight of her grievance, yet her tone was tinged with the satisfaction of anticipated justice.

"Of course," Grant assured her. He raised his voice, calling into the thickening woods, where shadows lengthened as the sun's rays began their retreat. "Kevin! Time to head back!" He bent and shoved the blanket into the pack.

Claire rinsed the last of their cups in the creek. "Kevin! Light a fire under those feet and move it," she called, then handed the cups to her husband. The forest seemed to swallow her words.

"Kevin!" he called again, a hint of steel underlying the fatherly timbre. "Let's go! We need to make it down before dark."

Silence greeted his command, the trees unyielding in their secrecy. The air grew cooler as the twilight hour approached. Claire's fingers clasp together tightly, the vestiges of her smile long gone, replaced by the knitted brow of concern.

"Kevin!" Grant's voice sliced through the stillness, his tone sharpening with every unheeded call. He strode toward the encroaching tree line. The forest floor yielded beneath his boots. Shadows reached out like tendrils from beyond the underbrush.

Lilly grabbed a hold of her mother's arm. Her anger at her brother had vanished and was replaced by fear and guilt for leaving him in the woods.

"Kevin, this isn't funny anymore," Grant intoned with a firmness that bespoke more of worry than anger. He cupped his hands around his mouth to amplify the urgency gripping his chest—a father's command laced with an edge of fear as he moved into the trees. "Kevin!"

Claire's breath caught in her throat. She watched Grant disappear between the trees. She trailed in after him, Lily holding tight to her arm.

"Where is he, Mommy?"

"Maybe he found a deer path and got distracted," she offered. Her words sounded hollow even to her own ears. The wind seemed to scoff at her feeble attempt at reassurance, rustling through the branches with a hushed disapproval.

"Kevin!" Her call echoed back, bouncing off the trunks, devoid of response. Claire's heart thrummed in her ears, a discordant drumbeat that quickened with each passing second of silence. Her eyes darted frantically from one darkened thicket to another, seeking a sign, any sign, of her son. She hurried her steps to catch up with her husband.

"Anything?" she asked, though her voice was barely audible over the din of her own mounting dread.

"Nothing," Grant replied, emerging from behind a redwood, his face etched with lines of strain. "He's not—"

Claire didn't wait for him to finish; she plunged into the woods, her movements erratic as desperation seized her limbs. Thorns and branches snagged her clothing, leaving thin red welts on her skin, but she hardly noticed—the sharp sting paled in comparison to the terror clawing at her insides.

Lily did her best to keep up with her mom, tears wetting her cheeks. "Kevin," she meekly called out.

Claire came to a stop. "Kevin!" Her voice was no longer controlled but raw and jagged, tearing from her like the cry of a wounded animal. It reverberated through the forest, a mother's anguish manifesting in sound.

"Please, baby, answer me!" Tears blurred her vision; the world reduced to a miasma of greens and browns, all indistinguishable save for the absence of a small boy with tousled hair and a mischievous grin.

Grant caught up to her, his features twisted into an unfamiliar mask of helplessness. Lily gripped her father's hand and wasn't letting go.

"Kevin, where are you?" Claire called. The plea was a mere whisper now, a ghostly echo of hope fading into the encroaching darkness.

Chapter Two
Unwanted Things

The forest murmured with the fading light, a shadowed tapestry weaving itself tighter as day succumbed to dusk. Amidst this hush of nature's subtle shift, a jarring discord—cries etched with panic sliced through the stillness, reaching the ears of Park Ranger Patrick "Paddy" Kipp. His boots, worn and faithful, quickened across the earthy path.

Paddy moved with practiced haste. Years as a Ranger for the army, added to the years as a forest ranger at Devil's Cradle State Park, provided training on keeping his nerves in check. Each call sharpened his focus. The calls grew louder, and he could feel the anxiety of each note calling out a name he could finally make out: Kevin.

He emerged into the clearing where a picnic site sat abandoned by Rees Creek. The remnants of familial joy were now tainted with palpable dread. He followed the voices across the creek and into the tree line and found a woman, her face gaunt and drawn in despair.

"Hello, ma'am," he said in greeting.

Claire turned toward the calm voice and nearly collapsed when she saw his uniform and badge. "Thank God."

"What?" came a man's not-too-distant voice.

Claire hurried, nearly tripping over exposed roots, toward the park ranger. "My son, he's not responding to my calls. He was right here, and his sister was with him," she said, words spilling faster than she could keep them straight in her head.

Paddy's eyes went to the man emerging from deeper in the forest and the young girl clinging to him with both hands, eyes wide and wild as a horse about to buck.

"I fully understand the urgency and panic, and I'm going to help you find your boy," Paddy replied. "Try to get your breath for a moment so you can tell me what happened."

"My name is Grant Marlow. This is my wife, Claire, and daughter, Lily," Grant said. His voice was rough and hoarse. "Our son, Kevin, he and his sister were both wandering in the woods over here after our lunch. Lily came back and said he'd thrown something at her and was teasing her. It was time to go anyway—"

"We called out, but he didn't come back, and he hasn't answered," Claire interrupted. Her fingers twisted around themselves.

Paddy crouched down and gave a friendly smile to Lily. "Hey, sweetheart. I know you're scared for your brother, but do you remember seeing him heading in a specific direction?"

Lily bit her lip, as fresh tears rolled down her cheeks. "I didn't look. I was mad. He threw a bone at me."

"A bone?"

"She thinks it was a bone," Grant said.

"A bone?" Claire said, shocked. "Honey, you didn't say—"

"She told me when we were out searching."

"But how did you—"

Paddy held a hand up to silence the girl's mother. "How big was the bone, Lily? Can you show me with your hands?"

Lily let go of her dad's hand and held her hands about six inches apart from each other.

"Oh, wow. That must have hurt. Are you okay?"

Lily nodded. "It landed in my hair. And then I threw it back at him, but missed."

"Do you think you can show me where that was before we go find your brother?"

Lily grabbed her dad's hand again and nodded.

"That'd be extremely helpful." Paddy got back to his feet and pulled a radio from his belt with methodical precision. "We'll find him." The static crack of the radio cut through the growing terror.

Claire's gaze clung to Paddy as if to draw strength from his assured presence. In her eyes, the ranger echoed every parent's nightmare, the unspoken horrors that haunt those who have lost a piece of their world.

"Base, this is Kipp. I need a search team at the west trailhead, possible missing child," he said into the radio. Each measured word was a testament to his experience in matters all too common in the deceptive wilds of the state park.

"Copy that, Paddy. Assistance is on the way," crackled the response.

"Kevin will be found," Paddy assured them once more. His confidence was a declaration of his own unyielding intent.

The radio crackled to life. "Kipp, this is Deputy Cabrera. I'm already up your way. I'll be there in five."

"Roger that, Deputy." Paddy clipped the radio back to his belt and turned his focus on the girl. "You ready to lead me to where you two were playing?" he asked.

Lily nodded.

Grant wrapped his arm around her small shoulders.

"Which direction was it?" Paddy asked.

"Back that way," she said, pointing.

Paddy offered her and her parents a reassuring smile as he pulled out his flashlight. "Mind showing me?"

She nodded.

"Let's show him where you guys were playing, alright?" Grant urged his daughter on.

She led the way, though she never released her father's hand.

"Up there," she said when they got to the last place she'd been chasing her brother. "He climbed up there, and then I left to tell Mom and Dad what he'd done."

Paddy looked the location over, observing the trampled ground, the footprints going round and round a large redwood, one set trailing up the embankment. "And where were you standing when you threw the bone at him?" he asked.

Lily pulled her dad along as she returned to the big rock she was standing at. "Right here."

"And what direction did you throw it?"

Lily made a throwing motion to where Kevin had been standing.

Paddy headed in that direction, swiping his flashlight back and forth, taking small, calculated steps. It didn't take long to find the bone. And it was in fact a bone. He picked it up and held it up. "You've got a great memory, Lily. Here it is."

"It's actually a bone?" Claire asked.

"There are plenty of animal bones in the park. Nature doing its work."

"What's it from?" Grant asked.

Paddy walked back to meet the family. "A raccoon, maybe. It's irrelevant. Lily, can I ask you one more question?"

Lily nodded. "Okay."

"Are you sure you didn't hit him when you threw it back at him?"

Grant and Claire exchanged a look of abject horror.

Lily nodded once more. "He was twice as far as I could throw it."

"Okay, thanks, Lily. You've been a great help. I'm going to go find your brother now. Folks, I'd recommend going back to the picnic site so the other rangers and deputies will know where we are, alright?"

They nodded. Paddy led them back to their discarded backpacks. "Wait here, and when the deputy arrives, send him my way," he said, pointing to where he would be.

"Yeah, okay," Grant said while nodding.

"We just wait here?" Claire asked.

"Best thing you can do is stay put. Stay where he knows he can find you," Paddy explained.

"But why isn't he answering?" she pleaded.

"Claire." Grant grabbed his wife and pulled her small frame into his, hugging her close.

Paddy gave them a moment before quietly reiterating his instructions. He returned to the clover patch and returned the bone to where he had found it. The idea skimmed into his head that a long bone such as this one could easily be mistaken as an animal bone but could very well be a child or human bone. He grabbed a stick and pulled flagging tape from one of the many utility pockets of his state-issued pants.

With that marked, he headed back to the embankment, climbing to the top and looking around. The treads of the boy's sneakers led deeper into the woods.

"Hey!" came a familiar voice behind him.

Deputy Eddie Cabrera, the eldest member of the Lost Grove Police Department, had a healthy head of grey-and-brown hair, and his already tan skin had soaked up the early summer rays, painting him a rich, golden hue. His bright teeth highlighted the youthfulness of his sixty-year-old face.

"Deputy," Paddy greeted the officer with a handshake, pulling him up to the top of the embankment.

"Lost kid?"

"So it seems. Likely wandered off." Paddy pointed at the tracks.

"The parents said he isn't responding to their calls. Anything out that way that he could fall down or…?"

"No real steep drop-off this direction, but there's any number of pitfalls he could have stumbled upon or into. Kids are more inquisitive than most scientists."

"I understand that well enough. Damn grandkids…Sometimes, I watch them and wonder how they're alive. Or how they haven't broken every bone in their body," he said as he pulled the radio on his shoulder close. "Debbie, this is Deputy Cabrera on the call for the missing child up at Devil's Cradle. We have a trail. Heading out now. Can you communicate with the rest of the team that we are moving southwest into the park toward…" He turned to Paddy. "What's off that way, landmark-wise?"

"Spencer's Butte," he replied.

"Spencer's Butte," Eddie said into the radio.

"Copy. Can do," replied Debbie, their switchboard operator.

Ranger and deputy followed the trail of the small sneaker prints into the wood, their flashlight beams intersecting. Another voice crackled over the radio, a voice Paddy was familiar with.

"Let me know if you need more officers, Paddy."

Paddy smiled. It didn't take much to remind him of the last time he'd communicated with that man over the radio. A stealth infiltration of the Orbriallis Institute that resulted in two rescued souls, but not a whole lot more. The government had swept whatever other unsavory experiments the doctors had been working on at the reputable and world-renowned facility under the rug. That hadn't stopped Paddy from occasionally leaking what little information he had stolen in a file transfer from a flash drive in his computer onto the internet.

What little light the low summer sun had left to offer did little to help them navigate their path. Night was coming.

"We need to find this kid before its pitch black out here," Eddie said. He knew Paddy understood that as much as he did but felt the need to voice it as if his own fatherly fears were creeping in. This wasn't the first time he'd dealt with a missing person. It happened all the time in Devil's Cradle and the surrounding forest area. But it always gnawed into his gut when it was a child missing. He could feel his stomach churning with worry already and knew he'd be downing Pepto-Bismol for the next few days, even when they did find this boy wandering around, having lost his bearings.

His words hung in the heavy summer air, a grim reminder of the urgency of their search. The shadows of the trees seemed to stretch and elongate as the sun dipped lower in the sky, casting eerie shapes on the forest floor. Paddy and Eddie followed the trail of tiny footprints that meandered through the undergrowth like a lifeline, leading them deeper into the heart of Devil's Cradle.

Paddy crouched. "He's running," he said.

Eddie surveyed the prints, the toe swiping through the dirt, indicating the boy was pushing off. Running. "Toward or from something?"

"He could have heard his parents calling. Got twisted around," Paddy said.

"Kevin!" Eddie called, putting a touch of grandfatherly love into the words. "Kevin Marlow!"

Both men paused and listened, holding their breath for any noise. Nothing came back to them except the sounds of the summer woods: the rustling of leaves, the distant call of a bird, and the creaking of branches swaying in the gentle breeze. The air felt charged with an unsettling energy as if the forest itself was holding its breath in anticipation.

Standing, Paddy's light caught the glint of something amidst the trees. "See that?" he asked, pointing.

Eddie bent down and squinted. "Yeah."

They moved toward it and stepped into a small clearing, where a flickering light danced against the trunks. Prisms of light danced off a crystal rock, smooth as an egg. Paddy picked it up and caught sight of something else white. He dropped the rock and moved to the object. "Another bone," he said, picking it up.

"A bone?" Eddie asked.

"Lily, the little girl, she said Kevin threw a bone at her. I flagged it back toward the camp. I would say this bone is pretty identical in scale."

Eddie pulled his eyes away from the bone and squatted down. His gaze fell on another discoloration seeping into the dirt. He crouched and touched it with his fingers. Residual warmth made his skin crawl and the viscosity was instantly familiar. "Shit," he said, lifting his fingers for Paddy to see.

Paddy closed his eyes and counted to ten in his head before looking at the small splash of blood Eddie knelt near. "There isn't much."

"No. But who is bleeding and why?"

Paddy took his next steps carefully around the clearing. His eyes scanned into the darkness of the trees, looked at all the low-hanging branches, and surveyed the dirt and ferns. "There aren't any more prints," he said, voice hushed as if saying the words were blasphemous.

Eddie looked at Paddy, then around.

Paddy moved to a pine tree and pulled a low branch down. A tiny droplet of red caught his eye. "There's blood here," he said, letting the branch go and stepping into the trees.

Eddie cursed, following Paddy's footsteps.

The trees seemed to close in around them as they ventured deeper into the forest, the shadows growing thicker and more menacing with each step. Paddy's heart quickened as he scanned the underbrush for any sign of the missing boy. He nearly missed the tiny droplet of blood on the forest floor.

"More," he said, pointing and already moving on.

Both men picked up their pace as night came on with force. The woods acted like a barrier between the dying sunset.

They skittered down a shallow slope.

"The terrain gets choppier here. Leading to the butte and caves down that way," Paddy said with a wave of his flashlight beam.

Eddie felt the pressure lock down on his gut. Images of his grandchildren played in his head. His lips moved in silent prayer, watching Paddy's beam of light swivel across the ground. Dread quickened his pulse until it was a steady thrum.

He couldn't say what he noticed first, the way the light stopped moving, the way Paddy's shoulders went rigid and his body stilled unnaturally, or the pale specter of a small hand and arm dangling in the air.

It was the arm he'd remember most. It reminded him of his grandson Dominic sleeping in the bunk beds when he came with his parents to visit during the holidays. Dominic thrashed in his sleep, limbs thrown out at odd angles. Eddie would go and check on his grandchildren in the night, watch them sleeping as he had done with his children before. Dominic's little arm would dangle over the side of the upper bunk, soft and relaxed, pale in the nightlight's soft glow. Eddie would carefully lift it and tuck Dominic back under the covers with love.

This arm cast from the shadows of the redwoods, tucked in a dark niche of rocks and crevices, did not belong to Dominic but instead to a boy named Kevin Marlow. And he wasn't going to wake up ever again.

Chapter Three
Behind the Redwood Curtain

He'd had far too much coffee on an empty stomach. He knew he should have gotten two more hours of sleep, which would have doubled the couple he tossed and turned through. That way, the Main Street Cafe would have been open and he would have indulged in a pastry or some homemade banana bread instead of having three cups of shit coffee at the station. His mind would also likely be operating at least half capacity as opposed to his brain feeling like a lead weight. This was not how he wanted to start his day. This week. This month. His chiefdom.

Seth Wolfe, big-city homicide detective turned small town chief of police, rearranged the contents of his desk to make room for the horrendous details of his latest case. He had been called to the scene at eight p.m. Eddie warned him it wasn't a pretty sight. An animal attack rarely is. But he was not expecting a scene so eerily similar to how he had found former sexual predator and kidnapper Raymond LaRange just two months prior. He could only hope this autopsy was more conclusive. An agent from the California Department of Fish and Wildlife had determined the fatal neck blow to LaRange was struck by a grey wolf, but Dr. Wes Hensley, the county medical examiner overseeing the autopsy, believed she wasn't confident in her determination. The bite marks confounded her. That shadow of doubt along with Mary Germaine's wild confession of being responsible still lingered in the recesses of his mind.

Seth's dark hair was a little too long and tousled from the wind. It reminded him of the days when he let it grow longer as a detective in San Francisco, back when life was a constant storm of late-night stakeouts and caffeine-fueled dead ends. His facial hair followed suit—a few days past a clean shave, rough along the edges, the kind of scruff that made him look like he belonged on the cover of some noir novel, cigarette smoke curling around his office.

But it wasn't just the face, it was the body, too. Once lean and wiry from chasing suspects through city streets, his new life, keeping tabs on the small town and its outskirts, had given him the time to carve muscle into his frame, an activity he hadn't indulged in since he left college. Broad shoulders filled out his button-down shirt, the fabric stretching just enough to hint at the strength beneath. His jeans sat low on his hips, well-worn, comfortable, like they belonged to a man who spent more time moving than sitting.

He set his notepad out on his desk and fired up his computer. Writing up reports never ceased to be tedious, but as he'd aged, Seth found reviewing the notes by transcribing them into a case report helped put the incident in perspective. Much like writing his initial notes by hand helped to keep the details in his brain.

The county sheriff had shown up to the scene, as was expected. The state park was under county jurisdiction. Sheriff Bernard Hayes was a stocky, well-built Black man with a fierce mustache. They'd first met at Wes's annual Red Shawl event, a fundraiser for missing and murdered Indigenous peoples. They formed a quick rapport and Bernard wasted no time letting Seth know he thought he was wasted as chief of Lost Grove police. Seth didn't wholly disagree but he'd already known that former chief of police, Bill Richards, was retiring.

Seth would never forget the look in Bill's eyes as he stood outside the Orbriallis Institute the night of The Event. The feds were swarming the site. Dr. Neil Owens was being carted off to the station. The dead body of a hired assassin was being loaded into an ambulance. Doctors and staff workers were boisterous, demanding answers as to what was happening, and the lights behind Bill's eyes had gone out. Seth had seen it before in young officers who found themselves not cut out for what they thought would be an exciting career. It was likely the same look Seth had on his face the morning he was called to Dolores Park in San Francisco to find a young woman overdosed on heroin, holding her dead infant child that she'd injected with the same drug. It was at that moment he decided he would take a leave of absence to come back home to help his ailing father as opposed to hiring someone.

So, it came as no surprise when Bill told him a few days into the new year that he was going to retire. He said that spending time with his family over the holidays had cemented his decision. It was time for him and Linda to do some traveling and spend more time with their kids.

Up until this time, Seth had struggled with whether or not to return to his job at the SFPD. His boss wanted him back. His partner, Kendra Washington, wanted him back. And quite frankly, Seth missed it. He missed the energy, the thrill, the danger. He missed the satisfaction of solving a big case and helping to bring people closure in their darkest of times. But his childhood home had dug its claws deep into Seth's soul. The town, the residents, the group of kids he'd grown so close with in such a short amount of time. Story Palmer.

Upon returning to Lost Grove, Seth quickly formed a deep bond with the town librarian—who, incidentally, was also its quietly acknowledged witch. What began as a connection rooted in shared understanding soon evolved into something more enduring: love. It was a feeling Seth hadn't allowed himself to entertain since high school. His former life as a lead homicide detective in San Francisco left little room for personal entanglements; sixty-hour weeks and relentless pressure had made sure of that. But in Lost Grove, working reasonable hours and shedding the weight of constant urgency—aside from the two weeks spent on the Sarah Elizabeth case—Seth found his guard lowering. For once, he didn't resist. He welcomed the rare and unexpected comfort of a real relationship.

Bill had told Seth that he wanted him to take his place as chief of police and gave him two weeks to make his decision. If Seth wasn't going to take the job, they would need time to find Bill's replacement. Story was well aware of Seth's internal dilemma on whether or not to return to his job in San Francisco and swore that she would not influence his decision in any way. She did, however, help him make one.

She'd sat across from Seth at her kitchen island while they were sharing a bottle of wine. Seth had laid out all the pros and cons for each scenario but was still torn on what to do. Story took what Seth felt was an impossible decision and helped to make it shockingly simple. Story set her forearms down on the counter and opened her right hand palm up. She'd said, "This is San Francisco." Then she opened up her left hand and said, "This is Lost Grove." She closed both fists and continued, "Now clear your mind. Throw all those pros and cons out the window and just look at my hands. Without letting yourself think for one second, when I throw each option up in the air, tell me where you look first." She tossed his choices up in the air and Seth looked toward her left hand. She said, "That's your gut."

Seth made his decision and never looked back.

Since then, Seth's department had built a solid working relationship with Sheriff Bernard Hayes, forged during the chaos of an officer-involved shooting. The county was sent to deliver an arrest on a man with an outstanding warrant. He was known to be a handful, but they hadn't expected just how much of one he proved to be. With other officers spread thin throughout the county, Seth and his officers were the closest to respond with aid for the wounded officer and her partner.

That was the thing about Lost Grove. It was a remote town amongst an outcrop of other small towns and even smaller police departments. All of them worked together. The town, the whole county, existed behind the redwood curtain. Those trees acted like a barrier between the rest of the civilized world and the outcrop of those who chose to live on the northern coast of California. It was like the Wild West still existed in this small nook of humanity.

Given the remote nature, cases that might fall under the county's jurisdiction sometimes got offloaded to the other police forces. Sheriff Hayes felt Seth could manage the Marlow case, as it seemed obvious the young boy was the victim of an animal attack.

A rap on his doorframe drew Seth's attention away from his notes.

"Morning," Peter Andalusian greeted him, stepping into his office.

"Morning," Seth responded.

Peter, the new sergeant of Lost Grove Police, had the kind of presence that made people sit up a little straighter when he walked into a room. Tall and built like he'd been carved from stone, he carried himself with the quiet confidence of a man who had seen more than his fair share of battle and walked away from all of it sharper, not broken. His time serving in the armed forces with his longtime friend Paddy Kipp, running special ops, clung to him in the way he moved—efficient, calculated, always aware of his surroundings.

His police uniform, black pants, brown-grey shirt, sat perfectly on his broad frame, the fabric stretched just enough over a chest that looked like it had never once skipped a workout. His belt was lined with the essential tools of the job, while a heavy-duty belt held a radio, cuffs, and a holstered sidearm. Everything about him was deliberate, no wasted space, no unnecessary weight.

Strong-jawed, dark-eyed, he had an easy but unreadable expression that made people second-guess whether he was about to issue a warning or crack a rare smile. There was something distinctly rugged about him, like he belonged more in the middle of a war zone than a small-town police station. But despite the hardened exterior, there was a depth to him. Peter Andalusian wasn't just another cop. He was the kind of man who could take a punch and barely flinch, who could track a ghost through the woods at night, and who, if it came down to it, would put himself between danger and the people he'd sworn to protect without hesitation.

He had also admitted to committing numerous crimes, including several felonies. Given the circumstances surrounding the crimes and that he was blackmailed into doing them under the threat of his family's lives, Seth made the decision to look the other way, especially considering it was Peter who helped him take down Dr. Neil Owens and save the lives of multiple children.

Besides getting off on the wrong foot, Peter proved his worth and made Seth promise not to hold his past deeds against him. Peter had the training and had excelled in the academy and forensic courses needed to land the job. He officially joined the department eight weeks prior, the same week Seth took over for Bill Richards, and thus far had proven to be highly dependable and capable at all aspects of the job.

"Did you get any sleep?" Peter asked.

Seth shrugged. "Some."

Peter nodded. He used to work as a guide at Devil's Cradle State Park. In the time he'd been an employee of the park, there had been countless missing persons. Young people, old people, skilled climbers, and newbies hitting way out of their league. There'd been accidental deaths and maybe a few well-hidden intentional ones. He'd been a part of any number of searches where the missing were never found and part of a few where they were. The children who went missing always stayed with him. He had the feeling Seth wouldn't be able to forget either. "If you don't need me, we got another call from the foreman up at the construction site. More property was defaced with paint and more protesters showed up."

The Orbriallis Institute had begun massive construction on virgin territory near their facility, just south of the Grouse River, nearly four months prior. The formerly wooded area had been cleared out to make room for high-priced homes and condos for the overwhelming number of doctors and staff that had been forced to live in unincorporated areas many miles from the facility. As crime increased in those areas, the doctors caused enough of an uproar to force the Orbriallis to hire contractors to go to work. The majority of Lost Grove residents were unhappy with the idea of more homes going up, much less the imminent threat of the unincorporated Goldenvale being incorporated into their quaint town. Environmentalists and activists had been peacefully protesting for months. Only recently had vandalism set in.

Seth sighed. "How many?"

"He said about ten to fifteen."

"Certainly pales in comparison to the Occupy Earth protests in San Francisco."

"Thousands?"

"Yep."

Peter chuckled. "I think we can handle this. Tell me about Kevin Marlow."

Seth nodded to his office door.

Peter shut it and pulled a chair up next to Seth.

Seth clicked on a folder that Wes sent him of the crime scene photos. He opened up the first picture, a full-frame photo looking down at the remains of Kevin Marlow sprawled across a large tree branch jutting out of a cliff. "This look familiar to you?"

Peter's brow drew tight as he examined the photo. "Unfortunately it looks all too familiar." He looked at Seth. "You think it's the same grey wolf?"

Seth gave a curt shake of his head. "Don't know. Would appear that way. And if it is, we'll need to get someone in here to track and relocate the animal. Or animals."

"Agreed. LaRange was on his last leg, but if we've got an animal aggressively attacking a child, we'll need to act quickly."

"And ensure the town it's being handled so we don't have someone racing through the woods, pegging off endangered species. Assuming it is an animal."

Peter raised an eyebrow at Seth. "Please tell me you're not still thinking Mary Germaine had anything to do with that prick."

"No. No, I don't. This is a child we're talking about, not a monster who hunts...sorry." Seth knew that the kidnapping of Peter's daughter Zoe was still a delicate subject. What happened to her during the hours she was locked in a room on a restricted floor at the Orbriallis was still unknown, but the options were horrific.

Peter gave a slight nod. "No reason to apologize. The point is valid and I'm glad you see it."

Seth closed his computer down and stood up. "Let's head out to the bullpen. I'd like to get everyone moving."

Peter slid his chair back, stood, and opened the door. "On you, Chief."

Officer Sasha Kingston leaned over the shoulder of Officer Joe Casey looking at his computer screen. Seth and Peter's entrance drew their attention.

"Morning, guys," Seth said, forcing his eyes wider than they were inclined.

"Morning, Chief," Joe responded.

Sasha lightly pushed the back of Joe's head. "He told you not to call him that. Morning, Seth."

Joe smoothed down the back of his blonde straw-straight hair. "Sorry. Seth."

"What were you guys looking at?" Seth asked.

"Joe's learning about animals." Sasha grinned.

"Mountain lions," Joe specified. "They often wait for their prey in—"

Seth held his hand up. "Love the initiative, but let's put that on hold for now. Wes is hoping to have results by this afternoon. Let's see if he can identify the animal, whether it's a wolf or—Joe—a mountain lion. This is going to be a hot topic. And a dangerous one."

"Hunters?" Sasha guessed.

"Exactly. I'm sure word has already started to spread, and the last thing we need is a bunch of renegade hunters going out into the wilderness shooting up any animal in sight. Or accidentally shooting each other. The farmers in Honeydew have been killing off coyotes over the past couple months due to livestock being killed. We don't need that here. I'm going to head into town and start squashing any rumors and spread the word that we have the situation under control."

"Nice," Joe said with a small fist pump. Sasha scowled at him.

"Sasha, find out where our newest recruit is and go pick him up. I want you two to head to Devil's Cradle and touch base with Paddy. He should be back there by now. I want you guys posted up at the entrance to check every car that comes through. If they have any firearms on them, licensed or not, send them back home."

"On it," Sasha said and headed to her desk to grab her things.

"Joe, I want you to accompany Peter, who's heading to the new building site."

"More vandalism?" Joe guessed.

Peter nodded. "Yeah, and protesters."

Seth looked between the two men. "Make sure things remain peaceful and see if you can find any clues as to who's doing this. Bag any evidence: spray cans, bottles, what have you."

"You got it." Peter walked over and patted Joe on the shoulder. "You ready, kid?" he asked, using the term affectionately.

"For sure," Joe said and locked his computer.

Sasha walked toward the front door. "Be careful of those protesters, Joe."

"I can defend myself," Joe said with an air of confidence.

Seth followed behind Sasha, pulling his keys from his belt, and then spun around. "Joe, forward the phones to the switchboard and lock the door on the way out. Eddie will be in early, but I told him to get some sleep."

Joe gave him a thumbs-up.

Chapter Four
Our Final Summer

Constance "Stan" Hensley soaked in the July sun with her head tilted back, eyes hidden behind a pair of cheap plastic sunglasses from the town drugstore. An oversized, cropped royal-blue sweater draped loosely over her frame, the sleeves extended just past her wrists, swallowing her hands. She stole an old pair of her older brother's khakis, cutting them off just above her knees. She cinched them at the waist with a simple brown leather belt. On her feet, she wore classic Chucks with mismatched socks peeking out above them. Sunlight glinted off her waist-length black hair and soaked into her already darkening skin.

Leaning back on her elbows at the picnic table, she admired the sweet, enticing aroma of vanilla and buttery waffle cones leaking out of the ice cream parlor. It made her mouth water and her stomach grumble. She opened her eyes and glanced over at the pickup window of the newly opened burger stand.

Noble Andalusian, with his long brown hair and six-three frame, towered over the other people waiting in line. He wore swim shorts that showed off his sculpted legs and a loose T-shirt with a pair of old running shoes so worn in they likely held together by sheer will. He smiled down at his girlfriend, Anya Bury. Her hair shone in the summer light as if it was mimicking the sun with its ginger-to-white ombre effect. She'd recently cut her gentle waves to shoulder length and added bangs. It made her look sophisticated. Stan thought she might have been trying to affect the easy French style of the town librarian and local witch, Story Palmer, and it suited her. Anya's skin had the luminous glow of morning mist hovering over a quiet stream and Stan hoped she'd brought sunscreen.

Noble reached out and tucked a strand of hair behind Anya's ear. The action made Stan smirk. He'd never been as expressive with his affection in his last relationship. Stan took it as a sign; what they felt was deeper, more adult, than the crushes of their youth, and honestly, it made her feel all warm in her tum-tum.

She checked her phone, awaiting a text from Ember after she finished her appointment at the Orbriallis Institute. One part of what their group of friends called the Power Twins, Ember still wasn't talking. Using her special powers of controlling thoughts and reading people's minds in a way she didn't know was possible, she had accidentally killed her long-time bully and fellow classmate last year in San Francisco. She hadn't spoken out loud since and rarely, if ever, used her powers to speak with her new group of friends. Unlike her brother, who was confronting his abilities head-on, honing them, pushing the limits, Ember wanted nothing to do with them.

Yet improvements had been made. She wasn't terrified to step outdoors or take part in social get-togethers. She was working on healing from the incident.

"One double cheeseburger and a strawberry shake," Noble said.

Stan spun around to dig into her food.

"And seasoned fries," Anya added, setting a large cup of fries beside the burger basket.

"Thank you! I am starving," Stan said, mouth salivating. She popped the top of her shake and dipped the fries in the creamy goodness. Salt and sweetness mixed on her taste buds in a perfect symphony.

Anya and Noble sat opposite her with their own burgers, fries, and drinks. It was Noble's day off from working at the horse ranch with his mother, leading tours down the Lost Coast to rugged Mourner's Beach and back again. What had been a lunch date with plans to head to the lake with Anya turned into a lunch date with Anya and his best friend. Stan was meant to go fishing with her father today, but he'd been called to the state park to deal with an animal attack yesterday evening, and it turned into a case he had to address sooner than later.

"So, was it a bad case?" Noble asked his best friend.

Stan shrugged, chugging her milkshake through a straw. "He had those vibes when he got home last night," she eventually replied. Noble got her meaning, but Stan elaborated for Anya. "Like, I could just tell it wasn't good."

"Does it have to do with the other animal issues?" Anya asked.

"The ones with the farmers in Honeydew?"

Anya nodded, mouth full of fries.

"Could be."

"But this was a person, right? Why else would your dad go out?" Noble asked.

"Yeah, it was a person."

Anya shivered despite the warm sun. Noble reached under the table and squeezed her knee. In turn, she slid closer so their legs were touching. Stan smirked, hiding it with another bite of her burger.

"I'm gonna need to see some IDs." Nate Abbott approached, wearing his volunteer police officer uniform and the cliche mirrored sunglasses.

Stan removed her sunglasses and glared at him. "You're an idiot."

Noble's laughter came easy, but seeing Nate in uniform created a knot in his stomach. Nate wore it as a volunteer with a whole future ahead of him and no secrets marring the shiny badge, but his father stepping up to fill the sergeant position wasn't as simple, because Peter Andalusian wasn't just another cop, he was a man with a past draped in shadows and secrets, and in a town like this, shadows never stayed hidden for long.

Noble thought of his little sister, Zoe, and what she might hear, what she might have to endure because their father had taken the job. People already doubted him, dismissed him, spat their rumors like venom. Was his father really ready for this? Was he ready for the scrutiny? Was Noble?

He forced himself to stay in the moment as Nate teased Stan. Nate, still lithe from his long-distance running, but more built than Noble due to his wrestling, stood at the end of the picnic table. "Ma'am, I'm the law in these parts."

Stan squinted her eyes up at his uniform. "Oh, let me fix that," she said, standing from the table.

"What?" Nate asked, looking at his uniform.

He didn't have time to dodge the punch she drove into his bicep, giving him a dead arm. "Fuuudgsicle," he said, noticing the kids all around. "Ow," he whispered.

"That's better," Stan said, returning to her lunch.

Noble laughed. Stan had five brothers by blood, but it was still like Nate was the brother she never had.

"Stop encouraging her, dude," Nate said to Noble. "What are you guys doing, anyway?"

"We're having lunch." Noble delivered the statement deadpan.

Nate rolled his eyes. "I see that. I meant after."

"Going to the lake," Noble replied.

Nate wrinkled his nose. "Damn," he said under his breath.

"Sorry, bro." Noble smiled. "Want some fries?"

Nate snatched fries from his friend's cup.

"You're the fool who wanted to gain field training credits," Stan said through a mouthful of burger.

"Yeah, and it will look good to my professors. I'll have loads of field experience and credit hours under my belt while you and all the other fools are just getting started," Nate replied.

Stan stared up at him. "I'm taking anatomy and medical forensics, you twat. I don't need to learn how to shoot myself with a taser." While Nate was dead set on becoming the FBIs top officer by the age of thirty, Stan decided to follow in her father's footsteps and pursue a career as a medical examiner, albeit with a side of cultural and natural preservation tucked in as a personal passion. She'd be attending Cal Poly Humboldt in the fall when Nate would be in the city at San Francisco State University.

Anya hid her giggle by taking a sip of her soda.

"That was one time," Nate grumbled.

The incident had been the butt of the jokes between them for over a month.

"And I'd say it's one time too many," Stan argued.

"Whatever."

"What are you even doing right now? Shouldn't you be patrolling or filing forms or something?" Stan asked.

"I'm on my lunch break," Nate said.

The old radio attached to a shoulder clip burst with static. The voice coming through was tinny and fuzzy. "Abbott, you there?"

Nate grabbed the mic and pulled it to his mouth, pressing the side button. "Ten-four."

Stan snorted and rolled her eyes.

"Where are you?" the impatient female voice asked.

"I'm up at Crampton Park by the new burger place."

"Stay put," demanded the voice. The radio went silent.

"Hey, you guys want to do something tonight? Ryker goes back to his weird Olympic training cult tomorrow. We should do something." Nate grabbed a few more fries from Noble.

"Olympic training cult?" Anya asked.

"Yeah, you know. It's all Foxcatcher and shit," Nate remarked.

"Those athletes actually won gold medals," Stan added in defense. She was getting to know Anya on a whole other level since her bestie, Noble, started dating her last fall. What little she knew of Ryker was he'd been offered a space at an academy on the East Coast to train for the Olympics in jiu-jitsu, and from what Anya said, he was dang good. She couldn't imagine one day watching a guy she grew up with on television take home an Olympic gold. It would be epic and surreal.

"Yes, true," Nate agreed. "But they were also basically just men slapping big man meat around while their wealthy benefactor got off. Oh, that's right, and he ended up shooting one of them, too."

Stan rolled her eyes and took a massive bite of her burger.

"So? Beach fire or something?" Nate asked.

Noble cleared his throat. "The fire warning is moderate to high."

Nate shrugged. "It's on the beach."

"By a bunch of dry dune grass," Noble countered.

"Chill out, Ranger Rick," Nate scoffed. "A small one."

"I'm down," Stan said.

"Yeah, alright," Noble agreed. "Can you come?" he asked Anya.

She nodded. "Yeah, probably." Her parents constantly reminded her to be a teenager and spend the rest of the summer with her friends before they all went their separate ways this fall. But she also had duties on the farm, especially since they'd agreed that what she wanted to pursue for her future was agriculture and taking over the Bury dairy farm. So, instead of wasting money on a college degree, much of what she learned would be hands-on. She'd acquiesced to taking as many agricultural courses as she could from the local colleges and would be attending Cal Poly Humboldt with Stan in the fall.

"Okay, gross, stop looking at each other." Nate pulled a sick face and turned to Stan. "Wanna tell Ember and Emory?"

"Yep, I'll text 'em," she replied.

"Nettie and Ryker?" he asked, looking at Anya.

"Yep, I'm on it!" Anya replied, already texting.

"I should get going. We've got a big case with the kid who got mauled up at the park," Nate said.

"Jesus," Noble scoffed.

"What?" Nate asked.

"It was a child?" Anya asked.

"Way to go fuckface. Talking about an open case," Stan teased.

"Everyone knows it was a kid. What are you talking about?" he argued.

"*Everyone* knows?" Stan teased.

"Pretty much," Nate said.

A squad car pulled up, and Officer Sasha Kingston waved Nate over.

"Gotta go, kids. Duty calls," Nate said, already walking away.

"Don't act like you're actually investigating anything," Stan called after him.

"Watch it, Hensley. I'll arrest you."

Stan scoffed. "Oh yeah, with what?"

"Oh no," Noble mumbled.

Nate sneered. "My dick."

"Okay then," Stan said dryly.

"Oh my God," Anya gasped.

"Whatever. He has one," Nate said, pointing to Noble.

"Huh?"

Noble patted Anya's knee. "Just ignore him. Please."

Nate waved them off and then discreetly gave Stan the finger before getting in the passenger seat.

"Charming as ever," Sasha remarked as he buckled in, and she put the car in gear.

"What's up, boss?" Nate asked, settling in with his arm out the window.

Sasha sighed. "I'm cursed to be surrounded by idiots."

Chapter Five
Ghosts of Orbriallis

Peter and Joe were cruising up the 211, the name of the country road that Main Street morphed into, with Peter at the wheel playing Pearl Jam's *Ten* album through the Bluetooth on his phone. Joe had stuck his foot in his mouth claiming that he too enjoyed some of Nirvana's songs. Peter had a look of such pained disappointment that Joe felt like opening the car door and rolling out onto the asphalt at 45 mph. Since then, Joe had been trying to make up for his faux pas by praising the heroics Peter had shown during The Event at the Orbriallis Insurrection. That's what Joe called it anyway. Not that he was there, but he heard the stories from Seth and Paddy and saw the aftermath outside of the facility that night.

"Where do you think Dr. Owens is now?" Joe asked conspiratorially.

Peter grunted. "Who knows. That old bastard probably got sent to take over another medical facility and is living in a mansion on the East Coast."

"Did he really have albino boys living with him in his penthouse?"

Peter shot the boy a baffled look. "What?"

"It was a rumor on Reddit."

"Reddit? What? No, there were no albino boys in his penthouse or anywhere else in the facility. What the hell kind of rumor is that?"

"There are all sorts of rumors and stories out there."

"I don't think Neil Owens had a proclivity toward any type of person, man, woman, old, young. The only thing I ever saw that indicated anything remotely sexual about the man was a bizarre painting he had in his library of two nude women riding a crocodile."

Joe's eyebrows rose. "A crocodile?"

"Yeah. And don't go posting that shit on your Reddit whatever."

"I won't post anything we ever talk about, I promise."

Peter looked at Joe out of the corner of his eye. "You're an appeasing sort of fellow, aren't you?"

"I…I just like to…follow—"

"Where are you from, Joe? Let's see if we can't get down to why you are the way you are."

"I'm from San Diego, but I don't really think that has—"

"Parents?"

Joe looked stumped. "Um, yeah, I have parents."

"No, no. What are their names? What do they do?"

"Oh, um, my dad is also Joe. And—"

"So, you're Joe Jr.?"

"No!" Joe spurted with a look of supreme annoyance on his face. "I mean, technically, yes, but fuck, I hate being called that."

Peter raised an eyebrow. "Okay, now we're getting somewhere. I think that's the first time I've heard you swear. I'm guessing things aren't so copacetic between you and your father?"

"He's whatever."

Peter glanced at him, seeing more pain than anger. "Was there a fallout? Or just a general lack of…"

"Caring? Yeah, you could say that. Neither of my parents ever cared what I did. They would just give me money if I ever had a problem or an issue or whatever."

"So, rich, distant parents? Is that what I'm gathering?"

"Yep," Joe said, drawing the word out.

"What do they do for a living?"

"I don't know. My dad's a financial analyst…or advisor, some stupid money job. Janice, my mom, used to be in real estate. Now she just goes to events or galas or hangs out on the boat."

Peter felt a wave of guilt for all the time he spent away from home on his numerous missions for Dr. Owens over the years. At least he showed Noble and Zoe his undivided attention and love when he was home. "Do you have any siblings?"

Joe guffawed. "Jocelyn. The one my parents fawn over. She's going to be a senior in high school next year."

"All Js, huh?"

Joe shook his head. "It's so stupid."

"So, I'm guessing that becoming a police officer wasn't your parents' idea?"

Joe chuckled. "What gave that away? It was my uncle Bruce. He's the only member of the family I really like. I mean, he's awesome actually. He's a fireman. He's like the cool black sheep on my dad's side of the family. I don't think he really likes any of the rest of our family either. He shows up for things, but he spends most of the time hanging out with the kids, playing games, telling stories. He likes telling embarrassing stories about my dad and their other brothers and sisters. He encouraged me to do something meaningful. Something to give back to the people, the city, the state or whatever applied."

"I think me and Uncle Bruce would get along," Peter said.

"For sure."

"So, how the hell did you end up here in Lost Grove?"

Joe looked over at Peter, the frustration from talking or thinking about his immediate family dissipating. "That was ultimately my uncle's doing as well. He knew I didn't want to stick around San Diego, so he suggested I go to college in his hometown, Sacramento. He thought it would be a good change of pace. It was cool. I liked going to Kings games."

"Did you play basketball?"

Joe laughed. "Yeah, right. I'm five-four. No, I played tennis."

"Okay, so you graduated I presume, and then what?"

"It was just a posting on a recruitment board. I really didn't feel like joining the force in Sacramento. I wanted to start somewhere…smaller, less…"

"Violent?"

Joe shrugged. "I guess. Anyhow, I googled Lost Grove and thought it looked pretty cool. When I came up to interview, Sasha had already been working here for a few years. Bill had me ride around with her for the day to see how I liked it. I guess her and I hit it off in a weird way. And Bill seemed really chill."

Peter glanced to his left to see the Orbriallis looming over the tree line. They were getting close to the new development. He looked over at Joe. "Hey."

Joe looked back at Peter. "Yeah?"

"You should stand up for yourself more. I can tell you two are really close, but I think she would respect you more if you fought back, gave her some shit for a change?"

"Oh man, I don't know. She's like twice my size. Have you seen her arms? I feel like she would put me in a sleeper hold and make me pass out."

Peter laughed. "No she wouldn't. Trust me. Tough respects tough."

"You mean like…what do you mean?"

"There was a guy in our Special Ops training with me and Paddy named Rick Schultz. He was maybe like an inch taller than you. Two tops. Wiry thin. Smoked like a chimney. But there was an intensity inside of him. Paddy called it a bubbling rage. You could just sense that he was tough well beyond his stature. We had a weekend off from training and it was your stereotypical situation. We were at the bar, everyone's drunk, and some big-ass dude bumps into Rick. Some of Rick's beer splashed over his glass and landed on this dude's arm. Big man calls Rick some very unkind names and Paddy and I both simultaneous say, 'oh, fuck.'"

Joe stared wide-eyed at Peter. "The bubbling rage?"

"The bubbling rage. Rick calmly set his glass down, turned around and hit this guy with a punch that I swear to God would have knocked out a bear. Three seconds later he has this dude on the ground, his arm bent behind his back, his foot on the back of this guy's neck, having him begging for mercy."

"Whoa."

"We've got to get some bubbling rage in you, young Joe."

"Yeah, I don't know if I have that capacity."

"Sure you do." Peter pointed ahead. "There's the site. You ready?"

Joe clenched his fists and summoned a deep, gurgling voice. "Yeah! Let's get the protesters."

Peter slowly turned his head toward Joe. "Don't force it there, big guy. You try that around Sasha and she just might put you in that headlock."

Gravel crunched under the tires as Peter steered the squad car through the open chain-link gates of the construction site. The protestors, a small but persistent group, watched, shifting their weight and tightening their grip on their signs. The air was damp with the scent of overturned earth and concrete dust, the distant murmur of the nearby river just audible beneath the occasional clang of metal and the hum of an idling generator.

"Not that many," Joe muttered, watching them through the windshield.

Peter let out a low chuckle, easing the car to a stop near the construction office trailer. "I would say for Lost Grove it's a fair amount.

Protesting takes a lot of patience and will." He turned off the engine and unbuckled his seat belt. "That or boredom and a lot of time on your hands," he said and exited the car.

Joe stepped out. The heat of the summer sun instantly made him wish he wasn't wearing a bulletproof vest.

A loose gust of wind sent dust skimming across the gravel, rattling the edges of the protestors' signs. They weren't doing much, just standing there, observing. Only two actually held signs—one woman with dark hair pulled into a messy knot had hers propped against her shoulder, the bold black lettering on white cardboard reading: RAPE THE LAND. PAY THE PRICE. Beside her, a younger man, long-haired and bearded, held his sign lazily at his side, but his eyes burned with silent accusation. ORBRIALLIS: CORRUPTION, GREED, POLLUTION.

The trailer, the reason for Peter and Joe being here, sat squat and unimpressive, except for the obvious act of vandalism splashed across its surface. Thick red paint streaked the walls, congealing on the windows in ugly rivulets, dripping onto the plywood steps like fresh blood.

Peter exhaled sharply. His gut told him this wasn't just some kids playing around.

"Looks boring," Joe said, eyes still on the protestors.

"Like I said, patience." Peter turned and surveyed each protestor. He knew all but the kid with the Orbriallis sign. His eyes settled on Jeffrey Tacet and Angus Weatherspoon.

Jeffrey forced a loud huff. "Look who it is. You gonna come over here and take a swing at me like your boy?"

"Guess they'll hire anyone there now that Bill's gone," Angus chimed in.

Peter kept his expression steady. Last fall, Tacet and Weatherspoon harassed his son Noble and daughter Zoe over rumors that Peter was behind the death of Sarah Elizabeth Grahams. It ended with Noble decking Jeffrey, Jeffrey returning a punch, and Seth Wolfe coincidentally being on the spot off duty to break it up. One of Seth's main concerns with bringing Peter into the department was the very real scenario that there were still people in Lost Grove who believed Peter was responsible for the eerily similar deaths of Kelly Fulson and Sarah Elizabeth and that these people might want to start something with him. Peter was not going to let Seth down, certainly not for a pair of losers like Tacet and Weatherspoon.

"Nope," Peter replied. "I think Noble did a good enough job."

Peter raised his voice. "You've all got every right to be here and protest peacefully. We're not here for you, so don't let our presence keep you from what you were doing."

"Hey there, I'm guessing you're Sergeant Andalusian."

Peter and Joe both turned to see a hulking man of at least six-foot-five and two hundred and fifty pounds holding his hard hat. He was wearing blue jeans, work boots, a white T-shirt, and the standard orange vest. He extended his hand toward Peter.

Peter shook it. "You must be the construction manager, Stephen Frazier."

"Yes, sir. Thanks for coming down."

Peter turned to Joe. "Stay here and keep an eye on the protestors. Especially the two looking to cause trouble."

"I'm on it." Joe took a few strides closer to the group of ten.

Peter followed Stephen Frazier toward the vandalized trailer. The site smelled of raw lumber and wet concrete, the metallic tang of exposed rebar mingling with the distant scent of river water. A half-built framework of townhomes loomed in the background, skeletal and waiting to be fleshed out, while a battered billboard with an artist's rendering near the trailer showcased the pristine, picturesque future the developers envisioned—a stark contrast to the gritty reality of the site.

Frazier let out a frustrated sigh, gesturing toward the streaks of red paint. "Came in this morning to find it like this. Bastards must've done it sometime after we locked up last night." He scowled. "We've had minor stuff before—trash dumped, an attempt at a slashed tire—but this?" He shook his head. "This feels like an escalation."

Peter studied the damage. The paint hadn't been haphazardly thrown; it had been deliberately smeared across the windows, dripping like blood over the plywood steps. A message had been scrawled near the door in the same red streaks: NO MORE GRAVES.

His stomach tightened.

Frazier folded his arms, his biceps flexing beneath his T-shirt. "You ever seen that before?" he asked, nodding at the message.

Peter kept his expression neutral. He'd seen plenty of threats in his time, but this one had an eerie familiarity to it. He wouldn't give Tacet or Weatherspoon the satisfaction of seeing him rattled. "We'll look into it," he said simply.

Behind them, Joe kept his post near the protestors, his presence alone ensuring things didn't escalate. Tacet muttered something to

Angus, earning a snicker, but neither made a move to push their luck. The long-haired kid with the Orbriallis sign kept his eyes locked on Peter, unblinking, as if trying to burn a hole through him with sheer willpower.

Frazier sighed again, rubbing the back of his neck. "I don't want my crew dealing with this crap. It's bad enough we've got protesters slowing things down, but now I've got guys worried someone's gonna come in and torch the site."

Peter glanced toward the open gate, where a few other construction workers lingered near their trucks, watching the scene unfold with wary eyes. They weren't just annoyed by the protestors—they were nervous.

"We'll get statements from you and your crew," Peter said. "See if anyone noticed anything out of place before they left last night." He pulled out his notepad. "You got security cameras?"

Frazier scoffed. "Yeah, but they're about as useful as a wet paper bag. Half the time, they cut out, and when they do work, they're blurry as hell. I'll pull the footage, but I wouldn't hold my breath."

Peter nodded, making a mental note to have the footage reviewed anyway. Even bad cameras could catch something. A figure, a vehicle, a time frame.

Frazier's jaw tightened. "You think this is just protestors taking it too far?"

Peter's gut told him it wasn't that simple. The words *No More Graves* weren't a generic eco-warrior slogan. They had meaning. And in a town like Lost Grove, where old wounds never quite healed, meaning could be dangerous.

"We'll find out," he said.

"The other stuff is this way," Stephen muttered.

Peter followed the foreman up the gravel path to the townhomes. He pulled up short in front of one with hanging wires and unfinished plumbing. Across the outside wall "Orbriallis Institute=Unethical Human Testing" was spray painted in bold red letters.

For nearly two decades, Peter had navigated the shadowy corridors of the Institute, slipping classified documents—likely filled with data on experimental tests—into briefcases for high-ranking government officials. Now he was on the other side, the side of good, working for the law. The irony was not lost on him.

"Hard to miss it," Stephen commented.

Peter had to agree. This message was hard to miss. He pointed to the spray cans on the ground. "No one's touched these?"

"No, sir. Left it all just as you instructed."

Peter pulled out latex gloves and a large evidence bag from his leg pockets. "We'll check for prints. Even if they're still there, I doubt they'll be in the system."

"I don't mean to be critical, but with protestors out here now for weeks, is there a reason you guys aren't patrolling the area?"

Peter looked up from a crouched position. "We have been. Our night man has been driving by once or twice a night. We had an incident last night in our state park that required most of the department's attention. And note that I said 'our night man,' one man. We don't have enough officers in a town of fifteen hundred to have someone staked out here the whole time you guys aren't working."

Stephen nodded, almost bowing his head. "Understood, Sergeant. I didn't mean to insinuate—"

"It's fine," Peter said as he sealed up the evidence bag and stood back up. "What I would recommend is telling your contact at the Orbriallis to hire some security. Trust me, they have the money to do so."

"I'll pass that along to them."

"Did you notice anything else, not as blatant, out of the ordinary when you got here today?"

Stephen looked around the site. "Nothing that stood out."

"Something else I would recommend from now on is to take a keen survey of things before leaving for the night. Maybe even take pictures. And then take the time in the morning to line it all up. If you notice anything missing, even anything moved from one place to another, you call me right away."

"I appreciate it," Stephen said.

"And you said you haven't had any issues with the protestors?"

"Nothing worth calling you in for. They yell stuff, chant stuff, but no one has crossed the property line."

Peter glanced back toward the entrance to see Joe chatting with one of the protestors. He looked back at Stephen. "I'd like to look around the site before I go if you don't mind."

"Sure thing." Stephen extended his hard hat. "I'll have to ask you to wear this for safety precautions."

Peter grabbed it and put it on.

"Anything in particular you're looking for?"

Peter shook his head. "No, just want to get a feel for the layout, look for any potential areas that might be targeted, see if I can find anything else suspicious lying around." Peter wasn't about to tell the construction manager that he was also going to be looking for any hidden explosive devices.

Stephen extended his hand once more. "I'll be around if you need anything. Thanks again."

"Sure thing." Peter shook the man's hand, turned around, and made his way deeper into the site.

The wind picked up again, rustling through the skeletal frameworks of townhomes, rattling loose tarps, and sending a discarded plastic cup tumbling across the gravel. Somewhere in the distance, a nail gun popped in quick succession, a reminder that, for all the disruption, work was still moving forward.

He moved deeper into the site, stepping over rebar and around stacks of lumber. The further he got from the trailer, the quieter it became, the sounds of the workers and protestors fading behind him. The river wasn't far from here. He could hear it now, a steady rush of water beyond the tree line, the lifeblood of Lost Grove and the reason why this development had been such a hotbed for controversy.

Peter stopped near one of the finished foundations, surveying the area. The vandal's message had been bold, direct. Not about the environment, but about the Institute. Or him?

NO MORE GRAVES.

That was what unsettled him. Were these two different messages, or were they meant to be conflicting to throw him off? The protestors outside were the usual mix of concerned locals and out-of-town activists, but someone with a deeper knowledge of Orbriallis had escalated things.

He crouched near a stack of cinder blocks, scanning for anything out of place. The site itself was in chaos by nature. Tools, materials, half-built structures. Peter knew how to look past the disorder, to find the things that shouldn't be there. A cigarette butt here, a misplaced footprint there. But there wasn't much to see.

Peter's breath came out slow, controlled, but his gut tightened. He stood and pulled out his phone.

"Sergeant, how can I help you?" Paddy answered.

Peter grinned. "I'm over at the construction site. Someone vandalized the place. Poured paint all over the office and spray painted one of the buildings."

"Artistic expression comes in many forms."

"Here's the thing," Peter continued. "They wrote out 'No more graves' on the steps of the office. And on the building, 'Orbriallis Institute equals Unethical Human Testing.'"

"I see."

"I could see this being a potentially dangerous situation."

"I agree," Paddy said, the typing of his keyboard sounding in the background.

"I know you have your hands full at the park, but do poke around and see what you can turn up."

"I was just getting ready to head back to the park now, but I'll dig in after I'm off. I'll probably swing by the bar and get some conversations going, see if anyone spills anything."

"Do your thing," Peter said and disconnected.

A distant crunch of gravel made him turn. Joe was heading toward him.

"Talked to a few of them," Joe said, jerking his head toward the entrance. "Nothing useful. The usual song and dance, evil corporation, greedy developers, 'think of the trees.'"

Peter nodded, but his focus drifted back to the messages.

Joe dusted dirt off his pants. "You think we're dealing with a local or someone from out of town?"

Peter glanced back toward the protestors, then toward the river, as if the answer lay somewhere between the two. "I don't know yet," he admitted. "But someone here knows more than they're saying. Let's go get statements from the workers."

Joe nodded and started toward the waiting construction workers.

Peter scanned the site one more time. Chances were that it was just one of the protestors. But whoever it was knew enough about the inner workings of the Institute to write what they wrote, and that didn't sit well with him.

Chapter Six
Coffee, Corpses, and Concerns

The Main Street Cafe was buzzing with a lunchtime crowd—twenty people instead of twelve. Seth wove past the cluster of loitering townsfolk outside, slipping into line with his ears tuned to the ebb and flow of conversation. Had word of Kevin Marlow's death already spread? And if so, how fast?

He was still adjusting to the lack of immediate scrutiny now that he was out of the sergeant uniform. Plain clothes offered a kind of camouflage. His toolbelt with walkie-talkie, cuffs, and his sidearm still marked him as law enforcement. Since stepping up as chief, direct stares had turned into double takes, which is what he was getting now.

"Hey, Seth, guessing it's been a long day for you, I'll get your order going right quick." Clemency Pruitt's voice cut through the collective hum of conversation like a knife.

So much for going unnoticed. Not that her greeting was unusual—the sister of the cafe's owner always greeted him like he was Norm from *Cheers*, but today it confirmed what he'd suspected. If she knew he'd had a long day, she knew about what happened at Devil's Cradle, and if Clemency knew, everyone knew.

The room hushed. Conversations dropped ten decibels, shifting to guarded murmurs—everyone except Old Tom King.

Tom, a town relic, had the bronzed skin of a man who'd lived a lifetime on the Florida coast despite never leaving Lost Grove, and a barrel-chested voice that belied his wiry frame. He was also hard of hearing.

"Now, I heard from Stew Massengill," Tom announced, unbothered by the hush around him, "who knows them parts as well as I know my grandkids, that it was a leopard who attacked that poor traveler boy."

Seth exhaled slowly. *Why did I think this would go any differently?* "Tom! Everyone!" Seth's voice carried, drawing every gaze except Clemency's. She was still chatting away with Louise Combs at the front counter, despite the fact Louise had her back turned to her, staring at Seth.

"For starters," Seth began, "there are no leopards in Lost Grove. Secondly, Stew Massengill was nowhere near the crime scene nor anywhere in Devil's Cradle State Park."

"That's not what he said," Tom uttered.

"I don't know what a 'traveler boy' is, Tom. But the child in question has grieving parents and an older sister who are staying in Lost Grove. So, please, be respectful and conscious of what you're saying and where you're saying it. Lastly, and most importantly, we do not have any answers as to what happened to the young boy. Rest assured that when those details are known, we will release them to the public. Do *not* spread rumors! Do not even *debate* over what animal it may have been! I will not have a militia heading into the woods shooting anything that moves. That is all. Thank you."

After a smattering of coughs, clearing of throats, and chairs shifting, dialogue amongst the patrons picked back up.

It felt familiar—standing before a crowd, commanding their attention. The last time he had to do this was during the search for Zoe Andalusian, when The Green Man, Raymond LaRange, had taken her. That night, he had rallied the town. Today, he was holding them back.

Seth felt a tingle crawl up his spine. It only mildly alarmed him that he knew what caused it. He turned around to see a radiant Story Palmer standing inside the cafe doorway, beaming at him. She wore a deep, earthy-brown blouse knotted at the waist. The fabric, crinkled and loose, revealed a teasing glimpse of skin beneath layered silver pendants that jump-started Seth's heart. The sleeves, casually rolled to her elbows, exposed delicate tattoos tracing the inside of her arms. The skirt—a billowing expanse of off-white gauze—fell in gentle folds, the perfect counterbalance to the raw, undone elegance of her top. Her favorite pair of lace-up boots peeked out from the flowing hem. He felt a mix of embarrassment and pride that she had been watching.

Story sashayed over to Seth, rose on her toes, and leaned in to kiss him softly on the lips. "That was highly arousing," she whispered in his ear. As quickly as the teasing came, her expression sobered. Her fingers curled around his, her grip gentle but insistent. "And also very sad. What happened?"

Seth looked around the cafe, seeing every chair filled. He glanced out the window and noticed the high table outside was free. "Why don't you go secure us that table so we can talk without eavesdroppers?"

"Okay."

"You want your usual?"

"Yes, please." She gave his hand one last squeeze before slipping outside.

Seth exhaled, then turned back to give Clemency the rest of his order.

The noise of the cafe had returned, but the weight in the air hadn't lifted.

Seth set his turkey and provolone sandwich and double iced latte on the table before dropping onto the stool opposite Story. He'd already brought her iced matcha latte and kale and locally made goat cheese salad, knowing her usual order by heart.

"I still miss your uniform," she said, sipping from her straw.

His eyes followed the movements of her lips, then wandered over the tattoos that inked her forearms. He followed them to the triskele tattooed between her exposed cleavage, feeling like a teenager. "It had just started to grow on me, too."

Story giggled, catching Seth's eyes taking her in. "You have time to come over after lunch?" she whispered.

Heat flushed through Seth's chest and settled low in his stomach, but he forced a chuckle, shaking his head. "Unfortunately, no. I have an autopsy to get to."

The rush of desire in Story's body vanished like a tide pulling out to sea. The warmth between her thighs turned to ice in her veins. Tears pricked at her eyes. "A young boy?"

Seth nodded, swallowing his bite of sandwich like it had turned to lead. "Seven," he said somberly.

She inhaled sharply, setting down her fork. "Jesus. That's awful."

Seth watched her dab at her eyes with a napkin, a twinge of something—love, admiration, envy—tightening in his chest. Almost twenty years as a homicide detective had worn down his ability to feel deeply about a case. He'd had to build walls; she never had.

Story glanced to her right to make sure the usual crew that liked to gather outside the cafe and talk for hours was still out of earshot. She leaned over the table, closer to Seth. "You mentioned an animal inside. Was it an animal attack?"

A muscle twitched in Seth's jaw. The image of the boy's ravaged body—the shredded skin, the missing finger—flashed behind his eyes. He forced a slow breath. It was no understatement that it was always worse with children. Children and animals. The most helpless and innocent. "That's the initial assumption. Based on the scene."

"Assumption?"

Seth glanced past Story to two young women ambling down Main Street, their arms looped in easy companionship, shopping bags swinging at their sides. Tourists—charmed by the old Victorians, the coastal air, the curated calm of Lost Grove. On any given week, they made up at least a quarter of the foot traffic. In July, it felt like half the town wore linen and sunscreen, especially with the county fair approaching. Locals smiled. Businesses stayed open late. Revenue flowed. The illusion of peace remained perfectly preserved.

Seth washed down another bite of his sandwich with his latte, nodding his head. "Some of the wounds look a lot like how we found Raymond LaRange. So, we could be looking at the same grey wolf, or pack of grey wolves."

A bubbling of anxiety quickly brewed inside Story's stomach. The demise of Raymond LaRange and what the medical examiner determined to be death by wild animal attack, specifically a grey wolf, was a point of unspoken and unknown contention between them. Just two months prior, Story's best friend Mary Germaine had shown up on Story's doorstep covered in blood, in a state of horrified shock. She confessed to Story, and shortly thereafter to Seth, that she had not only stalked and killed Raymond LaRange but that she had drunk his blood and even consumed some of his flesh.

Story had been aware of Mary's affliction for years, a heightened form of pica, or so the doctors told her when she was a young girl, that was so severe that it kept Mary from walking Main Street during the day due to the aroma of meat and blood emanating from the restaurants, grocery stores, and butcher shops. Mary had done deplorable things as a teenager to get blood and raw meat from butchers. Story helped Mary by not only giving her more natural, homeopathic remedies to treat her cravings but also being her emotional and mental support system, giving her confidence to believe she could overcome her affliction.

Last year, not long before The Event at the Orbriallis Institute, Mary admitted to Story that she had feasted on a dead not-child, one of Raymond LaRange's puppet children that were not fully human. The Green Man's not-children were a Lost Grove myth whispered about by a scant few who claimed to have seen them. Story might not have believed in them herself if she hadn't come into far too close contact with a herd of them one night when she was moonbathing, scampering behind a demented LaRange. Their eyes were empty and soulless, and their pearl-white skin was semi-translucent and didn't reflect light naturally, almost as if it were rubber, not flesh.

Story never told anyone of Mary's admission, not even Seth. She prayed that it was a one-time incident, Mary just happening across a dead not-child on the outskirts of the woods early one morning. But when Mary confessed to what she had done to LaRange, her conviction was hard not to believe. Every detail was vivid, her voice ravaged with anguish, her eyes pleading for leniency and forgiveness.

Seth had been relieved, and seemingly satisfied, with the findings of the wildlife expert who assisted Dr. Wes Hensley in the autopsy. Wes told Seth that it was impossible that a human could have been responsible for the attack, and Seth agreed. Story knew he would. Mary's affliction was not something tangible to wrap one's mind around. Story, however, had seen it firsthand, and she knew in her gut that Mary's wide-eyed story had been true. There was a series of desperate events, one violent and bloody, that she never shared with Seth. It would have felt like the harshest betrayal to divulge Mary's weakest moments with anyone else. Even her lover.

Story had allowed herself to bathe in the comfort that Mary was getting treatment and care at the Orbriallis Institute the past six weeks. She was happy to leave Mary's past behind, believing there was mental, physical, and emotional progress being made, perhaps even a cure one day. Now hearing Seth say the crime scene mimicked that of LaRange's felt like freezing water laced with razors running down her insides. But it was a child. No matter what Mary had done, she would never hurt a child. Yet the words *similar wounds* echoed in her head, and her matcha suddenly tasted sour.

"Story?"

She blinked, realizing she'd been staring into her kale salad like it might offer an answer. "Sorry. Did you ask something?"

Seth smiled softly, but there was a pinch in his brow. "Not yet. I knew you would take this harder than most."

Her lips twitched into something like a smile. "Yes. I just had such a vivid image in my mind of what happened to Raymond. Now with a child…"

Seth reached across the table, his palm warm over hers. "I know. Cases with children are always more brutal for me. For all detectives."

"Detectives, huh?" she teased lightly, catching his word choice.

"You know what I mean." He chuckled, but it didn't reach his eyes. Seth had never gotten used to being called a sergeant, and he wasn't sure he would ever get used to chief.

Story casually pulled her hand back, feeling a tremble in her free hand. "Would you mind getting a to-go box for me?"

Seth studied Story's expression, her rapid eye blinks, her uncharacteristic brief eye contact. "Is something else bothering you?"

She shook her head, maybe a beat too fast. "No. No, I'm just trying not to think about it. The boy. You said a boy, right?"

Seth narrowed his gaze. "I did, yes. Story, please tell me you're not worried that Mary—"

"No!" Her voice jumped out, too loud, too quick. "Of course not." God, she was terrible at lying. She didn't believe in lying. And yet here she was, withholding her feelings, her fears. She needed to contact Mary. See her. Look at her. If there was guilt, she'd see it. If Story was bad at lying, Mary was absolute shit at withholding her feelings, especially guilt.

Seth's brow furrowed. Story was clearly withholding something from him, and the concern etched on her face suggested she feared Mary might have been responsible. This was the last complication Seth needed. He had made peace with the conclusion of LaRange's death. It was the only explanation that fit neatly in his mind. And yet all the blood on Mary's clothes. The unwavering certainty in her eyes bothered him. No, he wasn't going to tumble down that rabbit hole again. He had an autopsy to get to, and it would surely waylay any ludicrous doubts that threatened to cloud his judgment.

Seth stood up to fetch them each a to-go container but leaned back over the table. "Mary would never harm—"

"A child, I know. Never."

The ride to the library was quiet, the kind of silence that pressed gently but persistently, like fog on glass. Seth drove with one hand on the wheel, the other resting on his thigh, fingers drumming softly. Story sat beside him in his department-issued Bronco, her gaze fixed on something far beyond the windshield—something he couldn't see.

The town passed by in slow motion: the familiar bookstore with its chalkboard sign changed daily, the bakery with the open window spilling the scent of cardamom and yeast into the street. It was all so normal. And yet her silence made it feel like the world had shifted an inch to the left, just enough to make everything slightly wrong.

Seth cast her a glance. She was twisting the edge of her paper lunch bag with one hand, her matcha long forgotten in the cup holder. He knew she adored children—he'd seen her read to them at the library, watched her fold paper into origami cranes and press them gently into little palms. That had to be what this was. Just grief. Compassion. She was an empath, after all. She felt things deeper than most.

Still, something about the way she kept swallowing, like she was trying to bury words before they rose to the surface, gnawed at him.

He pulled up in front of the library, the soft crunch of tires the only sound. Putting the Bronco in park, he turned to her.

"Come over tonight?" she asked before he could speak, opening the door and hopping out.

Seth leaned out his window as she made her way around. "I will. I promise."

Story looked at him then, her eyes a little softer than they'd been all lunch, but distant still, like the light in them had been dimmed by something she hadn't named yet. "You don't have to promise," she said quietly, her hand grazing his arm resting on the door. "I know the job can be unpredictable."

"I'll be there."

She nodded. For a second, it looked like she might say something else, something weightier, but instead, she leaned back in, kissed his cheek.

There was a time when daily life in Lost Grove was just that—predictable. Not lately. "I love you."

"I love you, too," Story said, and then she was gone, her ethereal skirt sweeping as she crossed the sidewalk, her figure folding into the tall doors of the library.

Seth watched her go, the hollow ache in his chest growing heavier the longer he stared at the spot where she'd vanished.

He didn't know what she was thinking.

But he knew deep down that she hadn't told him all of it.

Chapter Seven
Signs in the Flesh

The autopsy room had a profound heaviness. Walking through the steel doors felt like walking into some space station training room with less oxygen than humans needed to survive. Seth wasn't sure if that's how NASA rooms really were, but that's how he always imagined them in his head. Seeing the small, far too small, silhouette of Kevin Marlow's body under the sky-blue sheet on the operating table was a punch to Seth's chest. The age and the size of the body reminded him of a case in San Francisco in December 2022.

It was a double-homicide-suicide call he and his old partner, Kendra Washington, had received late one Saturday night. They arrived at the home of Catherine and Roderick Stevens to find Catherine, thirty-nine, in a nightgown holding her ten-year-old daughter, Abigail, wearing her pajamas, in the upstairs master bed, both shot through the head at close range. Roderick, age forty-three, was found in his office on the bottom floor, his head folded backward like a Pez dispenser over his leather rolling chair, naked, his registered 9mm gun on the blood-covered floor. A handwritten note on a blank piece of printer paper simply read 'Too much.'

It wasn't the first time Seth had walked into an autopsy room with a dead child on a table, but it was Kendra's first. As soon as they walked in and saw two covered adult bodies on separate tables and the uncovered body of Abigail under the bright lights of the operating table, Seth heard Kendra make a noise somewhere between a snort, a hiccup, and a growl. It was the swell of unbearable anguish making its way out of her body through her mouth. She muttered a high-pitched apology and left the room in a flurry. It was astonishing that the size of a human corpse could evoke such drastically different emotions.

For Seth, it was the same sensation as getting drilled in the chest by a line drive in baseball, his glove failing to do its job. Each time, it left him breathless. Today, this physical reaction was compounded by his frustratingly altered mental state. When he woke up this morning, all he could think about was the discovery of Kevin Marlow's body. Mary Germaine had been the last thing on his mind. But after dropping Story off at the library, thoughts of Mary traveled from the recesses to the forefront of his mind. It wasn't like Story to bottle up her emotions, and if it were only about the death of a child, she would have talked to him about it. Vividly recalling the conviction in Mary's eyes and voice the night she admitted to killing LaRange, combined with Story's silence, had Seth on edge in more ways than one.

Seth pulled his eyes from the body to address his friend, and old high school teammate, Wes Hensley. And apparently his older brother Cal. "Wes. Cal, wish I could say it's good to see you, but under the circumstances…"

Cal Hensley, two years older than both Seth and Wes, formerly an agent with the CDFW, was a reservation officer for the Wiyot tribe and an avid conservationist. The Native American brothers clearly looked related, with similar curved jawlines, curious dark brown eyes, and the same hairline, though Wes's hair was cut short and Cal wore his long black hair in a single braid. Wes had an inch on Cal at five-foot-ten, while Cal had fifteen pounds on Wes with broader shoulders, thicker arms and less of a paunch. Cal wore his chestnut uniform, slacks, short-sleeve button-up shirt, and cowboy boots, Wes his sky-blue operating coat.

Wes claimed his brother knew everything about every animal in Northern California, and possibly the country: attributes, tendencies, eating and mating habits, prints, bites, patches of hair or feathers. He wished Cal had been available to assess the wounds of Raymond LaRange back in May but he was out of town giving a speech at a seminar.

Cal greeted Seth with a handshake as he approached the table. "Never a good occasion when a child is involved."

"No," was all Seth could muster.

"Looks like you didn't get a whole hell of a lot of sleep either," Wes said, assessing Seth's eyes.

Seth shook his head. "Please tell me you were able to identify the animal or animals."

Wes and Cal exchanged a foreboding look.

"Fuck," Seth sighed.

Cal motioned for Seth to follow him as he made his way over to Wes's station, where roughly twenty photos were pinned up on a corkboard. "Wes called me up here early to take a look at the photos from the LaRange crime scene and autopsy in case there were similarities. Over here we have LaRange's body," Cal said, pointing to his right. "And obviously this is Kevin Marlow on this side."

Seth was thankful they were assessing photos rather than the body, though that was likely to come. He was familiar with LaRange's wounds, but this was the first time seeing the boy's cleaned up. "This poor fucking kid. All I can think about is the pain and fear he must have been feeling. Funny neither of those things popped in my head for LaRange."

"I can't say my feelings were much different," Wes admitted.

Seth glanced from Wes over to Cal. "Do you agree that the neck bites that killed LaRange were from a grey wolf?"

Cal shrugged. "There's only so much I can determine from photos, but I would agree that they would be consistent with wolf bites I've seen."

"What about the stomach? The CDFW agent Wes had in here apparently couldn't make heads or tails out of that area."

Cal fiddled with a chest-high button on his shirt. "I agree the claw marks on the stomach didn't come from the coyotes responsible for the legs."

Wes jumped in. "But tell him what you did notice—"

"I was getting to that, brother." Cal smirked as he turned to point at one of the photos of LaRange's midsection. "The claw marks that shredded the stomach open were curiously thick, wide almost. More so than a fox, a wolf, or even a mountain lion."

Please God don't say they were human, was all Seth could think as he held his breath, waiting for a response.

"They appear closer to an armadillo, a bear, or even an eagle." Cal turned around to face Seth. "A bear would be the only one that would remotely make sense, but still unlikely. I would expect much more damage if that were the case."

Seth rubbed his chin. "So…do you think—"

"I told Cal about your fear," Wes said.

"What fear?" Seth said, trying to keep his voice level.

Wes raised an eyebrow at him.

"A human," Cal offered. "Unless someone grew their fingers long enough to specifically file them into more of a claw shape, I would say you could rule that out."

Seth's stomach twisted. He wasn't saying it was impossible. "But let's just say for argument's sake…"

Cal looked at Wes and raised his eyebrows. "I don't want to argue my brother's stance, but given those highly unlikely circumstances, I suppose it would be possible."

Seth briefly closed his eyes and took in a long breath through his nose. "Okay."

"Is there something you're not telling us, Seth?" Wes asked.

"It's not that," Seth lied. Now was not the time to divulge Mary's ravings. If Wes or Cal were to tell him there was a chance that Kevin Marlow could have been killed by a human, that would be another matter. "It's just…we have coyotes, a crow, a grey wolf, and some other unidentified animal. That seems like an awful lot of animals for a body deceased just over a day in the woods."

Cal leaned over and tapped on Wes's workstation. "If someone came in here and set down a fresh, hot pizza and opened the box, how long do you think it would be before the three of us had a slice in our hands?"

Seth gave an exaggerated glance to the covered body of the young boy. "Can't say that your analogy works well under the circumstances, but I get your point. Tell me about the boy."

Cal nodded over at his brother.

"He likely died from severe blood loss," Wes began. "There is also a chance he died from heart failure."

Seth frowned. "Explain."

Wes turned and walked over to the operating table and uncovered the body of Kevin Marlow. Seth followed and stood opposite Wes toward the head of the body. Cal pulled up at the foot of the table, crossing his arms.

Wes extended the surgical light over the body and turned it on. "There were three main sources of the blood loss."

Seth's eyes traveled up the boy's body, from the torn-open stomach now cleaned and covered by a thin layer of mortuary tape, to the numerous pointed wounds in his chest, to what was left of his neck. Seth was blessed with an iron stomach. He never felt sick when encountering a gory or ghastly situation. The suppression of emotions and processing of information resulted instead in an acute headache, which was piercing the back of his skull now.

Wes extended a metal probe and pointed at the chunk missing on the right side of the boy's neck. "Obviously we have the neck. The carotid artery was decimated. Kevin would have been dead in a matter of seconds if this was the first point of attack. But the culmination of the injuries happened in far too quick of succession to determine what happened first."

"Does it matter?" Seth asked.

Wes shook his head. "The order of entry points is insignificant. Just making clear that this was quick." He sidestepped closer to the midsection and pointed at the stomach area. "There are numerous wounds to the intestines, and the liver is gone."

"This is common in most predatory animals," Cal chimed in. "The liver is filled with nutrients."

Seth felt an unfamiliar churn in his stomach. The act was so natural for a wild animal, but oh so unnatural to happen to a human, much less a child.

"Blood loss or possibly shock would have killed him if this was the first entry point," Wes said.

Seth looked from the stomach up to the chest. "Okay, so what do you make of those?"

Wes tapped his probe onto Kevin Marlow's chest. "Take a close look at these."

Seth leaned over to take a closer look at the pea-sized perforations. "Okay."

"These two right here pierced Kevin's heart."

Seth looked up at Wes with a sneer. "Jesus."

Cal walked over and stood next to his brother. "This is where things get really fascinating."

"Is that the word for it?"

Cal gave Seth a half smile. "For me, yes. And I think it might be for you once I explain."

Seth nodded for him to continue.

"A child's rib cage is quite small, of course, roughly half the size of a grown adult. And Kevin had no extra meat on him, as you can see."

Seth assessed the rib bones protruding through the skin. "And?"

"It wouldn't necessarily take an animal with the longest claws to reach the heart. Less than two inches, which would cover the vast majority of carnivorous animals in the state park."

"However," Wes interjected, "whichever animal this was pierced directly through the heart."

Mounds of wrinkles formed between Seth's eyebrows as he eyed the eight puncture wounds across Kevin's chest. Puncture wounds but no tears or gashes. He glared at Wes. "I don't get it. Why are these wounds so clean? Are you saying that whichever animal this was—"

"Intentionally pierced the heart? If this were a homicide and Kevin was attacked with an ice pick, then yes, I would say so. But considering—"

"Are you saying this could potentially be a—"

"No. No, I didn't mean to mislead you. The entry point of each pierce mark into his chest aligns with the angle into the heart, but the exit out the back of the heart is offset, indicating the curl of a claw."

"Or a talon," Cal interjected.

Seth took a step back and looked back and forth between the brothers. "Hold on here, guys. Talons?"

"As I said, this is where things get interesting."

"Don't tell me you think a bird joined forces with a fox or a wolf and—"

Cal calmly held up a hand to cut Seth off. "A few things here, Seth. For starters, there are only a select few animals native to Northern California that would have nails long enough to pierce straight through a heart, keeping in mind that the force of hitting the chest," Cal said, motioning down toward Kyle's chest with his right-hand fingers curved out like a claw, "could compress the distance it would take. And we can't say yet what animal was responsible for the neck or stomach."

"Come back over here," Wes said, heading back to the displayed photos above this desk. He pointed to a photo of the exposed rib cage of the boy. "What Cal is saying is backed up by the fractured ribs here and here," he said, pointing to the top and bottom entry points.

"With this in mind," Cal said, "we're talking about a black bear or possibly a mountain lion."

A morbid sense of relief began to overcome Seth. The force of what they were describing all but eliminated the frail form of Mary Germaine. "Okay, that makes some sense in theory. You mentioned talons, though."

Cal stepped next to his brother, pointing at the same photo. "What's most curious and perplexing here with the chest is this—the puncture wounds. With a mountain lion or black bear, I would expect to see claw marks, tears in the skin. This specific form of attack indicates to me an eagle or an owl. Especially with the two puncture wounds top and bottom, which is quite specific to the formation of the talons."

Seth huffed. "Are you telling me that Kevin was killed by a bird and then torn apart by some yet-to-be-determined animal?"

"Don't undersell the strength of an eagle or an owl, Seth. The speed at which they dive and the strength in their talons is enough to take down a deer or a wolf, among many other mammals."

"But would either attack a human? Much less a child?"

"It's quite rare, no doubt. And I would rule out the eagle due to it being near nightfall and that Kevin was in a heavily wooded area."

Seth held his hands up, starting to feel frustrated at the lack of definitive information. "So, an owl? Why on earth would an owl attack a young child?"

Cal exchanged a curious look with his brother. "Only reason would be if it felt threatened. But the real conundrum—"

"Why would it feel threatened by a fifty-pound child?"

"As you might recall from the statements by the family," Wes stepped in, "his older sister reported that Kevin threw something at her, which we know was a bone. And then Paddy and Eddie found another bone, from the same animal, by his dead body."

Seth nodded. He had seen the two bones that Eddie had bagged. "Okay, are you saying the determination of the chest wound is—"

Cal once again paused Seth with a lifted hand. "The conundrum, as I was saying, is that it would have to have been a massive—and I mean far beyond anything recorded—owl."

Seth waited for a follow-up to this piece of information. "Okay…so not an owl then?"

Cal looked to the floor, as Wes gazed over to the photos.

Seth raised his eyebrows, feeling an uneasy tension at the sudden silence. "Yes? No?"

"No," Cal said. He looked up and over to his brother, shaking his head. "No."

Wes looked his brother in the eyes and gave an imperceptible nod of agreement. "No."

Seth felt an alarming tingle roll up his spine. There was clearly something the Hensley brothers were communicating but not verbalizing. This was the most unwelcome trend of the day.

Wes looked at Seth. "Undetermined."

Seth sighed. "Okay, the two most important questions. One, is the attack on Kevin Marlow as identical as it looked to Raymond LaRange's?"

Wes shook his head. "No, certainly not in its totality."

"That sounds concrete," Seth grumbled.

"There was the finger, of course," Cal stated.

"Right, yes, each body had a missing finger," Wes replied.

Seth shrugged, asking for an elaboration.

"I don't see anything significant in it other than a scavenger picking off parts of its prey."

Seth rolled his eyes. "You guys aren't filling me with a great deal of confidence here."

"They're animal attacks, Seth."

"Which brings me to the most vital question. And I'm asking both of you about each victim. Is there any way a human being could have been responsible for *any* of this?"

Cal crossed his arms. "I don't believe so, no."

Wes strode back over to Kevin's body, Seth and Cal following. "The only thing that gives me any pause are the puncture marks on the chest. With my brother's assessment on which animals could have and could not have done this, the specific layout of the claw or talon marks, the improbability of a... I just can't say yet."

"Fuck!" Seth spun around and ran his hand through his hair again. "Wes, call your counterpart over in Oasis County and get his ass down here for a second opinion."

"That's unnecessary."

"I'd love to know why that is."

"Something I knew I should have done with LaRange," Wes growled with frustration. "We're testing for animal DNA."

Seth cocked his head to the side, feeling a little out of his element. DNA testing was standard practice as a homicide detective, but he had never come across a homicide by way of an animal in San Francisco. "And that's similar to—"

"It can be," Wes said. "Animal DNA testing takes hair or saliva samples to determine the precise species, and can actually narrow it down to the specific animal."

"I guess I shouldn't be surprised."

Cal chuckled. "What? You're telling me this didn't come up in the big city?"

Seth rolled his eyes.

Wes continued, "I should have trusted my instincts with LaRange. I knew that Agent Maretta wasn't concrete in her determination of the grey wolf, but I trusted her regardless. I'm going to correct that."

"You think it wasn't a wolf?" Seth asked.

Wes shook his head. "It's not that. It probably is. But if the same animal was responsible for Kevin Marlow, maybe we could have caught it sooner. That's on me."

Cal slapped his brother on the back. "No, brother. This is not on you."

"Either way, we can find out now."

Seth frowned. "What do you mean?"

"LaRange's body. It's not too late to exhume the body."

Seth felt the blood drain from his body. He placed a hand on the cabinet to the left of Wes's desk to steady himself.

Cal looked to his brother, who looked equally perplexed. "You okay, Seth? What is it?"

Seth had to pull it together, and quickly. There was no doubt that a DNA test would reveal human saliva. And from there it would be a matter of time before they traced it back to Mary, which would then all roll back on Seth. Mary would no doubt admit on record she told Seth what she'd done, and from there, Seth's career would be ruined. He turned back to the brothers. "Sorry, guys. It's been a long night—day. And I've got a town full of people on edge and hunters eager to go out and start shooting any animal they see."

"I can understand that," Cal said. "I'm willing to work extra hours to give you a hand here, Seth. Things at the moment are calm on the reservation. If I can help alleviate the tension in town, I'd like to help."

"I'd appreciate that, Cal. Thank you." Seth looked at Wes. "How long for the DNA results? The sooner we get them, the better."

Wes shrugged. "This will be my first time going down this path, but from what I've researched, we should get them within a week."

Seth ran his hand through his hair and sighed. "Well, see what you can do to get them sooner. We've got the county fair starting up next Friday. I'd love to get this wrapped up before we have thousands of people coming into town."

"I'll see what I can do."

Seth shook both brothers' hands. "I appreciate it, guys. Call me if you uncover anything else at all."

"Get some sleep, Seth," Cal offered.

Seth waved over his head as he headed to the door. With fears boiling over about Mary Germaine, what Story wasn't telling him, and now a possible DNA test coming from Raymond LaRange's corpse, Seth needed to get over to the Orbriallis to see what information he might be able to obtain from Dr. Bajorek about her work with Mary over the past few of weeks.

Chapter Eight
Layers of the Mind

Seth walked through the electronic glass doors to the Orbriallis Institute with two things in mind—to convince Lina Orbriallis to hire some private security for her construction site so he didn't have to waste any more time having his team babysitting it, and more importantly, to pry whatever information he could from Dr. Jane Bajorek regarding the ongoing treatment of his friend, and potential murderer, Mary Germaine. The first task he knew would likely be a matter of a brief conversation, but getting Jane to reveal information about one of her patients would be a dubious chore. The only leverage Seth had was that he was transparent with Jane about Mary's admission of what she had done and also that despite Dr. Wes Hensley saying it was impossible that a human could have inflicted the wounds upon LaRange's body; it was still wrapped up in a criminal case.

Seth spotted Seamus Owens, the nephew of the disgraced and disappeared former head of the institute, at the front desk, chatting away with new head of security, Vince Lashley. Seamus had been demoted from that position following The Event, a punishment he was more than happy to accept considering he was in mortal fear of being charged as an accessory to Neil Owens's misdeeds and deported back to Ireland. It wouldn't take much in these times. With the feds sweeping in to haul Neil away, along with any and all evidence of his unethical human testing, combined with Seth's own testimony to Seamus's legitimate solid performance as head of security, Lina allowed him to stay on.

The two men were a stark contrast standing next to one another—

Seamus standing at least six-foot-five, roughly 240 pounds of solid muscle, skin as pale as a blizzard, with shaggy red hair, Vince eight inches shorter and fifty pounds lighter, though still in supreme condition, rich ebony skin and a shiny bald head.

Seamus turned to see Seth approaching the desk. "Oye, Seth!"

Seth couldn't help being nudged into a mildly good mood seeing Seamus's wide toothy smile. Was it strange that Seth had actually become friends with Seamus Owens after the monster of a man held Seth out a seventeen-story broken window, threatening to drop him to his certain demise the night of The Event? Despite Seth's life flashing before his eyes while simultaneously hearing Sarah Elizabeth's scream from beyond the grave to save him, he believed Seamus when he told Seth he never would have done it, that he was just trying to scare him. It was also hard to hold a grudge against the man after Seth fractured his fibula and dislodged his kneecap during the melee, only to have the man react with mild annoyance.

Seth shook his hand. "How you doing, big man?"

"You know me, can't complain."

"Vince." Seth greeted the head of security with a firm handshake.

"Chief, good to see you. I heard about that unfortunate incident in Devil's Cradle. Just awful."

"Yeah, been a rough day."

Seamus shook his head. "A wee lad, too. That's just not right."

"I couldn't agree more," Seth said. "Obviously that's not why I'm here, though."

"No, Lina called me to give me a heads-up," Vince said. "I'll let your buddy take you up."

Seamus wrapped his meat slab of an arm around Seth's shoulder. "Up we go, mate!"

Seth was still trying to feel comfortable with the intimacy of Seamus's affection, in no small part because he knew that Seamus could snap his neck without exerting half his strength.

The elevator doors opened and the pair stepped in.

"Oye, Paddy texted me and said he wanted to get together at the pub tonight. You'll join us, yeah?" Seamus stated more than asked.

Seth grinned, knowing what the purpose of that invitation was. Peter informed Seth that he asked Paddy to "look into things," which would likely entail Paddy digging around on the internet in ways that Seth didn't want to know about, and also sapping information for the locals playing the role of "local drunk." Little did every patron of Reggie's Pub know that Paddy had been playing them for years, getting the locals to spill gossip and information he used to take down Neil Owens.

"I don't know, Sheam-O. You know the case I have on my hands. I got two hours of sleep—"

Seamus slapped Seth on the back. "Agh, you'll be there."

"Not sure I will," Seth murmured. "How's the knee coming?"

Seamus jumped up and down as the elevator passed the fifteenth floor, on their way to the penthouse, which would be the thirty-second floor.

Seth gripped the side rails and prayed that the cables didn't snap. "Okay, I think that's enough. So, good then?"

"Aye. What would ya think? Best doctors in the world here, yeah?"

"I mean, sure, but not really their specialty, is it?"

Seamus waved off the notion. "Ah, sure it is."

Seth frowned and decided not to argue the point.

"Not supposed to be jumping like that, but I feel great. New knee and all."

Seth raised an eyebrow at him. "You're welcome?"

Seamus burst into a fit of laughter and tackled Seth into the corner of the elevator.

"Yep, great," Seth muttered, just as the chime saved him from having to counter whatever Seamus was doing to him.

Seamus sprang to a standing, professional stance. "We're here, mate."

"Thanks for the heads-up," Seth said as the doors opened to Lina's, formerly Dr. Owens's, luxury two-story penthouse.

"Hello, Uncle Seth," came the voice of Thomas Jeremiah Grahams, followed by the tiny body of the two-year-old child of Sarah Elizabeth, who came charging around the corner in the distance.

"Jesus Christ," Seamus uttered, backpedaling. "Keep him away from me, Seth. Scares the bejesus outta me."

Seth used all of his internal strength not to laugh. There was no denying that young Thomas Grahams was the most unusual of all children, mentally, physically, and psychologically advanced far beyond his years, thanks to the research and testing of Dr. Owens, his team, and the willingness of Sarah Elizabeth to be a vessel. But to constantly see a man the size of Seamus genuinely terrified by a child not even three feet tall never ceased to amuse Seth.

Thomas jumped into Seth's arms. "I'm happy you came to see me, Seth. The atmosphere in the air today pleases me."

Seth ruffled his sandy blonde hair. "Good to see you, buddy." Seth spun around and stepped toward the elevator. "Say hi to Uncle Seamus."

Seamus sneered at Seth. "Shouldn't know the word atmosphere," he muttered as the doors started to close.

"Good day to you, Uncle Seamus," Thomas said in a high-pitched voice. "Hello, Seth."

Seth spun around with Thomas to see Lina Orbriallis approaching them. She was wearing beige slacks, a white tank top covered by a long, flowing brown cardigan, and no veil to cover her disfigured face, all drastic changes courtesy of Story Palmer's friendship and influence. Seth had grown up in Lost Grove, hearing all sorts of stories, rhymes, and songs about Geiger and Lina Orbriallis, and the Institute in general. As a young teenager, Seth would have believed that Lina looked like the Elephant Man, but the reality, which he encountered last fall, was so far from the lore it was a mystery how the rumors ever began.

"Hello, Lina. Thanks for seeing me."

Lina smiled. "Always."

"Where's Cleo?" Seth asked of Sarah Elizabeth's second child, just nine months old now.

"In her playroom. She'll be anxious to see you."

Seth looked to the boy in his arms. "Hey, Thomas? Could you go play with your sister while I talk to your gram-mama for a few minutes?"

"If it pleases you."

"It would," Seth said with a smile and set the boy down.

As Thomas ran back in the direction he had come from, Lina motioned to the seating area. "Please, have a seat. Can I make you some tea? Or bring you—"

"No, thank you," Seth said as he made his way over to sit in the plush armchair next to the couch Lina lowered herself on. "This will only take a minute. I assume you've heard of the protestors at the building site?"

Lina nodded, looking down to her lap. "Yes. I feel terrible. I never thought this would upset the people in town."

"It's not your fault, Lina. People, in general, don't like change. Lost Grove has had roughly the same population, the same houses, since I was a child."

"It's not just that. I've heard of the ecological concerns." Lina looked back up at Seth, her brows knitted together. "Neil arranged all of this. He'd been planning it for years. I've heard from the board that everything was signed off on by the city, that there wouldn't be any issues."

Considering how Dr. Owens went about the rest of his business, Seth didn't feel at all confident that palms weren't greased to get the permits signed off. "The construction is still in the early stages. It's not too late if you want to have someone come in to give a second opinion."

"Oh, I don't know." Lina wrung her hands together. "All the doctors and researchers are so anxious to move up here to get away from the unincorporated towns. They've had break-ins, property damage. I hear there is a drug epidemic as well."

"That is all accurate. But once these properties are up, roads are paved, a sewage system put in, it'll be too late to go back if something harmful actually does transpire with the surrounding forest or the river."

Lina looked up at Seth, her eyes starting to water. "Of course you're right. I should do that. It's just…no matter what I do, someone is going to be upset."

"I'm sure Dr. Bajorek would be willing to take some of this off your hands," Seth offered. After Dr. Owens's departure, Lina had assumed the role of executive director, and Jane had taken on the responsibilities of medical director and administrative director.

"Oh, I know she would, but she's got so much on her plate. It doesn't seem right to put this on her shoulders."

Seth's heart warmed. Lina was such a caring and loving individual, almost too much so. She had instinctively become a surrogate mother to Sarah Elizabeth's children after she died giving birth to Cleo. She cared for them fiercely. And she could have easily sold off her controlling share of the Orbriallis and let the board decide what to do with the company, who would run it. But Lina was the daughter of the man who built the facility from the ground up and she felt it was her duty to step into his shadow and take control after everything came crashing down after The Event.

"I'll speak to her," Seth said. "I need to go see her next to check on one of her patients, a good friend of mine."

"Oh dear, I hope they're okay."

Seth forced a smile. "Me too. Look, the main reason I wanted to see you, and you may have already received a call about this, but I think it would be wise to hire private security to watch over the site twenty-four hours a day."

Lina sat upright. "Did something happen?"

Seth scooched up on the chair, leaning in closer to Lina. "Nothing terrible. No violence or anything of that nature. But there's been vandalism. And the tension around the site is growing. I think the workers are constantly looking over their shoulders while trying to do their job to make sure the protestors don't cross the line. And I don't have enough people on my team to watch over the site at night."

"Yes, of course. I'll speak with Mr. Lashley. I'm sure he'll have a recommendation."

Seth grinned. "You might just want to send Seamus out there. I think his presence alone will deter any trouble."

Lina smiled. "He's such a kind man. I wish his uncle had been more like him."

Seth could only nod as he stood to his feet. "Well, thanks again for seeing me, Lina."

Lina stood and grabbed Seth's right hand and gave it a pat. "You know you're always welcome here. And I thank you for always checking on the children."

"It's my pleasure." And it was. Seth had felt an immediate responsibility to help watch over and protect Sarah Elizabeth's children. Even though he and Sarah had never met or spoken in the real world, they had an incorporeal connection. A psychic, supernatural link he couldn't explain. "Speaking of which, I should go see Cleo before I go."

"Yes, come, come," Lina said as she led Seth back to the children's playroom.

Every time Seth stepped into the rainforest-themed playroom, he was thrust back into his second time travel experience that Story had led him into when he was searching for answers about the Sarah Elizabeth case. It was this same room, with many of the same toys strewn about, where he first encountered Cleo, before they had met in the "real" world. Seth had been hoping to go back in time to talk to Sarah Elizabeth but had gone ahead in time where he stumbled into this room. Cleo told Seth that he was looking for Dr. Neil Owens and that the Green Man would lead him to where he needed to go. These were indeed the clues that helped him solve the mystery.

"Hi, Sef," Cleo said, extending her arms toward him, squeezing her little fists open and closed.

Seth grinned as he stepped into the room and sat down on the floor next to Cleo and Thomas. He adored her little lisp. The two were putting together a rather complex-looking puzzle of two rabbits running down a snowy hillside. Most children their age would have a twenty- to forty-piece puzzle, this one was five hundred. He grabbed Cleo's hands and gave them a gentle squeeze. "Hello, Cleo. How are you?"

"Well, fank you."

Even after nine months it was still difficult to process the advanced English both Cleo and Thomas spoke. "When did you start this puzzle?" Seth asked.

"Just this morning, Seth," Thomas answered.

Seth had to bite his tongue to hold back uttering an expletive. The puzzle was already two-thirds done. It would have taken him and Story two weeks to get this far.

"Extraordinary, isn't it?" Lina mused, standing above them.

Seth glanced at her, his eyebrows raised high. "It is." He looked back to Cleo. "I'm very impressed."

"Fank you, Sef. Will you be staying the day?"

"Yes," Thomas said. "Please do stay with us, Uncle Seth."

Lina crouched down. "Your uncle has a very busy day of work ahead of him, my children."

"It's true," Seth said. "But I'll come by this weekend to spend some proper time with you."

"Wif Story?" Cleo asked.

Seth laughed. "Yes, she wouldn't dare miss it."

Seth exited on the seventeenth floor and made his way to Dr. Bajorek's office, having paged her that he was on his way down from his visit with Lina. Her office door was open. He poked his head in to see her behind her desk, head down, writing, her long black hair covering her face. He knocked on the doorframe. "Dr. Bajorek?"

Jane looked up, brushing her hair to the side. "I told you to stop calling me that."

"Sorry. Jane."

"That's better. Come in, shut the door."

Seth stepped in, closed the door, and then grabbed the chair opposite her. "Thanks for seeing me."

Jane removed her reading glasses and set them on her desk. "Never a problem, Seth."

Seth swallowed heavily. There was something slightly intimidating about Jane Bajorek. Her razor-sharp eyes, sitting above her high cheekbones, always seemed to see right through him, deep into his mind. She radiated a superior intelligence and perception that rivaled that of the troubled, enigmatic, but brilliant Dr. Owens. Seth was also positive that she knew he found her strikingly attractive, a fact that Story loved to tease him about every time her name came up.

Seth cleared his throat. "Yes, so, I wanted to ask you about—"

"Czy chcesz, żebym odszedł?" the sultry voice behind Seth asked.

Seth jumped at least four inches off his chair, his heart rising up into his throat. "Jesus Christ!" He grabbed his chest and turned around to see one of Jane's highly disturbing and also stunning mothers sitting in a chair in the dark corner of the room. He should have known she would be there to taunt him as she tended to whenever he came by the facility. "Hi, Apolonia."

"Witaj, Seth."

Seth tried to avert his eyes from being caught in the vortex of Apolonia's hypnotic stare. Apolonia, who looked like Jane's older sister, had the same long jet-black hair, hers down to her waist, understood and knew English but refused to speak it. She could also read minds and put people in trances. That she was apparently possessed by her long-dead mother was the least disturbing aspect of her demeanor.

"Yes, Mother, I think it best if you leave. You got what you wanted."

Seth turned to look at Jane. "What did she want?"

"Just to see you."

"Uh-huh." Seth didn't like how she said that, as if it weren't undeniably creepy.

Apolonia silently walked toward the door, running her fingertips over Seth's shoulder.

Seth physically shivered, trying to maintain what composure hadn't leapt from his body.

"Będę cię mieć," were Apolonia's final words before she walked out, pulling the door slowly behind her.

"No, you won't, Mother," Jane called out as the door clicked shut.

Seth blinked rapidly. "What did she say?"

"Don't worry about it."

Seth slowly eased back into the chair. "I really wish I could say I won't."

Jane smirked. "You were saying?"

Seth cleared his throat once more. "Yes, I was hoping you'd be willing to tell me how Mary is getting along."

Jane leaned back in her chair. "You know I can't discuss—"

Seth held a hand up. "No, I know. It's just... Did you hear about what happened last night at Devil's Cradle?"

Jane furrowed her brow. "No, what?"

"Well, it's official police business, so..." Seth grinned with his eyes.

"Cute," Jane said. "I can't promise anything, but continue."

"It's not pleasant, but a seven-year-old boy was found mauled in the forest last night."

"That's terrible. I'm sorry you had to see that."

Seth shifted in his chair. "The thing is, the scene was eerily familiar to how we found Raymond LaRange."

Jane planted her elbow on the desk and set her chin in her hand. "I see. And you think, what? That Mary could have harmed a child?"

Seth quickly shook his head. "No, I truly don't believe she would. But I also never thought she was capable of what she claimed she did to LaRange."

"Claims," Jane said. "She has not wavered from her story."

"Okay... So, what, you believe her then? Despite what the autopsy said?"

Jane dropped her hand back to the desk. "You remember the story I told you about my mothers, yes?"

"About their affliction?"

Jane nodded. "Correct. You may recall that at first, I truly believed that both of my mothers were mentally disturbed. I was certain they suffered delusions. I searched and searched for answers in the world of psychology."

"Until the first time you saw your mother, Marcelina, become possessed, right?" The story had been seared in Seth's mind since he first heard it, helped in no small part by the psychic fuckery Apolonia unleashed on him. He had only met Marcelina once, who was incredibly kind, gentle, and not at all like her wife in terms of her disturbing nature.

"That's correct. Point being, I have yet to see Mary's affliction fully take hold of her. We've continued our counseling sessions while we run blood tests to try to understand what might physically be happening to her. But until I see it happen, the darkness that Mary says overtakes her, I can only believe that she believes what she's done. But, for the record, I saw Mary this morning."

"You did?" Seth raised an eyebrow.

"I did. And I saw nothing that would indicate that she had suffered a traumatic experience, much less anything violent in nature. Mary is transparent, a completely open book. I don't believe anything has happened since the night she encountered Raymond LaRange."

Seth let out a sigh of relief. At least for last night's tragedy. "Good. That's great to hear."

"Despite what Mary may or may not have done, she is innocent at heart. She is deeply caring and empathetic. I don't believe Mary would ever harm or want to see harm come to an innocent person."

"I do agree with that on all accounts."

"Is there anything else I can help you with?" Jane asked.

"Actually, if you wouldn't mind checking in with Lina. She's got her hands full with trying to figure out how to deal with protestors at the building site and deciding how to handle potential fallout to how Dr. Owens set this whole development in motion."

Jane sighed. "Oh, Lina. She's actually reminiscent of Mary in regard to her innocent heart. I've told her numerous times to let me help her with the operations of the facility. She doesn't like asking for help."

"I know."

"Of course, I'll go see her and help in any way I can."

Seth stood up. "Thank you."

Jane extended her hand. "Good to see you, Seth."

Seth shook her hand. "You as well, Jane."

Retrospective No. 1: Emily Bury

The summer of 1995 was hot, humid, and filled with electrical storms hovering out over the ocean but never making it to shore. The air hung thick over Lost Grove, the kind that clung to the skin like a damp veil. The sun was heading toward the horizon of rolling hills and towering redwoods, painting the sky in streaks of pink and gold as the cicadas buzzed their evening song. It was a perfect evening for baseball, the kind that made people believe nothing truly terrible could happen in a town like this.

Diana Bury wiped her hands on the dish towel slung over her shoulder and stepped onto the porch, calling out into the tall grass.

"Emily! Time to go!"

She expected a response—footsteps crunching against dry earth, a giggle from behind the old oak tree where Emily liked to hide. But there was only silence.

"You're gonna have to hoof it if you don't get your behind in gear right now! I'm finishing washing up, then grabbing my keys!" Diana called and headed back into the house. She hung the dish towel to dry and stirred dinner in the crockpot. Then grabbed her purse and keys.

Diana's eyes flicked to the barn, to the fences stretching toward the woods. The Bury farm sat on the edge of town, the land folding into the outskirts of Willow Creek Trailhead, which led into Devil's Cradle State Park. Emily knew not to wander past the fence line, but she was a curious child of ten, a restless one. Diana wouldn't be surprised if Emily had already wandered into town to sit with her father and watch her brother in the outfield.

"Emily?" she called again, this time louder.

No answer.

Diana glanced at her watch. They were running late. Assuming her daughter had, in fact, gone ahead to the game, she slid into the driver's seat of the truck and headed into town.

When she arrived at the park, she scanned the nearby playground and the concession stand for her daughter but didn't spot her. Her husband, Quinn, waved at her from the stands.

"Have you seen Emily?" she asked as she sat beside her husband.

Quinn blinked, his eyes still tracking their son at the plate. "No. She didn't come with you?"

"No. I assumed she'd already joined you."

Quinn barely glanced at her, his attention on Ethan, who was adjusting his stance, bat poised. "She's probably at the playground," he commented, throwing his thumb over his shoulder.

Diana nodded, but unease curled inside her. Emily always checked in. Always. She watched her son, Ethan, hit the ball past the shortstop and into the outfield. He made it to first base. The next player got him to third. He scored on the next run, and she cheered along with all the other parents.

"I'm going to check the playground," she said, already pushing off the bleachers.

The park was bursting with laughter. The shrieks of children echoed through the crisp evening air. She scanned the monkey bars. The swings. The slide. She called Emily's name, her voice getting lost in the din of kids.

No little girl with dark curls.

Her pulse thudded in her ears.

She quickened her pace toward the concession stand, where the older kids loitered, too old for the playground but too young to be anywhere else. "Hey, guys, have any of you seen Emily?" she asked a cluster of middle schoolers.

They exchanged glances and shook their heads.

The world tipped a little.

Diana swallowed hard and turned back toward the bleachers, her steps quick, a cold sweat gathering at the base of her spine.

"Diana." Her friend and fellow mom, Miranda, waved. Her youngest, a toe-headed little boy, hobbled behind with his fingers covered in sticky ice cream. "I'm glad I caught you. What are you making for the team bake sale?"

Bake sale? The words barely registered. Diana shrugged. "I hadn't settled on anything. Is there a dish we need?"

"Another cake would be good. Maybe a classic yellow with fudge icing?"

"I can manage that," Diana said, smiling. "Hey, have you seen Emily?"

Miranda frowned. "No. She's not at the playground?"

"No." Diana looked around, then to the dugout, where Ethan sat with his teammates. A prickle of dread ran up her arms.

"She has to be around. Did she wander back home?"

"Possibly," Diana admitted.

"Let's ask around." Miranda spotted Seth Wolfe, one of Emily's classmates, dashing past. "Seth?" she called.

Seth skidded to a stop. "Yes, ma'am?"

"Have you seen Emily today?" Miranda asked.

Seth shook his head. "Nope."

Diana's stomach twisted. "Are you sure?" she pressed, her voice a little too sharp.

Seth hesitated before nodding.

"Okay, thank you," Diana said.

Seth ran to catch up with his friends, Steve and Hart.

Diana couldn't breathe. The world around her was too bright. Too loud. The pop of a bat, the cheer of the crowd—it all grated against her ears. She tried to keep her voice steady as she spoke. "I thought she came here ahead of me."

Miranda grabbed her friend's hand. "She's around, Diana. We'll find her."

Diana nodded but didn't feel reassured. This was unlike Emily. She and her brother Ethan were well-behaved. They always checked in.

Cheers from the stands rattled her nerves.

"Where's Quinn?" Miranda asked, already searching the stands. "Has he seen her?"

"No," Diana answered. She started biting her thumbnail.

Miranda climbed into the stands and spoke with Quinn.

Moments later, he joined his wife. "She's not at the playground?"

Diana shook her head, her mouth dry. "No, Quinn, she's not here. She's not anywhere. Maybe she went home?"

"What's up?" Hank, Miranda's husband, asked. He'd noticed the two women talking and sensed something was amiss.

"We don't know where Emily is," Miranda replied.

"She's probably playing in the field. I saw a bunch of kids heading that way," Hank said.

Quinn stiffened. "Which field?"

"The one down the nature path."

Diana's stomach dropped.

Quinn was already moving, Hank close behind.

Diana's breathing hitched.

The nature path. The woods. The open field beyond. Too many places she couldn't see.

Miranda touched her arm. "We'll find her."

Diana looked nervously at Miranda. "Should I run home and—"

"Let's wait for them," Miranda interrupted. "She may be over there. Then there's no need to drive home and back."

Diana nodded, but the weight in her chest was suffocating. She once more looked to the dugout at her oldest. He was laughing with his friends. His two coaches were nearby. He was safe. But where was his sister?

They combed the field, Quinn's voice cutting sharper with each call of Emily's name. It wasn't just searching anymore. It was calling. Shouting. The kids in the field hadn't seen Emily. She wasn't with them. She'd never been with them. Afraid, the kids playing in the field trickled back to their parents, to the baseball field lit up with halogen lights as night approached.

Quinn continued calling for his daughter. Hands cupped around his mouth to amplify her name. Heads turned. Conversations faltered. Coaches paused mid-instruction, their gazes shifted toward the rising panic.

One by one, the realization rippled through the crowd.

A missing child.

A child gone.

Diana felt the word sink like a stone in her chest.

"What's going on?" a parent asked, their brows drawn together.

Miranda's voice was tight. "Have you seen Emily Bury?" She turned, addressing the parents perched on the bleachers.

The murmurs stopped. The air seemed to hold still.

One by one, heads shook.

No. No. No.

Ethan stood stiffly with his friends, his stomach twisting. He didn't like the way the adults' voices had changed, the way whispers spread like wildfire, bouncing from one person to the next. His parents—his parents were at the center of it. "What's happening?" His voice sounded smaller than he wanted it to be.

A firm hand clapped his shoulder. "I'll find out. Don't worry."

Ethan watched as the assistant coach strode toward the huddle of adults, speaking in hushed tones. Then he returned, leaning in to whisper something in the coach's ear.

Ethan didn't like the way Coach's mouth pressed into a thin line. Didn't like the way his stomach felt, tight and sour.

Something was wrong. Really wrong.

Coach turned back to the boys. "It's fine. Settle down." But his voice carried the weight of a lie. Then: "Ethan? Come here."

Ethan swallowed and stepped out of the dugout, away from his teammates' curious stares.

"Listen, Ethan," he started. His voice was calm, but his eyes weren't. "Have you seen your sister up here today?"

Ethan blinked. *Why? Why is he asking that?* He shook his head.

Coach exhaled slowly, nodding. "Alright, well, your parents haven't seen her either." He paused, choosing his next words carefully. "Okay, so we're just gonna check around, see if we can find her. Do you want to go with your parents, or stay here?"

Ethan hesitated. The question felt too big. He was twelve. He didn't know how to answer that. What did his parents or Coach want him to do? His stomach twisted again.

Coach tried again. "Do you want to go home? See if she's there?"

That made sense. That was something he could do. He nodded. His little sister was missing, and he had to find her.

"Okay, let me walk you over to them." Coach's hand landed heavy on his shoulder, guiding him toward the bleachers. The walk was only forty feet, but his legs felt unsteady, like they might betray him at any moment.

He should have been embarrassed—being steered along like a kid—but he wasn't. Not really. Because for those forty feet, he didn't have to think. Didn't have to acknowledge the weight pressing down on his chest. Didn't have to acknowledge the way the world suddenly felt too big. Too uncertain. Too wrong.

"Dad?" Ethan's voice barely made it past his throat.

Quinn pulled his son close. "It's okay. We're gonna go home and check to see if your sister is there. Okay?"

Ethan nodded. It wasn't okay. But he needed to believe it was. His mom was already peeling away in her car, speeding toward home.

Ethan climbed into the truck with his dad, his hands curled into fists in his lap. He couldn't shake the feeling that something was coming. Something cold. Something dark.

Something he didn't have a name for yet.

By the time they returned to the farm, dusk had fallen, and a sickly orange glow bled across the horizon. Diana rushed into the house, calling her daughter's name. Ethan jumped out of the truck and headed for the fields. He knew she loved to run down the far fence, past the woods, sometimes going into the woods to take a shortcut to Ms. Packness's house. She loved to watch the goats and feed them hay and grass. Mom and Dad didn't know she did that, but Ethan did. He ran like he was trying to make it all the way to home base on an inside-the-park home run. He even took the shortcut. The air inside the woods was colder by five, maybe ten degrees, and it smelled like ferns, dirt, pine, and cedar. He jumped over roots and slid down the narrow trail, further dirtying his uniform with black mud, not brown clay and sand.

He nearly fell headfirst over the fence to Ms. Packness's yard. "Emily?" he called. The goats all stared at him from inside their little house. It was more like a glorified shed. Ms. Packness had only got the goats this past spring. She was making goat cheese and goat's milk soap and selling it at the stores in town.

"Emily!" he yelled.

A light came on over the back porch and he heard a door click open. "Ethan Bury?"

Ethan stood on the bottom rung of the fence. "Yes, Ms. Packness. I'm looking for my sister."

"She isn't here, dear." Ms. Packness had a kind face and a strange way of dressing. She pickled everything and always smelled of sourdough and baked bread. She had a young face but an old disposition.

"You haven't seen her at all today?" Ethan asked.

Ms. Packness stepped out, shoving her feet into a pair of tall boots. "No, I haven't. What's wrong? Is she okay?"

"I… We don't know where she is," Ethan said.

Ms. Packness looked past him into the woods.

"She knows better than to go in there," he said defensively.

"Let me come help you look," she said, striding toward her back stairs.

"No," Ethan said, hopping down off the fence. "She's probably home."

Ms. Packness watched the boy run off. She grabbed her raincoat and flashlight from inside the back door and followed, heading toward the Bury farm.

Emily was not home. She wasn't in the barns. She wasn't in the fields. She wasn't in the house or hiding in the storm cellar.

They called the police. The search began in earnest—a dozen men with flashlights and dogs moving like shadows across the land, calling her name into the thick summer air.

It wasn't long before they found the first sign of her.

A single white sneaker, lying on its side at the pond's edge, just beyond the Willow Creek Trailhead. It looked too clean, too carefully placed as if someone had set it there rather than it having been discarded in haste.

Diana's knees nearly gave out.

"Emily!" she screamed into the dark, her voice breaking.

No answer. Only the whisper of the wind through the trees, the rustling of something unseen beyond the reach of their lights.

Night fell, and the search party grew. Flashlights flickered between trunks, voices carried through the trees, but Emily was nowhere to be found.

Days passed.

Flyers bearing Emily's face were stapled to telephone poles, taped to shop windows, pinned to the corkboard at the diner. The town held its breath, waiting for the news no one wanted to hear.

On the fourth day, it came.

A hiker on Kein's Island, miles from where she had last been seen, had called it in. He'd been following the Grouse River delta when he saw something caught between the reeds. At first, he thought it was driftwood. Then he saw the hair, tangled and dark in the current.

The voice of the chief of police, Conrad Richard, cracked over the radio as he relayed the discovery to his fellow officers and when he called in the coroner.

Emily Bury was dead.

Diana collapsed to the ground when he delivered the news later that night. Her hands clutched at nothing as if she could grasp the world before it shattered around her.

The body bore no bruises, no scratches, no evidence of struggle. It was as if she had simply lain down and let the river take her.

Except for one thing.

Her left hand was missing its pinky finger.

There was no explanation. No animal tracks, no defensive wounds, no logical reason why a ten-year-old girl had vanished from her own backyard only to be found lifeless on an island she could have never reached alone.

The town whispered, as towns do.

Some said she had been taken. Others said the forest had claimed her, as it had before.

But the truth? The truth was that no one knew. And perhaps no one ever would.

Chapter Nine
What the Forest Knows

Anya's skin still held the warmth of the July sun as she pulled up the long gravel driveway of her family's dairy farm. Her birthday surprise had been her father's restored 1987 Ford F-150, with a cream base, brown stripe, and pink detailing. He'd been secretly working on it for months, and it explained why she hadn't been allowed in the old barn for the duration of the restoration. The custom refresh of the paint job and the new leather interior were the only things he'd sourced out. Anya didn't think she'd ever fall in love with a car, but she sure loved her truck.

The scent of fresh hay and the distant lowing of cows welcomed her home, wrapping her in the quiet reassurance of routine. Her father, Ethan, came out onto the porch. He had a rugged, weathered intensity that spoke of long days under the open sky and a lifetime of lessons learned the hard way. His jawline, dusted with the shadow of a beard, was sharp enough to carve stone, and his piercing eyes held the quiet weight of a man who'd seen both nature's beauty and her brutality in equal measure.

He smiled when he saw her. It was the kind of slow and warm smile that told her she was loved.

Once, he had been all sharp edges and quiet grit, a man made of dust and determination. But somewhere between tea parties on the tailgate of his truck and letting her paint his nails when she was five, the roughness had eased. She had softened him in a way the land never could.

"'Bout time," he called out, voice rough but full of affection.

She grinned, shutting the door behind her. "Miss me?"

His chuckle was low and knowing. "Always. Did you have fun at the lake?" he asked.

Anya nodded, brushing a stray strand of hair from her face. "Yeah. I got a little sunburnt. Meanwhile, Noble and Stan both look like supermodels."

Ethan chuckled, then sighed, tilting his head toward the house. "I'm about to check on that momma cow, see if she's gonna get that baby out tonight or if we have another day. I thought I'd start up the grill afterward."

"Sounds good," Anya replied.

"Would you mind seeing if you can find your mother?" His voice was casual, but there was an edge to it. Anya knew why.

Ethan looked out to the edge of their property. Leith tended to disappear into the woods when she wanted to swim, slipping into the dark waters with the grace only one of her kind possessed. She moved through the trees with a confidence that made Ethan's stomach twist. Those were the Cursed Woods—the place where whispers of old superstitions mingled with newer, darker truths. Ethan had long since stopped stepping foot past their borders.

His sister had gone in once and never come out.

He could still hear his father's desperate shouts echoing through the trees, see the blur of flashlights cutting through the thick shadows as the search party scoured the woods. The memory of those frantic hours—the hours before hope had curdled into dread—was etched into his bones. Emily's name hung in the air, unanswered, until the search turned from rescue to recovery.

And when they finally found her, it had been too late.

Thirty years later, the woods still held her ghost, tangled somewhere in the dark canopy of branches and the thick carpet of leaves. Ethan wouldn't follow his wife in, no matter how many times she promised it was safe.

"Sure," Anya said, her voice easy despite the unease in her father's eyes. She knew the woods held no harm for her or her mother. Still, she understood his hesitation.

She headed toward their garage, which was more like an airplane hangar, and climbed onto the back of a four-wheeler. She gunned the engine and sped off toward the tree line. The evening air rushed past her, and the world smelled of damp earth and clover.

The air within Devil's Cradle was thick—damp and low, syrup-slow with the scent of moss and sweet rot. It clung to Leith's skin like a second layer, warm and chill at once, rich with the musk of fallen leaves and the scent of wet stone. The trees rose like cathedral columns, ancient redwoods so tall they swallowed the sky. Light filtered through in long, shafted spears, catching on the dust and spores suspended in the hush.

She had come to the woods to swim. The hidden pond deep within the Cursed Woods, ringed with mossy stones and shaded by leaning redwoods, was her quiet sanctuary. Her return to water. The place where she remembered she was not just a woman or a wife or a mother, but something bolder, ancient, and secret.

One moment she'd been heading across their property as cows lowed, watching her as she passed. The woods loomed ahead like an emerald wall at the edge of their land, inviting Leith in a way they would never be to her husband. Now, she was here, a half mile in, distracted, pulled off her usual path, blinking slow like a sleepwalker pulled from a dream.

Before her stood a redwood, ancient and wounded, marked with a glyph she'd never seen before. Not carved, exactly, but opened. Peeled. Like bark turned inside out, the shape exposed in slick coils of glistening pulp. It looked like a curled spine unraveling. The edges were stained with a slick blue-green lichen that pulsed faintly with violet edges in the shade.

The glyph grew brighter, the threads of fungus along its edge glowing like a shimmer beneath the bark. The longer she looked, the more it moved. Not in the literal sense, but her mind bent around it, trying to hold its shape. It shifted with meaning just out of reach.

She took a step forward.

The song in her blood began to rise. A deep, cellular hum. Her heartbeat slowed. Her vision doubled and rejoined, warped at the edges like a heat haze. Her breath came easier, though her chest ached. Her limbs felt heavy and numb.

Leith stepped closer, drawn like tidewater to moonlight. She didn't remember moving. Her fingers tingled. Her mouth was dry, but her skin was damp, and every inhale tasted of bruised greenery and warm iron. Her head was full of clicks and whispers, not quite words but suggestions of thought.

She reached out. Her palm hovered over the glyph. The fungus shimmered, threads of it quivering as if sensing her nearness. Her body became lighter and heavier all at once like she was floating yet anchored. Her thoughts scattered like minnows in light. Her brain became thick, not from dizziness but dissonance. The forest bent, trees swaying in rhythmless pulses, their bark slickening, their roots yawning open like mouths. She saw water where there was none, dark and still, reflecting a version of her that blinked out of sync.

A low hum began like insects tuning an instrument. Her vision filled with patterns. Bark became scales. Moss became fur. Leaves flickered like gills. The glyph elongated, and in its spiraled shape she saw tunnels, passageways into earth and mind, reflections of herself walking backward through time.

She did not blink.

The woods swelled. She saw something move behind the trees. Tall. Bent. Watching. It did not come closer. It did not need to.

"Mom."

The word was soft but wrong. Like it didn't belong in this place.

"Mom?"

The glyph flickered. The light shattered. The bark cracked.

"Mom—!"

The forest cracked, or rather, her reality did. Fingers, human fingers, gripped her arm, sharp and real, a sensation she forgot she could feel, and now it was alien and sent painful needles prickling up to the base of her skull and down into her fingers.

Leith gasped. Sound slammed into her ears—birds, wind, something scuttling in the brush. The stink of fungus filled her nose, no longer sweet but rancid and wet, like eggs rotting in water. Her knees buckled. She stumbled back, disoriented. Her foot slipped on a root.

"Mom!"

Anya. Her daughter's face, white with panic, flushed with sweat, appeared before her. Her eyes wild, cheeks flushed, her voice choked in panic.

"What the hell were you doing?" Anya asked, holding her mother's arms, pushing her hair from her face. "I've been yelling for—"

Leith fell to her hands and knees and vomited into the moss. It came up bitter and wrong, like pond water and bile. Her palms pressed into the earth, shaking. The hum was gone, but the echo remained. She sat back on her heels, wiping at her mouth with the back of her hand. Her body trembled, heart still trying to find a steady rhythm. Anya crouched beside her, face pale and tight with concern.

The sun had shifted and light had changed hands with shadow. *How long was I here?* Leith wondered.

"Mom? Are you okay?" Anya stared at her mother as if she was unrecognizable. For a moment there, she had been. Leith's expression was off. Her eyes, that impossible shade of sea green, always held depths that whispered of forgotten rivers and the songs of ancient tides. But now they were distant. Dark. Her pupils were dilated. The reflective layer behind her retina caught the glimmers of light like a silver sheen flickering unnaturally across her gaze. Like she'd just surfaced from a deep dive into the dark blue ocean.

Anya's shoulders tensed. "Were you swimming?" she asked. Her mother's skin was dry. Her summer shift dress didn't cling to her body. No damp tendrils of hair stuck to her skin.

"I...no. I was going to, but..." Leith's voice trailed off and she put on a smile. "I'm fine."

"You scared me," Anya whispered.

Leith nodded, forcing a breath through her nose. "I'm okay. I just... got dizzy."

"That wasn't dizzy," Anya said. "You weren't even blinking. You looked—God, I don't know what you looked like."

Leith reached for her daughter's hand. "I'm alright. Really."

Anya's eyes drifted over her mother's shoulder to the trees beyond, drawn to the tree with the glyph. Her brows pulled together. "Is that what you were staring at?"

The glyph held her gaze. It was pale and strange and mesmerizing, even without its glow. The hush of the woods pressed in, thick and expectant, as if the air itself were leaning closer. She moved toward it slowly, almost reverently. A soft breeze passed through, carrying the scent of wet bark and some muskier fungal note. Anya reached into her back pocket and pulled out her phone.

Leith turned her head slowly. The glyph no longer glowed, but the carved shape seemed sharper now, almost wet with clarity, and it stared. Her senses began to prickle. Something inside her recoiled. The space between trees felt too tight. Her skin began to itch with the residue of spores, her throat catching like something was crawling down it—tiny, invisible tendrils wriggling for purchase.

Anya lifted her phone. The click of the shutter sounded too loud in the hush. The screen flickered faintly, and a ripple passed through the air.

Leith felt it in her teeth. Her eyes darted to the space between trees, looking for a shadow. "Anya? Come away," she said.

Anya took another photo and blinked. It felt like the world was spinning. It was a sensation she recalled from when she was young, spinning and spinning with her arms out, then falling down in the meadow with her eyes closed, the world still swirling beneath her. When she was young, the sensation was exhilarating. It made her giggle. This was wrong. She felt like she'd been flipped and was being sucked into space, as if gravity was pushing her away instead of pulling her down. Her eyes shot open and she stumbled.

"That's enough," Leith said sharply, her voice crackling and raw. She lunged forward and grabbed Anya's wrist, yanking the phone down. "Don't take pictures of it."

Anya looked at her, startled. "But...I can look up what it is online."

Leith scanned the woods, nostrils flaring like a deer scenting the air. "Something's wrong," she whispered. "We're not safe here."

"Mom?"

"We're leaving," Leith hissed. Her gaze darted through the trees. Shapes seemed to shift just beyond clarity. Her mouth tasted like she'd taken a sip of rancid milk. "Now."

Anya flinched as her mother grabbed her wrist and pulled her back toward the pastures, toward the house, out of the woods.

They hurried through the trees, Leith leading with a pace just shy of panic, her hand gripping Anya's tightly. They climbed onto the four-wheeler, but even as they left the woods behind, the tension clung to them, the weight of something unseen pressing against their backs.

They rolled into the garage. Anya turned off the four-wheeler and regarded her mother, who stood on her tiptoes to look out a window toward the woods.

"Mom? What is going—"

"Don't tell your father."

"What?"

"About the glyph. About what happened."

"Why?" Anya's voice rose. "Mom, that was messed up! You looked possessed or something! And if there's something dangerous in the woods—"

Leith turned to face her, her voice low but firm. "Because your father doesn't need more reasons to hate those woods."

Anya fell quiet and looked away.

"He already lives with the fear that one day, something will take you. That the woods will swallow you the way they did his sister. He doesn't need this, too."

Anya's jaw tightened. "But what if this isn't something we can just ignore?"

"We won't ignore it," Leith said. "I'll figure something out."

Anya pulled her phone back out, unlocking it with a flick of her thumb. She stared at the photos she'd taken. The image of the glyph warped slightly on the screen, as though the lines refused to stay still. A wave of vertigo hit her. "Ugh," she muttered, rubbing her eyes.

Leith looked to her daughter and to her phone. She moved so quickly, snatching the phone from her daughter, that Anya let out a squeak of surprise. "Don't look at it."

Anya hesitated, then shook her head. "I'm telling Dad," she said, heading for the garage door.

Leith grabbed her. "No, no, Anya. I'm sorry. Here." She handed the phone back. "Give me a minute. Alright?"

"What is this, Mom?" Anya's brow wrinkled with concern.

"I don't know."

"You don't know?" Anya's eyes bloomed wide. She thought her mother knew pretty much anything worth knowing about the creatures and spirits inhabiting the Cursed Woods.

"I'll figure it out, little love," Leith explained, cupping her daughter's face. "I will."

Anya gave the slightest of nods. Her eyes shifted to her phone. "Then maybe we should ask someone who might. Like Story."

"Story Palmer? The librarian?"

"She knows a lot of esoteric stuff," Anya remarked. She'd seen the books on Ms. Palmer's shelves in her home on any of the numerous times she had gone with Noble to pick Zoe up. Her mind shifted to another person who would know about the Cursed Woods. "Or Stan. Someone has to know what it is."

Leith licked her lips and took her daughter's hands in hers. "I'll figure it out. I'm okay. We're okay…you're okay."

"You don't seem okay," Anya whispered.

"I am," Leith reassured her, smiling. "I promise."

"You scared me," Anya said again, quieter now.

Leith laughed, arranging her daughter's wavy locks, soothing them, touching her daughter as if she had almost just lost her. "I scared myself. But I'm okay. I swear. Okay?"

Anya's eyes glimmered with worry as the wind picked up, rattling the chimes on the porch. The woods whispered at the edge of the yard, just beyond the thinning veil of dusk.

Chapter Ten
Ashes in the Mouth

The sun had just slipped behind the trees when Story turned onto Rose Vine Lane. The white picket fence came into view, a soft silhouette against the amber hues of evening. Wildflowers, untamed and reaching, spilled over the edges of the walkway, painting the narrow garden in strokes of violet, saffron, and soft blue. Bees had long since gone to sleep, but the air still carried the sweet, green scent of crushed stems and sun-warmed soil.

Story's footsteps slowed as she approached the gate, her hand resting for a moment on the latch. The cottage stood still and inviting, white-trimmed windows aglow with the soft honey light of sconces, lace curtains fluttering faintly in the open windows. For a heartbeat, Story considered turning back.

But she didn't.

She knocked once—lightly—then again.

The door opened moments later to the warm scent of lemon and lavender, bright and clean, threaded with something recent and savory— roasted root vegetables, perhaps, and the faintest whiff of iron, like something metallic had passed briefly through the air.

Mary's face brightened. She was wearing a cotton blouse and wide-legged linen pants, her long dark hair loosely braided and slung over one shoulder. She looked rested. Calm. Her eyes sparkled the way they only did when she didn't know there was something wrong.

"Story! I didn't know you were coming by."

"I hope it's okay," Story said, already stepping through the threshold.

"I needed to see you."

"Of course it's okay," Mary said, shutting the door behind her. "I just pulled dinner from the oven. Are you hungry?"

"I'm alright."

"Tea?"

"I'd love some."

Mary padded into the kitchen, humming under her breath, and set the kettle on the stove. The house was pristine, as always. Not a stray book or dish out of place. The sitting room was quiet, a candle flickering on the mantel, casting gentle shadows across the pale lilac walls.

Story sat on the edge of the sofa, her hands folded in her lap, listening to Mary move around in the kitchen.

"I made a roasted beet and orange salad," Mary said. "The citrus cuts the earthy flavors so nicely."

"That sounds lovely," Story replied, though her stomach hadn't unclenched since lunch.

The kettle began to whistle. Mary poured the water over chamomile and lavender buds in two delicate porcelain cups, the kind she'd found at an estate sale last fall. She brought the tray into the room and placed it gently on the coffee table before settling into the armchair across from Story.

"So," Mary said, tucking a leg beneath her. "What's going on?"

Story picked up her cup but didn't drink. The heat of the porcelain seeped into her palms, grounding her.

"Did you have an appointment today?" Story asked.

Mary glanced over her cup, blowing gently. "Yes, this morning."

After weeks of gentle but persistent prodding—from both Story and Seth—Mary had finally agreed to consult with Dr. Jane Bajorek, known quietly in certain circles for treating conditions that defied conventional science. Since then, she'd been through a battery of tests—bloodwork, MRIs, CT scans, sleep studies. The physical assessments made her feel like a specimen under glass, a thing to be measured and documented. She hated the prodding, the cool fingers and bright lights and long waits in white rooms.

But Dr. Jane had surprised her. She wasn't just a scientist, she listened. She had a steadying presence Mary didn't know she'd been craving. The mental practices—the grounding work, the memory tracking, even the breathing exercises—were helping. Little by little, they were giving her back what she hadn't realized she'd lost: the right to think of herself not as a monster but as someone who could heal. Who deserved to.

"Have you heard anything or been online today?"

Mary blinked. "No, not really. Why?"

"There was a death."

Mary's face fell. "Someone from town?"

"No…a child. Visiting with his family. Kevin Marlow. He went missing in Devil's Cradle yesterday."

Mary sat up straighter, all playfulness gone. "What happened?"

"He was found this morning. Mauled. They're calling it an animal attack."

Silence settled between them, thick and sudden. The teacups steamed quietly between them.

Mary's brow furrowed. "Jesus. I had no idea. I—I've been in the house the past two days, only went out around dawn to water the garden after my usual run." She paused, her voice softening. "That poor family."

Story's chest tightened. She nodded, but her breath came slow and shallow.

"Did Seth tell you that?" Mary asked gently.

"He did."

Mary studied her, tilting her head slightly. "You're shaking."

"I know."

"You're not just sad."

"No."

Mary's expression changed. Not yet defensive, but more alert. Her fingers curled slightly around the armrest. "What are you thinking, Story?"

Story met her eyes. "I need to ask you something. And I hate that I have to."

A flicker of something—hurt, maybe—passed across Mary's face, but she nodded. "Ask."

"Where were you last night?"

The room didn't go cold, but the light inside it shifted. Slanted. The flickering candle on the mantel seemed to gutter.

Mary didn't answer right away. She stared at Story as though the question had come from someone else entirely.

"I just told you. I was here. I haven't left the neighborhood. I go out early—before the sun is fully up. Sometimes again after midnight. You know that."

Story nodded. "I do."

Mary's voice grew quieter. "Why are you asking me that?"

"Because the wounds… Seth said they were similar to LaRange's. And I need to know that you had nothing to do with it."

Mary stood. Slowly. Like a string inside her had snapped and left her hollow. "You think I did it."

"No," Story said, rising. "I *don't*. But I need to hear it from you. I need to see you when I ask."

Mary's cheeks were pale, her jaw tight. "You think I slipped. That I found a child in the woods and tore him open."

"Mary—"

"I trusted you, Story. You're the only one I've ever let in. I told you things I've never said aloud. You helped me believe I was more than this…this thing inside me."

"You are more."

"Then why are you looking at me like you're scared of me?"

"I'm scared for you," Story said, voice breaking. "Because I love you. And because I've kept things from Seth—because I've protected you in ways that I can't explain away forever. And now there's a dead child. And if there's even a chance—"

"There isn't." Mary's voice cracked on the words. Her eyes shone with unshed tears. "I would never, *never* hurt a child."

"I believe you."

"Then why does it feel like you don't?"

The silence that followed was the worst kind of truth.

Story opened her mouth, then closed it again. She set her teacup down with a soft clink that sounded louder than it should have in the still room. She laced her fingers together and stared at them for a long moment before speaking. "Because the last time you came to me covered in blood," she said gently, "you told me something I never expected to hear from you. You *hunted* him, Mary. You didn't just find LaRange. You stalked him. You made a choice—an intentional, deliberate one—and that shifted something in me."

Mary blinked, stunned into silence.

"I'm not saying I don't love you. Or that I don't consider you my best friend. But that changes a friendship, Mary. When someone you love becomes capable of something like that—even for a reason you understand—it makes you look at them differently."

Mary's brows knit, confusion painting her features. "I don't understand. I did it *because* of our friendship. Because of what he did to Zoe." Her voice caught again. "You were furious, Story. You said you'd hex him if you ever found him. That he was a waste of breath. That someone needed to stop him. I thought…" She trailed off, eyes wide, wounded. "I thought I was saving you from having to follow through."

Story's breath caught, her stomach folding in on itself. She remembered that night—wine-fueled and raw, after Seth had come home pale-faced and empty-handed, telling her LaRange had vanished again. She had said those things. She'd meant them in the moment. But they were just words. Frustrated, helpless words. Not a call to action.

"Oh, Mary," she whispered, voice thick. "I didn't mean it. I would never have actually… You know I couldn't."

"I know," Mary said quietly. "That's why I did it for you."

The guilt cracked through Story's chest like a fault line.

She looked at Mary, really looked at her—this woman she had nursed through tremors, calmed through bloodlust, whispered incantations over like prayers in the dark. And here she was, still trying to do good, and still getting it wrong in a way that left her more alone than before.

"I understand what I did," Mary continued. "But you don't understand what would've happened if I hadn't. If I'd told Seth—if I'd gone to the law—LaRange would've slipped through the cracks like all the rest. Like Dr. Owens. They just disappear, and the town forgets for a little while, until something else goes wrong. But it's never over. They come back. They always do."

"And maybe you're right," Story said, standing slowly. "Maybe justice in Lost Grove doesn't wear a badge. But that doesn't make what you did right, Mary. There was a better way."

"Not for people like me." Her words were soft. Matter-of-fact. Not bitter, but threadbare with truth.

Story sighed. "I've kept what I know from Seth. The real things. The things you've shown me. I told him the story about the woman in the fourteenth century, the Red Eater myth. That's all. I never told him about the deer. Or the not-child you found in the woods. Or how close you've come. Because it isn't my secret to tell."

Mary's breath hitched.

"But you have to understand," Story continued, her voice trembling now, "what that's doing to me. Loving someone—wanting to spend your life with them—and carrying this around in silence… It's not sustainable.

It's not fair. I don't regret protecting you. But the longer this goes on, the more I start to break under the weight of it."

Mary looked down at her hands. She said nothing.

The room, once warm and inviting, now felt colder. Like a space between two people had grown too wide to cross in one step.

"I just needed to know," Story said finally. "That it wasn't you."

"It wasn't," Mary said, barely audible.

"I believe you."

But belief didn't mend everything.

Their tea sat cooling on the table, untouched. The candle on the mantel flickered once, then stilled.

"I think I need some space," Mary said, not moving.

Story nodded and moved to the door. A breath passed. Long and sharp. "I still love you."

"I know," Mary whispered.

And with that, Story stepped back into the lavender dusk, leaving the door gently ajar behind her.

Chapter Eleven
Teeth of a Wolf

It was only eight p.m., but Seth was exhausted as he drove over to Story's from the station. Part of him wanted to just go crash in his apartment above his father's drugstore, but he told Story he would come over, and he still wanted to know what she was keeping from him earlier in the day. That, and he needed to tell her about the impending DNA test coming from Raymond LaRange's buried corpse. A DNA test that could open Pandora's box. Now, there was a chance that LaRange's body had decayed to the point where they wouldn't be able to pull saliva DNA from the neck or any other areas of his body, but they might find hair or fibers of clothing previously missed. Either way, going back to LaRange's body was opening back up a case and results he had believed to be buried.

Seth pulled over to the curb in front of Story's house and killed the engine as an unwelcome bout of anxiety coursed through his insides. His gut told him that whatever Story was keeping quiet somehow tied into whatever trouble Mary was potentially facing from unearthing LaRange's body. The fact that Story became uncharacteristically withdrawn when Seth described the scene of Kevin Marlow's death brought about implications he didn't even want to consider.

He exited his Mercedes, hating the feeling of not wanting to walk to Story's front door. She had done nothing but bring him happiness and open his mind to feelings and abilities he never would have imagined. She was the only woman besides his mother that he had uttered the words *I love you* to since his high school girlfriend. Story was an open book, deeply empathetic, tender and caring. She would tell him her deepest feelings, desires and dreams without a breath of hesitation. But now he was in a position where he needed to pry something out of her like she was a person of interest in an investigation.

Seth knocked gently on the door before stepping into her foyer. "Story?"

"Right in here."

Seth kicked off his shoes and peered around the corner to see Story curled up on the sofa in her den with a book open on her lap and a bottle and glass of red wine on the table in front of her. "That one of your grimoires?"

Story looked up and smiled, brushing her hair behind her ear. "It is. Grab a glass and join me."

Seth walked in and sat next to her on the sofa, not as close as he normally would. "Maybe in a bit. I just want to get off my feet for now."

Story could tell Seth was troubled, certainly from finding a dead child in the woods, but she also knew it was due to her and how she had shut down in front of him earlier today. "I understand. It's been a long day. You hardly slept. Have you eaten? I kept the oven warm so I can heat you up the eggplant parmesan I made earlier."

The truth was, Seth was starving. He had hardly touched his turkey and provolone sandwich from lunch. He had been fueled by nothing more than coffee and water since last night's dinner, but he needed to have this conversation before his tightening stomach could take in wine or food. "I met with Wes and Cal for the autopsy."

"Why was Cal there?"

"Bite marks. I'm not sure if it came up or not when you met him at Wes's fundraiser, but Cal used to be an officer for the California Department of Fish and Wildlife."

Hearing "bite marks" caused the hair on the back of Story's neck to stand on end. She wholeheartedly believed Mary had nothing to do with the boy, but memories from the past flooded her mind. "No, it hadn't. What did they find out?"

Seth sighed. "Nothing definitive other than confirming it was an animal attack. They're sending in samples from the various wounds in his body to test for DNA to determine what animal was responsible. But, Story…"

The way Seth said her name along with his pause kick-started Story's heart rate. She closed her book, set it on the table, trading it for her glass of wine. "What is it?"

"Wes is going to exhume Raymond LaRange's body from the public cemetery to run DNA tests, something he says he should have done in the first place. They want to see if the same animal was responsible."

The words landed on her like an anvil. There was no mistaking the ramifications of what this could mean. "Could they—"

"I don't know. It's been two months, but that doesn't disqualify every avenue of what they can test. Even if there's no saliva DNA left, there could be hair, fibers of clothes, remnants of a fingernail."

Story dropped her head into her free hand.

"There is a fair to good chance that they will uncover human DNA not belonging to LaRange. It could be circumstantial due to the report that I wrote up that Mary found the body, checked to see if he was alive and tried to resuscitate him. But if they find—"

"I need to tell you something, Seth," Story said, looking back up at her lover, her heart dropping.

Seth straightened, preparing to hear what he apparently was not going to need to pry out of her.

"I told you the story from my family's history about the Red Eater, and that I believed that's what Mary was. What I didn't tell you—what I should have told you long ago—were the stories that Mary confided in me, and the things I've seen."

Seth's breaths shortened as the feeling of impending doom washed over him. "Okay."

Story swallowed three mouthfuls of wine and set her glass back on the table, rearranging her body to fully face him. "I realize it might not matter, but I need to apologize in advance for keeping these things from you. I believed that I was doing the right thing in keeping promises I made to Mary. This is her life and her story. It isn't technically mine to share. And, admittedly, I was trying to protect her. But given the circumstances of what she…what happened to Raymond—I should have told you what I knew then."

Seth had sat across no shortage of people confessing to crimes they had committed, or crimes they were involved with, most of them homicides, but he hadn't been in love with any of them. Their words never tore at his heart. He chose to do what he did in all of those scenarios to get the best results, sit still and let the person speak.

"Obviously you know about her pica diagnosis, which is part of it. She has the symptoms of putting objects in her mouth, sometimes very absentmindedly, stones, paperclips, zippers, pieces of jewelry. I've told you, or rather alluded to, things she's done in her past to obtain raw meat and animal blood. But I've been present for moments when Mary is at her weakest, when her compulsions are at their peak. Her teeth," Story said, her eyes falling momentarily to her lap before looking back at Seth, "they grow."

The muscles in Seth's face went slack as his eyes widened. "What?"

Story forced her top lip to rise and pointed to her upper teeth. "The canines. They grow longer and sharper."

Seth unconsciously shook his head. What was Story saying? Why was his world, his sense of reality, constantly being upended? "What are you saying? That she's...a vampire? A werewolf?"

Story grimaced. How could she expect him to believe this when she still had a hard time believing the things she'd seen? "No, not in those exact terms."

Seth exhaled loudly. "Then in what terms? My mind is open to a lot of things, Story, but Universal horror creatures coming to life is not one of them."

Story's brows drew together, a flare of frustration rising. "Please do not turn this into a joke."

"I'm not trying to. I'm reacting to you telling me that Mary grows fangs. So, what are you saying she is?"

Story grabbed her grimoire off the table and set it in front of him. "A Red Eater. I tried to show this to you before. I think Mary was infected by the creature that bit her when she was a child. And I think it altered her...DNA," she said, rolling her eyes at the timely coincidence of terms.

Seth now consciously shook his head as he grappled with what he was hearing. "I don't understand. So, you're saying what? That her body gets low on iron, she craves blood, and that her teeth grow long and sharp? How else am I supposed to process this other than to think of a vampire, a werewolf, or some other creature that doesn't exist?"

Story's mind was racing furiously for a way to try to explain this to him. "Did you see The Wizard of Oz when you were a kid?"

Seth sneered. "What does— Yes, of course. But—"

"Do you remember seeing the Wicked Witch of the West for the first time? A green woman with a pointed nose and chin and long pointy fingers? Did you think witches were real?"

Seth let that settle with him. It was, of course, an excellent point.

"Okay, so Mary is something like those fictional characters, just... different?"

Story nodded. "Yes."

"And you've seen this?"

"I have. More than once. I first saw it when she called me from the alley behind the butcher shop. It was in the middle of the night and she was trying to break in. She was in so much pain."

"Jesus," Seth uttered as he dropped his head.

"The next time, she had convinced me to go running with her at night. You know I don't run. I'm not a runner." Story waved her hand. "That's not the point. She was of course much faster than me. She got ahead and she...I guess, caught the scent of it."

Seth looked back up. "Of what?"

"A deer. She chased it. She chased it, caught it, and killed it."

"With what?"

Story held her hands up. "Her hands? Her teeth? Maybe both."

Seth's heart rate picked up, as gooseflesh sprouted across his forearms and back. The image of anyone, much less Mary Germaine, running fast enough to catch a deer was hard to fathom. And then maul it with their bare hands, and what, eat it? "You said her teeth? Where did she...?"

"It's throat. Her face, her hands, her clothes, were all covered in blood."

"Mother of God," Seth sighed, clearly having adopted Bill's go-to utterance of shock. His eyes drifted as he imagined Mary huddled over a dead deer, blood flowing down her chin. That vision quickly morphed to Mary hovering over Raymon LaRange's corpse, causing ripples of fear throughout his body. His eyes shot back to Story. "Raymond LaRange."

Story feebly nodded. "That was my fear at the time. That's why I told you about the Red Eater. But then you told me the findings of the autopsy and I—I don't know—I wanted to believe that it was true."

"When she's in these states...are you safe? Is she even herself?"

Story's chest expanded, taking in a heavy, painful breath. "Yes. I mean, clearly she has a visceral reaction, but I guess I would equate that to anyone else in a reactionary state. It's not like she all of a sudden doesn't recognize me."

Seth's eyes darted back and forth, thinking back on the night he arrived to find Mary in a state of shock on this very sofa, seeing her blood-soaked clothes. He thought back to the autopsy, the wounds, the confounding teeth marks, Wes's suspicions and the CDFW agent's determination that it was a grey wolf. Seth suddenly stood up, bringing his hands to the sides of his head.

Story wrung her hands together as tears began to well in her eyes, knowing what Seth was piecing together.

Seth turned to face Story. "You said her teeth grow. Would you say they grow to the length of a wolf's?"

Story looked down at her hands. She was guilty of looking up wolves on the internet the day after Seth had told her about the conclusion of the autopsy to research exactly that. All Story could do was nod her head in confirmation.

"Story, what the fuck!" Seth started to pace the length of the living room. "Even after you brought Mary upstairs to go to sleep, you chose not to tell me any of this."

"I know. I'm so sorry."

"I would have handled things completely differently. I would have had to bring her into the station, logged her clothes in immediately. And the autopsy! How could you let me believe the autopsy was correct? You saw the relief take over my body and said nothing."

Story's bottom lip started to quiver. "I wanted to believe it, too. I made myself believe it. And maybe it's still true."

Seth spun around to face her. "And maybe it's not. And if the DNA, or further investigation into the body, somehow reveals or points to Mary, we're all in a heap of shit. I could lose my job. My entire career. Mary will have to be brought in for questions where she'll say on record that she confessed to stalking and killing Raymond LaRange."

"She wouldn't do that to you. I know she—"

"How do you know?" Seth threw his arms up in the air. "And now she's been talking with Dr. Bajorek."

Story couldn't hold in her tears any longer and started to quietly sob.

Seth gripped his forehead and forced himself to take a long, deep breath. Part of him wanted to go wrap his arms around her and bring her head to his chest. The other part of him wanted to punch a hole in the wall.

"There's one last thing I need to tell you," Story said, her voice strained.

Seth looked up to the ceiling. "Honestly, you probably shouldn't. This is already enough to try and take in."

"I have to," she said. "Even if you decide to leave me for good—"

"I didn't say that."

"I need to tell you everything. And I'll never keep anything from you ever again."

Seth squatted down to the back of his heels. He didn't want to stay towering over her as she wept on the sofa. But he also didn't feel like getting comfortable on it. "Okay."

"It was nothing else that I saw. It was something that Mary admitted to me. Something she made me promise to never speak of. Do you remember the not-children?"

Seth raised an eyebrow. "I mean, I remember hearing about them from Nettie, from you, from Mary."

"I know you never saw them, but there is a reason that we all call them 'not-children.' They're not human. Not fully."

"Okay, and where is this going?"

"It was last year, not long before Sarah Elizabeth's body was found. Mary was out for her early morning run and she came across the body of a not-child just off the road in the tall grass. It was dead, or just about dead."

Seth had a feeling where this was going, but he was past the point of shock at this point. He nodded for her to continue.

"Mary said that she gave into her cravings and drank some of its blood."

Seth's eyelids fluttered. "And then what?"

"That's it. She dragged the body a bit further into the woods, but left it there. And Noble saw her."

"What?"

"They go running at the same time early in the mornings. He saw her from a distance. He confronted her about it days later. She tried to explain it to him. She told him she was trying to resuscitate the not-child."

Seth ran his hand through his hair. "And just last night—"

"No! Mary would never harm a child. Not a real one."

"After everything you just told me, is that supposed to convince me?"

"I went to see her today. I confronted her about it. I had to ask. I promise you with all my heart that she had nothing to do with it. I may have harmed our friendship by insinuating it was even a possibility. I've never seen her so hurt before."

If Seth hadn't gone to see Dr. Bajorek early in the day to assuage his fears about this exact thing, he wasn't sure he would be able to take Story's word for it. But Jane was also positive that Mary wouldn't have done anything, and he believed she would have been able to tell. For that matter, Jane probably had her mother Apolonia in there, digging around in her mind. Seth stood back up. "Okay."

Story wiped the tears from her cheeks. "Do you believe me?"

Seth nodded. "I do. But you still put me in an awful position here, Story. I'm going to have to go talk to Mary myself. I really should bring her into the station to question her officially just to be safe."

"I understand."

"And then we just need to pray that digging up LaRange's body doesn't end up incriminating all of us."

Story dropped her head.

"Look," Seth said, "I have a lot to mentally sort through here. I've had almost no sleep. And I think for tonight, it would be best if I stay at the apartment."

Story swallowed another well of tears. She looked up and forced a faint smile. "I'm sorry, Seth."

Seth nodded and sighed. "I know."

Chapter Twelve
Last Flames of Summer

The wind picked up as Nate crouched beside the pit, striking the match against the box before tossing it onto the dry wood pile. The flames licked up instantly, illuminating his sharp grin. "There we go. Easy."

"You just got lucky it didn't blow out," Nettie teased, kneeling beside him to shift a few logs for better airflow. She wore a strapless, flowing dress with a jean jacket and her hair pulled up in a slick ponytail. Stress, as her family came to terms with a "healed" George, her little brother, had cost her several pounds she was in no position to lose. Only she was aware that her real brother had been returned to her, thanks to the now chief of police, Seth Wolfe. Meanwhile, her parents believed he had undergone a surgery that repaired his addled mind, and the tension of the years spent trying to convince them that her brother was not her brother all this time had not gone away. While she and George were reconnecting, the relationship would never be the same. He'd undergone too much in his time away. She loved her baby brother, and she thought she got him back. It took her a few months to realize he was never coming back. "Last time you tried to start the fire, you nearly burned your eyebrows off."

"That was wind interference," Nate shot back, plopping down on the sand as Nettie fed another branch into the growing blaze. "Besides, that's why I have you two fire-building professionals. I'm just the aesthetics consultant."

Stan snorted. "If by aesthetics consultant, you mean back seat builder, then sure."

Before Nate could retort, the hum of an engine cut through the night air. Headlights flashed over the dunes. "That'll be the lovebirds," he said, already prodding at the logs to coax the flames higher.

As the crackle of the fire came into view and laughter drifted down the sand, Anya stayed close to Noble's side, her phone still warm in her pocket from where she'd shown him the photo. He hadn't said much, just told her not to worry, that he'd help her figure it out. He tightened his grip on her hand and told her she should show it to Stan, that if anyone knew what those glyphs were, it'd be her.

Noble reached for Anya as they approached the fire, threading their fingers together like it was second nature. He bumped his shoulder gently against hers and murmured, "Hey, whatever's growing in those woods, it doesn't get to ruin our night."

Anya managed a smile, small but real. He leaned in and pressed a kiss to the side of her head, just beneath her ear, like a charm meant to ward off whatever still clung to her.

She didn't think the photo would leave her mind anytime soon, but for now, she let the warmth of his hand anchor her as the firelight flickered across the sand.

"Look who finally decided to show up," Stan called.

"Yeah, yeah, fashionably late," Noble said, leading Anya closer and hugging her to his body.

"We don't tolerate sex in public places, guys," Nate joked. "I'm going to have to cite you for indecent exposure and lewd acts on public property."

"Ha ha." Noble kicked sand toward his other childhood best friend.

Anya rolled her eyes but smiled. "More like, he wouldn't stop messing with the playlist he's created for tonight. You'd think he was going to Tennessee to train to be a DJ, not a veterinarian."

"Hey, I have eclectic taste," Noble defended. "Unlike Nate, who listens to the same ten songs on repeat."

"What can I say? Quality over quantity." Nate smirked. "Speaking of quantity—honestly, Ryker, you have to tell me what you've been eating. Is it pure protein shakes and the souls of your enemies?" he called out to an approaching figure.

The others turned as Ryker Hawley's broad form emerged from the dark, highlighted in flickering firelight. He was taller and more muscular than any of them had expected. In the nine months he'd been away, his lean frame was now solid, powerful, the kind of physique built for something beyond casual workouts.

"Nah, man. Just training." Ryker's voice was even, but his mind was a series of shifting thoughts and hidden narratives he'd never voice.

"Training for what exactly? This Olympic thing?" Nate pressed, skeptical. "You expect us to believe you're about to become the next big jiu-jitsu god? Win Olympic gold?"

Anya left Noble's embrace to give Ryker a hug. They were close friends; her tight-knit group had been her, Ryker, and Nettie. A lot had changed in their last year of high school. Outside forces had merged two friendly factions into one.

"That's the plan." Ryker dropped down onto one of the logs circling the fire.

Anya settled on the sand between Noble's outstretched legs.

"Right. And I'm about to be the next head of the FBI. I mean, I might be someday, but probably not the next one." Nate smirked, but there was an edge of genuine curiosity in his tone. "You swear this is real?"

"As real as it gets," Ryker said.

More footsteps announced Ember and Emory's arrival. Ember dropped down beside Stan with a tired sigh. She wore loose jeans and a sweater, her tight curls piled on top of her head and wrapped in a silk scarf. Their mother was in town from San Francisco, and it always made Ember nervous. Of all the people, she felt like her mom just knew something extra had happened that fateful day at school. Her mother was a lethal prosecuting attorney. It only made sense that she would have scrutinized the case and seen the inconsistencies.

Emory, with the slick black hair of their Asian father, and athletic build, took a seat on the opposite log. "So," Emory said, rubbing his hands together for warmth. "What are we talking about?"

"Are you going to tell us what you're doing at the Orbriallis?" Nate asked.

Emory laughed. "Bro."

Nate shrugged while the others around him laughed as well.

"You do not let it go." Emory flashed his white, straight-toothed grin at his friend.

"I'm gonna keep asking."

"Dude, let it go." Stan threw a stick at him.

Nate dodged the stick. "I think we should know. After all the shit they pulled."

"Nothing nefarious is going on," Emory said, his tone still playful.

"That you know of," Nettie mumbled.

Emory's eyes drifted toward her. Of all the people present, she held the greatest grudge, and he didn't blame her. "I set up the pill dispensary for the psych patients. Sometimes I fill out intake forms or transcribe notes. Once in a blue moon I'm allowed to observe patients in our clinical trials."

Nate snapped his fingers and sat forward, pointing enthusiastically at Emory. "That, that right there. What clinical trials?"

Noble laughed as he said, "Dude, the Institute has been researching real medicine for a while now."

"I know that," Nate said, voice exasperated.

"So," Noble quickly continued, "they still run trials on pills and other stuff."

"Other stuff?" Nettie asked, brows raised.

"You know what I mean," Noble explained. "Implants. That cochlear implant they've been in the news about, right? It's supposed to be revolutionary."

"I love that that's what they're in the news for," Nettie spat.

Anya shifted uncomfortably. She hated how mean-spirited Nettie had become since The Event. She had her brother back, her true brother, and the threat of Raymond LaRange had come to a decisive end this past spring. But the vitriol toward the Institute seemed to build with each passing day. Nettie had confessed to Anya that her brother was never truly coming back a few months ago, when the news of LaRange's death spread among them. She'd said, "Like it matters." Anya had found the reaction peculiar. "Everyone else is thrilled," she'd replied at the time. Nettie snorted and said, "My brother was ruined in that facility. What's done is done. LaRange being dead or Dr. Owens being gone doesn't change that my brother is never coming back."

Anya felt gutted that her friend had her hope taken away, and worse, still seeing that hope turn her into an acerbic pessimist.

Noble sensed the unease building in the group, especially when his girlfriend's muscles tensed against him. He knew the trouble Nettie was having finding the silver lining to her brother's return. The Event had drastically shifted her personality and Anya confessed she felt their friendship slipping away. He changed the subject. "Where'd you go this afternoon?" Noble asked Nate, kicking his friend's shoe.

"I had to do a patrol out at the state park earlier. We're worried all the press about that kid getting killed is going to bring a bunch of trigger-happy lunatics into the woods."

"*We're* worried?" Stan mocked.

"Yeah, *we*," Nate emphasized. "They see me as an equal."

"Oh, I'm sure."

Ember giggled at their teasing exchange. They were more like brother and sister than she and Emory.

"Are they saying it's the same thing that hit the livestock in Honeydew?" Noble asked.

"They don't know. No one's seen it, but whatever it is, it's got people scared," Nate replied.

"Anya, does your dad know anything?" Stan asked.

"I know the farmers have been shooting every predator on sight lately," she replied.

"Yeah," Nate scoffed. "The Department of Fish and Wildlife have had a number of calls."

Noble wrapped his arms around Anya and rested his chin on her head.

Anya glanced across the fire at Nate. "We've had weird things happen before, but this… It does kinda feel different. But my dad thinks people panic too easily. I'd have to agree."

"Maybe the Orbriallis Institute moving in and buying up all the land is forcing predators to find new hunting grounds," Nettie muttered.

That hit a nerve. The town had been in a state of protest for a while now, not just because of the new development going up. The nearby unincorporated town of Goldenvale wanted to become incorporated—absorbed into Lost Grove. Half were against it, half saw the positives, and others didn't see what harm it'd do. Then the subdivision went into development, a surprise no one in town saw coming. Dr. Owens, it was rumored, had slicked a few hands with bribes to get the housing development passed. The minute they broke ground near the Grouse River, activists came pouring into town to protest the changes the new houses, roads, and infrastructure would create with the flow of local flora and fauna.

"God; tell me you're not one of them." Nate sighed, falling back on the sand dramatically.

"One of who?" Ember typed in her text-to-voice app.

"One of the stupid activists picketing the construction site." Nate sat up and pointed at Nettie. "No joke, I hope you are not one of the idiots defacing private property."

Nettie rolled her eyes.

"I'm serious," Nate continued. "If you did, fine. But really, don't do it."

"You're not a real officer," she said, but her voice was sharp, filled with annoyance she'd meant to hide.

"He's right, though." Stan came to Nate's defense. "The fine and possible prison time on that is no joke."

"I'm just protesting," Nettie said. "I have more right to protest those assholes than anyone up there at the construction site."

Nate raised a hand. "You totally do. Just don't let it turn into doing something that could really get you into trouble."

"You guys sound like my parents. I get enough shit..." she said, standing and brushing sand off her butt.

"Whoa, where are you going?" Anya asked.

"I don't need to hear it from all of you."

"Nettie." Anya moved to stand. "No one is saying this to nag. They're worried. Nate's right; you could get in a lot of trouble."

"Stay, Nettie," Noble cajoled, like he was easing a riled-up horse. "Nate thinks he's the damn sheriff, true, but we all just want you to be safe."

Ember grabbed Nettie's hand and pulled her back to the sand. She typed in her phone. Seconds later, it spoke. "You're right to want to hold them accountable. It's good to keep an eye on them."

Nettie took back her hand and fiddled with her fingernails in her lap. "They are ruining the natural landscape there."

"Agreed," Emory said.

"Yeah, totally," Stan seconded. "I'm not saying we shouldn't protest. They're depriving the land of natural resources and erosion materials. But they've owned that property for ages. We had to know they'd eventually do something with it."

"Not enough housing around here as it is," Ryker commented. Everyone looked at him like he'd just shown up. "What?" he asked the people around the fire. "Forget about me?"

"No." Anya smiled. Then said, "Kind of."

They all laughed.

"You're so damn quiet, dude," Nate added.

Ryker laughed. "It allows me to hear a lot of stuff I'm not supposed to."

"What? Like Anya hasn't told you all about what happened while you disappeared into your Olympic cult?" Nate asked.

"She told me some," Ryker acknowledged. He might have thought she'd lost her mind if he didn't know there was more to worry about in the universe than fucked up human experiments. Not-children, the Green Man, kidnapping…she'd told him all those bits. Most interesting of all was how close she'd grown to Noble. It gave Ryker a peculiar comfort to know she was in a relationship with someone as decent as Noble. He had to be, the way he protected his sister.

Ryker wished he had more time to get to know Noble better, deeper. But his time away from his new training was precious and short.

"So, you know. It's not like we're revealing some big secret," Nate added.

"No. Not really," Ryker said, smiling.

"Wait," Emory addressed the group. "Has anyone else told someone outside of the ones who were present?"

They'd all been sworn to secrecy, not only by the authority figure, Seth Wolfe, but it became a quiet pact among themselves. Yes, in order to reunite Nettie with her actual brother, they had to keep mum about all they knew about LaRange and not-children but the experience was theirs, a bond deepening their lifelong friendships in a way no one could understand.

Everyone shook their heads.

"So, only you?" he asked Ryker.

Ryker shrugged and nodded.

"We both told him, really," Noble added.

Nate snorted.

"I spilled the whole thing about the cave and shit last week," Noble said.

"What cave?" Ryker asked, then laughed. "Don't worry. I know I can't talk about it."

"It's not like we care if you know," Stan said. "I don't, anyway."

"Nobody does," Emory said. "You seem like you have your own secrets. I doubt you'll spill ours."

Emory and Ryker held each other's gaze across the fire. Emory badly wanted to use his powers, but he had ethics. That was a line he wouldn't cross. No diving into the minds of friends, and Ryker had become a friend shortly after returning to get his diploma and graduating from

Lost Grove High.

Music filtered into the cool summer night. The ocean breeze carried the tunes up into the dunes, where nocturnal animals lifted their ears, curious if they should flee or if the noise wasn't a threat.

Noble grabbed the football from beside Nate and stood. "Okay, we need to shake off the doomsday vibes. Who's up for a game?"

They all jumped up, eager for a game on the sand.

As they played under stars twinkling above them like diamonds against a midnight velvet sky, laughter turned the cool air warm; huddles formed as tales exchanged became part memories now shared forever; adventures discussed sparked wanderlust within each person; stories unfolded woven deep within these souls who found solace among themselves amidst the chaos surrounding them. But tonight, it was just them on a beach. There were no threats, no jobs to worry about, no demands to be met. They all knew the summer couldn't last forever and then many were going their own way, but tonight, it was as if the only thing that existed was this small stretch of beach, these friends, and the limitless black of the Pacific Ocean stretching out to the heavens.

Anya jogged back toward the fire for some water. Her laughter from moments ago had faded into a quiet, internal hum. Her thoughts still snagged on the image of her mother swaying in front of that marked tree, blank-eyed and humming.

Stan joined her, flopping down beside the cooler.

"Can I ask you something?" Anya asked, handing her the water bottle.

"Of course."

Anya hesitated. "Noble said your family was from the Wiyot tribe?"

Stan smiled, wondering where this was going. "Mostly, yeah. My mom and dad are both part Wiyot, but Grandma Hensley is Yakama. You want a history lesson or something?"

Anya blushed. "Oh gosh. No, it's not that. Not really."

Stan chuckled. "What is it, you cute little weirdo?"

Anya briefly dropped her head into her hands. "This is going to sound insensitive no matter how I phrase it so…do either of your tribes have a way of writing?"

Stan blinked, then burst into a laugh—loud and bright.

Anya's cheeks flushed. "What?" she asked, grinning in spite of herself.

Stan tried to respond, but laughter overtook her again, drawing sharp little gasps as she clutched her ribs.

Anya's cheeks hurt from smiling so hard. "Like, I know Native Americans had carvings and drawings. I just meant, like do you guys have runes—stop laughing," Anya said, falling into a fit of giggles.

Stan wrapped Anya up in a one-armed hug. "I can't," she hissed.

Both of them dissolved into uncontrollable laughter.

"Runes?" Stan managed to wheeze out.

Anya gently shoved her with her shoulder and sighed, gaining control of herself. "You know, pictographs. Hieroglyphics that were maybe carved into trees."

Stan wiped her eyes. "I mean, no. I don't think so. Well, not that we've retained. We could have, but a lot of our Wiyot culture was wiped out during our genocide."

Anya sucked in a breath. "I'm sorry. I didn't mean—"

Stan reached over and gave her hand a reassuring squeeze, cutting her off. "It's okay. Why are you asking?"

Anya hesitated. The fire cracked behind them, the night settling in around their little circle of warmth. "Well…it's about the Cursed Woods."

Constance's brow furrowed. "Okay."

Anya exhaled. "I'm asking because my mom and I found something. Some kind of marking in the trees, just past our property line." She pulled out her phone and unlocked it, holding it out to Stan. "I took a photo."

The firelight flickered across her face as she studied the image. Her brow furrowed almost immediately.

"Is it just me," she said slowly, "or is this…hard to look at?"

"What do you mean?" Anya asked.

Stan tilted the screen, then brightened it. "I don't know. I can't focus on it. Like when your eyes try to refocus on 3D art or one of those magic dot posters. It's weird."

Anya's stomach tightened. "Yeah," she said quietly. "That's how it feels in person, too."

Stan looked up sharply. "You went near it?"

"My mom did. I…I don't know how long she was standing there before I found her. She was just—gone. Not passed out, but…not herself."

Stan stared at her for a beat. "She okay now?"

"She said she is."

Stan glanced back down at the image, then shut the phone off and handed it back. "I doubt they came from animal scratches. Too uniform. Too...deliberate." Stan didn't say anything for a moment, chewing her lip before adding, "I can talk to my uncle. He knows the old stories, so maybe he knows something about these."

Anya shook her head. "Nah, it's okay. I don't want to make a big deal of it."

Stan's gaze sharpened. "Anya, you just said your mom was—what—entranced by a symbol carved into a tree? That's a big deal." She leaned back on her palms. "Send me the photo. I'll look into it."

Anya hesitated, then sent it. "Thanks, Stan."

Stan tapped her shoe to Anya's bare foot. "No problemo," she said with a big smile, trying to ease her friend's concern.

They sat in companionable silence for a moment, the fire crackling between them. Across the way, Ember laughed at something Ryker said. Stan's gaze lingered on her for a second too long.

Anya caught it and smirked. "You like her, don't you?"

Stan gave her a sharp look, but there was no heat behind it. "Shut up."

"Just saying." Anya grinned.

The boys rejoined them, breathless from the game.

The fire burned on, bright against the darkness. Their last summer together. Their last night before things changed forever.

Chapter Thirteen
A Hesitant Inquiry

L eith hesitated at the entrance of the Lost Grove Library, her fingers tightening around her phone like it might fly from her hand if she let it. The building stood quiet, as unassuming as ever, with the gentle hush of late-morning sun filtering through high windows. Still, something about crossing the threshold made her uneasy. Maybe it was what she carried in her phone, the images. Or maybe it was the purpose of her visit.

The library smelled like it always had—old paper, waxed wood, a faint trace of lavender used to keep moths at bay. She'd come here only a handful of times since Anya was born, mostly in those early years of motherhood, seeking books on pregnancy and toddler development. The librarian had been someone else then, a white-haired woman who rarely looked up from her desk. Today, it was Story.

She found the librarian midway through shelving books, her dark hair shifting as she reached for the highest shelf. Story's attire was as flowing as ever, sheer fabrics draped over her form in a way that was both effortless and intentional. A glimpse of ink peeked through the folds—a hint of the swirling tattoos that marked her arms. She turned at the sound of footsteps, her sharp hazel eyes catching Leith in an assessing glance.

"Mrs. Bury." Her tone was smooth, a touch surprised but not displeased. "How can I help you?"

Leith offered a slight nod, uncertain how to begin. She and Story knew of each other—everyone knew everyone in a town like theirs— but they had never had reason to speak beyond polite acknowledgments.

Now, standing under Story's knowing gaze, she felt strangely out of place.

"I—" Leith shifted, glancing at the phone in her hand. "I wasn't sure if I should come. This might be nothing. I don't want to waste your time."

Story arched a dark brow, setting the book in her hand aside. "You don't seem like someone who wastes time."

Leith gave a thin smile. "I hope not. I just don't want to be too forward. We hardly know each other, Ms. Palmer. But Anya said—"

Story softly placed her hand on Leith's arm. "Call me Story. And you're here now. So, let's get to know each other."

Leith smiled. "Okay. Thank you. And call me Leith."

"I will. And your daughter is an absolute sweetheart, by the way."

"She is," Leith agreed.

Story quickly surveyed the library. "There's no one else in here. Just me and you. What would you like to know or ask?"

Leith sighed. "Well, we live on a farm just outside of town that's surrounded by the woods. The Cursed Woods. I've always liked to spend time in there, but lately everything feels...a little strange."

Story's expression shifted. She moved closer. "Strange how?"

"They just don't feel right. Something's changed. And I've seen markings, one in particular on a tree closer to the house. I don't think they're natural."

That caught her attention. The faint amusement in her expression faded, replaced with a careful seriousness. "Can you describe them?"

"I can do you one better." Leith held out her phone. "There are several."

Story took it without hesitation. The soft library lighting cast shadows over her face, highlighting the sharp angles of her cheekbones and the subtle curve of her lips as they pressed together in thought. She scrolled slowly, her brow furrowing deeper with each photo.

The pictures showed trees with unnatural markings, but more bewildering than that was how the markings moved inside these still images. They made Story dizzy the way they twisted and spun.

"These..." she murmured. "They're not just symbols. They're active. I can feel it even from these photos."

"I know," Leith said quietly. "They make me feel...odd. Looking at them on the screen, it's like they're still watching. It's hard to explain."

"No," Story whispered. She was curious at the word choice: watching, *still* watching. "That makes sense. I feel it too. Like pressure.

Or static under the skin." She tapped the screen. "This…this isn't a rune. It's older. Not a sigil either. If anything, it reminds me of a hieroglyph or pictograph."

"I've seen others," Leith said. "Deeper in. They all have presence."

Story's gaze lifted, pinning her. Again she was struck by Leith's choice of words. "Power," she corrected.

Leith nodded. "Yes. That's the word. They have power."

Story did not think it was the word Leith meant. She meant presence when she'd said it, but why? She'd always sensed a touch of the fae in Leith's daughter, Anya. That feeling was palpable on Leith, as if it was a beacon screaming, "I am other!" There were many things, beings, and ghosts in the Cursed Woods and Devil's Cradle State Park. Such vast wildernesses were always rife with wondrous unknowns.

A silence stretched between them, charged and uncertain. Leith glanced at Story then, really looking at her, and something flickered behind her gaze. An awareness, a quiet recognition that neither of them spoke aloud. Leith had always sensed Story was beyond human, though she had never pried. And now, standing so close, she could tell Story sensed the same in her.

Story tilted her head, considering. "And Anya thought I might have some answers?"

Leith smiled despite herself. "She did." Leith hesitated, her gaze dipping to the phone still warm in her palm. A beat passed long enough for silence to thicken between them again. "I haven't felt right since I saw them," she admitted. "The glyphs." Leith's voice grew quieter. "It wasn't just seeing them. I… I lost time."

Story's head tilted slightly. "How long?"

"I don't know, hours. I was going for a swim, same as always. But when Anya found me, the light had changed."

"Anya found you? She's seen this?"

Leith nodded, then rubbed her temple, eyes distant. "It was like waking from a dream I hadn't meant to fall into."

Story didn't interrupt, but her brow furrowed as she leaned in, watching Leith as if her words might reveal secrets hidden beneath her skin.

"I felt like I was being watched," Leith added. "Like the forest had turned its face toward me. Even now, it's still there. Under my ribs. In the back of my throat. Like the spores crawled inside and haven't left."

She exhaled sharply. "I'm jumpy. Guarded. I've never been afraid in those woods. Not once in my whole life. But now I feel like they're no longer mine to walk."

A flicker passed through Story's eyes at that. Familiarity, perhaps, or recognition of something spoken too late. She said nothing, letting Leith fill the silence with her breath and the faint hum of overhead lights.

"I'm sorry, I don't know why I'm telling you all of this. I won't—"

"No," Story said, grabbing her hand, feeling like she was about to leave. "I'm here to help. Anya was right in telling you to come see me."

Leith could see nothing but sincerity in her eyes. "Thank you."

Story gave her hand a gentle squeeze before letting go. "Of course. Tell me what you want."

"I want the glyph gone."

Story's voice came soft and even, a contrast to the tension humming between them. "It might not be that easy to erase."

Leith met her eyes. "Maybe not. But it's on my land. And I have a daughter."

Story nodded slowly, the weight of that truth settling between them like fog over the trees. "These may be dangerous. We don't know if going in and scratching them out may cause a reaction."

"I've never seen this before," Leith added, her tone urgent, annoyed.

"All the more reason to be cautious," Story said calmly, reaching for the phone. "Let me send the images to myself. I have a few ideas. I'll look into it."

Leith caught a shimmer of light, like a flame dancing in Story's eyes where there should be no such reflection. Leith nodded and, after a moment's hesitation, handed Story her phone.

Muffled voices of children entering the small library rose, followed by the softer tones of parents coaxing them into calm. Story Time was about to begin.

Leith glanced over her shoulder. "I should go."

Story nodded and gave her phone back. "I'll let you know as soon as I have information worth sharing. In the meantime, stay away from them." Story paused with what she wanted to offer next, but the panic in Leith's eyes drew her to voice it. She stepped close and whispered. "If you need something to help you forget that it's out there…"

Leith blinked. The words Story whispered settled in her mind like petals on a placid lake's surface. "No, thank you. I don't…no," she said, her lips curving into a brief smile. She lingered for a beat, then turned to leave, her phone clenched tightly in her hand.

Later, after Story Time had wrapped—a cheerful tale about forest animals and a paper-leaf crafting activity to follow—the children played among the beanbags and low shelves while their parents gathered near the back with coffee in hand. Story spotted Deanna Hensley crouched beside the children's activity table, coaxing her twin boys into finishing their crafts.

"Deanna," Story said, stepping closer. "Do you have a moment?"

Deanna rose with an easy smile. Her long dark braid had started to unravel, and a smear of green marker stained her hand from where one of the twins had grabbed her. "Sure. What's up?"

"Have you ever come across old tribal markings in Devil's Cradle? Glyphs maybe. Petroglyphs or pictographs. Carvings or paintings on trees or stone."

Deanna's smile faded just a little, curiosity sharpening her features. "There are some." Between her mother-in-law and the rest of the family, the ways of the Wiyot and Yakama tribes were remembered and warnings obeyed. Most of all, she, like everyone in the community who knew her, was reminded of the last time someone asked after pictographs in Devil's Cradle. "That's actually what drew Hannah Albrecht up here before she disappeared."

"Hannah Albrecht?"

Deanna nodded. "She was researching old Wiyot settlement traces. She'd begun to suspect the glyphs weren't just decorative or ceremonial, but part of a mapped system—an ancient, boundary-setting language leading to something central. Something important. She believed they marked the limits of a sacred site or perhaps even an entire settlement. She thought the Cursed Woods and Devil's Cradle had more to tell." Her voice softened. "She worked with my father-in-law a bit, but spent most of her time with Cal. He guided her during her time here. Walked trails with her, helped her get access to areas other researchers never even knew existed. Hannah was respectful. Curious. Bright. Not one of those outsiders who just wanted to write a paper. She listened. She came to dinners." A beat passed. "I liked her. We all did."

"And she went missing?" Story asked, a faint memory tugging at her—of a flyer on the bulletin board. A name. A face that looked almost surprised to be missing.

"She did. Up along the northern ridge of the park." Deanna's voice dropped. "I'm sorry I don't know the specifics. Cal might."

Story absorbed that quietly. "Do you think I could speak with him?"

"Of course. I can give you his number," Deanna said. She pulled her phone from her pocket and tapped it in. "He might warn you away from them though. Anyone of us will, you know that, right?"

Story smiled. "I don't plan on following them. Just curious if anyone knows their meaning."

Deanna nodded. "Here," she said, handing Story her phone with the number. She bent to get her boys ready to go as Story typed the contact into her own phone.

"Thank you," Story said, handing the phone back.

"You're welcome." Deanna smiled. "Be careful. Those woods have their own rules."

Story nodded in agreement and glanced back toward the children's section, where laughter still rang out beneath the soft flicker of overhead lights.

Her thoughts drifted to Seth. Their last conversation had left a small but persistent splinter lodged just beneath her ribs. She had told him the truth about Mary. About what she'd seen. The fangs, the grotesque shift of fingers into claws, and the weight of that confession had cracked something in him. With Wes pushing to exhume LaRange's body and test for DNA, everything hung in a fragile balance. Finding Mary's DNA in the wounds wouldn't just destroy the case, it would destroy Seth's career.

Since then, they'd barely spoken. She longed to tell him about the glyphs and the sick feeling that settled in her chest like mold when she looked at them. But she knew he had no room left in his mind for anything outside duty. Not now.

So she returned to her desk, waving goodbye to the children and their parents, and told herself she could wait. This wasn't his wheelhouse. It was her problem to solve, and she intended to start by tracking down former colleagues of Hannah Albrecht.

Chapter Fourteen
The Land Remembers

The reservation was quiet in the way small places often were, the kind of quiet that lets you hear the wind move through the trees and the low hum of a distant radio drifting from an open window. Stan parked her mom's van near the small police station, stepping out into the thick warmth of an early July afternoon. The air smelled of sunbaked pine and the salt that always came with the wind off the bay.

Stan was always Constance to her Uncle Cal. She spotted him just where she hoped: leaning against his patrol car, his broad frame relaxed in the summer heat. His dark hair was pulled back into a single braid, streaked with grey at the temples, his badge glinted in the sunlight and he was sipping a Styrofoam cup of something too dark and too hot for a day like this.

"Hey, old man," she called, grinning.

Cal squinted up at her, smirking. "Constance. You're late."

"You're early," she countered, stepping up beside him and sliding onto the hood of his car. She had called ahead of time, but getting out the door when her twin brothers were on the rampage was a feat meant for someone who had nowhere to be and all the time in the world to be there. They'd bogged her down with questions and stuck to her legs like human shackles.

Stan and Cal sat like that for a few moments, just watching the stretch of dirt road beyond the parking lot where cottonwoods rustled like whispers. Cal passed her the cup without asking. She took a sip, winced.

"Still tastes like overboiled road tar," she said.

Cal chuckled. "Grows on you."

She smiled, then grew quiet. He didn't press. He never did.

"Uncle Cal," she said, after a beat. "Can I ask you something a little weird?"

He arched his brow. "That's your specialty, isn't it?"

She nudged him with her shoulder. "Serious weird. About the woods."

Cal worked his jaw, squinting as he looked into the pure blue sky. "Hm," he grunted.

"Hm." Stan copied him, crossing her arms like his and frowning like he was.

Cal's frown lines disappeared, and a smile eased across his face. As a child, Constance had mirrored him a lot. She'd walk like him. Stand like him. She'd be his little shadow at family gatherings. For her to do it still, as a young woman, made him laugh.

"Why do you want to know anything about those woods?" he asked, still smiling at her actions. She was growing up, but he hoped she'd never grow up so much that she forgot she was her uncle's favorite niece.

Stan shrugged. "I'm asking for a friend."

"Oh?" He gave a nod. "Alright. Hit me."

Stan pulled out her phone, thumbed to the photo Anya had sent her, and handed it over.

Cal took it without comment. Seeing the image was a punch to the gut. He stared at it for a long time, jaw flexing as he studied the twisting, almost iridescent glyph burned into the tree bark. For a moment, the warm quiet of the day shifted, like the sun retreated just slightly. "Where'd this come from?"

"Near the Bury property," Stan said. "Anya and her mom found it. Leith acted weird. Zoned out. Like…real weird."

Cal's gaze didn't move from the screen. "And you brought this to me because?"

Stan shifted, her boot kicking lightly at the bumper beneath them. "Because it feels wrong. Because I've never seen anything like it. And because you used to talk about markings when Hannah was still around."

That pulled his eyes to hers. His voice was flat. "Constance, you need to stay out of it."

"I'm not in anything," she said defensively. "A friend came to me, scared I might add, and I'm just trying to help."

He exhaled through his nose. Handed back the phone. "I'm serious. Those woods have history. You think Devil's Cradle got that name because it sounded spooky? No. The old people called it cursed for a reason."

"I figured," she murmured.

"Our people never settled deep in there. We hunted the edges. Passed through when we had to. But the elders say there were rules. Places you didn't speak in. Trees you didn't touch. You know the stories." They were stories he wished Hannah had listened to more closely. Back then, he'd shared them with half a grin, not thinking that she'd disappear before he had the chance to tell her he believed them, too.

"I know some," Stan admitted.

Cal leaned forward, forearms resting on his knees. His gaze drifted out to the horizon. "My grandmother used to say the land there dipped because it was made to cradle something. Not hold it. *Cradle* it. Like how you hold something too wild to tame, just enough to keep it from lashing out. You ever hear the full tale of the Cradle?" he asked, not really waiting for her answer.

Stan shook her head slowly. "Just parts. Grandpa never liked telling it."

He nodded. "That's because it's not a story meant for comfort. It's a warning. One we keep telling so we don't forget." He leaned back against the windshield and let the words roll, not rushed or theatrical. "A long time ago, before the world looked the way it does now, Gudatrigakwitl, the creator of all, looked upon the empty earth and thought to fill it with life. From the stars above, Gudatrigakwitl pulled light and made the trees. From the waves of the ocean, he gathered mist and made the rivers that flowed through the valleys. And from the earth he took the strength of stone and made the creatures that would walk upon the land.

"But Gudatrigakwitl was wise and knew that for the world to stay in balance, there must be darkness to match the light. So from the deepest shadows, he created the spirits of the unseen, who would dwell in the places the sun could not reach—beneath the earth, in the darkest groves, and in the hearts of the tallest mountains. The spirits of the unseen grew restless. They were powerful spirits, and though they were meant to live in the dark, they longed for the warmth of the sun and the taste of the light.

"Among these spirits was the most cunning and fierce, known as Tsagallik, the Great Shadow. He traveled through the forests and the rivers, spreading his shadow wherever he went, turning the creatures of the land wild with fear. The animals cried out to Gudatrigakwitl, 'The light is fading! The shadows grow long, and we cannot see the path!'

"Gudatrigakwitl answered but he could not undo what had already been done. He called down the Wets'haw, the great wolf spirits of the sky, who had long watched over the land with patience and wisdom. The Wets'haw came down from the sky and they pursued Tsagallik through the forests. The Great Shadow fled, deeper and deeper into the heart of the woods.

"But Gudatrigakwitl was clever. He knew he had to trap Tsagallik, he could not simply banish him. So he called upon the spirits of the land, the waters, and the trees and they wove a powerful enchantment, one that would hold the shadow in place for all time. And thus, the Cradle of Shadows—what you now call Devil's Cradle—was born. Within this cradle, Tsagallik and his followers were bound, unable to escape, unable to roam the earth again.

"But we, the Wiyot, who had come to live in the land blessed by Gudatrigakwitl, knew that though the cradle held the shadows at bay, the balance was fragile. The spirits of the unseen still stirred within the woods, whispering their dark secrets to those who dared to wander too close. And so, our people became the watchers, the guardians of the Cradle.

"We learned the songs and the rites that kept the balance strong. Our Chustas, the shamans, would go to the edges of the Cradle and speak to the trees, calling upon the Wets'haw to keep the shadows bound. But we knew, too, that we must never enter too deep, for even the strongest spirit could be tempted by the whispers of Tsagallik. My grandmother used to say those symbols weren't made for us. They were made to warn us. Like barbed wire for the soul. You get too close, and something in you gets caught."

A long silence settled between them.

Cal sat up. "When our people were forced off the land, when they were slaughtered at Tuluwat and driven from what was ours, there was no one left to keep the balance." His gaze hardened, shadowed by something deeper than memory. "And the darkness spread."

Stan swallowed. She had grown up hearing about the massacre, about what had been stolen. But hearing it framed like this, a connection between her tribe's history and a legend, was something she hadn't considered before.

"You ever think about how we're all still connected to that?" Cal asked, glancing sideways at her. "Even now, it's in us. You, me, our family. You following in your dad's footsteps, going to school for forensic medicine? That's not just science, Stan. That's keeping our traditions alive, in a different way. The old ways are about understanding death, honoring it, not fearing it. That's part of who we are."

Stan nodded slowly. "I hear you, I do. But—"

"You heard about the livestock?"

Stan frowned. "Yeah. Some farmers think it's a mountain lion or wolves."

Cal shook his head. "Maybe. But I've seen mountain lion kills. This is different. And now, that boy getting mauled in the park?" He exhaled sharply. "Doesn't sit right with me."

Stan felt a chill at the reminder. "You think they're connected."

Cal didn't answer right away. Instead, he squinted at the invisible horizon blocked by trees and buildings and homes. The sound of the Pacific Ocean wasn't far off, and with it, the cold, coastal breeze broke up the piercing hot sun beaming down on their skin. "The balance was broken a long time ago. Without the shamans, without the keepers, things bleed through. Maybe it's just animals. Maybe it's something else."

"So the Cradle of Shadows is real?" she asked.

Cal exhaled, rubbing a hand over his jaw. "It's as real as the wind. The Cursed Woods, that's what they all call it these days. That's what happens when you leave something like that unchecked for generations. The rot doesn't stay in the roots, it spreads. Makes things sick. People too."

She shook her head to get rid of the cultural legends and beliefs taking up too much space, leaving little room for science and statistics. "People have lived next to the Cursed Woods for ages. Sure, we fear it, but we also live side by side with it every day. You make it sound like the legends are real. But if that's true, then why do people disappear from state and national parks all over the country? Not just here. Not just in Devil's Cradle."

Cal gave her a steady look. "Maybe that's the wrong question. Maybe you should be asking why this land in particular has always felt… different." He tapped the hood of the car lightly. "Science can explain a lot, and I believe in that. But I also know what our ancestors told us. The Cradle of Shadows twisted the land, warped things that should have stayed natural. Flora, fauna, even the things that hunt in the night."

Stan swallowed. "Like whatever mauled that boy?"

Cal nodded grimly. "The marks on him don't line up with a bear, mountain lion, or anything I've seen before. It's like—" He stopped himself, shaking his head. "Never mind. Just stay away from those woods, Stan."

Stan watched her uncle's shoulders. Their subtle shift could tell her everything she needed to know about his mood. She remembered those same shoulders turning away after the search for Hannah had been called off—how he stood in the rain outside the station for hours, hoping someone would come back with better news. "You're thinking about Hannah, aren't you?"

"I should've pulled her out. Should've insisted," he said softly. "Like I'm insisting with you now."

Stan watched him. There was something raw in his voice. Not regret, exactly. But close.

"She cared about what we lost," she said.

"She did," Cal agreed. "And that's what made it dangerous. She wanted to reclaim what was gone. But not everything that's buried should be dug up. The land remembers."

Stan looked out toward the woods, just barely visible beyond the low buildings. "She's my friend, Uncle Cal. I can't just tell her it's probably nothing and forget it. Anya was scared, she tried to hide it, but this upset her. A lot."

Cal nodded slowly. "Then let me help. Let me handle it."

Stan opened her mouth to argue, but he cut her off with a raised hand.

"But you stay away from it. I mean it, Constance. You're smart. You've got gifts. And that makes you appealing to the things that live out there. They notice you. That's why I'm telling you to leave it alone. Because when people disappear in Devil's Cradle, they don't come back." He looked toward the tree line beyond the low buildings, gaze drifting past the parked cars and mailboxes like he could still see Hannah's smile as she turned and watched him leave Grouse Ridge Market the morning she never came back.

His eyes found his niece's, and in them she saw something she wasn't used to seeing in Cal Hensley—fear. Stan felt a chill that had nothing to do with the summer heat. She slid her phone back into her pocket, her mind racing.

Cal patted her knee before standing. "Leave it alone, Constance."

Stan nodded and slid off the hood of the squad car. "Thanks, Uncle," she said and gave him a hug.

Cal squeezed her back. "Get home now, before it gets too dark. I don't like you driving on the 101 at night."

She swallowed hard, nodding and wondering what had happened with Hannah that scared her uncle so much.

Chapter Fifteen
Gulliver's Gully

The setting sun's gleaming burnt-orange rays shot over the tree line in the distance, illuminating the outfield of Garrison Park while the Lost Grove 16U traveling baseball team finished their drills for the evening. The snap of leather, cleats hitting dirt, and the crack of aluminum bats were a familiar sound for anyone walking by the park on summer nights. A small gathering of locals, mostly parents of the players, sat in the bleachers or in lawn chairs, watching on.

"Okay, guys, let's bring it in!" Coach Ray Bellanger waited at the pitching mound for the twelve players to circle around him. "Great work tonight. Let's bring that same energy tomorrow evening against Deerfield. Meadows, you bring that swing tomorrow, we'll be in good shape."

Clayton Meadows grinned at his best friend, Jasper Cunningham, who playfully rolled his eyes. The two had been friends since kindergarten and had been on the same baseball team since the eight-and-under league. At fourteen, they were two of the youngest players on the team, but also two of the best, Clayton known for his bat and Jasper for his glove and speed.

"The team bus will leave at five p.m. from the school parking lot as usual," Coach Bellanger continued. "If you're not on that bus at five sharp, I'll assume you're driving yourself or getting a ride from your parents. The wife and I will be hosting a late post-game dinner for anyone who wants to come."

"Corn dogs again, Coach?" Jasper asked, inciting some friendly chuckles.

Ray let out a hearty laugh. "That's about the sum of it. Okay, hands in the middle, guys."

Everyone clasped a hand over Coach's hand.

"Okay, on three, boys! One, two, three!"

"Go, Lasers!" The team cheered in unison and then headed off the field.

Clayton and Jasper walked behind the backstop to grab their bikes. Jason Collins, the team captain and their best pitcher, was walking toward them. "We're all heading to the pizza shop if you guys want to join us."

Clayton contained a smile. He loved that he and Jasper were embraced by the older players, already in high school. "Yeah, man, we'll for sure stop by."

Jasper nudged Clayton. "Remember, my mom wanted us to swing by real quick to help get all that gravel into the backyard."

"Oh, right." Clayton played along. There had been no mention of Jasper's mom or gravel. He couldn't even think of a reason they would need gravel in their backyard, but Jasper clearly had something in mind.

"Well, come by when you can," Jason said and headed to the parking lot.

Clayton waited until Jason was out of ear's distance. "What the hell was that?" he asked, leaning in closer to his friend. Clayton stood five inches taller than his friend at six feet even, handsome and well built for his age.

Jasper grinned as he took his hat off and rubbed his dark buzz-cut hair.

"What? What are we doing?" Clayton asked as he looped his glove around the right handle.

"I may have made some plans for us," Jasper said as he put his hat back on.

Clayton pushed his bike, leading them away from the park. "Like what?"

"I didn't actually make them. I more agreed to them."

Clayton glanced at his best friend and saw the twinkle in his eyes. "Dude, tell me you didn't hit up Angie. I told you—"

"I didn't hit up anybody, bro. Your girl's best friend—"

"She's not my girl," Clayton interceded.

"Marissa messaged me on Instagram. She said they're going to hang out at the gully tonight and that Angie really wanted you to come."

"Did she really say that?" Clayton asked, trying not to sound too hopeful. Clayton had had a crush on Angie Stokes since sixth grade. They had been friends, or maybe just friendly with each other, for years, but toward the end of elementary school, Clayton started to see her in a different light. Maybe it was his blossoming hormones, maybe it was her early development, whatever the case, all he could think about since then was what it would be like to kiss her.

Jasper laughed. "*Did she really say that?*" he mimicked. "Yes, dude, she did. I told you that she's into you, too."

"I don't know."

"Well, you're an idiot. Anyone besides you could see it clear as day."

Clayton's heartbeat picked back up, having just settled from practice.

"And Marissa said she got some weed from her older brother."

"Weed?" Clayton raised an eyebrow at his friend.

"Yeah, weed. They wanna get high, and they want us there with them."

"I don't want to smoke weed."

Jasper shot him an offended look. "Yes, you do."

Clayton dropped his head back. "No, I really don't. Especially in front of Angie. What if I freak out or something?"

"Dude, it's like drinking really strong tea or something."

Clayton laughed. "And you're saying I'm the idiot. What am I telling my mom?"

"That you're sleeping over. Which you will."

"What are we telling your parents?"

Jasper huffed. "Like they care. I'll just text them to say we're going over to Kev's to play GTA."

"Yeah, okay." Clayton didn't need a whole lot of convincing to agree to go see Angie for the first time outside of school. Exiting the park onto Tate Street, Clayton and Jasper both straddled their bikes. "Do we have time to stop at home and change?"

Jasper led the way, shouting back. "No way, they're probably already there."

"I'm all sweaty, though."

"It's like ninety degrees and humid as shit. We'd get sweaty again by the time we got there anyway." Jasper took a sharp right on 5th Street, the opposite direction of Main Street, which would be the route to Gulliver's Gully.

"Where are you going?" Clayton called out.

"We'll take the shortcut."

Clayton pushed to a standing position and pedaled harder to catch up. "Why would we do that?"

Jasper glanced over at his friend. "Um, because it's faster. And we don't want to bike past the pizza shop on the way out of town. They guys might stop us and ask where we're going. You'll cave in and tell them—"

"No, I wouldn't."

"And then they'll want to come. It'll turn into a whole thing. And Randy would make moves on your girl."

"What are you talking about?"

Jasper hung a left on Mulberry Street, which dead-ended at the path leading into the Cursed Woods. "I don't know. We want to get there sooner anyway. Takes forever to wind around the 211, cross the bridge… They might think we're not showing."

Clayton felt the dull weight of dread fill his stomach as he eyed the Cursed Woods entrenched in darkness, the sun having fully set. "I'm not sure going through there at night is such a good idea."

"Why the hell not? We've gone to the gully like ten times this way."

"In the morning. During the day."

"Like it matters," Jasper scoffed.

"Like it doesn't." The fact that he and Jasper kept daring to go through the Cursed Woods was probably stupid enough. It was like crossing the suspension bridge with decaying rope to get to the other side of the widest expanse of Reed Creek, something else they liked to foolishly do. It was just a matter of time before one of those wooden planks gave in. Going through the infamous woods at night felt like stepping on that plank.

They got to the end of the street and Jasper hopped off his bike, pulling it onto the dirt pathway that led into the woods. He looked back at Clayton, who still hadn't dismounted. "How is it any different?"

Clayton reluctantly got off his bike, raising his eyebrows. "Are you serious?"

"What, you think the ghosts of those creepy twin girls are gonna show up?"

Clayton swallowed down a wave of nausea. Ten-year-old twin sisters Nora and Nadine Carraway went missing during a family picnic back in 2001. Though their parents searched frantically, they found only Nora's bracelet near a small cave entrance—some claim to hear distant laughter echoing in that area of the Cursed Woods at dusk. Every kid knew the story, having looked it up on the internet wanting to see what the Carraway twins looked like. And every kid claimed they knew someone who had heard the echoes, despite the fact very few ever stepped foot into the woods.

"Why do they have to be creepy?" Clayton asked as he followed behind Jasper, who had started walking his bike down the pathway. "They were super adorable."

Jasper looked back over his shoulder, sneering. "Adorable?"

"Yeah."

"Sure, they looked cute in those photos, but I guarantee you they were creepy. Why else would they have disappeared in the Cursed Woods?"

Clayton grimaced. "What kind of logic is that?"

Jasper shrugged. "I don't know. Makes sense to me," he said as he pushed his bike into a row of bushes to his left. "Let's ditch our bikes here. We'll grab them on the way back."

Clayton let his bike drop into bushes. He peered into the woods as he took his hat off and rubbed the sweat from his forehead.

"Why do you look so freaked out?" Jasper asked as he turned the flashlight on his phone on.

"I'm not." Clayton attempted to sound convincing even though his heart was pounding in his chest, like it had little heart fists that were punching him in the rib cage for being so stupid. He took out his phone, sent his mom a quick text, and then turned on his flashlight.

Jasper laughed as he entered the woods. "I know why you're scared. You think the Carraway twins are still alive, living out here in the forest, feeding on young boys foolish enough to enter."

Clayton followed behind. The cracking of twigs beneath his feet sounded like fireworks reverberating off the maze of towering trees. "Not funny, dude."

"It's kinda funny. Look, forget about all the fairy tales and just focus on Angie Stokes. She's totally going to make out with you tonight. She might even let you feel her boobs."

Clayton pushed Jasper playfully in the back. "Shut up. And what do you mean fairy tales? The Carraway twins were real children. Their parents are real. And what about that one archeologist lady? That was barely two years ago she went missing."

Jasper felt a gust of breeze on his right cheek, like someone was standing right next to him blowing cold, dead breath on his face. He stopped suddenly and shined his flashlight around. "What the fuck was that?"

Clayton stopped next to him, chaotically moving his flashlight around. "What?"

"You didn't just feel a cold breeze just blow through here?"

"No, I… You better not be trying to freak me out."

Jasper turned to look at his friend, his eyes leaving no room for misinterpreting his seriousness. "How could you not have felt that?"

Clayton held his free hand up, trying to sense any breeze. It was so still the air felt heavy. There were no sounds of leaves rattling.

Jasper huffed. He refused to get sucked into the supposed eeriness of the woods. "Whatever, let's go. You probably just didn't notice it."

Clayton followed, his senses now at a fever pitch, his eyes constantly darting back and forth, following his light.

"We gotta pick up the pace," Jasper said, quickening his steps. "It's already nine thirty. They said they would be there at nine."

Clayton was oddly soothed by those words. It gave him something to worry about besides who or what might be lurking in these woods. The fear that the girls might bail, taking with them his first real shot with Angie, was something solid he could focus on.

"Keep your light ahead. I'll message Marissa that we're almost there." Jasper switched over to Instagram and quickly noticed he had no signal. "Shit, no signal."

"We've never lost signal in here, have we?" Clayton asked.

"Don't think so." Jasper turned his flashlight back on, and as he brought it back up, his beam caught movement to his left. He stopped and whipped the light back where he saw something move. There was nothing there.

"What is it?" Clayton asked, his voice cracking.

Jasper kept moving his light back and forth, searching for an animal. A tall animal. "Think it was a deer or something."

Pinpricks danced across the back of Clayton's neck. He nudged his friend in the shoulder. "Come on, let's keep going."

"Yeah." Jasper shifted gears into a spirited walk, almost a jog if it weren't for the abundance of impediments in the shapes of fallen branches, logs, boulders, and bushes.

As they made their way through the heart of the woods, Clayton felt a series of shivers run up his spine. The temperature had dropped precipitously. But more than that—far worse than that—Clayton had the inherent feeling that someone was behind him, that he was being followed. Fear ravaged his mind as he hurried to keep up with Jasper. He was too afraid to look over his shoulder. He just wanted out of these goddamn woods.

"We should have passed by the Howling Tree by now," Jasper said, short of breath. His forearms had sprouted gooseflesh from the chill that had weaved through the forest.

"I thought I saw it a ways back," Clayton said.

Jasper slowed to a stop and turned around. "Are you sure?"

Clayton spun around, finally feeling brave enough to look behind him. If Jasper hadn't seen anything when he turned to look at him, he was in the clear. So he hoped. "Yeah, I'm positive that I saw it over there, like five minutes ago," he said, pointing in the direction he believed he had spotted the twisted elm tree.

"Okay, good. Then we've got to be pretty close."

Just as Clayton turned back around, a series of heavy footfalls came from their right, quickly getting louder. Jasper grabbed onto Clayton's T-shirt like a life vest, stunned into frozen fear. Clayton instinctively aimed his flashlight in the direction of the thudding sound of someone running directly at them, his scream stuck in his throat like a trapdoor had slid across the top of his esophagus.

Jasper started to moan, a sound like a doctor told him to open up and say "ah" morphing into a wail as he crouched down to the ground, trying to pull Clayton with him.

Clayton gripped the wrist of Jasper's hand yanking at his shirt. He held his phone out in front of him like it was a magical shield, the flashlight illuminating no one as the running steps crescendoed and blew past them with no human form attached as Jasper screamed.

Clayton was shaking like he was being electrocuted.

"Fuck this shit," Jasper yelled as he sprung up and broke into a sprint.

"Wait!"

Jasper bolting away cracked the ice Clayton had been frozen in. He ran wildly to catch up to his friend, both of their flashlights swinging chaotically.

Jasper's foot landed on a large branch, causing him to stumble, but by sheer will he righted himself and continued running. He entered the open area of flat land not littered with trees, marking that they were roughly two hundred yards from exiting the Cursed Woods. He took the opportunity to look over his shoulder. Clayton had almost caught up to him.

Jasper pushed his legs to move at full force, as if he was rounding third, using every ounce of will power to score the go ahead run at the championship game.

Missssssssss…childrennnnn…

The whispered, ethereal voice sliced through Jasper's eardrums, causing him to lose his equilibrium and his heart to stop as he tumbled to the ground. He thrashed around like a wild raccoon, looking for who spoke those words. It took him four seconds, which felt like an hour of torture, to register that he didn't hear Clayton's feet hitting the earth. His arm shot out, holding his flashlight out in the direction they had been running. Clayton was nowhere to be seen.

Jasper scrambled to his knees and then to his feet as he shifted his body in forty-five-degree increments, searching the woods for his best friend. "Clayton!"

The woods answered back with a deafening silence.

"Clayton!"

After making a full three-sixty, Jasper spun around, facing the direction that led out of the woods. Had Clayton stormed past him while he fell to the ground and rolled around like a pig in shit? He must have. Maybe Clayton had already broken the barrier of the Cursed Woods and was making out with Angie.

"Clayton!" Jasper tried once more as he slowly started to move his feet.

Hearing nothing but a chirping bird and the distant woot of an owl, Jasper broke back into a sprint.

Jasper exited the woods, panting, sweating, his arms covered in lacerations. He planted his hands on his knees as he took in the gulley before him. He spotted the distant glow of a cell phone and took off in that direction.

As he got nearer, he only saw two figures huddled together and noticed the embers of a joint light up near Marissa's mouth, Angie standing by her side.

Hearing footsteps approaching, Angie turned around and spotted Jasper. "Oh my God, we thought you guys weren't coming."

Jasper continued to look around, praying to spot Clayton kneeling down or lying down on the ground, wasted from running or maybe already high.

"Where's Clayton?" Marissa asked.

Jasper pulled up next to the girls, reality crashing down upon him like a tsunami. He started to lose his balance, his head feeling like air. He dropped to his knees and felt like a boa constrictor slid down his throat. He dropped forward to his hands as he regurgitated on the gully floor.

Chapter Sixteen
Before the Hunt

B eams of light shifted and intersected throughout the Cursed Woods like a colorless laser light show, as Seth and his team methodically scoured the area for any sign of Clayton Meadows. Seth, Eddie, and Sasha had entered the west end of the woods through Gulliver's Gully, leaving Joe there to watch over Jasper Cunningham, Angie Stokes, and Marissa Daniels until their parents arrived. Angie had been the one to call 911, the call then routed directly to Seth. All three kids were shaken, none more so than Jasper, who had remained seated next to his vomit with his arms wrapped tightly around his knees, face pale, shaking like he had a fever. Angie and Marissa were clearly high and admitted as much before handing over a mostly smoked joint and two fresh ones.

Seth told the girls he wasn't going to enforce that they do community service or go to counseling, but strongly recommended that they both come clean to their parents, who would likely know within seconds of seeing them. Seth and his friends had done their fair share of smoking weed and sneaking beers when they were younger and they had a much bigger issue on their hands than underage consumption. It had only been six days since they found the body of Kevin Marlow and now they had a missing fourteen-year-old on their hands.

Seth pressed Jasper hard to get the necessary information out of him. He hated having to lean on a terrified boy, but every second that ticked by without sight of Clayton was vital. The route they had come into the forest and where Jasper exited formed a relatively clear line through the Cursed Woods. It was the non-logistical info that caused Seth's stomach to twist in knots. Running footsteps of an apparent ghost, whispered words that pierced Jasper's ears so badly that it literally threw him off balance, and Clayton, there one moment and then just completely vanished the next. It was the stuff of horror movies, but Seth had spent enough time in these woods to not question any of it.

Seth radioed Peter and told him to pick up Nate and head to the east end of the woods, letting them know he would find the boys' bikes likely around the same spot that he and Peter had entered the Cursed Woods just two months prior when they went searching for the remains of Raymond LaRange. He also told him to wait there for Bill, who Seth believed would be in his truck within seconds of his call. They needed every man they could get and Seth knew the recently retired chief of police would always be a member of their team when needed.

"Clayton!" Sasha's voice echoed in the distance, the furthest away from Seth, Eddie being in the middle of their line.

"Clayton Meadows!" Seth shouted. Every time one of them called the boy's name, Seth hoped beyond hope they would hear an answer but felt deep in his gut that all they would hear in response was their own echoes.

"Clayton!" Eddie yelled. "If you're afraid, son, don't be! We're the police and we want to help you!"

Seth appreciated Eddie's grandfatherly approach, not only because it was caring but because it was smart. It would be foolish to assume the boy was simply lost and shout in return upon hearing his name called. He could be injured, terrified, or confused. Seth saw beams in the distance swaying toward them like an out-of-control vehicle, followed by the soft echoes of Clayton's name. He grabbed his walkie from his belt and clicked it on. "Peter, this is Seth. We see you heading our direction."

"Yeah, we see you guys, too," Peter's voice came through.

"I assume you haven't got anything to report or we would have heard from you by now."

"That's a ten-four."

Seth headed in the direction of the nearest light opposite him. "No cell phone ringing?" He had gotten Jasper to unlock his cell phone so Seth could locate Clayton's cell number. Seth programmed it into his phone and had been calling it at regular intervals in case they could hear a ring or see it glowing.

"Negative."

"I'm going to keep trying it before we meet in the middle."

"I'll make sure Bill and Nate keep their eyes peeled and ears open." Bill no longer had a police-issue walkie and Peter had picked up Nate, ironically from his own home, who was hanging out with Noble.

Seth holstered his walkie and pulled his cell phone from his back pocket. "I'm calling his cell again!" he yelled out so Eddie and Sasha could be alert. He pressed Clayton's number, lowered his phone and looked around on high alert. A voice in the distance caused Seth's heart to jump.

"Clayton?" Sasha yelled.

Seth crouched down and laid his cell phone on the ground so he could grab his walkie again. "Peter, is that one of you or the boy?"

"That's Nate," Peter answered.

"Where is he?" Seth saw a beam directly across and closest to him shake wildly back and forth.

"See that light? That's me."

"I see it."

"Nate is the furthest light from me, on the northernmost end."

"Heading there now. Eddie, Sasha, you guys got that?"

"Got it," Eddie reported back.

"Running there now," Sasha replied.

Seth approached the rest of his team, the last one to get there, being the furthest away. They were all huddled around a small, open area of the forest. Seth couldn't see a body on the ground, which he supposed was a positive sign. He stepped in next to Bill and followed everyone's eyes down to a cell phone being illuminated by Nate's Maglite. "Shit."

"Wish I could say it was good to see you, Seth," Bill said. "But not under these circumstances."

Seth crouched down, set his Maglite on the ground, and pulled out gloves and an evidence bag from his utility pouch. "All the same, thanks for joining us, Bill. Much appreciated."

"Unless we're on vacation, I'll always be here."

Seth's heart warmed under the icy situation. He shuffled closer to the phone.

"I don't think you're going to like what you see, Seth," Peter cautioned.

Seth leaned over the phone and saw what Peter was referring to. There were droplets of blood. "Fuck," he muttered and looked up at Nate, who had been here the longest. "Nate, did you get a chance to track it? Or notice how far off the blood spreads?"

Nate felt surprisingly calm under the circumstances. Maybe it hadn't set in yet, but the sense of purpose was overriding any fear or inadequacies he might be feeling. Nate motioned with his flashlight from Clayton's cell phone over to a spot about six feet away. "That's the furthest I noticed any blood, Chief. I'm not trained to track yet and I didn't want to contaminate the scene so I haven't strayed from this area."

Seth nodded, impressed with Nate's instincts. "That's smart. Good work."

Nate nodded back, holding back a smile and perhaps the start of tears of joy that his idol just complimented him.

Seth stood back to his feet and looked around at his team. "Okay, Eddie and Sasha, I want you guys to survey this area over here," he said, clicking his Maglite back on and pointing it to their left. "Bill, you and Peter inspect this area." He shined his light to their right. "Look for any other evidence, more blood, or anything remotely suspicious. Call out the moment you come across anything. Nate, you stay here with me while I take photos and video and bag the phone."

"Yes, sir," Nate said.

Just as the rest of the team began to disperse, Seth added, "If we don't find anything else, I'll need two of you to stay here and wait for Wes to arrive so he can examine the blood. I don't want anyone out here alone. The rest of us will head back to Gulliver's Gully to talk to kids and their parents."

Having found nothing else of significance, Seth led the way back toward the gully with Sasha, Bill, and Eddie, while Peter and Nate stayed behind waiting for the medical examiner. Peter had more tracking experience than the rest of them put together times a thousand, so he offered to stay back to see if he could find a trail of multiple pairs of feet, a scuffle, drag marks, anything that might give them a better picture of what happened.

The fact that they found no discernable trail of blood, only the few spots near the phone, could either be looked at as extremely baffling or hopeful. The best-case scenario was that whatever injury occurred had been relatively minor, minor enough that Clayton stopped the bleeding on his own and maybe had escaped the woods through a route that they hadn't canvassed. There were far more ways in and out of the Cursed Woods than the two directions they had come from. The other scenario, the one Seth didn't want to consider, was that Clayton was bleeding badly and someone, God forbid some*thing*, had scooped him up and whisked him away.

As they approached the outer barrier of the woods, Seth saw too many lights and heard far too many voices coming from the gully. Certainly too many voices for Joe to handle by himself. "Christ," he muttered before turning to Bill, Sasha, and Eddie. "We've clearly got more company than we anticipated, guys. Be ready to contain the situation and make arrests if needed."

"I got you," Sasha said, picking up her pace.

Eddie and Bill followed behind Seth as he sprinted out of the forest and toward the gully where two trucks had been driven off-road and were parked with their headlights on near a group of at least fifteen people. Seth was relieved when he heard Paddy Kipp's booming voice as they approached.

"I'm not going to say it again! Put your goddamn rifles back in your vehicles and go home!"

Joe ran up to meet Seth before he arrived at the scene. "All the parents showed up right away, but then these assholes came charging in—"

"I get the gist of it, Joe," Seth said, making a beeline toward the two men standing in front of their trucks, holding their rifles, arguing with Paddy.

"I called Paddy right away," Joe shouted, trailing behind.

"Goddamnit!" Seth shouted, seeing who it was that had driven their trucks into the gully. "Jeffrey! Angus! You've got ten seconds to get in those trucks and get the hell out of here!"

Jeffrey Tacet started to head toward Seth, but Paddy stepped in between them, shoving Jeffrey back up against his truck. "Hey, that's assault!"

Seth arrived at the scene, seeing the group of scared parents and kids out of the corner of his eyes. "Jeffrey, I'm sure you want to help, but—"

"We have a right to help search!" Jeffrey spouted.

"Yeah!" Angus Weatherspoon chimed in.

"Actually, you don't. This is a crime scene and you're not allowed—"

"A crime scene?" a woman bellowed to Seth's right. "What happened to my boy?"

Seeing that Paddy had Jeffrey and Angus under control, Seth made a move to go speak to the couple, who were clearly Clayton's parents, but Bill stepped in front of him, placing a hand on his shoulder. "I've known the Meadowses for over thirty years. Let me handle it, Seth. It'll be better coming from me."

Seth patted Bill on his side, thankful for his friend's willingness to go above and beyond. "Thanks, Bill. I owe you."

"You owe me nothing," Bill said and turned to go meet the Meadowses. "Reid, Molly, let's go talk over here."

Seth turned back to his favorite town disruptors, relieved to see that Sasha and Eddie had commandeered their weapons. "I'm serious, guys. Now is not the time. If we need the town's help, I promise you we'll announce it."

Jeffrey threw up his hands. "This is bullshit, man! I've got a twelve-year-old boy. If there's some tiger out there—"

"There are no wild tigers in this country, you moron," Paddy interrupted.

"We have not identified any specific animal, nor made any information public about Kevin Marlow."

"That's because you don't know," Angus spat.

"You want me to arrest this asshole, Chief?" Sasha asked, standing near Angus.

"You can't arrest us!" Jeffrey yelled. "We didn't do anything!"

Seth held up his hands. "Quiet! Disobeying a police officer is a misdemeanor offense punishable by up to six months in county jail with possible fines. You've got ten seconds to get in your vehicles and leave before I have Officer Kingston and Officer Cabrera arrest both of you. One—two—three—"

Jeffrey and Angus exchanged a quick glance before starting to slither back toward the cabins of their trucks.

"Four—five—"

Angus hopped in his Ford Maverick and slammed the door.

"What about our guns?" Jeffrey said, holding open his driver side door.

"You can pick them up at the station tomorrow," Seth replied. "Six—seven—"

Jeffrey hopped in his Chevy Colorado, shut the door, and started to back up. Angus followed suit, as both men turned their trucks around and drove away.

"I was really hoping you got to ten," Sasha said.

"Me too," Seth agreed. He turned to Paddy. "Thanks for coming here. You didn't have to—"

Paddy slapped Seth on the shoulder. "Yes, I did. My brothers need help, I'll always be there."

Seth wondered at that moment if Paddy was going to ask to join the police force. "I appreciate that," he said, and focused his attention on the parents and children standing nearby, waiting for answers. He looked over at Bill, who had his arm around Molly Meadows while Reid Meadows had his head buried in his hands. The town was already percolating with tension. If they didn't find Clayton Meadows tonight, that tension was about to boil over.

Retrospective No. 2: The Fellmore Expedition

The forest lay submerged in an almost sacred hush—so ancient it seemed to hold its breath whenever men dared pass beneath its vaulted canopy. Each step pressed boots deep into a sponge of dark moss and loamy soil, the suctiony crackle of earth reluctant to release its claim. Above them, coastal redwood sentinels soared skyward, their gargantuan trunks draped in velvety green moss. Their intertwined boughs formed a dense lattice that choked the sun's rays, trapping the morning mist in swirling ghost wisps. Fern fronds, slick with jeweled dew, arced overhead like cathedral arches. Far off, a lone raven rasped, its echo drifting through the stillness.

Captain William Fellmore tugged his greatcoat tighter around his throat. A damp chill clung to everything here, and to his left leg, which screamed through sinew and bone at every breath. He'd taken the wound at Fort Lévis, on the edge of the St. Lawrence, where the cannons never seemed to fall quiet and the air itself trembled from powder. A burst of timber and iron lodged shrapnel deep into the muscle of his thigh. They got most of it. Not the shot, though. That stayed like a buried piece of the old world, nestled just below the bone.

"You feel that?" whispered Duke, the young ex-soldier, voice trembling like the mist.

Mace, the furrier, chewed a strip of jerky between cracked teeth and muttered, "Feel what?"

"The stillness," Duke repeated.

Fellmore didn't glance back. He recognized raw nerves when he heard them. Only Mekasin, the Yakama tracker, stalked on with impassive grace, his thick black braid swinging like rope, eyes narrowed beneath a leaf-stained brow. The man made no small talk, no sudden movements, and seemed somehow drier than the rest, though the fog clung to every surface like sweat.

They were a ragged sextet, hired at a princely rate by a panicked father unwilling to leave his youngest unaccounted for. Silas Dunney, the missing son. A trapper by fancy, not trade. Not the first to vanish in this wilderness, but the first whose name could summon a captain out of retirement.

At Fellmore's side, Silas's brother Laurence plodded forward with grim resolve, jaw clenched so tight his skin gleamed pale.

Mekasin halted abruptly and raised a single hand, finger slicing the air.

The party froze. Insects droned faintly somewhere close at hand. The forest closed in like a theater before the curtain fell.

Fellmore spotted it then: a bootheel, its leather split and frayed, jutting from a tangle of ferns. Dark, coagulated stains—like old bruises—streaked the undergrowth.

Mekasin fell back without a word.

Ambrose Tully, the boyish scribe tagging along, let out a soft whimper, as if someone had struck him in sleep. A curse slipped from Mace's lips.

When they edged forward, they saw a body—face up, limbs splayed in a grotesque parody of a scarecrow. But this was no straw man. The chest and belly were torn open in savage, jagged rips, as if some monstrous gaunt hand had clawed layer upon layer of flesh. The remaining tissue had turned a dull pewter grey, the blood long since congealed to black film. An empty socket stared skyward where one eye had been plucked out, and the left pinky finger lay missing, severed at the knuckle. Scattered entrails, slimy and half rotten, lay strewn about like discarded rope.

"No," Laurence gasped, stepping forward so abruptly the butt of his rifle nudged damp earth. "It's not Silas."

Fellmore dropped to one knee, the old joint protesting, and laid a gaunt hand on the corpse's shoulder. He turned the head slowly. Recognition bit him like a frost: Marcus Vey, one of Dunney's own. The throat had been carved—gouged so precisely it spoke of deliberate cruelty, not animal hunger.

Ambrose lurched sideways and retched into the ferns.

146

"What did this?" Laurence's voice cut through the quiet, too loud, too urgent.

Fellmore said nothing. Behind him, Mekasin emerged from the mist, silent as a shadow. The tracker knelt, studied the mutilation.

"Not bear," he finally declared.

"Wolves?" someone offered.

Mekasin shook his head once, flatly. "No tooth marks. No signs of feeding. This was not for eating."

Fellmore climbed to his feet, scanning the tangle of trunks and mist. No birds stirred. No wind. Even the drizzle had hushed. The hush pressed in, heavy as a tomb.

"We build a cairn," Fellmore said quietly, voice firm though the words felt sacrilegious beneath these ancient sentinels. "He won't lie here forgotten."

At first, the men hesitated. Disturbing the soil—already violated by unseen cruelty—felt like trespassing on some grim altar.

Fellmore's stare brooked no argument. "Now."

Duke was first, crouching to gather slick stones from the moss. The others followed: Mace grumbling, Laurence with trembling fingers but steady purpose. Their eyes flicked nervously to the gloom between trees.

Fellmore felt the forest's weight settle on his shoulders. He had seen cannons blast fields to smoking ruin, watched men die by the hundreds. But this—this quiet—was a darker violence, older than war.

He spotted Laurence's knuckles whitening around his rifle's stock as it creaked in his grip.

"That's three," the furrier muttered under his breath, as each man added another stone to the growing mound. "Three buried in this God-forsaken place. That's more than enough."

Fellmore lowered his hat brim over his eyes and answered only in a low growl: "Then pray we don't find a fourth."

The fire spit embers into the night, its thin flames lapping at damp wood that refused to burn with any warmth. Wisps of grey smoke curled upward, vanishing almost at once into the oppressive blackness of the redwoods. Here, darkness was not emptiness but a living weight, pressing in on every side. A cold seeped from the sodden earth—a gelatinous chill that crept through leather boots, numbing toes and ankles, and stirring ache in the marrow. Overhead, only narrow slivers of sky peeked between ancient trunks. Stars glimmered like distant pins of ice, framed by the gnarled, outstretched arms of redwoods standing sentinel in absolute silence. No wind brushed the needles, only the indifferent murmur of the forest: an owl's forlorn hoot far off, the soft scuffle of claws against wet undergrowth, a stifled cough echoing among the trunks—like a child stifling a cry.

Laurence crouched nearest the dying flame, shoulders hunched, hands pressed tightly between his knees as though collecting every ounce of heat from the embers. His gaunt face caught in the firelight cast stark angles and deep shadows, jaw muscles twitching with unspent tension. Fellmore sat a pace back, chin resting on the rim of a rust-stained tin cup that tasted of cold chicory and iron. Around them, the others picked at salt pork and beans that had swelled soft and lifeless in the pot, eating without hunger. Mace wordlessly passed around a weathered flask, its spirit sharp and biting; even Ambrose took a measured swig before wiping his trembling hand across his mouth.

They did not speak of the corpse they'd left half buried in moss and pine needles. Yet their silence spoke volumes—an echoing void more profound than any whispered thought.

"You mark the way back?" Mace broke the hush, voice rough as gravel. His gaze flicked toward Mekasin, who lingered at the tree line, arms folded, profile half lost in shadow.

"I did," Fellmore replied for him, voice low.

A dark chuckle. "Doubt I could find our trail even if it were paved."

Ambrose hugged his knees tighter. "Don't say that."

Fellmore offered the boy a faint, uneasy smile that faded in the flicker of darkness. The camp fell silent again, the crackle of the fire the only sound to fill the vast stillness.

"We should turn back," Mace said, tone flat as deadwood.

Fellmore's eyes never lifted from the flickering flames. "Not yet."

Duke nodded after a long pause, though the steadiness in his voice belied the darting look in his eyes. "I agree. We ain't gonna find anything out here."

Laurence's body stilled. "We're not going anywhere without Silas."

"Oh Christ," Mace hissed, sitting forward. "We've buried three men. You think your brother's gonna greet us with tea and a fuckin' hymn?"

"Say that again."

"You heard me."

Their anger snapped to life, sudden as kindling catching flame. Laurence bolted upright, fists clenched. Mace rose to face him, broad shoulders blocking the failing glow. Fellmore slid between them, hand flat against Laurence's chest, pressing him back.

"This isn't the place for bravado," he murmured, voice firm as steel.

Laurence's eyes, dark rims bright in the firelight, blazed. "Then what is this place for? We ride out into nothing but rot and shadows—if we turn tail now, what do I tell my father? That we found his trappers with their guts strung over a log and high-tailed it home?"

A sudden stillness. Mekasin's voice came, quiet and precise: "The boy may live. But he walks too far from the light."

Their gazes snapped to him. He remained motionless, silhouette etched against the trees, arms folded and eyes fixed on the impenetrable black beyond.

Ambrose's whisper trembled like dry leaves. "What does that mean?"

Mekasin did not answer. Only the hush returned, deeper, more absolute.

Fellmore swallowed against the bitter taste in his throat and shifted on the cold stone beneath him. His bad leg throbbed, reminders of shrapnel and shattered bone, memories of cannon blasts and men torn open in war. Nothing on the battlefield had felt as hungry as this forest, nothing bled with the same slow certainty.

Ambrose's teeth clicked. "Feels like the trees…are closer," he said, voice small. "Since yesterday."

No one answered. Above them, stars blinked indifferent between knotted branches. The woods pressed in, silent and watchful. A weight settled over the camp, a living pressure, as though eyes without form surveyed them.

A cloud drifted across the open sky.

That night, each man slept with one hand on his rifle, but none slept long.

By morning, the sky was the color of ash water and just as still. No mist, no breeze. The canopy above choked out the sun so completely that it could have been dawn or dusk. All around them, the forest crouched, unmoving, massive, quiet in a way that felt deliberate.

Fellmore rose slowly, back aching from too little sleep and too much cold, only to find a hole where Duke should have been.

His bedroll lay undisturbed. His boots were gone. No sign of a struggle.

They called his name until their voices cracked. Searched in expanding circles. Laurence's face was rigid with fear, lips dry. Ambrose muttered prayers constantly.

"What man deserts a camp without his rifle?" Laurence asked, jaw tight.

"A fool," said Mace. "Or a coward."

Fellmore stood apart, watching the wood line. "We don't know that he deserted."

"No blood," Mace argued. "No tracks. No cry. If he's gone, he's gone on his own legs."

Laurence shook his head. "He wouldn't run."

Mace spit into the mulch. "I don't know how that boy made it through the war without turning yellow before."

Fellmore glanced sideways. "He enlisted in '65. Didn't see much. A parade more than a campaign." He didn't say it cruelly. Just a fact. "He might've cracked."

The silence that followed hung like fog.

They gathered up the gear and fell into a thin, anxious line, now one fewer than before.

The trail—what little remained—led them deeper, where the redwoods pressed tighter and the air grew heavy. Here, the trunks thickened to monstrous girths, roots clawing aboveground like petrified serpents. The canopy above was stitched so tight that the light dimmed to a near dusk, even at midday. The ground was spongy underfoot, a carpet of rot and fungus that gave slightly with each step. When Ambrose slipped, his palm came up black with mildew. He gagged and wiped it on his coat.

Mekasin stopped without warning, one hand lifted.

A tree stood slightly off the path, its black-streaked and enormous form deeply scored with a single, peculiar mark.

The symbol was not large, but it arrested the eye. A winding knot of angles and curls that bent back on itself like a noose.

Fellmore's hair prickled. A low, humming vibration thrummed in his skull. The farther he stared, the more the forest seemed to tilt and sway, as if the ground itself had a heartbeat. A cold wave of vertigo washed over him; he turned away and vomited into the bracken, bile hot and acrid.

Ambrose stepped toward the glyph, blinking, hand reaching out. "What is it?"

"Don't touch it," Fellmore rasped, voice raw. "Not with a finger. Not with your eyes."

Mace asked, voice tight, "Which way, then? We're in thick now."

Fellmore drew his compass. The needle swung wildly, spinning one way, then another, then stalling as though seized by some invisible hand. He forced himself to meet Mekasin's unreadable gaze. The guide inclined his head gravely and pointed toward the west-southwest. No one questioned him.

They skirted the marked tree in a wide arc, each man keeping his distance. Their breaths came shallow, almost silent.

Beyond the scarred tree, the forest closed in.

Ahead, a rabbit burst from the brush. It darted to cross their path, then veered, violently, away. As if it struck something invisible and turned midair.

They paused. Breath misting, though no cold air blew.

A branch snapped in the near distance. Or was it the clap of a jaw?

Mekasin dropped to a crouch, still as stone.

Fellmore's body remembered what to do: He dropped low, joints screaming, rifle half raised. His throat went desert dry. Waiting—he had waited through ambushes before, when trees bled and all sound could explode into gunfire.

His hand brushed something cold and hard in the moss. Stopping his breath, he nudged away decaying leaves. A tiny bone, no thicker than a finger, lay white against the dark soil. He picked it up, turning it between forefinger and thumb. More bones lay hidden: little phalanges, shards of teeth. He scraped back the moss and uncovered a small jaw, teeth intact, ivory bright in the dim light.

A sick twist of nausea knotted his gut.

Mekasin rose and moved forward like the sound had been an invitation telling him which way not to go, but Fellmore's eyes remained locked on that small bone. His mind danced. The moss seemed to wave at him, curling toward him like the hair of a lover.

"Captain?" Laurence said behind him, drawing him out of his thoughts.

Fellmore didn't answer. He covered the bones again and rose with a quiet groan. The forest swallowed the sound.

They did not make camp that night. No one said it aloud. No one unrolled a blanket or dared to sit. They simply kept walking, torches lifted high, the flame shadows dancing against bark that looked black in the firelight. The night was colder now.

Fellmore's knee ached like it had been worked by a mallet. Each step ground the bone raw. The copper tang of blood clung to his teeth from where he'd bitten his lip an hour past, pushing onward.

He was beginning to believe Mace had been right. Silas Dunney—the spoiled heir with perfect teeth and poor instincts—was almost certainly dead. And what would the Caldwell family pay him for a name carved on a cairn?

Fellmore's thoughts stuttered toward his sweetheart, Anna's face—soft cheek, full laugh, the weight of her lock of hair still tucked in his breast pocket. He needed that money. He needed it to start a life. But did he need it *this* badly?

A sound broke through his thoughts.

"Where's Mace?" Ambrose's voice cracked the hush like a pistol shot.

They stopped. Turned.

The spot behind them was empty.

"Mace?" Laurence barked, already swinging his torch wide.

"Just a moment ago, he was—" Ambrose's voice failed.

They called for him. Again and again. The woods answered only with silence.

Fellmore spun in place, eyes scouring the trunks, the shadows, the paths behind them. "Mace!" he shouted.

Nothing.

Ambrose started to cry. Big, hiccupping sobs he tried to stifle in his scarf.

Laurence cursed so sharply it startled birds from a tree above.

"We need to go back. Please, Captain," Ambrose whined.

Laurence's voice cracked through the hush. "There is no back. We're in it now."

"You don't know that!" Ambrose cried.

Fellmore grabbed Ambrose by the arm—not hard, but firm. "Steady."

The young lad gulped air like it might run out. Laurence turned to speak again but faltered.

Mekasin stood still a moment longer, the torchlight flickering across the planes of his face. His eyes, dark and distant, fixed on the shadows coiling beyond the trees.

Then he murmured something low, barely a breath: "Tah-Tah-Kle'ah."

Fellmore didn't recognize the word, but it chilled him, curling down his spine like a whisper not meant for human ears.

Mekasin dropped the torch. Its flame hissed against the damp earth. Without another word, he turned and walked into the darkness to the left, vanishing between the trees like smoke drawn into a deeper night.

Fellmore cursed under his breath and followed him into the abyss of the forest at night, ignoring the grinding pain in his leg. "Mekasin! Come back. We don't split up!"

The guide kept walking, slipping between trees like a shade.

"Damn you, I said—"

"Captain!" Ambrose's voice, thready and desperate, came from behind.

Fellmore turned. The boy was wide-eyed, torch trembling in his hands. One more second, and he would bolt. Fellmore looked back to where Mekasin had vanished, then he turned around stepping back into the circle of light, but Laurence was no longer at the boy's side.

Only moments ago, Laurence had stood muttering to himself, torch high, boot planted in the same mud as them all. Now there was only empty ground. The air still held the echo of his last footstep, but no shape. No sign. As if the man had been unwritten from the world.

"Where—" Ambrose began.

"Don't," Fellmore cut in, voice hard. "Eyes on me. Keep close."

His own gut twisted with fear yet. This place had swallowed Laurence as easily as breath, and there'd been no sound. No shout. No parting of brush.

He grabbed Ambrose's shoulder. "You stay close. You don't turn around unless I tell you."

They walked again, the path narrowed to a trickle between ancient trunks. Abruptly, the forest fell away, revealing an outcrop of stone, a yawning cave in the distance. Fellmore knew what he was seeing was wrong.

Two trees flanked a far ledge. Each bore twisting, interlocking marks etched deep into the bark like scar tissue. The symbols glowed with their own impossible light.

He stepped forward, heart thudding.

The wind rose, sudden and hard. Ambrose shrieked, trying to protect his flame, but it guttered and died. Fellmore's went next. Pure, still darkness enveloped them, save for the luminescent glow of the marks on the two trees.

"Captain!" Ambrose's voice was moving. Running.

"Don't run!" Fellmore bellowed, but the boy was gone.

Fellmore turned in a full circle, eyes blind. No light. No shape.

Only memories.

He was in the fields again—hot wind carrying wheat dust into his teeth, Anna's ribbon around his wrist. Then the trenches. Screams. Mud. The reek of blood and burning gunpowder. His mother's lullaby twisted into a battle cry. Men broken open like fruit. The cold steel of the surgeon's blade twisting in his leg, trying to remove the shot lodged in his bone.

He blinked and found himself back in the dreadful, dark woods.

The symbols still glowed. His breath smoked in front of him.

He felt a presence around him as if the trees themselves had grown eyes. The sensation swelled until he could not breathe. He turned, stumbled. Ran.

Branches clawed at his coat. The forest buckled and bent. He didn't think, didn't stop. His leg blazed, every step a knife.

Behind him, the forest shifted in his vision, curled around him like a tunnel.

Branches lifted and swayed in ways they shouldn't. Not with wind. *Not with wind.*

He ran until pain became numbness.

Until the woods changed again, and the light came low through the limbs and a creek whispered nearby.

He collapsed there and wept.

Chapter Seventeen
Patterns Repeating

Story sat cross-legged on the floor of her office in the library, laptop open in front of her, a mug of cold coffee forgotten at her side. The Zoom call flickered once before stabilizing into the image of Dr. Elias Raines—a man with sun-lined skin, a thick peppered beard, thick eyebrows, long dark hair with wisps of grey pulled back into a ponytail. A book-cluttered study behind him, he looked more like a field researcher caught between expeditions than a professor.

"Ms. Palmer, hello! Thank you for agreeing to this call so quickly."

Story chuckled. "No, thank you, Dr. Raines, I'm the one that reached out to you."

"True, but seeing these photos with the information you provided triggered something in me, something that's been brewing inside since Hannah went missing. I feel as if I'm the one asking for a favor here. And, call me Elias, please."

"Well, hopefully we can help each other. And Story is fine."

"Story…a lovely name. Enigmatic almost."

Story shrugged.

"How much do you know about Hannah and her research?"

"Not a great deal. I did find her research grant online and read a bit about it, so I know she was looking to help the Wiyot Cultural Revitalization Project. The thing that had me most intrigued though…I read that her interest in this specific region and the glyphs or markers she wanted to research started with a strange little book—something like a pastoral travel memoir?"

Elias nodded. "Yes...yes, exactly. *Wilderness and Fortune: The Journals of a Gentleman Naturalist.* Penned by a minor aristocrat in the 1790s—more pompous than precise, but one passage stood out to Hannah. He recounts a tale told to him over port by a Captain William Fellmore, who'd led a doomed expedition up the Lost Coast. Hannah got caught on the glyphs Fellmore described. The way he said he still saw them years later, in dreams. She seemed sucked in by that. She latched on, tracked down further proof of the location, historical evidence of William Fellmore. She even managed to find evidence, very loose evidence, that confirmed the expedition did have a Yakama guide."

Story couldn't contain her smile. "I'm going to have to look this marvelous book up."

Elias laughed. "If you can find a copy. Come to think of it, I think it may have been scanned into the Project Gutenberg database."

"Good to know," Story said. "But back to Hannah..."

"Yes, so, she received a cultural preservation grant from our university to survey ceremonial signage and cultural artifacts that she hoped would lead to Wiyot heritage sites. She felt the glyphs were markers, leading to a massive discovery of an unknown heritage site. The odd thing about the glyphs, the reason she looped me toward the...before she went missing, was the fungal colonies inside the glyph cuts. I didn't fully understand what they had to do with her research at the time, the fungus, not the glyphs. Yet, since she went missing, I've had a chance to go through her field notes and photos and I...well to be honest I was alarmed at first. Confused. Her notes talk about peculiar things happening to her when in proximity to them. It reads more like madness than scientific notes. And that wasn't like her. Hannah was meticulous. Her field notebooks were practically literature—cross-referenced, color-coded, annotated like a linguist's bible." He sighed and ran a hand down his face. "I didn't know that, of course, not until I got access to her field journals. I wish I'd listened better when we spoke on the phone."

Story could see guilt weighing heavy on him. "I don't know your specific situation, but I spoke with people who knew her well and I got the impression she was incredibly driven. I'm not sure you could have done anything to prevent what happened to her."

Elias stroked his beard. "Perhaps not. Tell me, Story, your friend Leith, how did she come upon this glyph? You said it was close to her property?"

"That's right. There's a small lake within the woods by her family's farm that she often swims in. One thing that I left out was that she doesn't recall how she found the marking. She said she lost track of time. Perhaps hours. She hasn't felt right since. She feels paranoid and afraid. This is why I reached out."

Elias's eyes narrowed and grew serious. "This is troubling. In Hannah's field notes, she talked about losing time in the forest, having hallucinations around certain areas. Which is an eerie coincidence that aligns with an account by Captain Fellmore where he described being transported back into his memories, as if he literally left the forest and came back. Leith needs to stay away from these."

"I've already warned her to stay away. It's disorienting just looking at them. Do you know what they are? What's causing the bioluminescence or these memory losses, time slips, hallucinations?" Story released an awkward laugh and shrugged. "I'm not sure what I should be calling the effects."

"Nor am I. Her notes range all over the place." Elias looked down at the desk he was leaning on and turned pages in a notebook. "I sent Hannah's photos, which are in fact quite similar to the ones Leith took, to a colleague of mine, Dr. Rishi Patel at UC Davis's Fungal Lab."

"There's a fungal lab?"

"Indeed," he said with a smile. "He saw similar properties to the bioluminescence in Mycena lux-coeli."

"I'm familiar with forageable fungi but, what is…"

"It's a species of fungus found in the dark forests of Japan, often found on the Japanese islands. They're also called 'sky lantern mushrooms.' They look like glowing green mushrooms. Think of a glow stick that children have at Halloween."

Story's eyes grew large. "Ooh!"

"The thing is, they should not be growing in the redwoods of Northern California. Or anywhere in the United States. Have you seen mushrooms that fit this description?"

"I wish that I have. They sound lovely."

"Maybe to look at. Do you know the area in which Hannah was researching? She mentioned in her field notes that she was switching locations to a"—he paused and looked down again to read—"a path 'where the asphalt gives up.' The Old Timber Spur, she wrote. She has a note here of a name. Paddy?"

Story smiled. "Paddy is a ranger at the state park, so it makes sense he would have been helping her. I also know a local CDFW officer, Cal Hensley, was helping her as well."

"Do you know this path?"

She shook her head. "Sorry, I'm not intimately familiar with the wooded terrain surrounding Lost Grove, but if you give me a minute..." She was already typing in a search.

Elias was doing the same. "Ah, are you trying to find it?" he asked with a smile.

"Yes," she replied, clicking on a link for hiking trails. "I think I found something." She dragged the link to the Zoom chat.

Elias opened it. He pulled a physical map of the area into view and spread it on his desk. He caught Story smiling. "I'm old-school," he remarked.

"I understand," Story said, then asked, "Did she happen to mention anything about the Cursed Woods?"

"In fact, she did," he said as he found the spot and made a mark. "I wasn't sure if that was something she was just referring to them as, or if that was a known location."

"It is. And it is not a place many in our town enter. There is dark lore about the Cursed Woods, and there have been many incidents over the years."

Elias tilted his head to the side, raising an eyebrow. "Of what?"

Story briefly looked down and uttered a silent French prayer. "Well, as fate would have it, just last night a local teenage boy went missing in those woods. The police have been searching for him ever since."

Elias was quiet, contemplative. "I don't like this."

"No, it's terrible," Story said.

"The boy, yes, but if, as you say, this area in which Hannah was researching, where she disappeared, had these same glyphs... Can you tell me where on the map this was, and where the one your friend saw was?"

"Yeah, if you find Main Street, in Lost Grove...then find 5th Street, which goes east to Mulberry Street. Mulberry Street dead ends if you go north." She paused a moment before continuing. "That's where the Cursed Woods is. If you look northeast through the woods, you'll see a place called Gulliver's Gully in an open area past the woods. That's about the area the boy went missing. The Bury farm, my friend's farm, follows that finger of woods you'll see on the map, along Copini Road." Story waited as he traced all her directions.

Elias sat back. "I really don't like this. Your friend Leith found her glyph near civilization, and the boy…both those locations are nowhere near where Hannah was last reported to be researching. This could mean the organism is demonstrating dynamic behavior and shifting proximity without consistent human intervention. It could imply active environmental interaction."

"I'm afraid I don't quite follow."

"No, of course. Apologies. What this could mean, Story, is the fungus is demonstrating a biological intelligence of some sort. The hypothetical danger I have grown concerned about, rereading Hannah's field notes, would appear to be confirmed. It's spreading."

Story wrung her hands, her heart rate quickening. "What do I do?"

"You? You do nothing, Story. Other than to tell Leith and anyone else in her family to stay away from those glyphs."

"What about the police searching in these woods?"

Elias stroked his beard again. "I'm sure this would all sound so preposterous if you brought this to them."

The corner of Story's mouth curved upward. "Actually, I'm close to the chief of police and he's quite open-minded."

"Then warn him. The link between Hannah, her notes about losing time, correlates with Leith's accounts, and now this missing boy—this could be ecologically disastrous if left untouched."

Story felt her heart drop, unable to find a response to this.

Elias nodded and lightly slapped his table. "I'm coming up. I need to see these glyphs, investigate the area, and take samples."

Story's chest expanded, allowing a sigh to be released. This was more than what she was hoping for. "I can bring you to the spots."

Elias smiled but shook his head. "I wouldn't want to burden you or bring you to areas of potential danger."

Story's synapses were firing on all cylinders. "I'll get in touch with Paddy and Cal, I'm sure they'd be happy to assist us and they know the woods here intimately."

"Well, I would be indebted to them, and to you, of course. I have papers to get through this weekend, but I can drive up late Sunday, find a hotel, and then meet you and your friends Monday morning if that works."

"Yes, absolutely. I'll send you links to some of our lovely local B&Bs."

"That would be fine. Thank you."

"No, thank you, Dr....Elias," Story said with a gracious smile.

"I'm glad you reached out to me, Story. I have your number. I'll call when I'm in town."

"Speak soon," Story added.

The screen flickered as the call ended, but the weight of the conversation lingered in the room. It may not be the glyph itself causing the effects but a plant, a fungus, living within them. The idea sent a shiver down her spine. She needed to reach out to Cal and Paddy. Then she needed to head over to Mary's. If there was anyone who'd keep them safe in the woods, it'd be her. She only hoped that Mary would open her door to her.

By her lunch break, the enormity of the call still clung to her. She had more questions. She'd done more research on hallucinogenic plants and if spores could cause similar side effects, but lacked the knowledge to dig deep into the right questions. As afternoon approached, she got a call from Cal saying he could meet her for a quick coffee before he headed back into the search. She had one more box to check in this investigation, so she walked into town and down a street to the Victorian cottage with the white picket fence and knocked. Mary answered the door barefoot, hair wild, eyes curious, and paint on her fingers.

"Hi," Story said with a smile. "Can I come in?"

Mary stepped aside and nodded. As she shut the door she said, "I—"

But Story was saying, "Look, I'm..."

They both laughed gently.

"I'm sorry, Mary," Story said. "For the burden I put on you. For the way I approached the whole thing."

"No," Mary promptly interrupted. "I mean, thank you for the apology, but...I also wasn't seeing it from your perspective."

Story nodded slowly. "And I'm guessing...?"

"Dr. Jane and I have spoken about it. It's not that it didn't—doesn't—hurt but, yes, you had a lot on your plate and I put it there."

"Mary," Story said, reaching for her friend's hands and holding them tight. "I want you to rely on me. I've always been there and I always will be. My questioning you wasn't thinking less or worse or anything of you other than concern for you and your safety. It didn't come across that way and, again, I am really sorry about that."

Mary looked down at their hands and squeezed Story's fingers back, nodding.

"Are we good?" Story asked.

"Yes," Mary said, smiling.

Story released a heavy sigh. "Good, because I need your help."

"With Clayton?" Mary asked. "I already went out last night and tried to track him but—"

"No, not…" Story frowned. "You went out looking for him?"

Mary nodded.

"And didn't find anything?" she asked, heading into the living room. Mary followed. "I couldn't. It's kind of weird."

"Weird that you couldn't find him?"

"Weird that I couldn't sense anything. No trace at all."

"Mary," she continued, "have you ever seen any markings on trees or stones with a plant, a bioluminescent plant, growing in them?"

Mary sat on the edge of a chair as Story took a place on the sofa. "I…I have seen one or two."

"You have?" Story asked, excitement and worry both rushing through her insides.

"But they're not in this area and I stay away from them. When I've seen them, they gave me the creeps. Like…I don't know, like my senses went on high alert."

"Did your teeth…?" Story asked, implying the changes her friend had when moments of extreme emotions overcame her.

"Yeah."

"What did it look like?" Story asked. She pulled her phone out of her bag.

"Like a spiral. Why are you asking about them?" Mary grew hesitant. She desperately wanted to place something cool on her tongue.

Story held out her phone. "So, not like this?"

Mary frowned. Her eyes flicked from the screen to her friend's face. "No. Story, why are you asking me about them?"

"Leith Bury found this in the woods by their farm. She lost track of time and felt disoriented. Anya told her to come see me. I told her I would help." A thought occurred to Story. "Have you ever seen Leith in the woods?"

Mary shrugged. "From time to time. From a distance." She wasn't going to say anymore. It wasn't her place to reveal deep secrets of others when she had so many herself.

Story sensed there was more, but wouldn't press her friend. "Do you remember a woman who was in the area researching Wiyot sites? Hannah Albrecht. She went missing during her research almost two years ago."

"I mean, yes, I do."

"She was researching these, apparently. I've been in touch with her colleague at San Francisco State University, Dr. Elias Raines. He's a paleoethnobotanist. I spoke with him this morning. Hanna had photos of similar glyphs, and she also wrote of losing track of time when around them. Right before she went missing."

Mary's expression shifted. "Do you think this is what happened to Clayton?"

"Dr. Raines thinks it's a really strong possibility. He's concerned that they're spreading so close to civilization. He's driving up here Sunday night and wants to look into them on Monday, take samples. I told him I would help and…"

Mary leaned toward her. "You want me to go with you."

"I do," Story said. "You know the woods better than almost anyone. And not just the geography. You've felt the shifts out there. You've seen more than most. If something's changing, I want you with me when we go in."

Mary didn't answer immediately. She glanced toward the window, where the sunlight flickered through pine boughs like something breathing. "I won't let you go in there on your own, if you really insist on it. But I don't think you should."

"Mary," Story started. She scooted forward and caught her friend's eye. "Leith asked me for help and she needs it. If you'd seen the look in her eyes. This changed her, it hypnotized her, and, if Dr. Raines is correct about the effects of this bioluminescent fungus, not only could it bring us answers about Clayton, but it will help us protect others."

Mary bit her bottom lip so hard it bled. She hissed and stood, grabbing a Kleenex from the small mantel over her fireplace. "I'll go."

"Good! And now, we can go meet Cal Hensley to talk to him about it!" Story slapped her knees and stood.

Mary's brow furrowed. "Wes's brother?"

"I don't think there's another one."

"What does he have to do with it?"

"He guided Hannah around when she was here researching. I spoke with him yesterday and I got the impression that he feels responsible for Hannah's disappearance. I want to ask him to join us. He knows where she was working, where she found the glyphs. So, let's go!"

Mary dabbed her lip and shook her head. "I don't want to."

"Come on, you can get a strawberry shortcake latte! I saw the sign that they're back on the summer menu and I know you love them."

Mary continued protesting. "It's out with—it's day…there's people and—"

"And your therapist suggested you start branching out. To find a balance between your hermit lifestyle and the real world, right?" Story moved closer to her friend, reassuring her. "I'll be there. Every step of the way. And we'll take the long way round. We won't walk by the grocery or otherwise." She didn't even want to say the word out loud, knowing it would set her friend off. The butcher's shop was a trigger Mary would likely never be able to overcome. Instead, Story smiled and teased. "Strawberry shortcake latte," she said, drawing out the words.

Mary couldn't help but smile, and with many reservations and hesitations, she acquiesced.

By the time they'd ordered and sat, Cal arrived. He looked crisp in his taupe-and-brown uniform, which hugged his frame like something purpose-built. His hair was tied back into a braid, the tail of it dark with forest mist, and his boots bore the familiar wear of a man who lived more outside than in. He moved with quiet purpose, unhurried but direct, as though time itself bent a little to his rhythm.

He ordered a simple coffee—black—and joined Story Palmer, whom he'd met on a few occasions at fundraisers and community barbecues hosted by his brother. The woman beside her looked familiar, but he couldn't quite place her.

"Story," he said, reaching out a hand with a small nod of greeting.

Story stood and smiled warmly. "Cal, thank you for agreeing to meet up on such short notice."

"Of course." He reached out, warm hand clasping hers with a quiet steadiness, then turned to the other woman, suddenly remembering her name. "Mary Germaine, right? I thought I recognized you. You were in my brother's year, right?"

Mary blinked at him, nodded. "Yes," she said, a little too fast. "You look the same."

Cal chuckled. "And you don't look like you're in high school anymore. In a good way. Nice to see you."

She took his hand. It was rough and reassuring, and her brain flooded with such a sudden storm of nerves she nearly dropped the stirrer. Instead, she jammed it back between her teeth and bit down. Hard.

Cal slid into the booth across from them, easing his coffee down. "So," he said. "What's this about? You didn't really say."

Story reached into her coat pocket and pulled out her phone. She swiped through a few photos, then turned it around and slid it across the table to him.

Cal leaned in. The glyph stared up at him. Sharp, symmetrical, scarred into bark. He stilled with his thumb hesitating just above the screen.

Story watched him. "Do you know it?"

He didn't answer right away. Instead, his eyes narrowed, shifted, hiding something private.

"You alright?" Story asked gently.

He cleared his throat, leaned back. "I just saw this."

Mary's fingers resumed tapping.

"You mean the glyph?"

He nodded. "Yeah. A few days ago. Did Constance speak with you about this?"

Story tilted her head, understanding blossoming. "Anya," she remarked.

"What?" he asked.

"Sorry. That image was taken from a tree in the woods near the Bury farm."

"Ethan Bury?" Cal asked with redundant intention. Ethan had been in his class. They'd played baseball together.

Story nodded. "Leith came to me to see if I knew anything about the marking."

Cal nodded, slowly. "So that's how you're looped into this."

"Exactly. It makes sense that Anya would go to her friend about it. This thing has really rattled both of them, Leith especially. And then I saw Deanna and she told me you guided Hannah Albrecht around the area—"

Cal looked at the phone again, then up at Story. "What does this have to do with Hannah?"

"That's the other reason I reached out. I spoke with someone who worked with her—Dr. Elias Raines. Head of her department. He reviewed the glyph photos I sent him and…he's worried."

"Worried how?"

Story pulled in a breath. "He thinks it's not the glyphs themselves that are the issue."

Cal straightened. "What issue?"

"Well, he thinks it's what's inside them. The fungus you see," she said, enlarging the screen of her phone in front of him and tapping on it with her nail.

Cal leaned in and saw it. Yes, there was a strange, tiny fungal growth inside of the glyph. A peculiar color, almost glowing. The image went fuzzy and he blinked his eyes to clear them as Story continued.

"It could be a kind of mycelial colony that's growing inside the cuts. It might possibly be…hallucinogenic."

That pulled his attention, brow furrowing. "Like mushrooms?"

"Yes. But not any we've seen around here. And not ones that grow like this. He believes the glyphs are acting as some kind of growth channel. A conduit."

A long silence fell between them. Mary's tapping became erratic. She reached for another stirrer but Story gently laid her hand over Mary's, stilling her. She then slipped a wrapped lozenge into her palm. Mary gave her a quick, grateful glance and popped the homemade lozenge into her mouth.

His glances flicked between the two women and their movements. "He thinks the glyphs are causing the hallucinations?" Cal asked at last.

"According to the notes Hannah made and the details I recounted from Leith's interaction with that one," Story said, motioning to her phone still lying before him.

Cal stared down into his coffee, shoulders tense. "Wait," he said suddenly. "Hannah made notes about hallucinations?"

"Yes."

"She never said anything to me. Not once. We talked plenty. She'd send me photos, call about trail conditions. I'd ask how she was sleeping."

"She may not have wanted to worry you. But it's in her field notes. Along with references to time loss. Shifts in perception."

Cal scrubbed a hand over his jaw, eyes distant. She never said a word. Not when she was laughing over coffee. Not when she showed him the first glyph photo and asked if he'd seen anything like it before.

This wasn't a coincidence. First, his niece had brought it to him, a scrap of unease passed from a friend to her to him, and now Story, from an entirely different circle, had reached out with the same glyph, the same concern. The universe, or fate, or whatever thread wove lives together, wasn't being subtle anymore. It was pressing something into his hands and whispering, "look."

Story watched him closely. "I believe this is something you may need to look at."

He glanced up. He didn't answer right away. But he studied her, really studied her, and in her eyes, there was something hard to name. Wes had told him she was sharp, a hint of other meaning in the words, but now he was seeing it firsthand.

"There's more here than we understand right now," she continued.

"What do you need from me?" he asked.

"I was hoping you or Paddy might help Elias. He's coming up Sunday night. He wants to retrace Hannah's steps. Collect samples. Verify what we're dealing with, see how far it's spread. How dangerous it might be. I know you have Clayton to look for."

"I can make time. I owe it to Hannah. And I don't want anyone else to go missing." Cal leaned back again, eyes flicking between the two women. "I'd be happy to show him the trail. You can pass along my number."

"We were hoping to head out Monday morning. Old Timber Spur, is that right?"

Cal nodded once. His thoughts lingered on her choice of word, *we*. He said, "Alright. As I said, you can give me his number, I can coordinate with him."

"We'll be coming along too," Story added casually, but her tone left little room for objection.

Cal glanced at her, then at Mary. "You know the area?" he asked, figuring that perhaps it was the reason she was here. It would make sense for Story to gather people who knew the forest and the trails to show Dr. Raines around.

Mary shifted slightly in her seat. "Sure," she said, "but not that well."

Cal turned his glance to Story. "Then why come?"

Story offered a soft smile. "It's just something I need to see through. Besides, I love getting out in the woods when I can. There's still so much of it I haven't seen."

Cal turned to Mary again. "And you?"

Mary blinked, then shrugged. "Because Story asked me to."

Something in the simplicity of it caught Cal off guard. There was an ease in the exchanges between them, something unspoken but solid, like roots shared between trees underground. His gaze lingered on Mary a beat longer. He studied her. Her quietness didn't feel timid, more like an old spring clock, ticking inside. Mary's eyes met his, wide and flat as a lake, her fingers now tapping softly against her cup. She didn't hold his gaze long, suddenly looking away.

His lips quirked, almost a smile. He looked between them again. One with soft edges and secrets. The other humming like static. He didn't know what they were to each other—old friends, lovers (did Seth know?), something else entirely—but he understood that where one went, the other followed.

"Alright. Are we talking Monday morning?"

"That's the plan, yes," Story replied.

Cal nodded. He had a firm, thoughtful scowl. "But listen to me." His tone sharpened. "This isn't a trail ride. We stick together. No wandering off. You don't touch anything unless I say it's safe. No sniffing the weird fungus. We'll let Dr. Raines handle that part of it."

Story nodded. "Understood."

He took another moment to look at each one of them, then lifted his coffee. "Alright. We can meet at Grouse Ridge Market. Eight a.m. Monday," he said, then took a sip. He needed the caffeine as he headed into another long day of searching the woods for Clayton. *What does all this mean for the search?* he wondered.

"Great! Thank you, Cal," Story said, shaking his hand.

Mary gave a little two-finger salute. "We'll be there."

Cal slid from the booth and paused, one hand on the back of the seat. "See you both then," he said, then added, eyes catching Mary's, "Looking forward to it."

His departure was marked by the door swinging closed behind him, the bell above it giving a sharp, clear chime.

Mary sat perfectly still.

Story looked at her sidelong. "You okay?"

Mary nodded, but didn't speak, choosing instead to lean down and take a long pull from her frappuccino.

Story smiled softly and patted her hand.

Chapter Eighteen
Terror Rising

Earthquakes are a common occurrence for anyone who has lived in Lost Grove for a significant amount of time. The town sits above the Mendocino Triple Junction, an area of great seismic activity where three tectonic plates meet. Feeling the disorienting sensation of a house or building shifting is something most every resident of Lost Grove has experienced. A recent earthquake from early December the previous year was big enough to dislodge bottles off the bar shelves at the restaurant in the Lost Grove Victorian Inn and knock hundreds of products from the shelves at the Lost Grove Market. Back in December of 2013, Lost Grove was rocked by a magnitude 6.4 earthquake that caused extensive damage, numerous injuries, and even two deaths. Five buildings collapsed, gas lines were broken, glass windows of storefronts were shattered, homes were knocked off their foundations, and a section of Grovebridge collapsed, leaving the main route from the freeway into Lost Grove uncrossable.

The last town hall meeting in Lost Grove was held as a result of that earthquake. Seth wasn't present for that meeting; he was busy working a triple homicide case in San Francisco, but he heard all about it from his parents. It was a big deal. Many residents were displaced, there was severe damage to many gravestones at their historic cemetery, and there were major issues and concerns about how products were going to be imported into and exported out of Lost Grove. The town had to come together quickly and act decisively to put plans in place. Tonight was the first town hall since that night, and the residents of Lost Grove were jammed like sardines into Danish Hall at the city hall, brimming with fear, outrage, and questions desperate to be answered. Many questions Seth didn't have answers for.

Seth stood behind Mayor Diane Sumner, who was preparing to address the crowd. They had met briefly in her office, along with Wes and Cal Hensley, to discuss how they would handle the meeting. This had been Seth's first meeting with the mayor since he took over as chief of police from Bill two months prior. He found Mrs. Sumner genuinely pleasant, refreshingly direct, and highly intelligent. She had a clear understanding of people and how to anticipate their reactions and feelings. It was easy to understand why the residents of Lost Grove were so fond of her. Seth's mother, Amaranth, considered Diane to be a friend, which was enough of an endorsement for Seth. Amaranth was friendly with the majority of the town, but she also didn't mince words if she found someone to be phony or cruel.

Diane emigrated to Lost Grove fifteen years ago with her husband, Dr. Joseph Sumner, who had been offered a job at the Orbriallis Institute as a member of the research team for skin replacement. She was pregnant at the time with the couple's first child, Joseph, and two years later, they had their second child, Katy. Diane purchased a vacant storefront on Main Street the summer before Katy entered kindergarten and opened a bookstore. She quickly became popular amongst the townspeople, making friends with people of every age. After running the bookstore for five years, Diane decided to run for the open mayor position. She won in a landslide against a retired farmer who had very little interest in the position to begin with, becoming the first female mayor and, at thirty-four, the youngest since Frank Garbutt in 1934. She was coming to the end of her second term in November.

Seth surveyed the crowd as Diane's assistant, Kimberly, worked on getting the microphone to work. There were older faces that Seth had known since he was a kid and a whole host of faces of people he had gotten to know over the past year since he came back home. Faces of those he knew more intimately included Clemency Pruitt, his old high school art teacher Gretchen Young, his high school girlfriend Jaime Goodacre, who had reluctantly stopped hitting on him since he and Story became a public couple, Ethan and Leith Bury, Jolie and an off-duty Peter Andalusian, and Lord help him, Jeffrey Tacet and Angus Weatherspoon. Faces he was surprised to see were those of Nettie Horne, standing next to a man looking too old to have his arm around her, and, endlessly breaking his heart, Tommy Wilder, who smiled and nodded at Seth.

Further back in the crowd, leaning up against the wall, was Story Palmer. She gave a hesitant smile as Seth caught her eye. Seth returned a hint of a smile, but her presence brought about a tightening unease in his chest. And not because they were in the midst of their first row as a couple. Last night, she informed him of her conversation with Dr. Elias Raines and how Hannah Albrecht's field notes revealed that she experienced similar disorienting effects and loss of time being in close proximity to these bioluminescent fungal glyphs as Leith Bury. Dr. Raines was so fearful of the spreading fungus that he was driving up from San Francisco to examine them. Story said he mentioned the phrase "biological intelligence," which conjured the image of clone people growing in flower pods from the Donald Sutherland version of *Invasion of the Body Snatchers*.

Seth called Peter the second he finished speaking with Story and told him to grab Joe the following morning and head back out to where they found Clayton's cell phone, and from there search in all directions to see if they could locate a glyph that looked anything like the one Story texted him. If one or more were found, and they contained the fungus, it could go a long way in explaining Jasper's recollection of bizarre events they experienced.

Peter met him twenty minutes before the town hall back in one of the offices. They had in fact found a glyph carved into a tree about a hundred yards southwest from where they found the phone, which aligned with the path the boys took to get to Gulliver's Gully. And the glyph did harbor a fungus of some kind in the markings, which Peter extracted samples from and dropped at the station for Seth to pass off to Dr. Raines on Monday. Whether or not this explained what happened to Jasper and Clayton remained to be seen, but even if it did, he would be no closer to knowing where Clayton was now.

Although the situation was alarming and unnerving, Seth wasn't about to warn the entire town that a bioluminescent fungus was growing in ancient glyphs that might cause hallucinations or lapses in time. At least not yet. There was enough hysteria to contain as it was. He did, however, immediately communicate with his team to make sure they were aware of the potential danger and to be on the lookout for any glyphs in the woods during their continued search for Clayton Meadows.

"Hello, ladies and gentlemen, thank you so much for coming."

Seth glanced to his right at Mayor Sumner, finally with a working mic, and then to his left at Wes, Cal, and former chief of police Bill Richards. Bill told Seth he didn't want to step on Seth's toes, to which Seth told him to stop being foolish and that his presence would be nothing but a net positive.

The crowd quieted to a smattering of muffled conversations, allowing Diane to address the crowd. "I was standing right where you all are now, twelve years ago, after the collapse of Grovebridge, as concerned and nervous as anyone. Former Mayor Steven Donohue, who's with us tonight—hey, Steven," she said, waving to the former mayor. "Mayor Donohue knew moments after that earthquake hit that the town needed help, that the people needed help. So, he brought us all together and organized a plan of action to ensure that every resident would be taken care of and that businesses would survive.

"We've experienced something of our own earthquake, much more intimate yet no less affecting, over the past six days. Kevin Marlow, a young boy of just seven, was tragically taken from us in the rarest of animal attacks. And now one of our own, Clayton Meadows, the son of our friends Reid and Molly, has gone missing—both incidents occurring in the woods that surround our town. While our dedicated police department and numerous volunteers continue the search for any sign of Clayton, I know you're worried. I know you're afraid. I am, too. You all know my son, Joseph, and daughter, Katy. I would do anything to protect them, and I'll do everything to protect you and your children.

"At the urging of our chief of police, Seth Wolfe, with which I wholeheartedly concur, I wanted to call this town hall to be as transparent as possible with the efforts we're taking to find Clayton Meadows and to identify the animal or animals responsible for the death of Kevin Marlow. And with that, I'd like to turn it over to our chief of police, Seth Wolfe." Diane stepped to the side, motioning for Seth to take her place.

Seth nodded and walked over to the mic as the volume of conversations from the crowd rose. "Thank you, Mayor. Hello, everyone."

"It's been almost a week, Chief. Why haven't we heard anything about the predator out there hunting our children?" The question was blurted out by Vick Edwards, a dairy farmer married with three children.

Seth held up his hand. "That's exactly why I wanted this town hall, Vick. There was an article four days ago in the *Lost Grove Gazette* that some of you may or may not have read, detailing how we were unable to positively identify the animal or animals responsible for the attack."

"So, that's it?" Jeffrey Tacet piped in.

"Please," said Mayor Sumner, "keep your questions until the end."

"No, Jeffrey, that's not it," Seth said. "If you would let me finish, I think you'll find that a lot of your questions will be answered. And I understand the urgency of your questions. We all do. That's why we're here. Now, regarding the identification of the animal, our chief medical examiner, Dr. Wes Hensley," Seth said, motioning to his right, "has sent in DNA from the wounds in the body, which will tell us the breed of animal responsible, and in many cases, it can positively identify the specific animal."

"And how long is that going to take?" Vick Edwards asked.

"Let the man finish, Vick," chimed in Ethan Bury.

Wes took a step toward the crowd. "It can take anywhere from a week to three weeks to get results."

"Three weeks?" hollered Charles Winslow, a fourth grade teacher at Lost Grove Elementary. "What if a mountain lion comes charging onto the playground at recess?"

"First of all," Seth responded, "we don't know if it's a mountain lion, and don't go around spreading rumors that it is. We've already arrested two people sneaking their hunting rifles into Devil's Cradle State Park, which is not only illegal but incredibly dangerous."

"If I may, Seth," Cal stepped forward, his booming voice drawing everyone's attention. "Most of you here know me, having met at Wes's yearly fundraiser, but for those of you who don't, my name is Cal Hensley. I'm a reservation officer for the Wiyot tribe and a former wildlife officer for the CDFW. I was asked to come in and help my brother identify the animal in question, and I've agreed to split my time to help Seth with his investigation. I've heard rumors of no less than five different animals being responsible. I'd like to make some things crystal clear regarding hunting and our wildlife.

"It is illegal to hunt mountain lions. It is illegal to hunt bobcats. Grey wolves are an endangered species and very illegal to hunt. And we are not in bear hunting season. Each of these animals has been rumored to be responsible for Kevin Marlow's death. If anyone is caught killing any one of these animals, and believe you me, you will be caught, you will be fined anywhere from ten to a hundred thousand dollars and be sentenced up to a year in jail. Is that clear?"

The only response was the shuffling of feet and clearing of throats.

Seth was thrilled to have someone who cut more of an imposing figure than himself on his side. "The most important thing here is, folks, that renegade hunters pose more danger to our children, and each other, than any animal in our parks and forests."

"What do you expect us to do in the meantime?" asked Charles.

"I know that what we're asking you to do, Mr. Winslow—what we're going to ask of all of you—is going to be difficult, but I'm asking you all to be patient. Once we get the DNA results, Cal Hensley and a wildlife biologist from the CDFW will track down the animal or animals responsible and either relocate them or euthanize them."

"Relocate them?" Jeffrey exclaimed. "What the fuck kind of solution is that?"

"Mr. Tacet!" Mayor Sumner bellowed. "You will keep your dialogue civilized, or I will ask you to leave now."

Jeffrey shrank behind his cohort, Angus.

"It's the only solution," Cal responded, "if it involves an endangered species."

"That's right," Seth stated. "The best thing, the most logical thing, and the easiest thing to do in the meantime, is to simply stay away from the woods. Keep your kids away from the woods."

"That's easy for you to say, Chief," Vick Edwards voiced. "You don't have kids."

Seth sighed. "Mr. Edwards—"

"Keep your mouth shut, Vick!" Ethan growled. "You're not the only one with kids here. Almost every damn one of us has kids, and Chief Wolfe is the one in charge of protecting—"

"He can't be everywhere at once. There's only five damn officers in the department. I don't know about you, Ethan, but my kids don't always listen—"

"Everyone!" Bill yelled, stepping forward. "What is this? This isn't the community that I've been a part of for over five decades. You can either help be a part of the solution or hide behind your barbs and fears. I've been in those damn woods for almost twenty hours the past day and a half looking for one of Lost Grove's children. I didn't see you there, Vick. I didn't see you there, Jeffrey."

"You expect us to go into the Cursed Woods?" Jeffrey retorted.

"Would you go in there for Jacob?" Bill asked, referring to Jeffrey's son, to which he received no reply. "I thought so. Now, show Chief Wolfe the same respect you showed me for over thirty years."

Seth nodded his thanks to Bill and stepped back behind the mic. "Twenty-three years ago, when I wasn't that much older than Clayton Meadows, I got lost in one of our caves just outside Devil's Cradle. Oxygen drained from the spot I was stuck in, and I passed out. If it wasn't for the patience and persistence of one man," Seth said, looking over at Bill, "I would have died in that very spot." Seth looked back out to the audience. "You're right. I don't have any children. Not yet. But I've been in the same place as Clayton Meadows, likely lost and afraid, and I came to the precipice of death in the natural landscape of our town. And I, along with every member of my team and our volunteers, will do everything in my power to bring Clayton home safe and sound and to protect all of you from whatever animal may be a threat."

Seth spotted someone he didn't recognize raise a hand in the back of the crowd. Seth pointed to the man and said, "Appreciate you raising your hand, sir. Go ahead."

The man cleared his throat. "Hey there, Chief Wolfe. My name is Rip Rogers. I'm a cattle farmer south of town. Hearing you all talk about the attack on the young boy, I wanted to ask if you thought it could be the same animal responsible for the slaying of my cattle three weeks ago."

Seth's brow drew tight as he looked over to Bill, Wes, and Cal, who all had blank faces. Seth looked back at Rip. "I'm sorry to say, I haven't heard about your cattle, Mr. Rogers. Would you mind coming up to the front so we can all hear you?"

Rip made his way through the crowd, a stout man in his fifties with a peppered beard and long grey ponytail. He extended his hand to shake Seth's, who met it and offered him the mic. "Thank you, Chief. Most of you don't know me, but I was in town yesterday to get my wife, Rosie, a birthday cake at the Lost Grove Bakery, and saw the flyers for the town hall. A few weeks back, I woke up at three a.m. to a god-awful sound coming from my fields. I knew off the git that it was an attack on my cattle. If any of my fellow farmers here have heard the death throes of an attack on your animals, you'll know what I'm sayin'. I ran out with my shotgun to find three of my cattle on the ground, their throats torn open and cracks in their skulls."

Murmurs of "Jesus," "Oh my God," and one "fucking hell" swirled around the crowd.

"I took photos, wrote up a report, and called it into the CDFW. Someone came out to investigate, but I ain't heard nothin' since. Maybe you know?" Rip pleaded to Cal.

Cal stepped over and patted the cattle rancher's back. "Sorry to say, I haven't, Mr. Rogers. But I'll make a call first thing tomorrow and look into it."

Rip nodded and meandered back into the audience, making his way to the rear of the assembly.

"What about the construction?"

Seth looked for the source of the question, stunned to see it was Nettie Horne. "Hey, Nettie. Sorry, what about the construction?"

"The Orbriallis is upsetting the natural balance of the flora and fauna of our land. Isn't it possible that they've disrupted it to the point of upsetting the animals, forcing them out of their natural habitat, and causing them to react uncharacteristically and violently?"

The murmurs of the crowd intensified, Nettie hitting a sore spot with many in the community.

Seth locked eyes with Peter, exchanging an unspoken fear. It was predictable that Nettie would still hold heavy resentment for what the Orbriallis did to her younger brother, George. Would it be enough for her to deface the property? "I can't say that it's not possible, Nettie. We're very in tune with what's happening at the building site and understand the potential ramifications. We'll make sure that this is part of the discussion when we meet with the wildlife biologist from the CDFW."

"Actually, Nettie?" The voice from the crowd came from Jolie Andalusian. "I share your concerns about the development and the impact it could have on our river and the wildlife from that specific area. But whichever animal was responsible for that boy's death wouldn't be found in that area. The wildlife to be concerned about where the construction is happening would be beavers, otters, fish, and amphibians."

"Mrs. Andalusian is correct," said Cal. "The animals capable of the attack on Kevin Marlow reside deep within the woods. We may see them on the outskirts of town, but they keep to the woods and mountainous terrain."

"Someone should still do something about that development," Nettie responded with a scowl on her face.

Mayor Sumner raised her hand to draw Nettie's attention. "Ms. Horne, you're not alone with your concerns. I've spoken with many of our fellow residents who would agree with you. I've spoken with all the appropriate parties involved. I've had lawyers look over all the permits and contracts, and took part in the planning and zoning commission hearings. This is in no way to negate any of your concerns, but speaking on a purely legal level, everything was done above board."

Nettie mumbled something incoherent in reply.

"This is an open forum," Seth said. "We can, by all means, talk about the housing development, but I'd like to make sure all your questions are answered about Kevin Marlow and Clayton Meadows."

Old Tom King raised his hand. "Chief?"

"Go ahead, Tom."

"You reckon the same animal that killed that poor—"

"Don't say it."

"Traveler boy is responsible for the Meadows kid?"

Seth noticed the perplexed faces in the crowd at Tom's poor description of Kevin Marlow. "Let me make this very clear to everyone. There is absolutely no indication that Clayton's disappearance is the result of an animal or that of another human being. Furthermore, there is no indication that any physical harm befell Clayton." The minute amount of blood found on the scene didn't indicate a wound of any impending danger, but he was not about to mention that tidbit of information.

"Then what happened to him?" This question came from Bruce Stokes, standing next to his wife, Susan. "Our girl was out there that night. Should we be worried something might happen to her?"

"Are we talking about a kidnapper, like this past October?" asked Jim Peterson, the owner of the local car repair shop. "No offense meant," he said, nodding at Peter and Jolie.

Peter hugged Jolie closer to his chest and nodded at Jim. "None taken. It's a fair question."

"Is that guy still out there?" voiced Bruce Stokes.

"No," Seth said, "and we have no—"

"Read the papers, Bruce!" Old Tom King blurted out. "That kiddie fella's been dead for months."

"Doesn't mean there couldn't be another kidnapper out there," responded Bruce.

"Everyone, please," Seth pleaded. "There is no indication whatsoever of a kidnapping. As I literally just said, there were no signs of another human being present, outside of Clayton's friend, Jasper Cunningham.

And, no, Bruce, I don't believe there is anything of that nature to worry about with Angie."

"Chief Wolfe?" Jacquelynne Summerset, the reporter for the *Lost Grove Gazette*, raised her hand.

Seth pointed at her. "Ms. Summerset. Go ahead."

"Going just off the facts as they've been presented to me and from what I've heard here tonight, I have a question. Just over two months ago, I covered a story about Raymond LaRange's death, the kidnapper in question."

Seth and Wes exchanged a quick glance.

"Despite the man being on the verge of death, he was also killed by an animal. You were clear at the time that it wasn't necessarily an aggressive attack, that he could have just been seen as a source of food, but do you think it's possible that the same animal is responsible for the death of Kevin Marlow? And if so, why didn't you launch a more aggressive inquiry into the animal responsible then?"

One thing Seth was used to dealing with during all his years as a homicide detective was the media. "That's an understandable question and one we immediately asked ourselves when we arrived at the scene. What we believe—"

"Seth, if I may?" Wes interrupted.

"Go ahead, Wes."

"Jacquelynne, it was my determination at the time, after doing the autopsy on LaRange and consulting an officer from the CDFW, that due to LaRange's severe dehydration and malnourishment, the animals responsible were not seen as an aggressive threat. And a key point here is the word *animals*. We were able to identify at least four different species who were responsible for the wounds all over his body."

"And what species were they? That information was not disclosed at the time."

"And I'd like to leave it that way for now," Seth said. "Not to be evasive, but we've already had issues keeping hunters at bay, and we don't need to add any more fuel to that fire. Once we get the DNA results for the animal or animals responsible for Kevin Marlow, I'd be happy to give you our full findings on LaRange."

"Thank you," Jacquelynne said.

"Now, if there are no further questions for me or my team, I'd like to turn things back over to Mayor Sumner. We need to get back out there to continue our search for Clayton Meadows. And I'd strongly encourage any of you who would be willing to join us."

Chapter Nineteen
Summer Ride

The sun hung high in the sky as Anya pulled her truck into Stan's driveway. Zoe already chattered excitedly in the passenger seat. The eleven-year-old had been buzzing about this ride all week, eager to go on one of Noble's guided expeditions to the beach.

Zoe slid to the middle of the bench seat as Stan jumped in and buckled up. She smiled as Zoe continued speaking animatedly about her owl, Merryweather. They'd released the bird back to the wild once it was fit, but the owl had stuck around. They fed her raw chicken off the back porch. It was a sight to behold, one Stan was shocked to witness. The silence of the bird was uncanny as it swooped down out of the night sky and nabbed the chicken. Sometimes, she landed on the porch railing and ate her meal there. Even more bizarre, Merryweather would tap on the sliding glass door, asking to come inside. She'd hop inside like a dog and nestle onto the couch beside Zoe as they watched TV or perch on the back of her chair as she finished her homework at the kitchen island.

"And I just cannot wait to go on this ride!" Zoe exclaimed, bouncing in her seat.

"You act like you've never been on a horse before." Stan laughed.

"Not with you guys," Zoe shot back. "And not while Noble is technically working."

"Are you gonna be on your best behavior then?" Anya teased, glancing down at her. "Or are you gonna make him regret letting you tag along?"

Zoe gasped dramatically. "I am a perfect trail companion!"

"Uh-huh," Stan drawled. "Just like how Merryweather is a perfectly normal pet."

Zoe grinned. "She is normal—just...special."

Anya smirked. "You spend way too much time with Story."

"Story is the best!" Zoe declared, unbothered. "She says I have an old soul."

Stan snorted. "Yeah, like a mischievous old goblin."

Zoe elbowed her playfully. "I hope your horse throws you off."

Anya chuckled, pulling into the gravel drive of Ross Ranch. "He'll be half distracted the whole time, trying to make sure nobody gets bucked off. We'll probably just get to mess around and enjoy the ride," she said as they all hopped out of her truck and headed for the stables.

Noble was already speaking with a small group of tourists who were adjusting their stirrups and helmets. He spotted them, and a smile broke across his face, the kind that made Anya's stomach do a ridiculous little flip. His easy confidence, as effortless as always, had drawn her to him since they were kids. She still remembered the moment she first got that stupid crush—the way he had ridden one of her horses backward at her tenth birthday party, eating cake like it was the most natural thing in the world. He had always been fearless, always moving through life like nothing could shake him. But what she loved most was how he was with animals, how he understood them in a way she wished she understood people. Around others, she often felt out of place and awkward in her own skin. But with Noble, everything felt easy.

He strode toward them, eyes bright. "Right on time," he said, joining them. "I put you guys on Calamity and Shadowfax," he said to his friends. He quickly gave Anya a kiss while no one was looking. Zoe giggled. "And you," he said to his sister, pushing her into the ring where the others were getting into the saddle, "I put you on Woogie."

"The pony?" Zoe whined.

"Your legs are still too short to handle anything too stubborn."

"Hey!" Zoe objected, but she still took the reins to her pony, a sturdy little dun with a flaxen mane. "Might be small, but I could handle a wild one."

"Not today, you won't," Noble countered, ruffling her hair before handing Anya the reins to her horse, Calamity, who was not at all like her name. She was the sweetest mare with a pleasant countenance.

Noble pulled Calamity around so she blocked him from the group and his sister, and gave Anya another, deeper kiss. "I'm glad you're here."

"Me too," Anya said, beaming. The heat of the summer day painted her already blushing cheeks a deeper pink.

He squeezed her hand, then moved to boost Stan onto Shadowfax, an equally well-mannered but sometimes petulant dark brown gelding.

"Okay!" Noble clapped and swung onto his horse with ease. His smile was vibrant, and he addressed the paying customers. "Everyone ready?"

Many nods of excitement followed, and they took off out of the paddock and onto the trail.

As the group set off, Noble took the lead, guiding them through the familiar winding trails. The scent of damp earth and salty ocean air mixed as they rode under the towering redwoods. The tourists ahead chatted quietly, their voices rising and falling with the gentle clop of the ride, and Noble kept an easy pace, his voice occasionally drifting back as he gave tidbits about the area's history. He looked back now and then, scanning for stragglers and hazards with the ease of someone who knew the terrain like the back of his hand.

The trail was wide enough for the horses to walk two across, their hooves muffled by years of pine needles and packed dirt. Anya let her horse fall into rhythm beside Stan's. Zoe was just ahead, nudging her pony—Woogie—away from another particularly tempting fern.

"So..." Stan drawled, leaning forward on her saddle, "Did you hear about Nettie at the town hall yesterday?"

Anya's head snapped toward her. "Yes! My dad came home and asked me if she was doing alright. Said she got real heated."

Stan nodded. "Right? My dad said she practically shouted at the committee about the housing plans. Called the Orbriallis Institute a bunch of leeches or something. Like, chill."

"She needs to cool off with that," Anya muttered, adjusting her reins. "I get that she hates the Orbriallis stuff, but she's drawing attention. Like, the wrong kind."

Stan's brows knit. "I know. And I get where she's coming from, but sometimes it's like she wants to, I don't know, get in trouble."

Anya hesitated. Her horse sidestepped slightly as they passed a fallen log. "I'm not gonna lie... I've had my concerns that she might, I don't know, spill the beans."

Stan's eyes widened slightly. "About what happened? About her real brother?"

Anya nodded once, almost reluctantly. "Yeah."

"You really think she'd—?"

"I don't know. I... I feel like I don't know her anymore." She sighed. "I texted her last night. Told her my dad was worried, thought that might make her realize she overdid it. But she didn't even respond. She still hasn't."

"She's been weird lately," Stan said. "Quieter. Then—boom. Rage monster at the town meeting."

Ahead, Noble glanced back, slowing his horse until he could fall into stride with them. "Talking about Nettie's speech yesterday?"

Stan snorted. "Speech? More like a scorched-earth campaign."

"You heard about it too?" Anya asked.

He nodded. "Mom said she went a little hard about this whole..." He looked at his sister, who stuck out her tongue at him.

"As if I don't know what you are talking about," she said.

He stuck his tongue out at her and continued, "About the whole incident with the kid in the park being because of the Orbriallis. Mom said she had to mention that the land the housing development is going up on isn't land that a predator would inhabit. But"—he shrugged, calm as ever—"Nettie didn't seem to care."

"Look, she has a point," Stan said. "Orbriallis has been stomping all over prime habitat for shore birds and amphibians. But the yelling isn't gonna help."

"I just..." Anya lowered her voice, "I worry she's going to say something that can't be taken back. About her brother. About what really happened."

Zoe turned in her saddle, her small face serious. "They'd never believe her."

"Still," Noble muttered, his gaze fixed ahead, "truth has a way of leaking out when you least want it to." It was a concern he harbored secretly, a dread held in his stomach, that the secrets of his father would one day come to light.

They rode in silence for a few beats as Noble pushed ahead, checking on everyone before nudging his horse back beside his girlfriend.

Stan laughed before saying, "Did you hear what Old Tom is calling the child?"

"No, what?" Noble asked, smiling.

"A traveler boy."

"What is a traveler boy?" Zoe asked.

Stan shrugged, still laughing at the old man, recalling the way her dad told her mom about it last night. Her mom had remarked that Old Tom was worse than any busybody known to man.

"He probably means like a gypsy or something," Anya remarked to Zoe.

"Jesus," Noble laughed.

"What was the town meeting about?" Zoe asked, finally unable to keep her curiosity at bay. She'd asked her mom and her dad, but both had been evasive. Maybe she'd get more out of her older friends.

Noble sighed. "Did you ask Mom?"

"Yes."

"And what'd she tell you?"

Zoe looked over her shoulder, her big eyes large and sorrowful, pulling the classic little sister expression she knew would get him to crack. "Why can't you tell me?"

Stan lifted an eyebrow. "I am so glad I have younger brothers."

"Did you have a sad look for your older brothers?" Noble asked.

"Hell no." Stan laughed. "You think they'd fall for that," she asked.

They all looked back at Zoe.

"Actually…" Anya said.

"Yeah," Stan remarked. "They might have."

"So," Zoe prompted.

"It was about the boy who was killed by a predator in Devil's Cradle," Noble responded. "And the teenager that went missing."

"So." Zoe nudged Woogie away from some grass. "They think the teenager, that he's gotten eaten or something?"

"No," Noble said. He caught the questionable expressions from both his friend and girlfriend. "No, that's the point Seth was trying to make. We can't jump to conclusions. Maybe he's just lost," Noble added. "Like so many others who go into the Cursed Woods and never come out."

Anya shifted uncomfortably in her saddle, thinking how close that hit home for her father.

"You're not supposed to go in the Cursed Woods," Zoe commented.

Noble kicked ahead next to his sister and leaned down to whisper, "Hey, do you want to lead the group?"

Zoe's face split into a grin.

"Go on, then," he said, nodding her ahead.

Zoe kicked Woogie into gear and moved to the front.

Now that she was out of hearing distance, Noble could bring up what he thought was strange, or perhaps just interesting, about the scenario with the younger boy, Kevin Marlow. He hadn't had time to run it past Nate, but the two deaths stuck out to him. "You guys remember hearing about LaRange, right?"

Stan scowled and shook her head. "That he's dead?"

"Nah, the way he died. In the woods," Noble added.

Anya shook her head. "I think I was just relieved to hear he was gone. For good." Anya wrinkled her nose. "That sounds awful of me."

"No, it doesn't," Noble quickly said. He urged his horse closer to hers.

Stan pushed Shadowfax nearer as well, knowing they'd have to talk quickly and quietly.

"You guys don't remember what they said about him?" Noble asked.

"No," Stan said.

Anya shook her head.

"That he'd been mauled by animals?"

"Shit," Stan hissed. "I must have missed that. What do you mean, mauled?"

Noble shrugged. "I wasn't given all the details, just that he'd been found in the woods, his body mauled by an animal. That's what my dad told me."

"And Chief Wolfe?" Stan asked. "Did he corroborate that?"

"More or less," Noble replied.

"And then there are the cows being killed by a predator," Anya added.

"I keep forgetting about the cows." Stan swatted flies away from the horse's ears.

"So, are you saying this has been happening, building, since April?" Anya asked.

"Wait, what did they say killed LaRange?" Stan asked.

"I don't remember," Anya replied.

"They didn't say," Noble emphasized. "But there are two rumors going around. That Clayton may have been a victim to this same animal, or that he's been kidnapped."

Stan scoffed. "Let me guess who's flaming those rumors."

"Sure, Old Tom talks, but other people came up with the theories," Noble said.

Anya patted her horse's neck, unsettled by the idea that someone or something could have taken the healthy teenage boy without a trace. She couldn't help but feel some understanding for Nettie's vehemence against the Orbriallis Institute, recalling how Nate had also expressed at the beach fire last week that he felt like they all had a right to know what the Institute was getting up to. "Does anyone really think someone took Clayton?"

"No," Stan replied, though she immediately questioned that response. "Not really. Can they?" she asked Noble.

"I don't know. I imagine they're looking at every angle," he replied.

"I don't just mean the cops," Stan said. "I mean, well yeah, but more specifically, *our* cops. Like your dad and Chief Wolfe. Do they think…"

Noble held Stan's gaze for a minute. "You aren't thinking Orbriallis had anything to do with this?"

"LaRange got away during the cleanup," she immediately contended. "Who's to say other…people didn't escape."

Anya felt a chill down her spine so strong it made her visually shudder.

As if the woods themselves had been listening, the wind shifted and the energy around them changed. Noble noticed it first, his attention already snapping to the front of the line, to his little sister. A wind kicked up from the ocean, heavy with salt and a scent that turned the stomach. Branches swayed, and leaves rustled ominously, creating a symphony of eerie whispers that seemed to echo throughout the forest.

"Stay here," Noble instructed and urged his horse forward. His heart raced in his chest as he tried to ignore the uneasy feeling that had taken hold of him. His hands tightened on the reins as a shiver of dread ran down his spine. The horse beneath him snorted and stomped, sensing its rider's fear, but remained steady despite the mounting tension.

"Zo," he called, pushing his horse into a gallop. As he rode the edge of the trail, branches snapped at his legs, arms, and face. He pushed ahead to get to his sister.

Zoe clung tightly to the pommel of her saddle, her knuckles white with tension. Her breath came in short, ragged gasps as she struggled to control the mounting panic that threatened to engulf her. Her eyes darted left and right, taking in the sinister landscape around her. Panic bloomed from the pit of her stomach and pounded into her chest.

"What is that smell?" asked one of the tourists.

"I'm gonna check, give me a moment," Noble replied, pushing on.

Woogie snorted and stomped his feet.

Noble drew up beside his sister and took hold of the pony's reins. "Zo? You okay?" he asked.

Zoe shook her head. "What's happening?" she asked him with a wary voice.

"It's going to be okay, Zo."

Anya and Stan, disobeying the command to stay put, drew up beside them.

The horses stirred uneasily, their ears twitching. A pungent scent—something sharp and rotting—filtered through the air.

"What is that?" Stan murmured, nose wrinkling. She looked up the trail and narrowed her eyes at the sight.

An old tree with twisted limbs leaned dangerously over the trail, its roots barely clinging to the earth, the bark blackened and split. The rot spread like veins through its trunk, and the air around it felt heavy.

The horses whinnied and reared, their hooves striking the ground with a resounding thud. For a moment, it seemed as if they would all be thrown from their saddles.

"Whoa, whoa," Noble hushed the horses, easing them.

Anya stayed with Zoe, reaching down and holding her hand as Zoe did her breathing exercises she'd been taught by Dr. Jane. Sucking breath in through her mouth like she was sipping from a straw. Each breath in on a count to five and out on a count to five. It was merely a distraction, but it worked.

"Alright, everybody, stay calm," Noble called, expertly maneuvering his horse closer. "We're gonna go slow. One at a time."

Noble led each tourist through, guiding their horses by the reins and pointing them down the path to the beach. Once past, the horses seemed eager to move on and clopped onward, wishing to forget the behemoth in their path.

Stan gripped her reins, her pulse spiking as she maneuvered her horse around the tree. She wasn't the only one who felt it—the unnatural stillness, the way the air clung thick around them.

Maybe her uncle was right. Maybe the land remembered and it was best not to tempt the darkness to rear its head.

Retrospective No. 3: ————

C old is wrong. It makes the outside of skin sharp. Makes inside skin squirm. Like when the blue-sleeve nurse poked too far with a needle and made him go stiff and water come from eyes. Like that. Only slower. Not like before. Before was hot. Bright-hot. White on the top of the eyes and the chest thumping hard and big and fast. This cold is sharp. Like a bite.

He is out. He is outside.

That's what They said to him. *"Do you want to go out?"*

"Should we go outside?"

And he said, the big He, in soft words that were not sharp like a bite but soft like a blanket. *"Wouldn't you like that?"*

He did not say yes. But They smiled. They always smiled. White-white teeth and soft sounds. Bright coats. One with a badge. One with a name he almost remembers.

Out is this. This night-wet. This cold. The green-black all around. The underfeet crunch that isn't room-floor. The *outside*.

He likes the bright. But this outside is not bright.

"Sit," They say.

So he does. He folds legs. Back not right. Head too high.

He watches the above. It is full of blink-eyes. Not people eyes. Not soft light. Not light orbs.

Voices near from the They persons talk like gravel.

"It's fucking unsettling the way it doesn't breathe. It has to breathe, right?"

"Yeah, it breathes… It's just quiet about it."

He doesn't know what breathe is. Maybe it is the chest moving. In-out. In-out. He tries but his chest doesn't care to play.

Before, there was the Bright Place.

The clean place.

He was born in it. Maybe.

He woke in it. Definitely.

He woke in the clear box. He remembers the light most. White on top of his face. Warm on bones. Always warm. There were tubes, yes, and pokes, and cold metal, but the air smelled like lemon and water. He had blankets. They tucked him in. They made sounds with soft lips.

He was good there.

This place is not that.

He is not sitting anymore. His legs took him up. He wanders. That's the word one of the They persons said.

"It's wandering again, fuck's sake."

He doesn't know what the word means, but it means someone comes. A hand grabs his skin. Pulls him back. Makes him sit again.

He mimics the grab. Touches the They person's arm.

"No," They say. "Stop." They go back to the other They person. "I hate this."

"Orders are orders."

He knows that sound. He heard it in the Bright Place too.

Orders are orders. Always said before they poked him. Or took blood. Or moved him from one box to another.

He misses the first box. The warm-glass one. This place has no glass. Only cold. And damp that sticks in his joints.

Before, the They people smiled. White teeth, blue gloves. Gentle hands. Blankets.

These They persons don't smile.

They bark. They grunt. They fiddle with the new box. In this cold-dark. In this wide room.

This box is not glass. Not like before.

This one is rough. Dark. It doesn't hum or hiss. It smells like wet and old things. The lid opens with a cough of air. His had air. His glass box. It made a huff sound when They opened it.

Inside the box there is a him-but-not-him.

"Help me with this other one," They say.

The Other One needs help like he needed help. Needs foot movement help. Needs stand up help. But They do not help the Other One. Not like the other They people in the bright place. They helped him.

They don't help the Other One out. They just grab it.

In the glass place, when he lay still, they waited for him. They rubbed his arms. They said soft things like *you're okay, you're safe.*

Now there are only fingers. Tight fingers by the arm fold.

He goes where the hand says.

He tries to grab a shoulder, like they grabbed him. But he's told No. Always No.

He can be grabbed, but he cannot grab.

He walks to the box.

The dark box.

The mildew box. It smells like old things. Not like lemon-wash and clean needles. Not like the warm-bright.

He doesn't like it.

He can't say it. His mouth isn't right for saying yet. Just a hum in his throat that no one listens to.

"What's it doing?"

"Just put it in."

The fingers press again. He is bent, lowered. Set inside.

Flat. Like the Other One. Like before.

He remembers being flat in the glass box. But there was a soft beep there. There was a warm voice counting his fingers.

This place counts nothing. Just cold and splinters.

Then the bite in his leg.

Leg fire. Small sharp. Skin bite.

His eyes flash open wider but he doesn't scream. He doesn't know how.

He thinks maybe when he wakes next, it will be the glass place again. The warm place.

Or maybe…

Maybe there are *more* places.

Places he hasn't seen.

Places not warm or cold, just *other.*

Maybe this is how you go there.

They close the box. It slams.

He doesn't like it. He wants the light. The hot-white when he first was outside.

His leg kicks. Or tries to, but nothing moves.
No move. No feel. No blink.
He does not close his eyes. He cannot. He lies still.
Waits.
Feels the weight start to press down.
No up-down in his chest. No breath.
Only in. And *in* is not where the light lives.

Chapter Twenty
Exhumation

It was early morning, just before the break of dawn. The sounds of birds chirping were interrupted by the sharp metallic sounds of shovels hitting the earth. Four battery-operated LED work lights lit the scene as Seth stood next to Wes, both holding to-go coffee cups, watching on as two gravediggers were in the process of exhuming Raymond LaRange's body. An environmental health officer and archaeological supervisor stood opposite them next to Glen Larson, the cemetery manager, clipboards in hand, ensuring the exhumation was being done safely, respectfully, and technically correct. The grave was in the furthest corner of Lost Grove's historic cemetery, marked only with a small concrete slab the size of a paperback book with the number 416 etched into it.

Just a day and a half removed from the town hall meeting, Seth was still stunned to be gathered here so soon. The only case Seth had been involved with in San Francisco where an exhumation had been required, the court order and permit had taken six weeks. Glen Waters, the district attorney of Laresa County, was clearly concerned enough by the recent mauling of a child and another child gone missing to have pushed things through, calling Seth on Sunday to issue the go-ahead. Glen had already called the cemetery manager, ordering him to get things in order for the following morning. He told Seth they couldn't afford to have another fatality, and if the same animal was responsible for both Raymond LaRange's and Kevin Marlow's deaths, they needed to track it and kill it immediately. Seth respectfully informed him that, depending on what animal it was, euthanasia might not be an option, but the point had been made.

Working around the clock the past week, searching Devil's Cradle State Park, the Cursed Woods, and the greater redwood forest for any sign of Clayton Meadows, left little time for Seth to do anything but sleep. The sparse bouts of time he did have were spent with Story, continuing to work through their first real bump in the road as a couple. It was impossible for Seth to remain upset with Story for more than a day after she metaphorically punched him in the gut with her admission of what she had seen and heard regarding Mary Germaine's affliction, a word he still found unsuitable for the things she'd done and what apparently happened to her body. Putting himself in Story's shoes, he understood the position she was in, understood her devotion to her friend.

Seth believed Story when she promised him that she would never keep anything from him again, and maybe more importantly, he believed Mary when he went to see her the following day to inquire as to her whereabouts the night Kevin Marlow was killed. She had been visibly surprised to see him on her doorstep. He hadn't gone to see her by himself since the night she showed up at Story's house covered in blood. He had only seen her once since the day he and Story went to have an intervention with her, telling her she absolutely must go seek help with Dr. Bajorek. Seth had told her the results of the autopsy on Raymond LaRange, that a grey wolf had been the culprit of the attack, to which she responded only with a mix of facial contortions, ranging from offense, to confusion, to a sad acceptance.

Now, Seth stood here, with roughly a foot more dirt to be dug out, waiting for LaRange's body to be exhumed, beset with the brutal truth that it likely had been Mary Germaine, not a grey wolf, responsible for putting him here. He could, of course, lean into Wes's autopsy results in that LaRange was already on death's doorstep. But the fact remained that a death blow had been struck, regardless of the fact that he could have been only twelve hours away from starvation. The only solace in Seth's soul at the moment was that he was certain that whatever human DNA might be pulled from LaRange's corpse, it would not match the DNA results from Kevin Marlow's body.

"Have you found anything yet to back up the notion that Clayton may have gone missing due to hallucinations brought on from the glyphs?"

Seth shook his head. "We collected samples of the fungus found in the glyph by where we found his phone, but they won't be evaluated until later today when Story and your brother meet up with Dr. Elias. But even if he determines that there are hallucinogenic compounds within, that proves nothing. And furthermore, even if it somehow proves that he was infected by these compounds, he's still missing. It doesn't help our search one bit."

"Other than to stay away from glyphs," Wes offered.

Seth laughed. "True enough. Have you come across any cases where you found hallucinogenic compounds in a body?"

Wes raised an eye at Seth. "You are aware that I wasn't stationed in San Francisco with you where I would have been supplied with numerous bodies a day?"

Seth moaned. "I forget that fact often with everyone. So, that's a no?"

"That's a no. Though I am wildly curious to what the effects of inhaling these spores would do."

It was Seth's turn to raise an eyebrow. "You in the mood to experiment?"

Wes grinned. "I would wait for Dr. Elias to analyze the fungus first, but I wouldn't be opposed to it."

"Wes Hensley," Seth said, impressed. "I'm learning new things about you every day."

"I'm not saying I would go into the Cursed Woods to partake, mind you. In the comfort of my basement or backyard."

"I'll see what I can do."

Wes looked at Seth, registering his wry grin, and laughed.

"I hope you and your brother have put a tracking device on Stan. I don't like that her and that renegade group of her friends are poking around asking questions. The last time—"

"You don't need to tell me. The message has been made crystal clear, believe me."

"Good." Seth still planned on checking in on the overly curious group of recent graduates and putting his own two cents in the mix.

"Ancient glyphs. Alluring and horrifying," Wes pondered.

Seth finished off the rest of his coffee and set the cup on the ground behind him. "I don't know what's more disturbing, strange and dangerous glyphs, or digging this fucking guy up."

"Bodies don't frighten me."

"No, I imagine not. I'll make rounds today to talk to all the kids and nail home the point."

Wes patted Seth on the back. "I'd appreciate that."

A loud thud announced contact had been made with LaRange's coffin.

Seth stepped forward and peered down into the grave.

One of the two gravediggers, both clad in white coveralls, hoodies tied tight, rubber boots and gloves, and face masks, looked up, pulling his mask down to speak. "You mind throwing down the ropes and chains?"

Seth and Wes carefully lowered down the length of chain and rope and then stepped back toward the replacement coffin, which they would use to transport the remains back to Wes's offices. Wes explained that he could potentially get the samples he needed there at the gravesite but wanted to reexamine the body in a controlled environment.

Once the gravediggers exited the grave, having prepped the coffin for removal, Seth and Wes assisted them in pulling it up and out. They put on their latex gloves while each gravedigger brought it closer to the replacement coffin and pried it open. The body Seth had exhumed in San Francisco had been underground for two years in a pricey airtight titanium casket, so the decomposition was on the slower end, the body in decent condition. LaRange was in an admittedly cheaper coffin, probably the cheapest. The city wasn't going to put up any more money than necessary for an unclaimed body of a child sex offender, but it had only been two months, so he wasn't expecting the body to be in too poor of condition.

"Okay, ready to remove," said one of the gravediggers, prying gloved fingers under the lid.

Seth stepped to the head of the coffin, Wes doing the same on the foot end.

The gravedigger flipped the lid open and fell on his ass, instantly recoiling, covering his mouth. "What the fuck!" he exclaimed, crab-walking backward. The other gravedigger turned away and vomited on the ground.

"Holy Christ!" Seth blurted out, covering his mouth in an attempt to block out the vile stench, eyes wide in horror. Shivers ravaged his body.

"What in God's name?" Wes uttered, staring in disbelief at what lay in the coffin.

Glen Larson approached and looked on with a grim, unnerving curiosity.

The health officer and archaeological supervisor stepped up to see and promptly backpedaled, expressing their disbelief in expletives and holy words.

Seth couldn't process what he was seeing. The most alarming part wasn't the fact that the naked body was clearly not Raymon LaRange, the skin darker, the frame longer and larger. It was the concaved forehead and pools of dried blood and brain matter that had seeped out of the ears. It was the entire right side of the torso that looked as if it had deflated, the bones of the rib cage missing, as if they had turned into dust. It was the left leg that had lost all human form, as if every bone from the fibula to the big toe had been removed, leaving a flat mound of flesh filled with putrefied muscle. The state of the body was so foreign that it was like being at the most disturbed and sadistic wax museum imaginable. But there was no mistaking that this was a human body.

"Seth," Wes said, grabbing his attention.

Seth tore his eyes away from the unholy sight. "What is this?"

"I don't know. But that sure as hell isn't LaRange."

"I can assure you the proper body was buried. And clothed," said Glen Larson.

Seth looked at the man, attempting to gauge the truthfulness in his eyes. He appeared sincere. Shocked. Also morbidly curious as to the unholy state of the body before them. "How long after the body was buried before anyone attended to it? Or placed this marker here?"

Glen looked back at Seth before his gaze periodically returned to the body. "We typically wait six months before placing gravestones on plots. But considering it was just a state marker the size of a brick, we placed that in just two weeks ago. Regarding the grave site itself, we do daily walkthroughs to assure nothing is disrupted."

"I'd like to think you would have noticed if someone dug up this casket and swapped bodies."

"After the earth settles, sure. But if it were done while the plot was still fresh, and done carefully, it's possible it could have gone unnoticed."

"Well, clearly it did." Seth looked over at Wes, who was glaring at the body with grim curiosity. "Is there any medical explanation for this? Putting aside the fact that it's not LaRange."

Wes shook his head. "I've been running through scenarios in my head, but nothing that makes sense so far. Aside from a very bizarre and violent murder. But even then…"

Seth ran his hand through his hair, glancing back at the body. Who would have wanted Raymond LaRange's body? His first thought was the

Orbriallis Institute. But only if Dr. Owens was still in charge. Having thoroughly questioned Dr. Bajorek and Lina Orbriallis after The Event last fall, Seth was certain that neither of them had any knowledge of LaRange living at the institute. Jane had only seen a confidential file with his name on it, but had no context. No one knew the whereabouts of Dr. Neil Owens. It was possible that he was somehow connected to this. Perhaps the bigger question was, who was now in this wooden casket?

"Here," Wes said, already moving to the coffin. "Help me get the lid back on. We can't transfer this body."

Seth tried to shake the shivers out of his body and bent down to grab the front end of the lid, as Wes walked down to grab the bottom end. They set it back on top, uneven and wobbly from the bent nails. Seth turned around and grabbed the loose rope lying next to the grave. "Let's just tie it shut."

"Here, I can help," said the gravedigger who hadn't vomited.

Seth handed him one end of the rope as they began the process of getting this casket and the remains over to Wes's coroner's office.

Chapter Twenty-One
The Stillborn Orchard

The morning was a rare one—quiet, almost forgiving. The dew still clung to the meadow grass, and mist threaded through the trees like breath not quite taken. Peter Andalusian walked beside his son up the winding trail that sloped away from Ross Ranch, carrying a chainsaw slung across one shoulder. Noble walked ahead, glancing back now and then, the ever-present rope coil on his hip bouncing against his thigh.

"You know, you didn't have to come. I could've handled this," Noble offered with a sideways grin.

Peter smirked. "That's what I said to your mom when she dragged me out of bed this morning."

Noble laughed, and the clear, boyish sound drifted into the trees like birdsong.

"Even though I've spent the past three days out in the woods looking for Clayton, this is far more relaxing. Plus, I've got to soak up as much time as I can with you before you're off to Tennessee."

Noble felt a tightening of his heart. It took a couple months to fully process and get over what his dad had done in all the events surrounding the Orbriallis Institute. But they had bonded more over the past few months than ever before. He was going to miss his dad. He was going to miss everyone.

"Did you know him? Clayton."

Noble looked back over his shoulder. "I didn't know him, know him. But I've seen him play some games for the Lasers. Has a hell of a swing. What do you think happened to him?"

Peter picked up the pace to pull up next to his son. "I think he simply got lost. Talking with his friends and parents, he didn't have a lot of experience trekking through the woods, no experience traversing the caves. His best friend, Jasper, said they had taken the same shortcut to the gully a handful of times, but never at night."

"But it's been over three days now. Wouldn't he have found his way out by now?"

"The entirety of the redwood forest is over a hundred thousand acres, Noble. Over forty miles long. Once your internal compass gets thrown off, you become disoriented, confused. Most panic, which only worsens the situation. People get lost all the time in forests. Forest much smaller than the redwoods."

"Which is why you've always told me to stay close enough where I can see the ocean or landmarks."

"That's right." Peter wrapped his arm around Noble's shoulders. "And you've got the experience. You also inherited your dad's elite internal compass."

Noble laughed. "Real modest, Dad."

"Hey, you don't end up as a lead tracker in Special Ops if it isn't in your blood."

Noble spotted the ancient tree hanging over the trail, just coming into view. "Do you think you'll find him?"

"I hope so. The thing that worries me the most is the fact that we haven't found a trail, which really opens up the search area. The good news is that we've got a number of Search and Rescue groups joining the search today. We've got to find him before he goes too long without food and water."

"Can I help?"

Peter looked at him. "You're old enough to make your own decisions. All volunteers are welcome."

Noble smiled. "You think Mom would be mad?"

"I think she would feel better if you were with me, but she would be proud."

"Cool. I'll join you after we clear this," Noble said as they approached the crooked tree.

Peter examined the tree, the dead limbs, the exposed roots barely hanging on to the earth. The bark near its base was bloated, weeping sap like a wound that wouldn't close.

"It's worse," Noble murmured.

"Since yesterday?"

"Yeah."

"And it wasn't this bad? What about before then? The tour before?" Peter asked.

Noble had been wondering the same thing. He had been down this trail more times than he could count, and the tree had never stood out to him before. It was like a giant had come through the trail at night and pulled the tree down, tearing its roots from the ground. "Not so much that I noticed. The horses got spooked when the wind hit it." He tapped it with his boot. "Dry rot?"

"Not sure," Peter said, setting the chainsaw down. The tree looked odd, and the smell was more like ammonia than the subtle rot of wood. "Are you ready for Tennessee?" he asked as he prepped the saw.

Noble hesitated. "Yeah. Nervous-excited, I guess."

"Are your grandparents ready?"

"Yeah," Noble said with a smile. "They've already cleared the room over the garage."

Peter chuckled. "You'll be the best set-up kid there. That 'room' is bigger than any room on campus and probably most apartments in the area."

Noble nodded, smiling.

"Enrollment's not till August, right?"

"Yeah, the eighteenth."

"Have you narrowed down the courses yet?" Peter asked, lifting the saw and pressing the primer.

"Think so. Intro to Animal Biology, Chemistry, Equine Science… general ed stuff. Trying to get a work-study at the ranch, working for Grandpa."

Peter raised an eyebrow, nodding with the pride he never quite said aloud. "And Anya?" he asked.

That earned a pause. Noble bent to inspect the base of the tree, his back turned. "She's…"

"Are you guys good?"

"Yeah, we're great." Noble couldn't help but smile.

"And you guys are gonna do the long-distance thing?"

"Yeah," Noble said instantly. He couldn't imagine not staying with Anya.

Peter held up his free hand. "Okay. I didn't mean anything by it."

"No, yeah…sorry. It's not that. She's just been…"

Peter paused, waiting for his son to continue. "What?"

"Her mom's been acting weird lately," he admitted. "Like zoning out as she stares out the window, and she sleepwalked the other night. Anya's really concerned about her."

Peter glanced over at Noble. "Sleepwalking, huh? Has she ever done that before?"

Noble shook his head. "Not that Anya's known about."

"I can't say I know a lot about that," Peter said, fussing with the chainsaw. "Might want to ask Seth. He was a psychology major."

"Really? Did he like, double major or something?"

"He did. The man is very intuitive. He can see through bullshit from a mile away." Peter grabbed the starter handle and was about to pull it when Noble interrupted.

"Hey, do you or Paddy know anything about markings in the woods? Or in the park?"

Peter was wondering when this would come up. Leith talked to Story, Anya talked to Stan. He was sure the entire group of his son's friends knew about them. Worse yet, they were curious. "Noble, look at me."

Noble looked up at his dad. "What?"

"We're well aware of the glyphs. We've already been out looking for them. There might be something wrong with them."

Noble's brow furrowed. "Wrong?"

Peter sighed. "I'm telling you this as your father, and I'm warning you as a sergeant of the police department. We believe there might be fungus in them that causes hallucinations."

"What the fuck?"

"We found one by where Clayton went missing. We're getting some of the samples tested later today. This needs to stay between you and me. And I mean really between us. No girlfriend, no Stan—"

"Does Nate know? If he does—"

Peter raised his hand. "He does. He's out searching for Clayton. But he's not going to talk. I don't know if you've noticed, but Nate is taking this opportunity seriously."

"I have," Noble admitted. "I have to tell Anya though, Dad."

"Just tell her, and all your friends, to stay the hell out of the woods. Tell them it's not safe."

Noble nodded. "Okay. What about Anya's mom? Do you think—"

Peter opened his mouth to respond, but the wind shifted, and the smell hit them.

A rank, sweet-sour musk worse than rot. It was the scent of something pretending not to rot, like plastic melting in a microwave filled with spoiled meat.

Noble took a step back, his face twisting. "God, that's new."

Peter moved toward the base of the tree. "Probably a dead raccoon inside. Hollow trees do that."

They began cutting, leaving the conversation of glyphs behind. First, the limbs snapped under the chainsaw's bite. Then, the trunk, the center oozing sap the color of old nicotine.

Peter worked methodically down the trunk as Noble hauled the wood away. His hand jolted. The sound of a crack drew his attention. It wasn't the clean crack of splintering wood but a wet one. Muffled and sickly.

The tree's top tipped forward, then twisted, spilling something from its center. A tangle of limbs, cloth, flesh. Bodies. Not one but six or eight. They tumbled out like dolls knocked from a shelf, limbs flopping too loosely, one head hitting a root with a soft, hollow thunk. Their skin shimmered pale under the canopy, translucent and stretched with dark smudges beneath the surface like bruises never earned. One arm bent the wrong way, boneless. One face bore no eyes at all, just collapsed sockets like thumb-pressed clay. Mouths hung slack with jaws too thin and small. Skulls hairless, save a few feeble wisps. Some had teeth, some didn't, and all of them smelled wrong.

Peter stood frozen. The chainsaw idled at his feet, forgotten.

Noble stared, his breath short, his hands twitching at his sides. He started feeling lightheaded as the stench made its way into the base of his chest, causing him to bend over and begin to wretch.

Peter quickly snapped out of his brief befuddlement and ran to his son, placing a hand on his back. "It's okay, get it out."

Noble spat bile onto the trail ground, tears filling his eyes, images of what he had just seen playing back like a mind-control torture video on the back of his eyes.

Peter spun Noble away from the tree and walked him over to a fallen log. He guided him to face away from the horrifying scene behind them and sat him down. Peter squatted down. "Hey, look at me. I need you to take a slow breath in. Purse your lips and inhale on a five count with me. One, two, three, four, five. Good."

Noble exhaled just as slowly, his eyes darting around as his mind processed what this was. "Not-children," he whispered.

Peter narrowed his eyes. "What did you say?"

Noble looked at him, eyes wide. "Not-children," he repeated, a little firmer now.

Peter stared at his son for a long moment. The forest buzzed with quiet. "Not-children?"

Noble nodded.

Peter exhaled, sharp and short. "Okay, Noble? I need you to stay here while I check the area and examine the rest of the tree."

Noble looked down to the ground, trying to focus on dirt, weeds, anything tangible. "Can't you wait for Seth to get here? You should call Seth?"

Peter squeezed his son's shoulder, knowing he was in shock. Understandably so. He needed to get a closer look at the bodies, but at first glance, there was something very wrong with them. They didn't feel right. "This is my job now, Noble. I need to make sure there's no one else out here, check all the bodies, then I'll call Seth. Can you stay here for me?"

Noble nodded.

"If you start feeling lightheaded, put your head between your legs. Okay?"

"Okay. Yeah."

Peter patted him on the back, got to his feet, and began to canvass the area. He hadn't heard signs of other people since they were out here, but he also had a chainsaw running half the time. He quickly made his way back to the bodies to make sure there wasn't anyone still alive. He looked down upon what his eyes had already seen: a pile of bloodstained limbs, some boneless, and bodies at varying stages of decay, some of the skin spotted with dark welts, and some of the skin was simply not right. It looked like bodies or limbs wrapped in rice paper. The features on the faces were no less disturbing. Mouths much too small, inverted noses, missing eyes, sealed eyes. What was this? Noble said "non-children." Had he heard him mention this before?

There was no mistaking one very important thing. There was no life left in any of the bodies. Whatever they were.

After Peter felt secure that the surrounding area was safe and free from any other bodies or potential evidence, he checked on Noble and then returned to the twisted tree. This wouldn't be enjoyable, but he needed to clear out whatever else was left inside the hollowed-out area. He took off his T-shirt and tied it around his face to block out as much of the rancid odor as possible. He then put on his work gloves and reached inside the cavity of the tree, and began to pull out the rest of the limbs and bodies.

Thankfully, the majority of the contents had already spilled out, but holding the limbs in his hands confirmed how wrong this all was. He pulled out an arm, which had coagulated at the shoulder, and it felt like holding on to a tube-shaped waterbed. There were no bones, not even in the hand. The other two intact bodies felt like he was pulling out vile, deprived, and insanely expensive sex toys, made to look and feel like the real thing, but most decidedly not.

Peter finished emptying out the hollow and arranging the bodies and limbs as best he could. He pulled off his blood and substance-covered gloves and pulled out his phone to call Seth.

Seth crested over a dune at the south end of Mourner's Beach and spotted Peter and Noble standing by the shore, staring out into the ocean in conversation. Seth looked over his shoulder. "They're right over there," he said, pointing.

Wes, a few strides behind Seth, hoisted his crime scene bag over his shoulder. "Would be nice if we had a four-wheeler."

"It's already been a long day, and it's not even close to noon."

"Long and completely fucked."

"And somehow that's an understatement," Seth said, heading toward the Andalusian men. Once they got back to Wes's autopsy room, Wes and two of his assistants did their best to keep the body intact as they transferred it from the broken casket to the operating table. The preceding two hours transformed into the most bizarre and surreal autopsy of all time. Seth couldn't fathom there was another autopsy on record where the body was determined, rather quickly, to be—not human.

"So, you said what Peter told you was vague? But he estimated, what, eight bodies?" Wes asked.

"Yeah, and that they had fallen out of a tree trunk that had decayed and fallen over a trail. He said it was impossible to describe what he was seeing, and it would be better for us to just come out and see it for ourselves."

Wes shook his head and let out a long sigh. "Are we actually in a nightmare right now? Like, a shared, completely insane nightmare?"

Seth couldn't argue he'd wished for it to be. "I've been hoping the same thing."

"Seth. Wes," Peter said, greeting the men as they approached. "Think we're going to need to increase our staff if things continue at this rate."

"It's crossed my mind no less than thirty-five times this past week," Seth admitted. "Noble, you doing okay?"

Noble nodded. "Yeah, I'm okay. I think I would be more messed up if they were real kids."

Seth and Wes exchanged an incredulous look.

"What is it?" Peter asked.

Seth ignored the question. "What do you mean, Noble?"

"The bodies. They're not-children. Like not-George."

Seth cocked his head to the side, processing the connection between the body they uncovered in Raymond LaRange's grave and the kid Noble and his friends always referred to as not-George. Is that what not-George was? Last year, the night before The Event when everyone was gathered at Story's, Nate told Seth the story about how the Green Man had taken little George Horne when he was a child and replaced him with an identical child and only Nettie knew. No one believed her. Nate told him about how the Green Man traveled around with his not-children and that they weren't real, but Seth processed it as hyperbole. It never occurred to him that they might actually be whatever it was that he and Wes had just been performing an autopsy on.

Seth ran both hands through his hair. If that's what not-George was, he was now in the hands of the Orbriallis Institute and Dr. Jane Bajorek. Was she aware of the not-children? Was she a part of their unholy creation? Or was it something Dr. Owens kept under the radar with his close circle of doctors who disappeared after The Event? Either way, she had to be aware of it now, wouldn't she?

"What is it?" Noble asked.

Seth shook his head. "Nothing. How far away are the bodies?"

Peter turned and pointed to the rocky incline leading up to the woods. "Ten-minute walk, most of which is getting up that."

Seth gauged the terrain and looked back at Wes. "That's going to be a challenge."

"My team's not going to be able to get our van up there to load the bodies."

"They're going to get their exercise then."

"How far off are they?" Peter asked.

"Probably fifteen, twenty minutes," Wes said. "They had to get the bigger van and load up enough supplies to accommodate the number of bodies."

Peter placed a hand on Noble's shoulder. "You want to wait here for Wes's team and lead them up, while I take these guys up now?"

Noble nodded with some eagerness, clearly okay staying away from the bodies. "For sure."

Peter was relieved that Noble had pulled out of his earlier shock. "Go get the horses if it looks like it will help."

"Will do, Dad."

Peter led Seth and Wes up the hill and waited at the top for them to catch up. "You guys want to tell me what that look was about? Have you come across these not-children before or something?"

"Not children…" Wes cryptically answered.

Seth wiped his forehead with his forearm, the sun beating down on them. "If you had asked us this last night, I'm sure we both would have looked as perplexed as you might have anticipated."

"So, what the hell?" Peter asked, continuing forward toward the pile of bodies awaiting them. "Does this have something to do with LaRange's exhumation?"

"I'm afraid so," Seth said. "I didn't want to say anything in front of Noble, but LaRange's body wasn't in the coffin."

"What?" Peter asked, his eyes wide in disbelief.

"Our best assumption at this point is that someone dug up the grave—"

"Someone?" Peter exclaimed. "The Orbriallis. No one else knew about him."

Seth shrugged. "Whoever it was, dug up the grave, I'm guessing it was within days of the burial, and swapped out the bodies."

"With who?"

"That's the thing," Wes interjected. "It's not a *who* but a *what*."

Seth continued, "I'm guessing it might be something similar to what we're approaching, but ours was a fully formed, so to speak, adult."

The trio continued on in silence for a brief spell before something occurred to Peter. "Does this all tie back to George Horne and the… not-George thing?"

"The thought hadn't crossed my mind until Noble mentioned it down there, but I'm starting to think that it does," Seth admitted.

"But not-George was a real boy, wasn't he?"

"Real enough to fool his parents for years."

Wes looked over at Seth. "I've always wondered what that was. It was very difficult to understand when you first told me."

"Well, I didn't know everything that we've learned today."

"Not sure how much we've actually learned yet."

"Not sure how much we'll be able to learn," Seth said, frustration leaking into his voice. A trip back to the Orbriallis was at the forefront in his mind. He just needed to remind himself that Clayton Meadows was still missing. He couldn't let this mess of inhuman bodies take priority over finding the missing teen.

"What did your body look like?" Peter asked Wes. "Did you get a chance to examine it?"

"There were certain parts of the body where the insides just disintegrated, or liquified," Wes said. "An entire leg, the right chest cavity, the brain and top of the skull. Somehow most disturbingly to me were the fingerprints. They were, I'd estimate, twenty-five percent there."

Peter shook his head. "I didn't think to look for fingerprints, but the rest of what you described sounds like what we're coming up to. What the hell is happening?"

"We don't fully know yet," Seth said. "But, as insane as whatever this morning has brought us, we have to remember there's a missing child out there we need to focus on. I can't see there being any connection between the two. At least not at the moment."

"Jesus," Wes uttered, spotting the line of children's bodies and limbs ahead of them.

All three men cautiously approached the scene, careful not to disrupt anything.

"What in God's name?" Wes said, covering his mouth, getting a close look at the bodies. There were immediate similarities with the unidentified body back in his autopsy room—the same translucent bluish skin, epidermal thinning, deflated limbs.

Seth looked from the bodies over to the fallen tree. "And why the hell were they stuffed into a tree?"

Peter grunted. "I think I was too absorbed with dealing with the bodies and limbs to even bring up that very logical question in my head."

Seth looked back to the bodies. "How would anyone process this falling out of a hollowed-out tree?"

"How do we process any of this?" Wes asked.

Seth coughed, the familiar and vile scent seeping into his nostrils. "Smells the same," Seth said, staring on in repulsion. "It's crazy. In one aspect, they look so human. So real."

"Yet the eyes, the limbs," Wes replied, crouching down to get a closer look.

"The lack of eyes. Looks like those ones are melted shut," Seth said, pointing.

"That semi-translucent skin."

"I've stood in front of more than one pile of bodies," Peter said, bringing an instant graveness to the air. "They don't feel like this. There's no sense of humanity here. No essence of loss. It doesn't yank out part of your soul just staring at it."

Wes nodded. "I haven't seen the horrors that you have, Peter. But I've seen death. And you're right, this isn't it."

"Agreed," Seth said. "I've been at enough murder scenes over the years to grow what feels like an immunity to it. But seeing this, seeing that…man, earlier today, it reminds you there's something missing. You talked of soul, Peter. Maybe that's it."

"How do we even report this?" Peter asked. "Like, where's the paperwork for this?"

Seth shook his head. "There's certainly no guide for anything like this. I think we just approach this as we would any other death scene, any other autopsy, and then we see where we're at. I'll have to assume at this point that there won't be any records of the man-thing back at Wes's autopsy room or any of these…not-children on file anywhere."

Peter looked up at Wes. "Did you get a chance to open up your guy yet? See what's inside?"

Wes nodded. "Enough to find a liver and kidneys that look, on the surface, normal. There was a heart, but it was undersized, fibrous, with no chambers. Would appear to operate more like a pressure pump than a true muscular organ."

Peter looked from Wes to Seth. "You know this has Dr. Owens written all over it."

"I agree that would be the most prudent place to start," Seth said and looked back at the bodies. "But to what end? We have no clue where he is. And what's the purpose of this? Everything associated with

Sarah Elizabeth, Kelly Fulson, it all revolved around human childbirth. Augmented or altered, but not this."

Peter stared at the scene, not even sure where to begin that trail of thought. A sound down the trail grabbed his attention. "Looks like your team got here sooner than you thought, Wes."

Seth glanced over his shoulder to see Noble, followed by Wes's team, who were lugging a stack of stretchers.

Wes stood back to his feet. "We can take it from here, Seth. Get back out there and find Clayton."

"We will. But, Wes, I think the most important thing here is to try to ascertain a timeline. I don't even know how you would do that, but we really need to know how long these...bodies have been in this tree. We know the LaRange swap-out had to have happened in the last two months, but these..."

Wes raised his eyebrows. "Believe it or not, we didn't cover this in college."

"Funny." Seth nodded at Peter. "I know you haven't had much sleep, but are—"

"You think I'm taking a nap while Clayton is still out there?"

"Nope. Just testing you."

Peter grinned. "Noble's going to join us."

"Great. Let's grab him and go meet the team."

Chapter Twenty-Two
Unfinished Stories

Monday dawned pale and cool. The trailhead sat at the end of an old, rutted road, where cracked asphalt surrendered to gravel, and gravel surrendered to earth. Mist coiled like slow smoke through the undergrowth, threading itself among the damp skeletons of ferns and the leaning ghosts of fallen trees. Morning light pressed against the canopy but could not pierce it—only fractured into strange prisms that clung to the mossy boles of ancient redwoods.

It smelled of wet bark, churned soil, and the breath of trees older than memory.

Story stood near the weathered trail marker, jacket zipped tight against the early cold, her hands stuffed into her pockets. Beside her, Mary shifted her weight from foot to foot, arms crossed.

Cal leaned against his truck, impassive, his gaze roving the tree line, cataloging every sound. The last time he walked this trail was during the frantic search for Hannah. He hadn't been back since and he hadn't planned on it until Story approached him. He was not about to let her, Mary, and an out-of-town professor follow Hannah's final path on their own. And the outside chance that they might uncover some clues as to her disappearance gave him a sliver of hope.

The crunch of tires on gravel announced the arrival of Dr. Elias Raines.

His vehicle was modest—an older Subaru thick with dust. Elias stepped out with the unhurried economy of a man built for long roads and longer silences. He was broad-shouldered and rangy, skin sun-browned and lined from years outdoors, his dark hair, pulled back into a ponytail, was salted with grey. His clothes were field-worn: canvas jacket, heavy boots. His eyes, dark and steady, missed nothing.

He didn't rush to close the distance between them. He simply stood for a moment, breathing in the air, as if greeting the land itself before turning to the small gathering.

"Story Palmer?" he said, voice low and gravelly.

"Dr. Raines," she greeted, stepping forward and offering her hand. "Thank you for coming."

"Elias," he corrected with a small smile, clasping her hand in a firm but not aggressive shake. He turned to the others.

"This is Mary Germaine," Story said. "And Cal Hensley."

Mary offered a shy, brief wave.

Cal stepped forward to shake his hand.

"You're with the department of wildlife?" Elias asked.

"I was. I work as a tribal officer now," Cal responded.

"Oh, change of pace?"

"Something like that," Cal acknowledged.

"Well, it's good to meet you," Elias said. He meant it. His presence was not performative; he simply settled into the space as if he belonged to it. He reached into the back seat of his car and removed a battered pack. "I brought the map I built based on Hannah's field notes."

They unrolled it on the hood of his car. They all leaned in to get a look.

Elias pointed to two places, marking them with a capped pen. "Here's the Bury farm—where the new glyph was found. And here"—he tapped again—"is the area Hannah catalogued most of her later observations." The two locations were on opposite sides of the park.

Cal nodded slowly. "Yeah. That's the area she began focusing on."

Elias pulled out her field book and laid it flat next to the map. "Here are her notes. I think the first glyph she marked as the 'entrance' to the path is here," he said, pointing to the map. "Does that look right?"

Cal studied the notebook, her handwriting, a looping scrawl he could still see in his dreams. For a heartbeat, it felt like she was just out of sight, about to step from the trees with a crooked grin and some clever quip. The illusion twisted something sharp inside him. "Yeah, it's not too far up that trail there," he said, pointing.

"Then it continues, you can see." Elias ran his finger along the map, an imaginary hand drawing Hannah's path based on her notations of latitude and longitude. "By her notations, she walked along here, down to follow Semper Creek for a while, before turning back in, up to the Caldorn tree."

"Yeah, that's where we found her tracks stopped, her pack…" Cal trailed off.

Elias took a beat. "What is the Caldorn tree?"

"Local legend, named after a man, Jacob Caldorn. He built his cabin in front of that tree three times. It was ruined by natural disasters, and each time he rebuilt it in the same damn spot. In 1854 he disappeared, and so did his house. Only thing left is that tree," Cal explained.

"That's eerie," Story said. "I've never heard that legend."

Cal smiled. "It's not a common one and some say it's not even true."

"I love a good yarn," Elias said with a smile. "But it has nothing to do with Native legends?"

"No," Cal responded. "It doesn't hold any significance to her research, if that's what you're asking."

"Precisely what I was trying to discern. Thank you." Elias returned to the map. "How long do you suspect this will take? Can we look at this whole path in a day or…?"

"We should be able to cover it today, saving any unforeseen issues." Cal pulled out his old CDFW hat where he'd tucked it in his back pocket and pushed it on. "You need to grab anything else? Ladies?"

"All good," Story said.

Mary nodded.

Elias folded the map and put his pack back on. "Let's go."

They set off through a dense trail network, Cal leading. The forest began to lift with the rising sun, sending spears of light through the redwoods. Everything felt half awake, holding its breath. Mary moved like she belonged to the woods, barely disturbing a branch. Elias kept glancing at his map and journal, comparing tree formations and topography.

The forest swallowed them. Each footfall was muffled, absorbed by a bed of needles and the behemoths that towered into the sky, enveloping sound, emitting some of the freshest, coolest air on the planet. Story, dressed in gothic military pants and an old cropped T-shirt with black hiking boots, reveled in the majesty of the ancient conifers and the blessedly cool air. It wasn't a bad way to spend a Monday morning in the summer, avoiding the glaring sun.

Elias moved with quiet reverence, pausing often to listen and watch. He pointed once to a set of barely perceptible pictographs on a rockface, almost lost beneath lichen.

"Age is hard to judge out here," he murmured. "But Hannah believed the older pictures and glyphs—like the ones near the Caldorn tree—have been here for centuries." He shook his head. "They're something else."

Story glanced at Mary, who was tense, alert. Cal had fallen behind them, ever watchful. He squinted at the barely visible pictograph as the others moved on. Hannah had been onto something, but her curiosity, her gluttonous cravings for knowledge and acknowledgment, got her in trouble.

Mary stiffened as they continued, and Story took that as a sign they were nearing the first of the glyphs marked in Hannah's notes.

They came upon it as any hiker might, only they were looking for it. It was carved into a massive cedar, so old its bark was armor-thick. The glyph shimmered with a faint golden light that was hard to distinguish from the dappling sunlight. It outlined a strange symbol like a claw intersecting a circle. The fungus within the wound glowed not with simple luminescence but with a living pulse, like the slow throb of a deep-sea creature.

Without a word, Mary knelt beside a small rock—a smooth, rounded pebble warm to the touch—and placed it on her tongue. Story, startled, moved subtly to block her from view. Neither man had noticed.

Elias unslung his pack and set it down. He removed latex gloves and a mask. "Want one?" he asked his companions, holding the masks out.

Story took two and handed one to Mary.

"I'm not getting close to that thing, Story," Mary said in confidence. "And neither are you."

"Alright. Just hold on to it," Story said. She squeezed Mary's shoulder and ran her hand down her arm in a soothing gesture.

Cal took one and approached it with Elias. If Truth be told, it wasn't visible unless you knew what you were looking for. This one was different from the one Constance showed him. It was more overgrown. It blended in. That sent a shiver into his core. He'd never seen anything like it—not in his childhood hikes or years in uniform. But Hannah had. And whatever she'd found here, it had taken her. That realization gnawed at him. He was supposed to protect this place...and her.

Elias exhaled through his mask, awe bleeding into wariness.

"Gorgeous," he whispered.

He set to work, unrolling a sterile swab kit, scraping fungal tissue into vials. He murmured notes into his recorder: "Distinct bioluminescence. No adjacent fungal growth on neighboring bark. Fungus adheres exclusively to the glyph wound."

As he worked, Mary stood stiffly nearby. Her stiffness turned to pacing. Story caught her rubbing her palms down the sides of her leggings, the sound of the rock in her mouth clicking with a feverish pace.

She went over to her. "You alright?" Story murmured.

"Feels like we're standing in a mouth about to close," Mary muttered back.

Elias straightened, glancing at them. "It's natural," he said. "Old places don't always like to be touched."

Cal grunted. "Some things aren't meant to be touched at all." He watched Mary shift from one foot to the other and noted the way Story took her hands and brushed the palms. It was hidden from view, but he swore he saw her drawing something there, a hush falling from her lips in a foreign language.

Elias flicked through the pages of Hannah's notebook. "This matches Hannah's description of the 'Cross-Claw.'" He held up a page from her field guide and handed it to Cal.

He read the entry:

"The Cross-Claw equals Sanctuary.

Description: *Difficult to spot at first glance.*

Fungal Pattern: *Radiant, golden glow. Almost warm to the touch.*

Notes: *Sat within this grove for an hour. Unbothered by insects. A hummingbird landed on my pack.*"

"It's no sanctuary," Mary whispered.

Cal closed the notebook, his gaze flicking toward Mary.

"I've got what I need here," Elias assured them, not hearing Mary's words.

They pressed on, following the path Hannah had once taken. Elias walked with more purpose now, his strides lengthening as he read from her notes between glances at the forest around them. He compared tree growth patterns, slope grades, and changes in flora. With every landmark they passed that matched Hannah's sketches, his brow furrowed deeper.

"She was right," he said to the group, stopping to stare at another pictograph painted into a small rock formation jutting between the massive roots of a redwood. "She was right about all of it."

There was a kind of reverence in him now, mingled with a gentler emotion, like sadness. The delight of discovery was tempered by grief, as if every confirmation brought him closer to knowing how much had been lost with her. Her mind had walked these woods first, marking turns and naming paths where no paths had existed before, and now, retracing them, Elias felt less like a trailblazer and more like a guest moving through a construct someone else had designed.

"She was brilliant," he said quietly to Cal, snapping pictures of the pictograph with his camera.

Cal nodded, his jaw tight. "I know."

The woods grew stranger the deeper they moved. The redwoods thinned into gnarled oak, twisted pine, and slim white birch. Elias took samples, photos, observations as they moved. Story and Mary often drifted away, though Cal warned them always to stay within view.

Elias theorized on the glyphs, the native paintings, and the fungus. Story occasionally offered knowledge or counterpoints. Cal was quiet for most of it. He couldn't help but notice that Story had a peculiar knowledge of many things. Then again, she was the librarian. *Did all librarians have deep fonts of knowledge?* he wondered. He looked back at Mary, who kept to the tail end of the group. He caught her eyes always darting, her mouth constantly working on a lozenge or some sort of candy he occasionally heard click against her teeth. She seemed, for lack of a better word, at home in the woods, but annoyed as they neared each marked glyph.

Deep down he had hopes that this would lead to…something. Not salvation, perhaps not even closure, but maybe a shape to the pain. A direction for the guilt. He knew Hannah was gone, but silence is a cruel ending, and he wasn't sure which haunted him more—the mystery, or the possibility that he might have missed something that could've saved her.

They made it to the Caldron tree, then continued on, following her detailed notes and directions. The trail dead-ended at a rise in the ground where moss-covered stones curved into a cave. They all paused. Faint glyphs glowed near the base. Inside, the air turned dense and primal. Scratch marks adorned the stone—some high, as if made by hands that climbed or creatures much taller than any of them.

Elias stepped forward.

Cal caught his arm. "What are you doing?"

"I'm going inside."

"No you're not. If Hannah went in there, she didn't come out."

"And I'd like to know why." Elias moved.

Cal kept a firm hand on his arm. "I'm not making the same mistake. No. We're not going in there."

Elias backed up. "You can stay here." He looked at the others. "I'm not asking you to follow." He unslung his pack and pulled out a flashlight, pointing it inside. "See those?" he asked.

Story and Cal came close to take a look. Just beyond the threshold, illuminated by the shifting beams of Elias's flashlight, a mural sprawled across the stone. Lines of ochre, coal black, and faded crimson curled and sprawled in a style unlike any modern graffiti—primitive and yet deliberate.

Cal stepped forward, something tight in his chest loosening at the sight. "That's...Wiyot," he murmured, reverently. His voice carried a weight that hushed the others.

Story's heart caught in her throat.

The central image was a massive tree, its roots snaking deep into stylized earth, its branches reaching a heavy sky where a blackened, almost eclipsed sun hung over all. Around the tree, human figures bowed or writhed, diminutive against its sprawling form. At the base of the mural, a dark and churning ripple pattern rose up, devouring the land, dragging away the tiny figures.

Elias carefully moved closer to examine the pigments. He bent low, almost whispering to the stone. "This... It could be a flood story," he said. "Or an earthquake. A catastrophe. It's...a cultural memory encoded in imagery." He pulled a camera out of his knapsack and clicked off a series of photos.

He paused then, lowering the camera, his face lit not just by the flashlight's beam but by pride, grief, and awe. His throat worked before he could speak. "She was right," he said, softly, like a benediction. "Damn it, Hannah. You were right." He turned to Cal, eyes wet with unshed tears of joy and sorrow. "This is what she was chasing. Not hallucinations or folklore, but this. A site like this—preserved, untouched—this is a once-in-a-lifetime find. It confirms her theory of a real cultural node." Elias shook his head in wonder and lifted the camera again. "This needs to be catalogued. Carefully. Deliberately. With respect. I can file for a preliminary report, pull in tribal liaisons, notify the anthropology board—hell, we could finish her paper, Cal. Her work deserves to be published, and this…this could finally draw the attention she never got."

Cal said nothing for a long moment. He simply looked at the mural, the dark sun, the writhing figures. He thought of Hannah's boots on this very floor, her hand brushing these same stones. Thought of how hard she'd worked to be heard and how she never got the chance.

"Do it right," he said at last, voice gravel and steel. "Don't let her get lost twice."

Elias nodded once and stepped deeper into the cave, as he lifted his mask over his face, taking precautions with the delicate drawings. He raised his camera, snapping careful photographs.

Story stared at the black sun. It felt wrong. Heavy. She thought, irrationally, of eclipses, of things slipping across the face of the world unseen.

"The Howling Tree?" she suggested, her voice barely above a whisper.

Cal nodded slowly, but his face was clouded. "Could be. Could also be the mouth of the Cradle. We heard stories, back when I was a kid, about how the river would swallow the world when it was angry."

Mary shifted uncomfortably at the entrance, her arms wrapped tightly around herself, unwilling to step any further.

Deeper in the cave, additional paintings unfolded, older and harder to decipher. Spirals twisted like whirlpools, stick figures with arms thrown wide, odd, angular marks that didn't look human at all. Elias, drawn by the pull of ancient knowledge, drifted forward without thought, chasing the next layer of mystery.

The snap of the flash from his camera drew Story's attention away from the mural.

"Dr. Raines," Story called sharply.

He didn't respond.

A sound began. Not heard so much as felt. A low thrumming. The infrasonic resonance vibrated inside their bones, made their teeth ache. Story felt her ears pop, her balance shift. Mary, still at the mouth of the cave, flinched like it touched a nerve deep in her skull.

Cal looked up to call the professor back and noticed the subtle shift, the oppressive breath in the stone. "Elias," he barked, his voice cracking the heavy silence.

The air seemed to compress and then split. From deeper within the cave, a shadow detached itself, massive and impossibly fast. It rushed past, grazing Elias with a force that sent him stumbling into the wall, his breath escaping in a pained grunt.

Mary moved faster than thought. Her fingers extended. She felt the pain in her gums as her teeth revealed themselves, bared like a predator cornered. She rushed into the cave, pushing Story aside to shield her, crouched low and defensive.

The shadow fled, swallowed by the labyrinth beyond.

Silence crashed back like a wave, broken only by Elias's ragged breathing and the faint, pulsing hum that seemed to seep from the very bones of the cave.

"What the hell was that?" asked Elias.

Cal moved and helped him up. His voice came hard and sure. "We're done here."

No one argued.

Mary gripped Story around the wrist, and she felt a sharp pain in her soft flesh but let Mary pull her out, to the light of day.

"Anyone hurt?" Cal asked, letting Elias go once they were outside.

Elias shook his head. "No. What was that?"

"It's the perfect home for any large predator," Cal said. He scanned the surroundings for scat or marks that would tell them what kind of animal was making that cave home, but he found nothing of interest. He pulled off his cap and ran a hand over his forehead, back into his hair. "That was stupid," he grumbled. "We just had an animal attack and I just…" His eyes fell on the bright red mark along Story's arm. "You're bleeding," he said, moving toward her.

He saw Mary flinch, pull her hand back from her friend's arm. Her fingers looked different, wrong, too long and too thin.

Story lifted her arm. "It's nothing."

"We should get it cleaned," Cal remarked as he watched Story put a reassuring grip on Mary's shoulder and spin her around, urging her back down the trail.

"We can at the car," Story said. She looked at the scratch, already knowing it wasn't life threatening.

Cal turned to the professor. "You get enough for the time being?"

"Yes. I have all I need to approach the board." Elias nodded and pushed up from the small boulder he was sitting on.

They started on their way back. Ahead, Cal was certain he could hear Mary crying, but he couldn't catch the gentle whispers the women exchanged.

Back at the cars, the tension had not entirely lifted.

"Come to my place," Story offered, brushing hair back from her eyes. She dabbed carefully at her injury with a Kleenex. "I made something light—a late lunch. I think we could all use a breath and a regroup. This has been exciting for you, I'm sure," she said, looking at Elias before her gaze flicked to Cal. "And emotional."

They all agreed lunch and time to breathe and digest what they'd found was necessary.

As they packed up gear, Cal paused beside Mary. He didn't ask. He didn't flinch. Instead, he said softly, "I've seen beings who don't belong to either world. You're not the first." He put a hand over hers, resting on the trunk to push it shut.

Mary blinked. Something fragile and rare passed between them, settled like fog into the silence.

They got into their cars and followed Story's taillights through the trees.

Chapter Twenty-Three
Luminescent Lullabies

S eth quietly opened the front door to Story's house and stepped into the foyer, exhausted and mentally spent after a day filled with non-human corpses and miles trekked in the redwoods still with no sign of Clayton Meadows. He got a text earlier in the afternoon from Story letting him know that she was having Cal, Dr. Raines, and Mary over for a late lunch after their excursion into the Cursed Woods to follow the trail Hannah Albrecht had left behind. He hadn't been thrilled that any of them were venturing into that labyrinth, but he felt secure knowing Cal would be leading the way. And if they were able to learn anything new regarding the bioluminescent fungus etched into glyphs that was reportedly causing hallucinatory effects, then all the better for him, his team, and everyone else out there searching for Clayton.

He slipped off his boots as he heard the singsong voices of Story and Mary emanating from the kitchen.

"You're wrong, Mary. He's genuinely interested in you," Story's voice carried.

"No one is," Mary's soft voice hummed.

"Oh, will you stop being so self-deprecating."

"That's what Dr. Bajorek says."

"And you should listen to her. And to me," Story said and laughed.

Seth heard Mary giggle as he approached the kitchen, gliding down the hallway in his socks.

"Do you find him attractive?" Story asked.

"Will you stop?" Mary whined.

"I mean, he is."

"Who is?" Seth asked, stepping into the light of the kitchen.

Story jumped, hand to her heart, as Mary squeaked and backed into the pantry door. "I swear, you have the most silent footfalls of anyone I've ever known," Story said, crossing from the kitchen island to meet him with a hug and a kiss.

"Feet of a ninja, Kendra used to say." Seth held Story's hips to keep her from pressing into his body. He felt like he was covered with the death film of not-humans. He noticed a Band-Aid on Story's arm. "What happened there?"

Story shook her head. "Nothing, just a scratch."

"Who's Kendra?" Mary quietly asked, holding her clasped hands together in front of her chest.

"Seth's old partner from San Francisco," Story answered. "Are you okay?" she asked Seth.

"I've had better days. Most of them, in fact."

"Oh no. What happened?"

Seth's eyes were drawn by Mary shuffling around the island.

"I'll go," she said, evading Seth's eyes.

"Actually, Mary?" Seth held up a hand, halting her. "I was hoping you'd still be here. If you weren't I was going to ask Story to call you back over."

Mary's head dropped. "Oh."

"It's nothing bad, Mary." Seth rolled his eyes at himself. "I mean, it's actually pretty horrendous, but nothing to do with you. I could actually use your help. Both of you."

Story walked over and put her arm around her friend. "Mary, stay. Have another glass of wine."

Mary nodded. She stole a quick glance at Seth before walking back around the island and sitting on the barstool near her almost finished glass of merlot.

"I'm going to take a quick shower and change," Seth said.

"We'll be here," Story said, grabbing a new bottle of wine from the rack in her pantry.

Seth turned to head to the staircase, but then spun back around. "Oh, and who were you talking about?"

Mary looked up from her glass. "Hm?"

Story laughed as she uncorked the wine. "Cal. I think Mary has a crush on him."

"Story! I do not."

Seth grinned. "I don't blame you, Mary. He's a good-looking guy. And single."

Mary covered her blushing face.

Seth returned to the kitchen in dark grey sweatpants, a moss green T-shirt that fit snug around his shoulders and biceps, hair still damp and feet bare. "I could use a glass of that," he said, motioning to the bottle between Story and Mary, who were huddled together on the far side of the island.

"I could sense that," Story said, pointing to the full glass right in front of Seth.

Seth looked down. "Oh. That for me?"

"Mm-hmm," Story cooed.

Seth winked at Story and sat down on the barstool, about four feet separating them across the island.

"Any progress with Clayton?" Story asked.

Seth shook his head, swallowing a healthy gulp of merlot. "Still no trace."

"I'm sorry."

"Me too. How did your excursion go?"

Story and Mary exchanged a weighted glance.

"What?" Seth asked, worry seeping into his voice.

"Oh, nothing really," Story said. "It was very productive overall. For one thing, and I think it's rather important culturally and as a scholar, what Hannah had been trying to find, we found it. There is a significant Indigenous heritage site out there. But as to what you're likely most interested in," she said with a sly smile, "Elias took plenty of samples and specimens."

"*Elias*," Seth teased.

"*Jane*," Story retorted, grinning.

Mary looked from Seth to Story, befuddled.

"Okay, and?" Seth urged her on.

"He's going to send the specimens directly to his friend at UC Davis's Fungal Lab. The samples he's going to bring up to Cal Humboldt to have them tested first thing tomorrow. He said he should have results fairly quickly. He's hoping it gives us some answers about the effects of the spores coming from the fungus."

"Sounds horrifying," Seth said flatly and took another sip of wine.

Story shrugged. "I think it's fascinating."

"Of course you do. So what was the culturally significant find?"

"An old Wiyot pictograph on the inside of a cave. It was gorgeous," Story enthused.

"It might be a warning," Mary added.

"Of what?" Seth asked.

"Of where not to tread."

"Oh, great. And you guys were all there."

Mary looked back at Story, urging her with her eyes.

Story nodded and looked at Seth. "Yes, well, coincidentally, there was a large animal of some kind in the cave—"

"A predator," Mary interceded.

"That quickly flew by us."

"Flew?" Seth asked.

"Knocked over Dr. Raines," Mary said.

"Is he alright?"

"Everyone's fine," Story said. "And I don't know if it flew."

"It didn't make any sound," Mary added.

"But we couldn't make out what it was."

Seth looked between the two women. "And that's it?"

Story nodded. "That's it. We left right after that."

"Cal made us go back," Mary said.

"Good," Seth said. "And please tell me you're done following Hannah's trail?"

Story swallowed a sip of wine. "Well, depending on what Elias discovers, he might want to go back out for more samples. But I'm done."

Seth eyed her wearily.

"I'm not going back out there," Mary said definitively.

Seth nodded. "Okay then."

"What did you need our help with?" Story asked, changing the subject.

Seth sighed and then downed the rest of his wine. "May I?" he asked, motioning to the bottle.

Story raised her eyebrows. "Oh! This must be bad," she guessed, sliding the bottle across the table. Seth rarely had more than one glass of any liquor on any given night.

Seth grabbed it, refilled his glass, and stood to his feet, leaning his hands on the countertop, deciding on where to start. He looked at Mary, whose eyes flickered back and forth between the table and then met his eyes. "What can you tell me about the not-children?"

Mary's eyes opened wide.

"The not-children?" Story asked.

"Why do you want to know about them?" Mary asked suspiciously.

"You've um…well, you've seen them, right?" Seth asked. "You've come into contact with them?"

Mary's eyes darted to Story, fear gripping her.

Story grabbed her hand. "It's okay, you can—"

"Mary, it's fine," Seth jumped in. "I know you know that I know about the incident with the one who…had expired. I don't care. That's not what this is about."

Mary stole a glance back at Seth, unease racing through her eyes.

"Okay, look, I got a call from Peter late this morning. He and Noble were clearing out a fallen tree from a trail leading to the ocean. Noble had come across it on a guided tour yesterday. The thing is, the widest part of the tree overhanging the trail split, and…the bodies, and parts, of about seven children—"

"Oh my God!" Story gasped, covering her mouth.

"Not-children, sorry, fell to the ground."

Mary's eyes widened. "I had nothing to do with it. I would—"

Seth held his hands up. "I'm not saying you did. That's not why— the thought literally didn't even cross my mind, Mary." As Seth said the words he was honestly shocked the thought hadn't crossed his mind.

"Are you sure they're not-children," Story asked, her eyes welling up.

"He would be sure," Mary said with certainty.

Seth nodded. "Yes, as Mary said, there is absolutely no mistaking these…things, for human children."

Mary's shoulders began to ease, as curiosity overtook her. "What happened?"

"I have no idea," Seth admitted. "I went there with Wes and we treated it like any other crime scene. At least for now. That's why I wanted to talk to you. What can you tell me about them? When and how often have you seen them? When's the last time you've seen them? What does their skin look like?"

"I haven't seen one since before the Green Man died."

The statement hung heavy over the entire kitchen, everyone now fully understanding the circumstances surrounding LaRange's death.

"Since months before," Mary clarified. "Much like he was dying from starvation, I think his not-children were as well. They used to always travel together, but ever since The Event, I think they got disbanded. As you know, I couldn't find the Green Man for months. But I saw his children, usually alone, sometimes in pairs, in the distance. They looked weak, lost. I wanted nothing to do with them. They're not right. They never were."

"And how so? In what ways?" Seth asked.

"Their eyes. There's nothing behind them. The structure of their faces. Sometimes it's close to that of a real child, but others...others are misshapen, mouths too small, ears not level."

"What about their skin?"

"It looks real enough from a distance. And maybe it is. I've only seen one close enough to touch," she said, looking back down to the table.

"It's okay, Mary. Go on."

"The one I came upon. He had, as you said, expired. But I don't think he was weak. It was an animal attack. His neck," she said, pointing to the side of her neck, "had been torn open. The skin was normal. Normal enough. The weak ones. The last ones I saw earlier this year, their skin was more...see-through."

Seth nodded. "That's what we saw. The bodies of the ones from the tree, the skin was more translucent than not."

Mary stared ahead, deep in thought. "He buried them." She looked back up at Seth. "In the tree."

Seth lifted an eyebrow. "Did he kill them?"

Mary shook her head. "No, he would never. He loved them in his own delusional way." Mary paused to consider the situation. "Yes, it makes sense. He couldn't go back to the Orbriallis after The Event. He had to live in the wild on his own, fighting for food, searching for water. He would have had no shovel to dig a grave. It only makes sense that he found a place to put them that he thought no one would come across."

Seth looked over at Story, who was gripping her wineglass. She felt his gaze and looked up, giving him a weak smile. Seth looked back to Mary. "I'd like to ask you about their blood. I'm sorry to be so blunt, but we've got so little to go on here and—"

"It's real blood. Human blood."

Seth furrowed his brow.

"No," Mary said. "I've never...my blood. I have only ever tasted my own blood from cuts, accidents. Everything else has only been animal blood. It's different. They fill them with human blood."

"They?" Story asked.

"The Orbriallis," Seth and Mary responded in unison.

Story nodded. "Of course. I just…I don't understand."

"Nor do I," Seth said. "I understand what Dr. Owens was striving for with his fertility experiments. As deluded and off course as he got, the impetus was from a place to help, to cure. But this? I have no idea."

"Do you think Jane knows about them?"

"I honestly don't know, but—"

"I think she might," Mary interrupted.

"How do you know, Mary?" Story asked her friend.

"I told her about them. I could tell. I think she was alarmed by the idea of them, but I sensed some recognition."

"Not-George," Seth said.

"Yes," Mary agreed.

Story, concerned and confused, looked from Mary to Seth. "You mean to say the boy who had been living at the Horne house for all those years…"

"That's my hypothesis at any rate," Seth answered.

"But how would they not know?"

"He was different from the ones I saw in the woods," Mary interjected. "Not as primitive."

Seth sighed. "Well, I need to talk to Jane about him, about the not-children in general. And about why the hell they wanted the real George Horne to begin with."

"You said she had no knowledge. And no records were discovered from what Paddy retrieved."

"That was true at the time. But she has to have learned something in the past months. She has not-George there and she's still seeing the real George for therapy sessions," Seth said, running his hand through his hair. "What a fucking mess."

Story looked deep into her lover's eyes across the island. "I'm so sorry, Seth. What an awful situation to have to deal with."

Seth let out a long, slow exhale. "I wish that was it."

"Oh. Did something go wrong with the…" She nodded her head in communication.

"You could say that." Seth quickly glanced at Mary.

"What? With what?" Mary asked.

"Raymond LaRange," Seth answered. "We exhumed the body first thing this morning."

Mary's eyes fell. Seth had told her what was planned, the DNA testing, and what that could mean for her.

"What happened?" Story asked.

"His body was gone."

Mary's head snapped up to attention.

"What?" Story said. "It was empty?"

Seth shook his head and took a long sip of wine, wishing he hadn't, as the image of what they uncovered popped back in his mind, souring the taste. "Would have been better if it was empty."

A whimper escaped Mary's throat. "I swear, I—"

"Mary." Seth stopped her. "This happened likely within forty-eight hours after he was buried. I know it has nothing to do with you."

"What was there?" Story asked.

"*What* is the operative word," Seth replied. "The best I can describe what we found in his place is that it was a not-man."

Mary looked from Seth to Story.

"An adult?" Story asked.

Seth nodded. "Yes. Mary, have you ever seen a—"

"No, never. What did he look like?" she asked, fascinated.

"It wasn't good. I'll just say that whoever, or whatever, the man was, he suffered multiple injuries and…I don't know, malfunctions?"

Story placed a hand on her friend's back. "So, does that mean…"

Seth sat back down on the stool. "Well, obviously we can't pull DNA from a body we don't have."

Story gave Mary's shoulder a gentle squeeze.

"But I'd like to ask you both a favor. Something I would never do under normal circumstances. But we're not talking about humans here. Or at least, not humans like we currently know them."

"Not much disturbs me," Story said. "But this most certainly does."

"What do you need?" Mary asked Seth.

"Well, you've got a unique experience and history with these not-children. As far as I know, you're the only person who has come into close proximity with one of them. If you'd be willing, I'd like you to come up to Wes's coroner office and have a look at them. It could be very beneficial—"

226

"Yes. Whatever I can do to help. I want to help."

Seth nodded. "Thank you, Mary."

"And what can I do?" Story asked.

Seth looked over at Story, deep into her eyes. "We know nothing about them. If there's any way—"

"You want me to see if I can find something. In their past. Their memory."

"Yes. If they have memories."

Mary grabbed Story's hand and gave it a squeeze.

Story smiled at her friend and looked at her lover. "Whatever I can do."

Chapter Twenty-Four
The Real and the Replicated

Seth approached the front desk at the Orbriallis with one task to complete before heading up to see Dr. Bajorek.

"Seth, good to see you." Vince extended his hand.

Seth gave it a firm shake. "You as well, Vince. Where's Seamus? I was actually hoping to talk to both of you."

Vince looked over to the cafeteria, where Seamus was chatting away with two male doctors, both laughing at whatever anecdotes Seamus was conveying. "Seamus!"

The big Irishman looked over and saw Seth. He gave a salute and then patted one of the doctors on the shoulder and could be heard from a distance saying, "Gotta go, boys, the chief is here!"

Seth waited for Seamus to join them, wondering how much in the realm of actual security detail he did on a given day.

Seamus approached and looked at Vince. "The chief is here."

Vince grinned. "You don't say."

"How goes it, Seth?" Seamus said, shaking his hand.

"Not great, Seamus. Not great."

Seamus furrowed his brow, seemingly perplexed that Seth could have a bad day.

"No news on the boy?" Vince asked.

"Afraid not," Seth said, motioning them away from the front desk, out of earshot of the two receptionists.

"Sorry to hear that. Seamus and I joined one of the search teams on Sunday."

"We were out there with fifteen other people and I still felt lost," Seamus said. "Hope the lad is okay."

Seth nodded.

"I got the security system set up at the construction site," Vince said.

"I heard. One of my deputies said he saw the cameras up."

"I doubt he saw all of them."

Seth raised an eyebrow in question.

"We got six cameras installed in clear view, two by the entrance, two by the office, and another two by the townhomes going up. But I got the security team to install four more micro cameras in secluded areas in case someone takes out the main cams."

"Excellent," Seth said, impressed. "I wanted to ask you guys for another favor."

"You name it, Chief," Seamus said.

"Within reason, of course," Vince added with a smirk.

"The town is understandably on edge."

"I've sensed it."

"And we're still awaiting DNA results on the animal that attacked the young boy last week. So, we've got a missing teen, a dangerous animal yet to be identified, and the county fair is starting up Friday."

"Ah, love that fair," Seamus said. "Didn't have 'em where I grew up."

"Great. Then you won't mind spending some extra time there."

"What do you need?" Vince asked.

"I know it's asking a lot," Seth said. "And I appreciate you guys already helping with the search for Clayton. But I'd feel a lot better if we had some beefed-up security at the fair this weekend."

"In case the animal attacks?" Seamus asked.

"In case anything. It's been over a week now with one disaster after another and I'd like to avoid any more. I know the county will have their own security there, but if you've been there and seen them—"

"Say no more," Vince said.

"Bunch of old men and kids," Seamus added.

"Ill-equipped to handle any potentially dangerous situations," Seth said.

Seamus chuckled. "Sure, however you want to say it."

"I'm game," Vince said. "I'm off at six Friday. I'll see if I can get off early. And I'm all yours Saturday and Sunday."

Seth patted him on the back. "Thanks, Vince."

"I'm off Friday," Seamus said. "Just tell me when and where. Working early Saturday and Sunday, but can shoot over afterward."

"You're the best, Sheam-O. I'll have you guys fill out some paperwork so you'll be official reserve officers."

"Look at that! Do we get badges?"

Seth smiled. "Sure, I'll get you a badge if you'd like one."

"Well, yeah."

"You want us armed?" Vince asked.

Seth briefly pondered the question. "Yeah. I'd rather be on the cautious end."

"We'll be there."

Seth nodded. "Thanks, guys. Seamus, you want to take me up to Dr. Bajorek's office?"

"Let's go."

Seth entered Dr. Bajorek's office, quickly surveying the space.

"She's not in here," Jane said from behind her desk with a wide smile, knowing that Seth was looking for her mother, Apolonia.

"Sorry, no offense meant."

"None taken. Have a seat."

Seth motioned to her open door. "Do you mind?"

"Please."

Seth shut the door and sat in the seat opposite Jane. "Thanks for seeing me on such short notice."

"Of course. You said it was a serious situation. Is this about Mary again?"

"No, no, not at all. I wanted to ask—" Seth stopped and looked over his shoulder up to the corner of the room, where he recalled a camera being last year.

"We removed the cameras from all the doctors' and researchers' offices almost immediately after Dr. Owens was taken away."

"I guess I hadn't noticed in the few times I've been here since."

"It was so unnecessary and invasive," Jane said. "This must be quite serious if you're looking for cameras."

"Yes, as I said." Seth had been pondering how to approach this situation since he started putting the pieces together yesterday. He trusted Jane. She had been nothing but helpful and compliant since the Sarah Elizabeth case last year. But he also knew this situation and line of inquiry would delve deep into the institute's undisclosed research and past infractions by Dr. Owens and his inner circle. "I need to ask you about the…boy we exchanged last year."

Jane raised an eyebrow. "Okay."

Seth locked eyes with her. "What can you tell me about him?"

"In what regard?"

"Any regard."

Jane shifted in her chair. "We call him Liam."

"Why is that?"

"We thought it best to have a clean slate."

"Has he communicated to you yet?"

Jane swallowed. "In his own way, yes."

"How has he responded to being here?"

Jane placed a forearm on her desk. "As you may recall, he is operating with very low faculties. His response has been nominal."

Seth observed her breaths were becoming shorter. "And have you figured out why that might be? His low faculties, as you put it?"

Jane began to fiddle with her pen. "Well, of course this is confidential information between doctor and patient."

"Right, but is it? Under the circumstances?"

Jane took a heavy breath. "What is this all about, Seth?"

"What else could you tell me about him? The boy. Liam."

Jane tried to remain expressionless, but an air of despair seeped into her face and the room. "I see."

Seth held her gaze, all friendliness and rapport built over the past year pushed to the side. They studied each other like poker players. Or like a detective and suspect, trying to ascertain what the other knew. Seth sensed the slow dawning of realization fall upon Jane. The realization that he knew what not-George was.

"Now I wish my mother was here," Jane said.

Seth couldn't tell if she was being serious or facetious. He remained quiet.

"That was a partial joke."

Seth still gave away nothing.

"Your reputation as a detective is very apparent. I wouldn't like to be on the other side of the table from you in an interrogation. Or is that what this is?"

"No. If I was coming here under that pretense, I would have come with a warrant. Which under any normal circumstances would have been quite easy to come by."

Jane straightened her posture. "I assume you're not talking about

George Horne being held here in the first place."

"We obviously already tried going that route. The feds had other plans."

"Yes." Jane brushed her long black hair behind her ear. "I hope you'll believe me when I tell you I had no knowledge of Liam's creation."

Seth purposely relaxed his posture, wanting to put her at ease. Hearing her verbalize what he came here to discuss was enough to know she would continue to be as cooperative as she always had been. "I believed that before I walked through the front door."

"Did you? It doesn't feel like it."

"Interviewing technique."

Jane nodded. "How did you find out?"

"What is he?" Seth countered.

Jane sighed. "Truthfully, we're still trying to figure that out. We've run every blood test imaginable. X-rays and MRIs have revealed... abnormalities. EEG tests on the brain have revealed functions unlike anything we've seen. And not in a good way. Same with pet scans. Troubling and unprecedented."

"Do you have nothing else to go on?"

"We have no records of whatever project this was. We've questioned every doctor and researcher here with the threat of dismissal if they weren't forthcoming. It's possible that someone is lying, but as best we can tell, there's no one left here that was any part of it. Perhaps you could question them. I can't fathom anyone would hold up under that pressure."

"With your permission, I think that would be highly beneficial."

"You have it. I'd like to know more than anyone."

Seth leaned in toward her. "I also have something that might help your research into finding out what exactly the boy is. If I can call him that."

Jane shrugged. "That would of course be a matter of heated ethical and medical debate. What do you have? I assume something led you to this discovery."

"I've got an absolute disaster on my hands. I keep trying to think of a more apt word. A catastrophe?"

Jane narrowed her eyes. "A catastrophe that might help me?"

"Well, I think it could help both of us. But I would need you to be as transparent with me as possible."

"I would like to think that's possible, but I would need to know the circumstances."

"Has Mary ever told you about the not-children? The ones that used

232

to follow Raymond LaRange around?"

"I have heard about them, yes."

Seth gave a slight shake of the head. "Well, I've got the bodies of eight of them at our county coroner's office."

Jane's eyes grew exceptionally wide. "My God. Eight? Where did they come from?"

Seth laughed, with no humor. "A tree. The not-children came from a hollowed-out tree on a trail in the woods near Mourner's Beach."

Jane's jaw dropped, unable to find words.

"As fate would have it, the son of Peter Andalusian was the one that stumbled upon the tree that had fallen over a trail used for expeditions. Peter went out with him yesterday to help him cut it down, and out came the bodies and limbs of eight not-children. Their discovery has thankfully been contained."

"I don't even know what to say. Why were they in a tree?"

"Well, Mary seems to think that Raymond LaRange buried them there. Without a shovel and so forth."

Jane shook her head. "I'm not sure how to even process this."

"I understand, believe me."

"Has your coroner autopsied them yet?" she asked.

"He has."

"Can I speak with him?"

"I was hoping to do you one better," Seth said. "We're at a loss, Dr. Wes Hensley and I. We've got bodies with incomplete organs that don't abide by human mechanics. The fingerprints are either incomplete or have partially or, in some cases, completely vanished. Whatever they once looked like, they're not human. Based on your admission, they don't have any parents or relatives outside of the doctors who once worked at this facility. There are no laws written for this in my realm of police work. The bodies began here and I'm hoping you can take them back."

Jane's head jutted back. "Oh…I guess I'm not sure what you were going to ask. Yes, of course. If that's okay."

"As I said, there is no legal precedent for this situation. I could run this up the chain of command, but I have a feeling it would turn into a complete clusterfuck that would ultimately bring the same feds to the door to take the bodies and bury it all. I'd rather have you and your team figure out just what these things are, and then we can use your documented medical findings to do some good. Maybe use it to track down Dr. Owens and his circle of doctors that disappeared."

The corner of Jane's mouth morphed from a smirk to a sneer. "I would enjoy nothing more. Anything I can do to make him pay for what he did to Sarah."

"Good, because there's another matter of even greater concern to me."

"I can't fathom what that might be."

Seth rubbed his stubbled chin. He hadn't shaved since Clayton went missing. "It's not just children."

Jane cocked her head to the side.

"The same day—the same morning, Wes and I uncovered the body of a not-man."

"A man? Where?"

"We were exhuming the body of Raymond LaRange yesterday morning—"

"What for?"

Seth paused, weighing his words carefully. "We were hoping to get some DNA from his wounds in case the same animal, a grey wolf, was responsible for the boy who was found mauled last week."

"Right. Okay, and where does this not-man come into play?"

"Well—"

"Wait, you're not saying Raymond LaRange is a—"

"No, Raymond was most definitely a human. He was also most definitely not in his casket. In his place was the not-man."

Jane's brow furrowed as her eyes fell to her desk, deep in contemplation. After a weighted moment, she looked back up, alert. "You think it was Dr. Owens?"

Seth nodded. "I do. No one else even knew of Raymond's existence. His body was likely taken within forty-eight hours of the burial, and I want to know why. We've already dusted for fingerprints and taken numerous samples of DNA, but I'm not holding my breath. I know it's a long shot, but I'm hoping maybe you and your team can, I don't know, find something or learn something that might give us a clue."

Jane had grabbed her pen and was lightly tapping it against her desk. "We'll certainly do our best. I'm still stunned by this chain of events."

"I can only stay stunned for so long. We still have a missing teenage boy to find."

"Of course."

"And the transparency I requested? I'm hoping that won't be—"

"Not an issue," Jane said, slicing her hand through the air.

"I appreciate that. And I mean everything. Even if it's medical jargon you think I won't understand. Wes will."

"Absolutely."

Seth nodded and then grinned, knowing what he was going to ask next and how it might be perceived. "I'd like to ask you an additional favor. Actually maybe two."

Jane held her hands out, palms up. "I feel as if I'm in no position to say no."

"Once we transport the bodies, I'd ask that you allow Mary and Story to come see them."

Jane grimaced. "That's an unusual request."

Seth shrugged.

"I'm sure you could just as easily bring them into your coroner's office. If you'd prefer to do that here, then I will certainly allow it. Can I ask why?"

"Mary may have already told you, but she's been in close proximity with a not-child. A deceased one at that. An animal attack. I think she may be able to help us to determine the time of death. Or at least give us a ballpark idea."

Jane nodded. "I understand this. And may I ask about Story?"

Seth gave Jane a guarded smile. "You can ask her if you like."

Jane thrummed her fingers on her table. "I think that I will."

Seth slapped his hands on the armrests. "Okay, then. I'll have Wes reach out to you to coordinate."

Jane stood up and smoothed out her lab coat. "You could have given me a hundred guesses of why you were coming here today and I never would have come close."

Seth studied her eyes as she said this, content that she had no idea that not-children had been roaming the woods. He stood, extended his hand, and shook hers. "I had a night filled with moral debate over what to do about this. I hope I made the right choice."

"You did."

Seth stopped at the door and turned back around. "The not-children. The not-man. Whatever all of this is, would you have supported this..." Seth twirled his hand in the air. "Creation?"

Jane grinned. "I'm a doctor, Seth. I would need to fully understand the purpose, the research, and the development to truthfully comment on that."

Seth considered this and nodded. "Fair enough."

"On that topic…" Jane stopped Seth before he opened the door. "The files. The ones your…Paddy, was that his name?"

"It is."

"I assumed he kept copies. Is there any chance that—"

"I doubt it. Paddy scoured every file in there. If he had come across anything about creating not-human beings, or partially human, he would have told me."

"Too much to hope for," Jane said with a sigh.

"I'll certainly ask again, though."

Chapter Twenty-Five
Where Water Calls

The sun hung heavy and golden over the Eel River, its light brushing the slow water into molten ripples. The air smelled of wet stone and sweetgrass, the hills beyond the bend blurred by a lazy haze. They had found the perfect spot: a sweeping, pale stone beach embraced by redwoods, distant enough not to upset Stan's dad or Chief Wolfe, and crowned with smooth slabs just warm enough for lounging, just cool enough not to burn.

Anya stretched out a leg, laughing breathlessly as Nate, Ember, Stan, and Noble batted the birdie back and forth across a makeshift line scratched in the sand, occasionally calling half-hearted jeers when one of them missed. Zoe, absorbed in the battered pages of a mystery novel, barely glanced up from her perch atop a sun-warmed boulder right behind her.

The laughter echoed through the trees as the girls finally managed to gain the lead on the boys, eliciting cheers from Anya. This was a moment they would cherish, another memory to hold onto when Noble left for Tennessee to attend college.

He looked over to his sister, who was smiling despite being engrossed in her recent library borrow. Anya's laughter, her brilliant aquamarine eyes, was an image he didn't ever want to let go of. And Stan...how was life going to be without Stan? She'd been his sidekick, his ride or die, his daily dose of weird and goofy, a reminder to always be himself. He knew he'd miss Nate, too, but nothing would compare to not having these three girls around, and that thought ached deep inside him. He reminded himself of his mother's advice and focused on enjoying the last days of summer.

Anya felt a similar tug deep down when she knew each day was one more day closer to Noble heading off to live on his grandparents' horse ranch. The emotion was dulled, only the slightest, knowing he was pursuing a degree in something he loved. Though she was smiling and laughing, a part of her was silently worrying over the changes in her mother. The way she zoned out, the silent murmuring, and last night's sleepwalking incident.

A strong breeze kicked up, chilling all their flesh and rustling the boughs of the ancient trees nearby. What Anya hadn't noticed was that she'd begun sketching lines into the sand at her feet.

The pasture unfurled before her like a half-forgotten dream: wavering grasses whispering against her bare calves, the heavy golden light of afternoon turned syrup-thick around her. Leith walked barefoot, dress billowing softly around her ankles, the air with the scent of crushed clover. She didn't feel the stones underfoot or the thistle spines brushing her skin. The world was far away now, muffled, slowed.

Ahead, the tree line of the Cursed Woods waited: a wall of shadow, pulsing gently like a heart under the skin of the world. A low thrumming began under her feet—not just in the soil but in the space between things: the roots, the stones, the very air.

Come.

The invitation was soundless, yet Leith heard it, clear as a bell tolling underwater. Her heart beat in strange new patterns, matching the slow throb of the woods ahead. As Leith crossed the invisible threshold from pasture into woodland, the world changed. The temperature dropped a dozen degrees. The smell of iron and wet moss thickened until it clung to her tongue. Light, which had once been bright and forgiving, became dappled and strange—broken into lurching shadows that flickered and folded in ways no sane sunbeam should. The ground grew soft and spongy beneath her feet and a low, resonant hum began to rise.

A sound like the earth itself tuning its voice, sharpening its hunger.

A prickling sensation had begun to creep up Anya's spine. A whisper beneath the brightness, a wrongness weaving through the hum of the river and the shriek of distant hawks. Her skin itched. Her heart thrummed a beat too fast.

The forest folded tighter around Leith, a cathedral of rot and wonder. Filaments she'd never seen or noticed before draped from the high branches, pale as drowned hair, swaying gently in currents of wind that did not touch the ground.

A fallen tree loomed ahead. A titan cracked open by time and sickness, its carcass stretched across a shallow hollow choked with moss and slick, dark growth. Beneath it, something stirred. A thin, wheezing hiss cut through the hum of the woods. Leith froze, head tilting in slow, marionette-like curiosity. There, tangled in the weave of fungus and loam, lay a creature.

Anya kept dragging a fingertip through the sand in sweeping, repetitive curves. A symbol unfurled under her hand, coiled and sinuous. Cold, persistent anxiety twisted in her belly. The world, once sun-splashed and safe, suddenly pressed too close, too sharp, as if unseen eyes lurked just beyond the reach of sight.

Stan, halfway through a sarcastic remark, paused mid-sentence. Her gaze sharpened. She watched Anya, confusion flickering across her face. Anya looked pale. Her eyes wide like a spooked horse.

Noble served a clumsy shot; the birdie arced wildly and thudded into the sand near Anya's feet. "Babe?" he called, grinning. "You spacing out?"

"Dude, get it together," Nate commented over his shoulder to Noble, striding to retrieve the birdie.

"Anya?" Stan asked quietly.

At first, Leith's mind scrabbled for a name. *Bird*, it insisted, clumsy and wrong. A fledgling perhaps, fallen from some monstrous nest. But it was the length of her forearm, maybe longer. Its feathers were still wet and clumped in irregular patches. The bones of its wings jutted at unnatural angles. Its talons, though curled and weak, gleamed wicked and sharp as knives.

Leith felt a low, sweet ache behind her ribs. She knelt slowly, reverently, hands trembling as she reached toward the creature.

A low, primal instinct surged up inside of Anya: Run. Hide. Water. Before thought could catch action, she bolted. Sand sprayed from her heels as she raced for the river, her form a pale blur against the stones. In an instant, she plunged beneath the surface, swallowed by the slow-moving water.

"Whoa!" Nate backpedaled out of the way as she went flashing by.

"What the—?" Stan slowly lowered her racket, letting it fall to the sand at her feet.

"Anya?" Noble called after her.

They watched her splash into the cold river water and dive under the gently rippling surface.

"Can she swim?" Nate asked offhandedly. He hadn't thought she liked swimming. She never got in the water.

Time ticked by as they glared at the water, waiting.

Zoe slid off the boulder, clutching her book to her chest. "Noble?" she asked, her voice almost too quiet to carry over the burble of the river. "Why isn't she coming up?"

"Anya?" Stan called.

Still, she hadn't surfaced.

"Anya!" Noble shouted, panic gutting his voice. He sprinted after her, tossing aside his racket.

"I'm coming!" Nate dropped his racket and followed his friend into the water.

Zoe started toward the water's edge.

"Stay here, Zoe!" Stan barked over her shoulder as she dove in after Noble and Anya.

Ember moved to stand near the younger girl and was shocked to discover Zoe slipping her hand into hers and holding on tight.

The river clutched at Noble's legs, colder than it should have been for July. He kicked through the sluggish current, heart hammering as he searched. Then a glint of pale skin below. He lunged down, arms closing around her.

They broke the surface together, Noble gasping. For a moment, chaos reigned—the river swirling, Stan beating a swift freestyle paddle to catch up to them, Nate shouting from waist deep, Zoe yelling from shore. But then Noble saw her—really saw her.

Anya's hair, usually a delicate melt of carrot orange into pale white, now burned pure ginger, catching the sunlight like fire underwater. Her eyes, wide and disoriented, shimmered unnaturally. The pupils refracted light into strange, slitted patterns, like a cat or something not wholly human.

She saw the recognition in his face, and horror twisted across her features. With a cry, she tried to pull away, ducking beneath the surface again, but Noble instinctively clutched her tighter.

"Anya—no, hey, it's okay, I've got you!" he rasped against her hair, his voice low and urgent. "You're okay. I promise. You're safe."

She struggled once, twice, then sagged against him, shivering. He wrapped his arms tighter around her, buoying her weight as he waded them slowly back toward the beach. His mind had no clue how to process what he'd seen, how she had physically changed from literally just entering the water.

"Is she okay?" Stan asked, swimming alongside them. It took her a moment to realize the color of her hair was more striking, too striking. "What the hell?" she murmured.

Nate glared openly as they stood and walked to shore. "Wha...?" he voiced to Stan as she walked by, wringing out her long black hair.

Stan looked at him with wide eyes, a clear communication that she was just as puzzled as he was, and followed Noble to the beach. Anya remained tucked under his arm, shielding her face into his chest with her hands over her face.

Zoe ran and retrieved two towels. She clutched them tightly, trying to keep them from dragging in the sand as she returned and gave them to her brother, her face pale and solemn. Her eyes widened at the shimmering sparkle of Anya's golden orange hair and caught the fleetest glance of her hands, a subtle bit of pale, nearly translucent webbing between each finger that was nearly undetectable it was so gossamer thin. She sucked in a quiet, shocked breath.

Noble guided Anya up onto the sand, kneeling beside her, wrapping her in the towel, and gathering her into his lap like a fragile and precious thing, wondering if they were going to have to rush her to a hospital. But for what? Anya tucked herself against him, still burying her face into his chest, trembling.

Stan, Nate, and Ember kept their distance, staring, bewildered.

Nate leaned close to Stan. "Why is her hair all orange? Is that, like, a special dye?"

Stan's neck nearly snapped as she turned to look at him. "Special dye?"

"Yeah? Like you have all that fingernail crap that turns color in hot or cold water," he commented. "My sister has some anyway."

"I don't know, Nate," Stan hoarsely whispered. "Honestly, I hope it is, otherwise…"

"Anya?" Noble asked, gentle as he would if he were approaching a wild animal.

"Don't look at me," she whispered into his chest. The sound was further muffled by her cupped hands. "I didn't want it to happen like this."

"Anya, I don't…" Noble began and sighed. He rubbed his hands up and down her back as she continued to shiver uncontrollably. "Look at me. Hey, look," he said, carefully pressing her away and lifting her face to his. Her eyes were still stunning, so deep blue they looked like he was staring at pools of a Caribbean Sea, but there was an uncanny sparkle to them. The pupils had changed. No longer round, they were stretched and slit-like, refracting the light in fractured, iridescent lines, as if each held a fragment of a broken rainbow.

Her eyes held fear like she expected him to recoil, to push her away, to turn his back and run. She was waiting for all of them to run.

Noble reached out and cupped her face, brushing his thumb along her cheekbone, ignoring the way her skin felt cooler than usual. *I didn't want it to happen like this,* she had said. Whatever was happening to her, she knew it. She understood it. It was something she wanted to share but didn't know how. Which likely meant they didn't need to run to the hospital. He couldn't look away from her. Even when his brain screamed "unnatural," "impossible," his heart only knew: *This is Anya.*

"Hey," he whispered, voice rough with confusion but unyielding. "You're okay. I'm here. I'm not going anywhere."

"Anya?" Zoe reached out and pressed her small hand to Anya's shoulder.

Anya resisted turning. She didn't want to frighten Zoe. "I'm okay," she said, only partially turning her head, resting her fingertips on Zoe's.

Stan hovered nearby, dripping and wide-eyed. She turned to Ember, then Nate, hoping someone had a glint of understanding as to what they were all seeing. They did not.

Ember met her gaze and said into her head, *Is she okay?*

"I don't know," Stan responded and moved closer.

Nate followed. "Does someone want to explain…any of what just— what is happening?"

Stan frowned, glancing down at the sand where Anya had been sitting before her sudden flight. "What is that?" she muttered.

"What?" Nate asked, stepping close.

242

Noble remained focused on murmuring reassurances to Anya.

"This symbol," Stan said, crouching to trace the pattern lightly with her finger. "Did you draw this?"

Anya shivered harder but didn't lift her head.

"She did," Zoe piped up. "She kept drawing it, over and over. Before she ran into the water."

The teens looked at Zoe—surprised, impressed.

After a long, shaking breath, Anya finally spoke, her voice muffled against Noble's chest. "I... I felt something. Like something was coming after me." She lifted her head slightly, just enough to meet Noble's gaze with dark, haunted eyes. "I ran to where I feel safe."

Noble brushed a soaked lock of hair back from her forehead, his fingers trembling slightly. "Safe...in the water?"

Anya hesitated. Her jaw worked as if chewing over whether to speak, whether to trust them. Finally, she nodded. "My mother," she whispered. "She's...she's not like everyone else. She's a naiad."

Stan sat down hard in the sand, her mouth open. Her thoughts chased themselves uselessly: *Wiyot mermaids? Naiads? Lost Grove has naiads?* "So...she's a mermaid?"

"They're not mermaids," Zoe offered sagely, plopping down beside them. "Naiads are freshwater spirits. They guard streams and springs and rivers."

"What the hell is a naiad?" Nate asked.

Zoe said, "Like a nymph."

"What's a nymph?" Nate asked.

Zoe looked up at him like he was an imbecile. "A fairy."

"A fairy?" Nate exclaimed. "I thought fairies were small things with wings and shit. Not mermaids."

Zoe sighed. "She's not a mermaid. They're so totally different. There are all kinds of fae, Nate," she said with exasperation and a roll of the eyes.

Anya gave a tiny, broken laugh that quickly dissolved into tears. "Smart kid," she murmured.

"Fairies aren't real," Nate said.

"You don't know that," Zoe countered. "There are all kinds of things in the world."

"Oh? Says who?"

"Says Story." Zoe scowled at him.

"Oh," Nate laughed, hands flopping at his sides. "The witch. Sure. She would believe in fairies."

"They are real, and I've seen some."

"What, her?" Nate pointed to Anya.

"No." Zoe once again rolled her eyes. "Not a naiad. A fairy."

"What. Is. The. Difference?" Nate leaned over, holding his hands out.

"Can you stop arguing with a twelve-year-old for two seconds?" Noble proclaimed, glaring at his friend.

Zoe sat cross-legged beside Anya, pulling out her phone.

Noble tightened his hold, resting his chin atop her head. "You're safe," he whispered again, fiercely. "Whatever it was…it didn't get you. We're here."

For a while, the only sound was the river murmuring against the stones, a lazy, endless lullaby. Anya huddled against Noble's chest, her damp hair a curtain between her and the world. His hands moved in slow, soothing circles across her back, anchoring her as if afraid she might slip away again.

Nate moved close and squatted beside them. "Anya, you're safe. We wouldn't let anything happen to you. But do you mind me asking what you thought was coming to get you?"

"It was just a feeling," Anya explained. "Like…someone in the woods."

"Like a peeping tom?" Nate looked into the woods, trying to see into the dark beyond the edge of the wood.

Anya shook her head. "Like the trees themselves. I don't know, like a creature or something."

Nate stood and observed the woods with squinted eyes. "What about something like Raymond LaRange?"

Zoe tensed and looked over her shoulder, and Noble had to keep himself from swearing a blue streak and punching his best friend in the gut. "LaRange is dead," Noble said firmly.

Nate looked nonplussed. "Come on, we all thought Nettie was out of her mind and the Orbriallis Institute was a state-of-the-art medical research lab. We had no idea they were impregnating young women with mutant babies and stealing kids with telepathic powers to study in their labs. You telling me nothing else from Owens's lab got loose during the feds' 'cleanup' after The Event?"

Noble started to get up but Stan beat him to it. She socked Nate in just the right place to make his arm go dead.

"Ow, Jesus!"

"Are you completely daft?" Stan said in his face.

"He's dead, we all know he's dead," Nate said, glancing at Zoe. "But I'm just saying, what if something else is out there. Something like a mermaid."

"She's not a mermaid!" Stan and Zoe said in unison.

Nate raised his hands in defeat. "Okay, okay. I'm just saying."

"Yeah, we get that," Ember's electronic voice said.

Nate turned back to Anya. "Was it like an animal, you think? Like the one that killed Kevin Marlow? I just want to help out."

Anya shrugged.

Stan stared at the strange symbol in the sand, squinting at it like it might blink or move if she looked long enough. She brushed her fingers lightly across the spiraling lines, tracing the shape Anya had carved almost without thinking. Her stomach turned uneasily. "This is like the one you showed me," she said.

Anya looked over her shoulder and then cautiously spun, keeping as small as she could, to look at what she'd been drawing. Stan was right. It was like the symbol they'd found in the trees, the one her mother had stared at for hours. Anya's brow furrowed, her face pale and wary. "Yeah," she said slowly. "It does look like the one by our house. It's…not exact, but it's close."

Stan's mouth tightened into a thin line.

Zoe looked up from her phone and said, too casually, "Like the glyphs Story called that professor about? The ones from that missing lady?"

The words dropped into the air like a stone breaking the river's reflection.

Stan jerked upright. "What?" Stan blurted. "Wait—you mean Hannah?"

Zoe blinked at her, a picture of calm innocence. She shrugged. "I don't know her name. The one who went missing."

Stan pushed to her feet, sand sloughing off her shorts. "Yeah, that's Hannah."

"Wait. Wait." Nate held up his hands. "Anya's seen the glyphs? What else don't I know?"

Stan took a long breath. "Anya found her mom in a trance in the

245

woods staring at a weird symbol with fungus growing in it. I asked my uncle about it and he said Hannah found symbols like that too. She was researching the glyphs as a part of restoring Wiyot history and culture. Then she went missing."

"We've been told to stay away from a certain part of the park," Nate muttered. "Chief Wolfe said they think the fungus inside the glyphs might be some kind of psychoactive agent. He told me Saturday morning, said Dr. Raines is doing research. That's what my patrols have been. That's where I'm going after this, I mean, we have patrols in general, but like… we're keeping people away."

Stan gave him a flat look. "And you're just now mentioning this?"

"I can argue the same thing." Nate put his hands on his hips. "Why don't I know anything about this? It's clear you all know. You guys didn't tell me Anya had seen them. That her mom had. I didn't think it was connected. Why would I connect them?" Nate replied, then looked at Anya, uneasy. "I guess… I didn't know it was this close. The sector Dr. Raines is working at is on the opposite side of the park. It's nowhere near the Bury farm. Why wouldn't you guys tell me?"

"I didn't know about it either," said the robot voice on Ember's phone.

"Because she came to me about it," Stan explained. She gave Ember a shrug and an I'm sorry sort of look.

Ember shrugged back.

"Yeah, but if this is, like, a problem, you could have let me know. Does Chief Wolfe know about Anya's mom?" Nate asked.

Stan caught him looking at her as if she had the answer. "How would I know?"

"You know everything else," he countered.

"It's safe to say if Story knows, Seth knows," Zoe said. She'd scooted closer to Anya and her brother, but was still busy on her phone.

"True, but…" Nate ran a hand across his short hair.

"Look, you guys have been busy looking for Clayton," Noble interrupted. "And there's a professional working on these glyphs, right, the hallucinogens? So everyone seems to be doing their part. What would Seth do, anyway?"

Nate nodded slowly.

Staring hard at his little sister, Noble asked, "How do *you* know all this?"

Zoe thumbed at her phone, screen lighting up in the bright, pulsing sun. "Story told me," she said, as if that explained everything. She tapped a few more times, wholly unbothered, while the others traded glances.

Anya twisted in Noble's lap, worry shadowing her eyes. "There's more," she said quietly. They all leaned in instinctively, the small gravity she spun pulling them tighter. "Last night," Anya said, "my mom went sleepwalking."

Stan opened her mouth, but Anya held up a trembling hand to stop her. Everyone looked at the nearly imperceptible webbing between each finger. Anya snatched her hand back.

"It was the middle of the night," she continued, meekly "Bear, you know, our dog? She started barking, woke dad up." Her voice thinned. "He followed her. All the way to the fence by the Cursed Woods."

Stan's face drained of color. Even Zoe looked up sharply now, the gravity of the words sinking deep into her young bones.

Anya clenched the towel tighter around herself. "You don't understand. My dad doesn't mess with the Woods. Ever. His sister..." She swallowed, struggling to push past the thick knot in her throat. "His sister disappeared there, ya know? When he was a kid."

Stan and Noble knew what had happened to Emily Bury, simply because they'd grown close to Anya.

"What happened to his sister?" Nate asked.

"She went missing. When they found her..." Stan didn't want to say the rest in front of Zoe.

Silence fell heavy over them, heavier than the heat, heavier than the river's slow song. Stan swore softly under her breath, pacing two steps toward the water and back.

"And it's not just the sleepwalking," Anya went on, a desperate, broken laugh escaping her. "She's been...zoning out and leaving bowls of water around the house like some...some crazy shrine." She scrubbed a hand through her damp, tangled hair. "I haven't been sleeping well with these weird dreams."

Noble tucked her closer again, his hand firm and steady against her back. "You didn't tell me."

Anya shrugged. "It seemed more like anxiety or worry, but now... I'm not sure that's the case at all."

Stan stopped pacing and planted her feet, squaring her shoulders. "We need to do something," Stan said, voice tight with urgency. "We can't just sit here waiting for it to get worse."

"Talk to someone?" Anya whispered, not daring to hope.

"Yeah," Stan said. She kneeled in front of Anya. "I'll find something out."

Anya took her hand and leaned close. "I'm scared, Stan. Like really scared."

Stan could feel her still shivering. Though her eyes were surreal and strange, Stan knew the emotion pouring out of them. Fear was etched across her face and the way she held her body. "Crap, what time is it?" They all searched for their phones. Stan found hers and checked. "I've got our family dinner. This is perfect. I'll talk to my uncle again. I'll really press him this time, I promise," she said to Anya.

Anya nodded.

Zoe's phone pinged again, a sharp digital chime that sliced through the thick, humid tension. She glanced down, thumbed a few words, and looked up with eerie calm. "Story said to come over. Now."

The gravity shifted again—the lazy, golden afternoon snapping into sudden, urgent focus.

Stan didn't wait. She grabbed her hoodie, tossed Zoe her sandals, and jerked her head toward the trail. "C'mon," she said. "Let's move. You guys can go to Story's and see what she says. I'll talk to my uncle."

"Wait," Nate said. They all paused. He continued, "Are we gonna… like come on. A naiad?"

Anya shrunk.

"We're not gonna ask anything about that? Like, all this time?" Nate asked her.

"Now is not the time," Noble said.

"What are we gonna say to anyone else? Does Nettie know?" Nate asked Anya.

"No one knows," Anya replied.

Nate looked around at his group of friends. "Don't make me look like the bad guy. This is weird. We're talking about a fictional creature."

"She's not a creature," Noble said, standing.

Ember hated the tension. She hated the way Anya had curled up, like she wanted to disappear into a shell. Before she knew what she was doing, Ember suddenly moved. She fell to her knees in front of Anya and took her hands. "There is nothing wrong with you. You're perfect, just the way you are."

The group collectively gasped, then held their breaths.

Anya blinked her peculiar eyes, a second nictitating membrane flashing across them.

Ember stiffened. "Someone had to say it," she quickly expelled the words, then stood and took off up the river to the path.

Stan looked after her before moving, "Wait, Ember!" She jogged after her.

Noble helped Anya to her feet, keeping his arm slung firmly around her shoulders.

"That's not how I meant it," Nate explained. "I didn't mean it, Anya. I didn't."

"It's okay," she said. "I get it."

Nate nodded. "I'm just like…"

"Curious?" Zoe asked, her sandals on, book in her arms.

"Yeah," Nate replied. He looked down at Zoe. "How are you so much smarter than my sister? You guys are going to the same school, right?"

"I read," Zoe said with a smirk, before moving onto the path. The others followed.

"No one's going to mention Ember just spoke? Out loud?" Nate asked from the back of the line as they headed back into town.

Chapter Twenty-Six
Roots of Caution

C al's house was a quilt of noise, patched together with the scrape of wooden chairs on the floor, the clang of dishes, and bursts of loud, overlapping conversation. The air smelled like frying onions and grilled corn, underpinned by the rich, smoky scent of brisket that had been in the slow cooker all day.

Someone had opened the windows to let in the evening breeze, and it carried the scent of wild sage and dust from the nearby gravel road. The kitchen was crammed with bodies. Wes flipped tortillas in a hot pan. Deanna whipped together a salad with greens from their garden. Their eldest son, Mark, strained iced tea into a heavy glass pitcher, ice clinking like soft bells.

Cal leaned against the doorframe, sipping a beer, his face golden from the sun. Stan's middle brother, Sam, leaned over the table trying to teach a cousin, little Josie, how to fold napkins into triangles. Josie was more interested in making paper hats.

Through it all, Grandma Hensley sat at the head of the table, old hands resting gently on the polished wood, eyes crinkling at the edges every time the kids giggled or someone cursed too loudly.

Stan, weaving her way through the chaos, nudged Cal with her elbow. "Hey, can we talk for a second?"

He glanced at her, eyes narrowing a bit. "What's up?"

Stan jerked her chin toward the back door. They slipped outside to the small, covered porch where the light was softer and the noise of the house faded into a muffled hum. Cal leaned against the railing, his broad shoulders relaxed but his eyes watchful.

She kept her voice low. "I wanted to talk about the glyphs again."

Cal's face stiffened. "Constance—"

"No, just listen. Nate told me there might be a psychoactive fungus involved. Story told Anya and Noble that Hannah's professor friend— Dr. Elias Raines—is running tests on the spores and stuff. Why wouldn't you have told me that?"

Cal took a long, slow breath and set his beer down on the railing. "I didn't think to tell you because it's none of your business. I told you that I'd handle it," he said firmly, heading back inside and grabbing a serving dish from the counter as he moved to the dinner table. "Leave it alone."

"What are we leaving alone?" Sam asked as he poured chips into a bowl, eyeing them curiously.

"Nothing," Cal muttered.

Stan followed, irritation heating her cheeks. She sat down at the long, scratched wooden table, the clatter of dishes barely covering the tension now trailing behind her. She crossed her arms, jaw set stubbornly. "No, actually, it isn't nothing. I want to know about the glyphs in the Cursed Woods. About the fungus growing in them."

Wes, setting down a plate of tortillas, grumbled low, not quite meeting her eyes. "I told you to stay out of the woods."

Deanna, wiping her hands on a dish towel, paused. "Have you been in the woods?"

"No," Stan replied.

"Good," Mark chimed in from the sink. "Keep away from them."

Stan shook her head, stubborn as ever. "I'm not talking about the woods. I'm talking about the glyphs."

"What glyphs?" Sam asked.

"No glyphs," Cal responded.

"What are glyphs?" Stan's younger brother, Caleb, asked.

"Symbols," Deanna said, brushing his hair from his face as he took another bite of corn.

Wes turned to face his daughter, his expression unreadable. "They're in the woods. Means the same thing. Leave it be."

"Why?" Constance pushed. "You can't just tell me not to ask questions—"

"We most definitely can," her grandfather chimed in. "Don't go disrespecting your uncle and father. Or your brothers."

"I'm not. And why just the men? Are you saying I can disrespect my mom? Grandma?"

"That's not what I meant. Don't go twisting—"

"You better not disrespect me," Deanna teased.

"Look, I'm not trying to go stomping through the woods or anything," Stan said as everyone sat and began passing around food. She handed the platter of corn on the cob to one of her cousins sitting next to her and leaned across the table to speak with her uncle. You guys keep telling me to stay out of the woods, I'm staying out. All I'm asking is what is it? What does Dr. Raines know?"

Cal shook his head. "I don't know. He's running tests."

"But it's a fungus?"

"Constance," her mother shushed her.

"I can't ask?"

Cal replied, "You can ask but it doesn't mean I'm gonna tell you."

"Why not? Look." Stan scooted forward, fully directing her conversation with her uncle. "My friend Anya is really upset. She just told me she's been having strange dreams and her mother is acting weird."

Cal sighed and leaned on the table. "Can you be sure they are staying away from the one near their property? Are they staying out of the woods?"

"She said they are."

"But are you sure?" Cal asked.

Stan lifted her arms and let them flop at her sides. "Anya told me they are. Why shouldn't I believe her?"

"I'm not saying that." Cal speared some meat onto his fork and took a bite.

"You seem to be. Anya's not a liar." Stan defended her friend, internally thinking she may have kept a big secret, but there was no way she was lying about staying away from the woods and the glyph. Stan just knew she was being honest. It was in her fearful gaze and pleading voice. Anya needed help. "Why aren't you taking me seriously?"

"Alright, enough," Wes said. "Do you really think we aren't taking this seriously? A professional is looking into it."

"But you're not listening to me." Her voice rose along with her anger. "It's like I'm telling you there's a stalker and you're all like, there's nothing we can do about it until something bad happens."

Cal's fork dropped to his plate with a clang. "Not even close, Constance."

"Isn't it?"

"No," Deanna forcefully said to her daughter.

"I think it is," Stan continued. "I'm literally telling you they're staying away, but it's still affecting them and you're all like, 'Leave it alone.'"

Cal took a deep breath. "Okay. I'm listening. What do you want me to do?"

"I don't know. Tell me they should go to the hospital? I mean, should they? Do they need to get some Narcan?" She let her hands flop on the table. "Dad, have you found stuff in someone's system recently? Like, psilocybin."

Her dad arched his brows. "Recently? As in?"

"I don't like what you're implying," her mother commented.

"As in the boy, Kevin Marlow?" Stan asked bluntly.

"Who's Kevin?" Phoenix, the other twin, asked with a mouth full of bread.

Grandma Hensley tsked her grandson, wiping at his chin. "You talk with your mouth full again, and the spirits might think you're calling them with crumbs."

"Dad?" Stan asked her father, sitting on her side of the table.

"I'm not going to answer that," he said.

"That's clearly a yes."

"Respect," Grandpa Hensley remarked again in warning.

"How long can something like psychedelic mushrooms stay in one's system?" Stan pressed.

Wes wiped his mouth. "They can be detected in the bloodstream for up to twelve hours after ingestion, but there are variables. How much did a person take, how much do they weigh, what kind of activities did they undertake."

"So, tell me it doesn't sound, I don't know, weird, unlikely, fucked up—"

"Stan swore, Mom," Caleb interjected, shoveling corn into his mouth.

"Watch the mouth, Stan," her brother Sam remarked.

Stan continued, "—that they're both still feeling the after-effects of having been near it one time."

"We don't know what it is," Cal replied. "We don't know the strength of it, or what it does. We have to wait for the specialists to tell us. There isn't really a whole lot more we can do. So just leave the glyphs alone."

"The same glyphs Ms. Albrecht was looking at?" Grandpa Hensley asked.

Cal nodded, taking another bite of food.

Stan sat back, lips pursed. She took a sip of her lemonade and ate a bite of the brisket. She tapped her fork on her plate. Her uncle had a point, but it left her feeling useless.

After a pause, her grandfather cleared his throat. "Still doesn't sit right with me," he said, looking across the table. "That girl… Ms. Albrecht. A good head on her shoulders. Smart. Careful. She wasn't out there taking selfies on cliff edges."

"Selfies?" Stan asked, impressed.

"I know more than you think I do."

Cal glanced down at his plate. The familiar weight of guilt returned to his shoulders like a well-worn jacket.

"She seemed like she was being careful," Sam remarked.

"Sometimes that means nothing," said her uncle Bruce. Heads nodded in understanding. The forest takes what it wants.

Cal looked up, eyes scanning his family's faces.

The table fell quiet for a beat.

Sam cleared his throat and spoke carefully. "So, what, do you think these glyphs you guys are talking about had something to do with it?"

Cal nodded. "I don't know what else to think. Her notes suggested she found a pattern in the symbols, each one denoting a boundary."

"Boundary?" Grandpa Hensley raised an eyebrow. "Like a fence? Keep something in or out?"

Cal offered a small shrug. "Nah. Don't think so. She thought there was a center point, and when we went out Monday, we found that cave and that painting I told you about."

"Ah, right. With the mural and the animal."

Wes looked at his brother. "There was an animal in the cave you found?"

"Yeah," Cal said offhandedly.

"You didn't mention that part."

Cal shrugged. "It just ran off."

"What kind of animal?" Phoenix asked. He was swinging both feet back and forth and tapping his fork on the brisket on his plate.

Grandma Hensley, her hands still resting on the table, answered, "Tah-tah-kle'ah," she whispered, the word rolling out like a low wind over water.

Both Wes and Cal snapped to attention. "Mom," they said in unison, like they'd rehearsed it.

Stan frowned, eyes darting between them. "What's that mean?"

Grandma reached across the table and took her granddaughter's hand, her skin cool and soft. Her voice was low, deep, and full of warning. "Some things, child, aren't meant to be found or followed. They wake up when you poke at them. Better to let sleeping spirits lie."

Stan swallowed hard but didn't look away. "But what is that?" she asked, looking at her dad and uncle. "Why did you react like that?"

Cal set a dish down hard, finally losing his patience. "It doesn't matter!" he snapped, rubbing the bridge of his nose. "Just old stories. Nothing more. People let them get in their heads and start seeing things. You keep poking at it, and you'll start seeing things, too."

Wes cut in, voice firm and final. "I know you're eighteen, Constance. I know you think you're grown. But I'm telling you right now to drop this. Leave it alone."

She opened her mouth to argue, but the weight of his stare kept the words stuck in her throat. Her uncle busied himself with his plate of food. Only when he looked up did Stan see his eyes begging her not to say more, not to do more. She'd never seen him look that way, or felt the weight of unspoken things between them.

Wes turned back to his meal, clearly done with the conversation.

Grandma Hensley squeezed Stan's hand one last time, then let go, folding her hands back in her lap. Her face was thoughtful, but she didn't say anything more.

Stan chewed on the inside of her cheek, stewing in the uneasy silence that followed. The food smelled good, the house was full of laughter and noise, but something darker hung in the corners, just out of reach, like a shadow that refused to be banished.

Chapter Twenty-Seven
Prowlers and Vigilantes

Nate sat in the passenger seat of Sasha's police cruiser, heading to answer a call about a prowler in someone's backyard, his mind still frazzled by what he had seen earlier at the river. *You would think having friends who can speak inside your head would have prepared you for this,* he thought to himself. But Ember and Emory were still human. Albeit humans with supernatural powers. Anya had changed right before their eyes, her hair, her eyes, her hands. *What the fuck was that?* And what were they all saying? A naiad? A fairy? A nymph? All made-up creatures from fairy tales. And was a nymph the same thing as a nympho? He didn't think so, but he couldn't rule anything out at this point. And why was everyone but him acting like it was no big deal? I mean, seriously, they all just witnessed Anya mutate in front of them and acted like she had just gotten a scrape from a rock in the river. And Noble, glaring at him, scolding him like he was being malicious when he only wanted to openly talk amongst friends about what was happening. *You're perfect, just the way you are,* he said. "What a loser."

"You okay over there, buddy?"

Nate looked over at Sasha. "Did I just say that out loud?"

"You sure there's nothing you want to talk about? You've been acting weird ever since you got to the station. Like, you're quiet."

"Pfft," Nate scoffed. "You're quiet." What was he going to tell her? My best friend's girlfriend is a mermaid? *Sounds like the title of a shitty romance book*, he thought.

They were just outside town limits on the Wildcat Highway heading south to their destination. "Okay, whatever you say. I just find it a bit ironic that you've been asking me personal questions nonstop for a month, and the first time I ask you to express yourself, you clam up."

"I don't ask you personal questions."

"Are you fucking kidding me right now?" Sasha spouted. "You asked me if Angel and I showered together or separately on a daily basis."

Nate waved her off. "I did not. That was Seth."

Sasha laughed so hard she could hardly bring herself to stop. "Seth is the most respectful, professional, and decent person I have ever met. *You*, on the other hand. It's like you transported here from the nineties."

Nate puckered up his face at her. "The nineties? What does that even mean? That I like shitty music or something? Because I don't."

Sasha shook her head. "I give up with you."

"Well, I'll never give up on you."

"I don't even know how to take that."

"I'm your partner and I'll always have your back."

Sasha rolled her eyes. "Please stop with the cliches. You're not even an official member of the department. How could we be partners?"

"Oh, don't start that again," Nate said. "What am I doing riding shotgun with you on the way to investigate a prowler then, huh?"

"A prowler?"

"Yeah, the lady said someone was lurking in her backyard. Sounds like a prowler to me."

"Her name is Michelle O'Ryan. And just make sure to call her—"

"Mrs. O'Ryan, I know. Unless she tells us to call her by her first name. I don't need to be told anything twice. I have an iron memory."

"That's not a phrase. Oh, here we go," Sasha said, pointing at a mailbox on the side of the road being lit up by her headlights. She turned onto a long, dirt pathway surrounded by a pitch-black forest.

"Where the hell is the house?"

"Probably close to the shore."

Nate looked around the wooded area. "Why would someone be way out here, creeping behind someone's house?"

"I was thinking the same thing. Keep an eye out for any movement, any lights, maybe a car off the path."

Nate didn't see anything by the time they arrived at the house, but he was getting creeped out by the darkness that surrounded them and the idea that someone could be out there watching. "I wouldn't want to live out here. It's a perfect setting for a horror movie."

Sasha turned off the vehicle. "Thanks for putting that in my head. Once we get in and make sure Mrs. O'Ryan is safe and that there's no one in the house, I'll search the perimeter while you stay inside with her."

"I'm not letting you search out here by yourself."

"It's not your call, young one. Now, let's go," she said, and got out of the cruiser.

"Young one," Nate said, shaking his head while he got out and headed toward the front door. He turned in circles, shining his flashlight into the woods, hoping he didn't see a face peeking out from behind a tree. Or worse, a masked face. It was colder this close to the ocean. The crashing waves were so loud he didn't think they'd hear anyone approaching them. A perfect trap.

Sasha knocked on the door. "Mrs. O'Ryan, it's the police!"

Nate noticed a woman peer through the closed curtains of the front window, presumably Mrs. O'Ryan. She had said she was home alone, that her husband worked the night shift.

The front door opened, Michelle O'Ryan holding the door tightly. She was a short woman in her late forties, Sasha guessed, wearing grey sweatpants and a navy-blue sweatshirt that said "Colorado" with a snowy mountain on it.

"Hello, Mrs. O'Ryan, I'm Officer Kingston and this is Officer Abbot. May we come in?"

"Of course. Thanks for coming so quickly. Please, come in. And call me Michelle," she said, and stood aside, allowing Sasha and Nate into her home.

"Thank you, Michelle. Have you seen or heard anything since we last spoke?" Sasha asked, shutting the front door behind her.

"No, no I haven't heard anything, but I also haven't been looking out the windows."

"Can you show us where you saw this man?"

"Yes. This way," she said, walking past the living room area.

Nate looked around. The house looked a lot bigger from the inside. It had the vibe of a fancy, fully furnished cabin that someone would rent out on Airbnb. "Are there any other doors to the outside in here, Mrs. O'Ryan?"

Michelle walked into the back den, a library of books on dark oak shelves, a comfortable loveseat, a lamp on each side emitting warm light, and a drape-covered window behind. "Yes. A back door by the butler pantry," she said, pointing to her right. "And, please, just Michelle."

"Did you lock everything like we told you?" Sasha asked.

"Oh, yes. All the doors and windows."

Sasha walked behind the loveseat and pulled open the curtains to the window looking into the O'Ryans backyard. "Through here, I presume?"

Michelle joined Sasha at the window. "Back there, right by the tree line. The motion sensor floodlight came on. I figured it was a deer or a raccoon. We see lots of both of them. I peeked out and saw the man back there, right behind the first line of trees."

Nate gazed out the window and couldn't see a thing, just pure blackness.

"Can you describe him to us the best you can?" Sasha asked.

"I wish I could," Michelle admitted, hanging her head. "The light barely reaches that far back. He had a beard and…I don't know, I got so scared I immediately closed the curtains, ran to make sure the front door was locked, and called you."

Nate exchanged a glum look with Sasha. If the man had a beard, it certainly wasn't Clayton Meadows. They shared an unspoken hope when they got the call. Neither of them even verbalized it for fear of jinxing things.

"Was he tall? Short? White? Darker skinned?" Sasha inquired.

Michelle wrung her hands together. "He was white. Or lighter skinned at least. Normal sized, I suppose. Not too tall or too short."

"How about clothing?" Nate asked.

Michelle stared ahead, trying to recall what she had seen. "I'm sorry, I don't know. Nothing that stood out. No bright colors or anything."

"Do you mind if we search the house while we ask you a few more questions?" Sasha said.

"Of course," Michelle said and stepped out from behind the loveseat. "It's just the one story. I grabbed a knife and looked through the rest of the house to be sure no one had somehow gotten in."

"Smart," Nate commented, following Sasha through the dining room, into the kitchen.

"Has anything like this ever happened before, Michelle?" Sasha asked.

"No, never. Not that I've noticed anyhow."

Sasha walked down the hallway, looking into the first doorway, a bathroom. All the lights in the house were already on, which was good. "Do you ever have friends, neighbors, or relatives that show up unannounced?"

"Not without calling, no."

Sasha continued down the hallway. Nate exited the room on the left. "Bedroom. All clear," he said.

"Do you have issues with anyone? Any recent arguments or incidents of any kind?" Sasha asked, stepping into the next room, an office with more shelves filled with books. A well-read couple apparently.

"Oh, no, not at all," Michelle said, peering into the office from the hallway. "Samuel and I get along fine with everyone."

Sasha stepped out of the office and nodded at Nate, who was walking into what looked like the master bedroom. "And you said your husband works at the hospital? Did you call him?"

"He's a nurse. Everyone likes him there. We've gone to holiday parties and everyone is so nice. I texted him. I haven't heard back yet, but that's not uncommon. He doesn't like to be tied to his phone when he's at work."

Sasha looked into the last room on the left, across from the master bedroom Nate was still inspecting. It was a third bedroom, likely for guests, no family photos on the wall or any personal knickknacks. "That makes sense. It's an important job. When is he off?"

"Three in the morning."

"Is there someone you can call to come stay with you until he gets home?"

Michelle shrugged. "No one all that close."

Sasha walked back into the hall, where Nate was waiting for them.

"All clear," he said.

"Let's go back into the kitchen," Sasha said, leading the way. "Michelle, I'm going to go out and search the perimeter of your house. Officer Abbott will stay in here with you."

"Okay, thank you."

Nate motioned to the stools around the kitchen island. "We can sit if it's more comfortable."

Michelle motioned to the stool nearest Nate. "Yes, please sit. Can I make you a cup of tea or get you a cup of water?"

"Tea would actually be great, thank you. How long have you and your husband lived here?"

Sasha stepped outside, shutting the front door behind her, relieved that Nate was already engaging Michelle in friendly conversation. And of course he said he would have tea. She doubted Nate had ever drunk a cup of tea in her life. When she heard the deadbolt latch behind her, she pulled out her Maglite and gun, placing one wrist on top of the other, and stepped into the front yard. Not that there was much of one, basically a gravel driveway surrounded by woods.

She checked on the right side of the driveway, walking about fifty feet into the woods, carefully searching for any signs that someone had recently been out here. Michelle O'Ryan must not scare easily living out here. The dense woods were constricting and utterly silent, too far away from the highway to hear cars passing, and no previous complaints or calls had been logged by the family of two. She made her way back toward the driveway and checked the other side of the forest area.

Finding nothing of note, Sasha made her way to the backyard, the motion light activating, alert for any movement or sounds that she could hear over the roar of the waves beyond and below. The houses along this stretch of the Wildcat were few and far between. The thought of a bearded man wandering through the woods back here was ominous, no question about that. It could have been a neighbor out looking for their dog. And although the chances were slim, she supposed it could be someone out searching for Clayton. They had had hundreds of volunteers over the past week, the town all coming together in hopes of finding the boy.

If it wasn't that, Sasha couldn't think of another good reason for someone to be roaming around back here. She walked inside the first row of trees where Michelle had stated she saw the man, Maglite pointed to the ground, looking for tracks and any debris left behind. Every tree she passed, Sasha couldn't help but examine it for any strange glyphs, hoping she wasn't inhaling toxic spores or hallucinogenic fungus.

Weaving through the trees, going deeper into the woods toward the ocean, the sound of her own footsteps crunching leaves and twigs started to unnerve her. They were her footsteps, weren't they? Sasha exited the forest and walked up to the ledge overlooking the ocean. She did a full sweep with her Maglite to ensure she was alone. So far nothing suspicious had caught her eye. She inched toward the edge and peered over. It was a good hundred feet down to the rocky deathtrap below. Sasha wasn't especially afraid of heights, but the thought of a bearded man rushing out of the forest to push her over the edge was enough to get her quickly backpedaling away from the ledge.

Sasha reentered the woods, marking a different pathway back to cover more ground. Right as the lights from the back windows of the house came into focus, she heard a rustling to her right. She spun, aiming her Maglite toward the sound, and saw a pair of eyes reflecting back at her. Sasha yelped and dropped to her knees, aiming her gun at what turned out to be a raccoon. She let out a sigh of relief as the creature just stared back at her. "A fucking raccoon." she sighed.

"Would you stop laughing? You would have been scared shitless out there, too."

"It's not that," Nate said. "I was already creeped out before we even entered her house. It's just the first time I've heard you sound or act like a girl."

"That is so sexist. Dudes yelp."

"Real men don't yelp."

"Jesus Christ. And you're a real man, are you?"

"I would have been more like, 'oh fuck!' and got ready to fight."

Sasha glared at him. "Ready to fight a raccoon?"

Nate shrugged. "Whatever. Whoever."

"I don't buy it. If you had a firearm, which thankfully you don't, you probably would have reacted and fired a shot off. I doubt you've ever been in a dangerous situation in your life."

"Look, I don't have to have been confronted by armed robbers or vigilantes to know danger."

Sasha laughed. "Vigilantes. Not only is your social awareness from the nineties, you're like stuck in a Stallone action film from back then."

"Cobra."

"Exactly."

"It's almost midnight. Are we going to meet up with Eddie and— hey, look at this asshole!" Nate exclaimed, pointing at a person in the distance walking on the side of the highway.

Sasha leaned forward. "It looks like a man."

"A drunk man. Look at him, he's weaving all over the place. Oh, I bet that's our prowler. Probably couldn't find the right house."

"I'm going to approach slowly."

"Don't hit him."

"I'll pull in front of him, but not too close."

"What do we do if he runs?" Nate asked.

"Run after him."

"Now we're talking. Looks like he's wearing some sort of outfit or…"

Sasha gave a wide berth as she approached the man to ensure he didn't stumble into the vehicle.

Nate peered out the passenger window. "Ew, this dude is dirty as shit."

Sasha pulled past the man, happy he didn't take off running.

Nate looked in the side mirror. "Man, this dude looks like he crawled out of—holy fuck."

"What?" Sasha asked, pulling the car to a stop.

Nate looked at Sasha, wide-eyed. "I think it might be Clayton."

Sasha dashed out of the car, Nate following just a step behind her. She brought her Maglite up and lit up the man's face. The boy's face. "Oh my God. Clayton? Clayton Meadows?" She had been deceived by the boy's height.

Nate slowly approached with both hands held up in peace, the boy's features slowly coming into focus beneath the layer of dirt, mud, or whatever was covering him. "Clayton?" he attempted, getting no reply but what could only be described as "crazy eyes." "Dude, he must have been around the glyphs," he said quietly to Sasha.

Sasha lowered her light enough so it wasn't blinding Clayton. Not that he had any reaction to it, or their presence at all. He was mumbling to himself, tripping over his own feet, staring at who knows what he was seeing. "Clayton? My name is Officer Sasha Kingston. I'm with the Lost Grove Police. We've been looking for you. Your family misses you." Still no response. She closed the gap between them, and Clayton started flailing his arms, like a windmill on acid, causing Sasha to quickly back up.

"Whoa! Hey man, it's okay," Nate offered, getting nearer to Sasha now. "We're here to help. Get you home. Maybe get you a burger or something."

Sasha and Nate continued backpedaling. "Call Seth," Sasha said. "Right now, Nate."

Nate grabbed his phone, one arm still held out toward Clayton, quickly finding and pressing Seth's contact.

"Clayton, I'm going to need you to get in the car with us. Or we can call an ambulance. Are you hurt?" she pointlessly asked. He didn't have any visible wounds and wasn't responding to them.

"Seth, it's Nate. We've found Clayton… No, I'm sure, he's standing right in front of us. Or walking… Sasha, she's trying to get him into the back of the squad car." Nate was watching Sasha, who had jogged backward to open up the back door. "I don't think so. I don't see any blood or wounds, but he's also covered in dirt, and maybe shit, he doesn't smell too good… No, but we're pretty sure he must have been around that fungus you told us about, because he's acting all sorts of crazy."

Sasha stepped to the side of the car, getting in position to hopefully funnel Clayton into the back seat.

Clayton's mumbles started to form into words. "No more of that, I don't want any more of that!"

"That was him," Nate said into the phone, making his way around the front of the squad car on the other side of Sasha, so he could help block Clayton off. "Not really. He swung his arms in circles once, but he hasn't been aggressive."

Sasha held her arms out, Maglite back in her belt, and prepared to guide Clayton. "I need you to get in the back seat, Clayton. I'm going to put my hand on your shoulder, okay?"

"Hold on, Seth." Nate placed his phone on the hood and prepared himself like a defensive end in case Clayton made a mad dash.

Sasha placed her hand on the back of Clayton's shoulder and his arm whipped back. Sasha ducked, grabbed his arm, and twisted it behind him. "Help me get him in!"

Nate rushed up and grabbed Clayton's wrist on his oncoming swing.

"Never!" Clayton yelled. "I won't go back. You won't find me!"

Nate grabbed the back of Clayton's head, putting his years of high school wrestling to use, and pulled it down while Sasha pushed the boy in from the side as they successfully wedged him into the back seat. Nate grabbed a hold of Clayton's kicking feet, just now realizing he was wearing cleats. "Ow!" He kept hold of them, forced them behind the front seat and fell back so Sasha could shut the door.

"Nice work, partner," Sasha said, falling back against the car as Clayton pounded on the window, screaming.

Nate got to his feet and looked at his hands.

"You okay?"

Nate wiped his hands on his slacks. "Fine, just a bit of blood," he said as he grabbed his phone. "Hey, Seth, we… No, we got him. He's in the back seat… Yeah, I think that's a good idea… Yep, we'll see you there."

"He says we should meet him at the hospital?" Sasha guessed.

Nate nodded. "Yeah. That window gonna hold?" he asked, pointing at Clayton's fists attempting to break through.

Sasha patted the window with her palm. "Bulletproof."

Nate raised his eyebrows, skeptical, and made his way to the passenger side of the car. "Gonna be loud in there."

"Yep." Sasha opened up her door to get in, and Clayton's voice boomed out.

"Too small for me, I've seen those eyes, ain't no mice!"

"Oof," Nate uttered and opened his door to get in.

Chapter Twenty-Eight
Hospital Relief

Seth impatiently waited for the elevator at Darcy Medical Center to reach the fourth floor. It was one of those elevators that sounded like there were two grizzled operators living in the subterranean basement who manually pulled the car up to the desired location. It wasn't that he didn't believe Nate that the boy he heard in the background was in fact Clayton Meadows, it was just that every day this past week had brought nothing but bad luck and curveballs, so it was hard to accept a win.

Seth was out of Story's bed and in his car in less than two minutes. As soon as his phone connected to his Bluetooth, he called Reid Meadows's cell phone. Clayton's father had been the one to take all calls since his son went missing. He answered after the first ring, his voice a volatile mixture of hope and fear. Seth told him that two of his officers found Clayton wandering up Wildcat Highway and positively identified him, the boy still wearing his baseball uniform, and that he was currently being treated at Darcy Medical.

The chime for floor four mercifully sounded and Seth muscled the doors open, believing he could get through them quicker. He immediately spotted Sasha at the reception desk and sprinted to meet her.

"Hey, Seth, Clayton's in with doctors now. Nate's perched outside the door like a bodyguard."

Seth laughed. It felt really good to laugh. He stepped away from the desk and lowered his voice. "Have the Meadowses showed up yet?"

"Not yet. I can't imagine what they're feeling on the way here."

Seth shook his head, still in disbelief that the boy was found unharmed. "As positive as they've remained, every parent knows the statistics. The relief must be indescribable. Though they're likely holding that in until they see his face, which I'll be honest, I'd like to see myself."

"You don't believe us?" Sasha cocked an eyebrow.

"I do. I'd still like to see."

Sasha led Seth down the hallway to where Nate was standing post.

"Hey, Chief. Good news, huh?"

Seth patted Nate on the shoulder as he looked through the window into the room, seeing the side of Clayton's face. There were two doctors and a nurse surrounding the bed. "That's an understatement. Have you heard anything yet?"

"Couple different doctors have been in and out of there, but I didn't want to interrupt them."

"You can always ask for an update."

Nate nodded. "Noted."

"Did he say anything else on the way here?"

Nate exchanged a look with Sasha. "I mean, nothing that made any sense. He talked about the darkness a lot."

"Which could mean anything under the circumstances," Sasha said.

"Circumstances that we don't fully know yet," Seth corrected. "Anything else? Any words or phrases that stood out?"

Sasha sighed. "Mostly unintelligible. Mice?"

"Claws," Nate added.

Seth looked back through the window and caught the eye of one of the doctors. Seth motioned for him to come out and got a nod in return. "Any context to either of those things?"

"Definitely not," Sasha answered.

The door opened and out stepped a young male doctor, Asian, stout, well built, who extended his hand to Seth. "It's a good night. I've been following the search."

Seth shook his hand. "Chief of Lost Grove Police, Seth Wolfe."

"Dr. Yun."

"How is he doing?"

"Vitals are stable. Physically, he's well. He was dehydrated, but we—"

"Is it him?" A woman's voice carried from down the hall.

Seth turned to see Molly Meadows running toward them, followed by Reid. Quickly closing the distance, she grabbed a hold of Seth's hands. "It's him, Molly."

Clayton's mother wrapped her arms around Seth. "Oh my God."

Reid looked at Dr. Yun. "How is he, Doctor?"

"I was just updating Chief Wolfe."

"Can we see him?" Molly asked. "Please, I just—"

Dr. Yun held up his hands. "In just a brief moment. We're finishing taking some blood samples. Most importantly, he's in good physical condition. He was quite dirty, but once we got him cleaned up, we found no broken bones, no fractures, just a couple minor scratches and bruises."

Reid placed his hands on his wife's neck and rubbed the tension out.

"He was quite dehydrated, but we've got him on IV fluids. The only area of immediate concern was his state of mind."

Molly closed her hands over her mouth. "Oh no."

"He was incoherent and physically agitated upon arrival, which is consistent with what Officers Kingston and Abbott described when they found him. His eyes were dilated and he was having issues responding to any verbal questions or prompts. I would describe his state similar to what we see when people are high on mushrooms."

"Mushrooms?" Reid said.

Seth exchanged brief glances with Sasha and Nate.

"We'll see what the blood results are, but he's been sedated for now. He needs fluids and rest."

A nurse exited the room with a plastic dish of blood vials. "Hello," she greeted the parents and officers and then looked at Dr. Yun. "Dr. Richardson says you can come in now."

Dr. Yun pushed open the door and extended his arm to Reid and Molly. "Come in and see your son."

Seth waited for Clayton's parents to enter the room and then said to Dr. Yun, "I'll be in in a moment."

Dr. Yun nodded and let the door shut.

Seth turned to his team. "Nate, can you call and update Eddie, Peter, and Joe? And then call Bill and tell him to reach out to all the local volunteers."

"On it," Nate said and headed toward the reception area.

"What do you need from me?" Sasha asked.

"Call Cal, Paddy, and Sheriff Hayes. I'll see if there's anything we can get out of Clayton. I'll call Mayor Sumner as soon as we're done here."

"You got it." Sasha turned to go.

"Oh, and Sasha? Get some sleep tonight. Wes said he's hoping to get the DNA results tomorrow for the animal that attacked Kevin Marlow. That along with the start of the fair—"

"It's going to be a long weekend," Sasha said.

Seth nodded and headed in to see Clayton.

Chapter Twenty-Nine
Break Ground

They moved like ghosts across the gravel, feet muffled by soft-soled boots, breath kept low in their throats. Nettie's heart was pounding, but not from fear...at least, not the kind that warns you to turn back. This was the good kind. The kind that hummed in her blood, loud and chaotic, like something wild finally being let loose.

The chain-link fence had already been clipped in one spot, the cut edges curling outward like silver thorns. Jesse slipped through first, glancing back once, his dark eyes glinting behind the strip of green bandana over his mouth. His shaggy, sun-warmed hair curled under his beanie, and tattoos peeked from the sleeves of his threadbare flannel. Inked vines twisted up one arm, the word *hollow* inked just beneath the crook of his elbow. He gave her a cocky, two-finger salute and turned forward again, moving like someone who didn't care if he set the whole place on fire.

Nettie followed, crouched low. The bandana she wore smelled faintly of fabric softener and spray paint. Behind her, Valerie, in her early thirties, climbed through the fence last, calm and composed as ever, her sleek ponytail tucked into the back of a faded baseball cap, black cargo pants tucked into her boots, knife at her belt like this was a normal Thursday. For her, it kind of was.

They didn't talk. Valerie had a rule about silence during ops. No names. No chatter. No lights unless you had to. This wasn't just protest, it was resistance, and resistance didn't need words.

Nettie remembered the first time she saw them. She'd gone to the picket at the edge of the site mostly to watch. To *feel* like she was doing something. Her friends had already moved on. Noble was holding Anya's hand like none of this had ever touched his sister. Stan joked about it and had cozied up to the newcomers to town, the ones being studied like lab rats themselves by the very same institute. Nate had stopped pushing his conspiracy theory investigations, saying he'd "outgrown all that." They all treated The Event like a thing that happened *then*, as if everything went back to normal after it was over.

But Nettie lived in a house where the lie had worn her brother's skin for years. Where her *real* brother, the one she fought for, came back a stranger. Fourteen years old now, but aged in some other dimension that had been quiet, drowsy, gentle, foreign, and all of it forced on him in a drugged-up state so he barely recalled a single thing. He wasn't charismatic and goofy like he used to be. He wasn't the kid she'd spent years trying to save.

So when she saw Jesse and Valerie standing at the edge of the protest line—Valerie with her arms crossed, silent and assessing, and Jesse sprawled across the hood of a gutted van covered in mossy stickers—something inside her tilted. Valerie looked like control. Jesse looked like chaos. Nettie had no idea where she fit between them. She just knew she wanted to stand near them.

When Jesse caught her staring, he'd grinned. It wasn't mocking or leering. Just that lazy, charming kind of interest she didn't know how to handle. She never thought someone like him—older, feral—would look at someone like her. But later that night, after the protest, he asked if she wanted to see the bus he lived in. She said yes, and when she curled up on the bed beneath the strings of colored lights and heard him rant about pipelines and logging companies and synthetic seeds, she nodded along.

Later, after the three of them became a group and Jesse kissed her, after they'd done more than kiss, she ranted about the Orbriallis, about how they conducted strange experiments and stole people and impregnated them with genetically mutated babies, and he listened. He truly listened and he got angry with her.

She never told him the whole truth, but as they lay in the hard bed of his converted van in the cooling breeze through the small window, she let a few rumors slip. Maybe she let him think the Institute was more than it let on because it was and someone should do something about it.

The Orbriallis Institute's expansion site was all wooden skeletons, unfinished electrical, and poured foundations. The frame of a house—a nurse or doctor's future dream home—jutted out of the dirt like a broken rib cage. The whole place reeked of new lumber, sunbaked dust, and quiet greed.

They moved through the building site and slipped between the work trucks and generator stacks, spray-painting the cameras. Red, green, black—whatever cans they'd found last minute on sale or in Nettie's garage.

Valerie painted red Xs over the cameras. Jesse cracked one clean off the siding with a length of rebar.

This wasn't right, but it was better than feeling helpless. Her real friends—the ones she used to build forts with, drive out to the beach with—told her to be careful. Nettie tried to explain to her oldest friend, Anya, and she would bite her lip and say "I get it," but she didn't. She had Noble occupying all her time.

Stan and Nate had both said, "Don't get in trouble. Don't do anything stupid." Well, they hadn't spent their entire childhood arguing with their parents over not-George, going to countless appointments of pointless family therapy as if not-George might suddenly change. He wouldn't and he hadn't because he wasn't real.

Valarie tossed her another can from her pack and Nettie jogged to the camera above the office door. She stood on tiptoe and sneered beneath her mask. She stuck out her tongue too, then sprayed over the lens, thinking, *Screw you. Screw all of you.*

Nine months ago, she thought she'd finally won. The world had cracked open, and the truth had come spilling out. The Green Man was Raymond LaRange, a man tried for child molestation and sentenced to a mental institute, then transferred to the Orbriallis Institute. The not-children were real, living in caves and following LaRange like a demented Pied Piper. George, the real George, was being tested, experimented on, in the dark lower levels of the Orbriallis Institute. She'd been right. George wasn't George. Not-George was a lie, the rot in the foundation of her family, and she'd known it from the moment she was eight years old and saw the Green Man come for him and warned her parents to keep him safe, but they hadn't. She'd lived years looking at a stranger. She'd lost any hope of a relationship with her parents because she refused to give up on her real brother.

But when the real George was returned—weak and thin, his skin too pale, his voice strange and quiet—nothing was resolved. They'd covered it up with excuses, which she understood was the only way she'd get to keep her real brother. Nettie did understand that. So there was no parade. No justice. No apologies from the Institute or her parents. Just... explanations. Storylines. A tumor. A "cure."

What she hadn't understood was she would never get her brother back. He didn't like the same music. He didn't laugh at their inside jokes. He tolerated her attempts at affection and sibling kinship, but didn't need her anymore. And he liked Emory Graff better than he liked her.

God, *Emory*. The cool, brown-eyed, wide smiling jock who rescued her brother. Him and his hip sister, down from the city, and now he was working for them. Emory was actually helping those unethical doctors inside the institute like they weren't moments away from shoving needles filled with disorienting drugs in their arms and kidnapping them from their families to be studied like animals without sunshine or other human interactions.

It killed her that Emory was the one George always talked about. He smiled when he mentioned him. He loved going to the Institute for his routine visits to work with Emory.

She hated him.

She hated them all.

They took her brother.

They gave him back wrong.

And now they were building houses on stolen land.

Nettie grabbed the rebar from Jesse's hand and swung it at the camera on the makeshift light pole as they headed deeper into the site. They had plans for a more permanent kind of damage, something that couldn't be painted over or washed off with turpentine and soap.

Jesse caught up with her, wrapping his arm around her shoulders and pulling her in close as he took the rebar back from her. He swung the rebar up into a freshly installed window, all the stickers and plastic still on it. The window split open with a cathartic shatter and they all ran down the dirt road, high on the idea they were morally in the right.

They paused inside the makings of a series of connected townhomes. Jesse was crouched by the frame of a garage, giving her a wild grin. He had that easy, crooked kind of smile that could get him forgiven for things he absolutely shouldn't be forgiven for.

She liked him. Maybe a little too much. His ethics were fuzzy. He wasn't in this just for the trees or the frogs. He liked watching people squirm. But Jesse understood her pain, the way it manifested in anger and the need to yell, bite, scratch, scream. He understood what it meant to feel righteous and furious and small all at once. He didn't try to fix it. He just held her hand and joined in. And when he kissed her—quick and careless and hot like stolen matches—she didn't feel like a kid still stuck being the pariah, the girl who thought her brother was a changeling from some fairy tale. None of it had been a fairy tale.

They were at the back of the site now, where new foundations were waiting to be dug. They reached the excavator. A rusted yellow beast with its claws raised to the dark like it had been caught mid-pounce. Jesse climbed first, nimble, cocky, already reaching for the controls.

"This the part where we make 'em bleed money?" he said through his mask.

Valerie nodded once. "Do it fast. Quietly if you can."

Nettie climbed in beside Jesse, heart thudding. The cab reeked of oil and sun-heated vinyl. She braced herself as Jesse flipped the ignition.

The machine roared to life louder than expected.

"Subtle," Nettie muttered.

Jesse grinned. "You love it."

"Do you even know how to drive this thing?" Nettie asked, joking.

Jesse flexed his fingers over the controls. "How hard can it be?"

Jesse fumbled, cursed, then yanked a lever with more confidence than understanding. The excavator's arm extended, and landed on the ground in front of them, groaning like a dying animal. The whole cab shook and Nettie grabbed onto Jesse's shoulders.

"Whoops," he said, still grinning under his mask.

Nettie playfully slapped his shoulder.

Outside, Valerie rolled her eyes, then waved her hand, making the "get on with it" sign, telling them to hurry it along.

Jesse found a lever that kick-started them out of gear, and then they started rolling. He pressed the gas, a little too hard, and the machine jolted forward.

Nettie fell back into the plexiglass. "Careful!" she harshly whispered.

Jesse waved a hand, pushing more buttons, toying with more levers. "Alright," Jesse muttered through a grin, working the levers like he was born for it. "Let's give 'em a new floor plan."

The excavator rumbled forward, treads chewing into the loose-packed soil. The steel arm lifted and rotated, jerking like a drunk puppet. They moved toward the homes with windows, siding, nearly done except for the interior finishing touches. They were going to wreck this place and the Orbriallis was going to pay out the nose to get these homes rebuilt.

Nettie gripped the edge of the seat with both hands, nerves buzzing. This wasn't the kind of destruction she'd pictured. It was clumsier. Realer. "You sure you know what you're—"

But before she could finish, Jesse slammed a lever downward. He'd meant to swing the arm sideways but his hand slipped.

The excavator arm plunged down. A thunderous crack exploded beneath them. The soil rippled under the machine. Dirt collapsed with a bone-deep protest, a slow-motion convulsion of the earth itself.

"Jesse…" Nettie's voice came out thin.

He yanked back the lever, but it was too late.

The ground beneath the excavator cracked open, gaping like a wound in the world. The front treads dipped forward as the machine continued its steady plod forward and the ground gave way beneath them.

The machine tilted and groaned. Then it dropped.

"Out!" Jesse bellowed, already shoving at the door.

They slammed it open. Nettie jumped first, boots scraping the tread as she leapt. The force of her landing jolted through her legs.

Jesse jumped behind her. The machine screeched again, metal screaming against stone as it slid deeper, teetering as the ground decided whether it would have such a monstrosity or not.

Valerie met them halfway, eyes wide but face calm. "Come on, guys! Come this way!"

They scuttled across the ground, finding their feet tangled beneath them, their bodies responding too slow to what their brains were telling them. Behind them, the ground caved in where the excavator had struck, but it continued, radiating outward like the blow had broken the seal of some buried hollow. The front half of the excavator tipped fully in and vanished with a sound like a mountain swallowing its breath.

Dust, debris, and earth blasted upward in a choking wave. They ducked, shielding their faces.

It felt like a disaster film, all motion and wind and sound. The dust was dense and dry, blinding. Nettie coughed, gagged, pulling her bandana off because she couldn't get enough air as she coughed on the grime swirling around them.

The air had turned wet and sour with the scent of rot and guano. The smell hit them like a wall: urine-sharp, fungal-damp, like the inside of a cellar full of animals that had never left.

"What is that?" Jesse wheezed, choking back a cough and waving his bandana around in front of his face to clear the air.

Valerie didn't answer.

She was still, her posture taut. One foot shifted back unconsciously. Her hand hovered at the blade on her belt.

The pit steamed dust into the night air.

It churned upward in heavy swells, dragging the moonlight with it, catching the blue-white glow and scattering it through the haze like light thrown through dirty glass.

"Do you hear that?" Valerie asked.

At first, Nettie thought the sound beneath it was just settling rubble. Just stone and machine shifting into the aftermath of collapse, but it wasn't. There was something too coordinated in the movement, a shifting rhythm.

The dust swirled, refusing to settle.

Skrrk. Skrrrk.

...pause.

Chk. Chk.

They stilled, listening to the cadence. It repeated like something moving deliberately beneath the ground, gently brushing softly against the walls of a cavern that should never have been touched.

Valerie flinched and stepped back as a darker shadow rose among the cloud, sweeping and swirling the dirt and grime. It wasn't a form, more like spirits slipping between worlds. It wasn't solid, but it hadn't been smoke either as it rose and disappeared into the night sky.

Another one danced behind the dust. It bent moonlight around its form, draped in deeper blacks, shifting greys, the softest variations of void.

This time, Nettie gasped and tumbled back into Valerie. Beside her, Jesse stood slack-jawed, unmoving.

The smell hit them again as another shadow passed behind the static of the dust that refused to settle.

Nettie's eyes watered.

Jesse's voice broke like a snapped string. "Maybe...maybe it's a gas leak."

Nettie shook her head. She didn't know why. She had no idea what a gas leak would look like or smell like, not truly.

A sound crept from the pit, too low. Too wet. Too familiar.

It came from somewhere inside the churned-up dark. Not a voice. Not words. Just a breath, staggered and ragged, like someone startled. Like a young woman gasping.

Nettie's eyes widened. Her throat refused to close, as if her body knew better than her mind not to scream. Her legs locked. She didn't breathe.

Another deeper shadow swooped overhead, fast and low. The air pressure dipped like a sudden thunderclap.

They all ducked.

Valerie didn't shout, she just grabbed Nettie's arm with iron fingers. "Run."

Boots hammered the gravel. Masks forgotten. Rage forgotten.

The earth behind them shifted again, a soft, wet chuff of breath in the dark.

Nettie's lungs clawed at the air. Jesse, beside her, panted, no grin left in him. Valerie ran, watching the sky with her shoulders hunched like someone expecting impact.

They didn't look back.

But Nettie knew in that primal, marrow-deep way that something had been down there.

And now it wasn't.

Chapter Thirty
A Tunnel of Bones

Seth turned off the 211 onto the recently paved road heading into the new subdivision being built by the Orbriallis, eyeing the finished townhomes to his right. They were finely crafted structures without being audacious, yet lacked any real character, especially for a town populated with Victorian homes. This would be the case with almost any new housing development, of course, but they felt especially out of place here. It was no surprise that the current residents of Lost Grove would be opposed to the construction. Seth had underestimated just how upset they would get. He had expected people grumbling about it at coffee shops and stores, not protests and vandalism.

After almost two weeks of one disaster after another, Seth felt like the town had turned the corner when Clayton Meadows was found last night. He had actually gone to bed with a feeling of something akin to relief. But then he got the call from Peter at a quarter after seven in the morning telling him that the vandalism had turned into destruction of property and that an excavator had collapsed through the earth. The first day of the county fair was not starting off on the right foot.

Seth finished the remainder of his triple cappuccino as he approached Peter's vehicle, spotting the giant yellow excavator sticking up in the air, half buried in the broken ground below. "What the hell?" he muttered. For some reason, Seth interpreted Peter's description of the scene as if the excavator dipped into a ditch, not like it had fallen into a giant sinkhole.

Joe approached Seth as he exited his vehicle. "Hey, Seth, great news about Clayton, huh?"

"To say the least. This"—Seth paused and pointed ahead—"not so much."

"Crazy, huh?" Joe glanced over his shoulder. "It, like, fell through the earth."

"I see that."

"Here, come look," Joe said and led Seth toward the scene. "There must have been some sort of tunnel or something."

Seth slowed his steps as the obvious realization dawned upon him. He had literally traversed an underground tunnel last fall and seen more than one offshoot. If this was one of those it would really open up what he had conceived of the world underneath Lost Grove. How many tunnels were there? How far did they stretch? Were they natural extensions of the cave system or were they man-made? Clearly the one leading to the Orbriallis had, at the very least, been augmented with lights, floors, and a door.

Joe approached the taped-off area surrounding the excavator and turned back to Seth. "There's a couple guys down there from the construction team."

Seth surveyed the area, seeing the finished house not far from where the excavator had taken a nosedive. "I imagine that was their target," Seth posited, pointing to the house.

"That's what we're thinking."

Seth shook his head and stepped underneath the yellow tape, walked up to the edge, and peered down. It was at least fifteen feet down to where the machine had hit solid ground. Two men with hard hats were down there moving large chunks of earth off the excavator. "Hey, guys, I'm Chief of Police Seth Wolfe. You uncover anything interesting down there?"

A man with a solid three-quarter handlebar mustache looked up and Seth noticed he was holding a bone. "Hey, Chief. I'm Alden Page, the foreman for our crew. This is Bobby Viola. And this," he said, lifting the bone up, "is one of a shit ton of bones down here."

Seth ran his hand through his hair. "Are you able to tell if any of them—"

"I know what you're thinking. I'm no archeologist or whatever, but they all seem like animal bones to me."

"We haven't found a human skull or anything," Bobby added.

"Well, that's something," Seth responded. "If you guys wouldn't mind leaving the bones where they are, just in case."

Alden dropped the bone. "You got it, Chief."

Seth squatted down, leaning his head into the hole to see if he could make out a tunnel. There certainly seemed like there was an empty space behind a massive mound of dirt behind Alden. "Does that lead anywhere?" Seth asked, pointing.

Bobby grabbed a flashlight from his belt, turned it on, and pointed it toward the opening. "As far back as we can make out. Some sort of cave system."

"I'll tell you this," Alden said. "Whoever did this actually did us a favor. If we had begun construction on the townhouses mapped out to this area, we could have had either a massive accident on our hands, or worse yet, the structures held up until someone moved in and then bam, some poor sap and his family fall through their kitchen and have their home come tumbling down on top of them."

Seth stood back up, considering the unintentional "favor." "I guess that's a glass-half-full way of looking at it."

"Don't really see another way, to be honest."

"Fair enough." Seth looked back at Joe. "Where's Peter? Any clues yet? Peter said all the main cameras around the site were smashed."

"That's exactly what Peter's looking into," Joe said. "He went with the construction manager, Stephen Frazier, to check the recordings. The only thing we found so far is over here." Joe walked past the taped-off area toward a small orange flag in the ground next to a purple cloth. "This bandana got left behind. All the crew members verified it wasn't theirs."

"If we strike out on the security footage we should at least be able to pull some DNA from this. Getting a match in the system is another matter."

"Have you heard anything from Clayton yet? Any idea what happened?"

Seth sighed. "Nothing yet. He was speaking in grunts and riddles last night. We think he might have come into contact with the fungus in the glyphs. We should get the blood results today."

Joe leaned toward Seth and spoke conspiratorially. "The Lost Grove subReddit has a theory that he was taken by a cult."

Seth frowned. "SubReddit?"

Joe's eyes grew wide. "Yeah, there's this story that deep in the Cursed Woods there's this—"

"Seth!"

Seth turned to see Peter coming his way, along with Stephen Frazier, and looked back at Joe. "Fill me in on the cult story later, yeah?"

"For sure!"

"One hell of a mess," Peter said, approaching. "Did you, um, see the—"

"Cave? Bones? Yeah." The men exchanged a knowing look. "We can look into that when everything gets cleared out. Any luck on the footage?"

Peter grimaced. "Uh, yeah, actually we did get lucky. So to speak."

Seth narrowed his eyes. "And for some reason this isn't good news?"

"It's great news," said Stephen Frazier. "Those hidden cameras paid off."

Seth looked from Stephen back to Peter, trying to grasp what Peter's hesitation was.

Peter looked over Seth's shoulder. "Joe, stay here with the crew. I'm going to walk Seth back to the trailer."

"You got it." Joe gave a quick salute and headed back toward the excavator.

Seth followed Stephen and Peter through the construction site and was happy to see that the office trailer hadn't been further desecrated after they painted over the "NO MORE GRAVES" graffiti. He stepped up into the trailer as Stephen walked over to a group of three monitors. Seth saw the video was paused with the front end of the excavator just entering the left side of the frame and a person with their back to the camera lower right.

"Pause it at the same point I had you freeze on," Peter instructed.

Stephen tapped the play button and Seth watched as the excavator jerked wildly into frame, the arm with the shovel claw contraption careening from a raised position and then hitting the ground.

"Things aren't as easy to drive as one might think," Stephen muttered.

"Would have never thought to try," Seth said as he watched the person standing on the ground wave their arms, motioning them to head to their right. That's when he noticed the second person in the cab sitting behind the driver. The night vision on the security system was impressive but he still couldn't make out either of their faces with their bandanas still on. The steel arm jerked upward, then quickly plummeted back down to the ground. "Uh-oh."

"Yep," Peter said.

The ground caved in from the impact and the front end of the excavator dipped into the collapsed tunnel below. The two people in the cab jumped out, one after the other, while the person stationed on the ground ran up to meet them.

"Here comes the big one," Stephen warned.

The ground beneath the excavator further collapsed, the machine plummeting, causing a cloud of dust and debris to explode out. The three people waved their arms in front of their faces to clear the air while one took off the bandana and turned right toward the camera. Or rather, she turned and looked almost directly into the camera, which is where Stephen paused it.

"Shit."

"You know this girl or something?" Stephen asked.

Seth stroked his stubbled chin and looked at Peter, now understanding his cryptic look before. "Yeah. We do."

Stephen unplugged a flash drive from the computer and handed it to Peter. "Here you go. Done copying over."

"Thanks," Peter said and extended it out to Seth. "You want to hold on to this or—"

Seth's phone ringing interrupted the question. "Chief Wolfe," he answered. "Yeah, okay, put him through… Hey, Ethan, what can I do for you?… And you just found them?… No, you did the right thing. I'll be there in ten minutes."

"Ethan Bury?" Peter guessed.

Seth nodded. "Animal attack."

"Fucking hell."

"Yep."

"You want me or Joe to come with you?"

"No, I got it," Seth said. "Finish up here and then…well, go pick her up and bring her in."

"Yeah, okay," Peter replied glumly.

Chapter Thirty-One
Rolling Pastures, Quiet Dread

By the time Seth Wolfe turned off the county road and onto the broken asphalt lane leading to the Bury farm, the sun was climbing toward its midday throne, scattering soft gold across the pastures and the worn hills that unrolled gently toward the redwood-cloaked ridges beyond. The mist had already burned off the low ground, leaving only traces lingering in the shade-heavy hollows. Summer here was never dry and still, it shifted constantly, a living breath between coastal fog and wild inland wind.

Lost Grove's dairy country was a kind of quiet most people didn't understand anymore. The silence wasn't empty. It was made of distance and space, of wind whispering through red alders and black locust, of cows lowing in the far pastures, and the sigh of rusted gate hinges that hadn't been oiled in decades.

Seth drove slow. Not because the road required it—though the ruts were deep enough to jostle his teeth—but because he liked seeing where he was. Seth slowed as he came around the bend, the white Victorian farmhouse rising into view like something out of a forgotten storybook, tall and elegant with deep porches and shining windows, shutters freshly painted and flower boxes spilling nasturtiums and ivy. A line of laundry danced on a clothesline near the side yard, brilliant white against the deep blue of the sky. It was a scene straight out of a movie, a book, or a painting, and he wondered if Story would ever desire a property like this. Seth had spent eighteen years in a one-bedroom apartment in San Francisco. As lavish as that apartment was, one that he was still subleasing, it now felt like a prison looking upon the grandeur of the Bury farm.

His eye caught on something new: a smaller paddock tucked near the barn, fenced off with fresh posts and rope wire. Inside were three cows—short-legged, shaggy beasts with expressive eyes beneath woolly forelocks and horns like curved crescents of weathered driftwood. They looked like oversized stuffed animals, more dog than bovine, and two of them were barely the height of a golden retriever.

Seth couldn't help but grin.

He pulled the cruiser into the graveled lot and stepped out just as the farm dog padded up, silent and massive. She was a striking mix, all muscle and coat, her thick fur a swirl of cream and ash, eyes sharp as polished stones.

Seth paused, tension pulling in his shoulders. She was a gorgeous dog, but he was a stranger on her property.

The dog studied him. Then her ears flicked forward. She wagged once.

"Bear," came a voice from the porch.

Ethan Bury strode down the steps with an easy gait, ball cap in one hand. "She'll scare the hell out of you, but she's a marshmallow once she knows you're not here to steal the chickens."

Seth extended a cautious hand. Bear pressed into it, grunting, tail swishing once more before she turned and lumbered off toward the distant cluck of hens foraging in the high grass.

"She's beautiful," Seth said. "And seems highly intelligent."

"Too smart for her own good."

Ethan offered a short nod and a handshake. They weren't close. They had never been more than two boys from the same town who happened to pass each other in the hallways—Ethan a senior when Seth was a sophomore. Still, their familiarity ran deep in the way it does in small towns—the kind built more from proximity and memory than true connection. But last year Seth dropped his daughter off after a mishap in town and Ethan had been forever grateful, knowing Seth Wolfe was back in town protecting all of them.

Seth nodded, glancing back toward the paddock. "Those little cows...new additions?"

Ethan exhaled like he'd been waiting for the question. "Highlands. And two minis. My wife's idea, but really it's my daughter's doing. Leith calls them her therapy cows. Don't let the fluff fool you, they've got opinions."

Seth chuckled. "I believe it."

"I suppose we should get to it then."

"I'll follow your lead."

Ethan motioned to his truck. "Hop in. Ol' Julia is built for this terrain."

Seth followed him. "Might I ask?"

They climbed into Ethan's truck. It was dust-coated, work-tired, and humming with the smell of sunbaked hay and diesel.

"Stiles. My dad passed the truck down to me when I was a junior in high school. I had watched *10 Things I Hate About You* about ten times at that point."

Seth chuckled as Ethan started up Ol' Julia. "I'll have to admit that we shared that crush."

Ethan gave Seth a warm smile as he shifted into first gear.

The road through the pasture curved past the old barn, which stood like a sentinel near the mouth of a gentle gully, its aged red siding faded to rust. Ivy clung to one side, clawing its way toward the cupola. Seth swore he noticed a strange carving on the side as they passed but couldn't get a good look at it once they'd gone by.

The land unfolded around them in long, sighing waves, the kind of pasture that looked like it might never end. Tall grass danced in the wind, green and gold where the sun angled through thinning cloud cover. Wildflowers speckled the fence lines. Lupine, Queen Anne's lace, orange poppies still half asleep. Off to the north, the dense reach of the redwoods loomed, dark as myth, their trunks like cathedral pillars rising in silence.

"Did you ever miss it?" Ethan asked suddenly. "Lost Grove, I mean."

Seth's hands tightened slightly on his knees. "Some parts."

"Not the parts full of mutilated livestock, I take it," Ethan joked.

Seth laughed. "I can't say I was all too clued into the state of livestock when I was in high school."

"I suppose not. I know you came back after your father had his stroke. Do you think you would have come back if that hadn't happened? Apologies if I'm being too personal."

"No, not at all." Seth thought back, as he too often did, to the pivotal morning at Dolores Park just weeks before his father's stroke when he and his partner were called to the horrific scene of a drug addict mother and her eight-month-old baby with two heroin needles sticking out of her, both dead. "I guess you could say there was something starting to pull me back here."

"And you stayed."

Seth swallowed, his city apartment feeling further and further away. "I have, yes."

Ethan raised his eyebrows as they crested a low ridge, and Ethan pointed. "There." He pulled to a stop and shut off the engine.

Two shapes slumped in the far paddock, a patch of flattened grass smeared dark, as though the ground itself had been struck sick. The cows lay oddly, their limbs twisted in ways that didn't look like simple collapse. No flies yet. Not many, anyway. No birds circling overhead. The stillness felt off.

Ethan jumped out of the pickup.

Seth stepped out and walked slowly forward, highly unnerved, each footfall muffled by the soft, spongy earth. He had approached countless bodies over the years, but there was something about the innocence of animals that stung his heart. And there was something ominous about this scene that heightened his senses. It didn't feel right. Story would say he was tapping into his abilities. Seth would argue it was his years of experience. Maybe they were both right.

They walked the last stretch in silence. The air thickened as they approached, the smell shifting from sweet hay and salt to something raw, a coppery tang, and the deep, wet rot of spilled innards left out too long in the sun.

Seth crouched low beside the nearest body. What he saw stopped his breath short in his throat.

The hide had been raked open over and over. Parallel gouges ran across the shoulders and flanks like a giant had dragged curved knives through the flesh, peeling back skin in brutal fans. The meat beneath was exposed, muscle cleaved with precision and savagery. He pulled a pair of gloves from his back pocket and traced the edge of a wound. The angle and the depth looked familiar.

Kevin Marlow's body had looked like this—slashed across the ribs like something had tried to gut him.

Bite marks, or rather holes that looked like someone had taken an apple corer to the animal, riddled the underside of the jaw and neck. Whatever made them was narrow and sharp. But it was the eyes that struck Seth. They were missing. Not pecked or torn but carved out clean and deep, the sockets hollowed like someone had scooped them with intent. Chills rolled down his back. He had just left an underground tunnel filled with animal bones, and now this. This entire week Seth had an ominous feeling about the start of the county fair and the quick succession of events this morning were darkening the clouds he felt looming overhead.

He stood slowly, glancing at the other cow, and noticed the same pattern. Mauled, yes, but methodically. The rib cage on that one had been opened. Split wide like something had gone inside it.

Ethan shifted his weight, arms folded tightly across his chest. "I haven't seen anything like this in years," he muttered.

Seth looked over. "Years?"

"Not since before I met Leith. We had a calf show up like this once. Torn to hell, eyes missing. Vet chalked it up to a bobcat gone rabid."

"That was a long time ago."

"You don't forget a sight like that."

"Do you remember well enough to recall if the marks looked similar? Or if the eye sockets were this cleaned out?"

Ethan stretched his back out, contemplating the question. "I guess I don't recall those specific details well enough to say for sure."

"Okay. Did anything else disappear back then?"

"Two hens. A barn cat. Thought it was just nature doing what it does."

Seth let that event go for now. It had to have been twenty years ago. He focused on the scene before him as if it were a crime scene. He took photos. Wide shots. Close detail with a ruler. The only footprints in the dirt were his and Ethan's. No drag marks. No tire tracks.

"You hear anything last night?" Seth asked.

Ethan shook his head, then hesitated. "No. But Bear was pacing before dawn. Growling. Didn't think much of it."

"Could've happened during the night, then."

"Came out around six and found them like this. They were fine yesterday afternoon. I walk this paddock every day."

"Any prints? Scat?"

"Nothing I could see."

Seth nodded slowly. "I'll file a report. You can submit it for reimbursement with the ag board. But I wouldn't wait to fence that lower ridge again. If whatever it was came once…"

Ethan exhaled, glancing toward the trees. "We fenced it last summer after Emily's cross was found torn up."

Seth didn't respond because there wasn't anything to say. He remembered that summer Emily Bury went missing. His mother had been on edge, upset, and had cried so hard when the news came it was as if the little girl had been her own daughter. He didn't understand at the time, being only ten, but he had an idea now why it had been so heartbreaking.

He crouched again, tracing one of the slashes with a gloved fingertip. "These aren't gouge wounds. This is more like…rending. Like it knew exactly where to hit."

"You think it could be a person who came in and did it?" Ethan asked, voice low.

"No. That's the problem," Seth said. "If this were human, it'd almost make more sense. How methodical this feels. But the marks are consistent with recent animal attacks, so…"

They stood in the wind, the silence stretching long and uneasy. The tree line beyond the pasture loomed, shadow-dense, the edge of the Cursed Woods drawing a dark line beneath the horizon. Seth stared out toward the dark fringe of the forest, where the sunlight seemed to stop short, unwilling to step over the invisible line. He felt a chill run through his body. It felt like there was a gravitational pull coming from the woods, asking him, begging him, to come in.

"Is that part of the Cursed Woods?" he asked, knowing the answer.

Ethan's mouth twisted. "Locals still call it that. I've lived here my whole life and never liked that name. But yeah. That's the line."

Seth considered bringing up what he'd heard from Story about Leith, but this was not the time to drag the man's wife into the conversation. *Keep it about the cows,* he told himself. "Have you noticed any animals in the woods lately? Anything unusual?"

Ethan's body stiffened. "Not personally, no. You think whatever did this came from in there?" he asked, fear slipping into his voice.

I do, Seth thought. "I don't know. Just thinking out loud."

Ethan looked down to the ground, kicking the tip of his boot into the ground. "I don't really go in there."

Seth didn't blame him. He wondered how Ethan felt about Leith traversing the woods. Probably not too favorably. Seth finally tore his attention away from the woods and looked back at Ethan. "Do you mind if I call Wes and see if he can send someone out here to take a look?"

Ethan raised a brow but nodded. "Fine by me."

Seth pulled out his phone and rang Wes as he waved at Ethan, stepping away.

"Hey, Seth. Please tell me you're not calling about another body."

"Not a human one if that's any consolation."

"Then what's that got to do with me?"

"The marks," Seth said. "Something attacked and mutilated two of Ethan Bury's cows sometime in the middle of the night. They look almost identical to the marks on Kevin Marlow's body."

"Shit."

"Yeah. If you have time, I'd love to get you out here to take a look, get some photos and DNA."

Wes sighed. "Well, on this exact note, I'm eagerly awaiting a call on the DNA we pulled from Kevin. I can send Leon out. Should probably give Cal a call as well."

"That was next on my list."

Seth came back over to Ethan after speaking to Cal, who agreed to come out. "Wes said he'd send one of his assistants out to get some samples, if you don't mind."

"Not at all."

"I'm also going to have his brother Cal come out. He used to work with the—"

"We were in the same class, Seth," Ethan said, brightening. "Always liked Cal. He's a solid dude."

Seth gave a quick shake of his head. "Right. I should have put those pieces together. You've kept in touch?"

"Enough."

"Great. Well, they both shouldn't be more than an hour out," Seth explained.

"I'll be around." Ethan smiled.

Seth smiled back. "Alright. Well, let's head back. I've got what I need to secure you a report for reimbursement."

They bumped over the pasture roads as they headed back to the house. It was slow going, but it was a moment for Seth to gather his thoughts. There was some connection here with the glyphs and the fungus getting closer to civilization, and now the animal attacks. The timing couldn't be ignored. Just what that connection might be was far beyond anything Seth could surmise. He was waiting for Story to get a call from Dr. Raines with results from the samples he took, and if Wes was correct, they would be getting DNA results today telling them what animal attacked Kevin Marlow. Hopefully between the two, he could start connecting the dots.

A new thought jumped to the forefront of Seth's mind, a part of the job, like many recently, he'd never had to know about while working in San Francisco. "What's your plan for the carcasses?"

Ethan, squinting against the glare of the sun, rubbed the back of his neck, a hint of weariness in his eyes. "Well, composting's out," he said. "Illegal in California unless you're part of a research project or have special permissions. And I don't have the setup for that anyway."

Seth nodded, recalling the regulations he'd read about.

"Burying them on-site is an option," Ethan continued, "but it's not ideal. I'd have to dig deep enough—at least six feet—to prevent scavengers from getting to them. Plus, there's the risk of contaminating groundwater if it's not done properly."

"Rendering?" Seth suggested, recalling some handbook or email that had come across his desk due to recent events with animal attacks on the nearby farms.

"That's the plan," Ethan confirmed. "There's a facility in Petaluma that accepts livestock carcasses. I'll need to transport them there, but I have to coordinate the logistics. It's a bit of a drive, and I'll need to ensure the carcasses are properly stored in a cool, dry spot until then. Why do you ask?"

"Well, like I said, the marks are similar to other recent attacks. There's a chance that Wes or Cal might want to look a little deeper into the wounds."

Ethan looked over at Seth. "The boy?"

Seth kept his glare ahead steady. He'd likely said too much already.

Ethan nodded. "Well, I can keep them stored for a few days just in case. Just let me know."

"Appreciate that."

As they pulled into the driveway, the sun was high in its corona. Bear came trotting out of the big barn, tongue lolling, then stopped and looked back. Both men got out of the truck and watched Leith walking slowly across the gravel, barefoot, holding something wrapped in a towel.

"Afternoon, Leith" Seth called.

She didn't even glance their way.

Ethan didn't look. "Probably checking on something. She's been doing that a lot lately. Says it helps her sleep."

Seth watched her disappear into the shadow of the old barn. He didn't say what he was thinking.

"Thanks again for coming out," Ethan said.

"It's my job," Seth said with a smile. "You guys coming to the fair this weekend?"

"Of course. I think Anya's heading up with Noble later today. If she ever gets home first," Ethan only mildly grumbled.

Seth nodded. The comment stirred a quiet ache he couldn't name. Because being a girl dad—he imagined—wasn't just about knowing how to braid hair or tolerate mood swings or pretend not to hear whispered phone calls at two a.m. It was trust. It was fear. It was loving someone so completely while knowing the world might never be soft with her, never fair, and it was letting her walk out the door anyway, keys in hand, heart worn somewhere on her sleeve.

"Will we see you and Story up there?" Ethan asked, eyes locked somewhere behind the house, trailing after where his wife had disappeared.

"I'll be there on duty tonight," Seth said, snapping out of his curious thoughts. "I'm sure we'll go together later in the weekend or next week."

Ethan looked back, a smile on his face but his eyes distant. "Look forward to seeing you both."

Seth nodded. "Yeah. Same." Seth climbed into his Bronco and headed down the driveway. The road curved between the paddocks, the hills spreading wide and wild on either side.

Just before he reached the main road, he spotted Noble's Crosstrek.

Anya sat in the passenger seat, hair caught in the breeze. Noble raised a hand in a tired wave. Anya followed suit, her expression unreadable in the shifting light.

Seth nodded back, then drove on.

Chapter Thirty-Two
Not Just a Name on Paper

The air in the station felt stale, like it hadn't quite recovered from the heat the day before. Fluorescents hummed overhead, just a little too bright for how little sleep Seth had gotten after waiting for hours at the hospital the previous night in hopes that Clayton might snap out of it and say something. Having just returned from the Bury farm, Seth was not looking forward to what was next on his list. He rubbed the bridge of his nose, a headache whispering behind his eyes as Peter Andalusian leaned against the doorframe of his office.

"She's been quiet," Peter said, arms crossed, one foot hooked behind the other. "Hasn't asked for a lawyer. Barely said a word. Just stares at the table."

Seth nodded. "You pull anything useful?"

"Yeah," Peter said, thumbing through a slim folder. "It wasn't hard. They've been making themselves known throughout town. Up at Reggie's Pub, getting coffee and chatting with locals at Main Street Cafe. But, uh, Joe already had a list of names and places, after the last call. He'd done some digging. The two she'd been hanging out with…" Peter scanned the paper inside the folder. "Valerie Whitaker and a kid named Jesse Semens."

"Semens?" Seth asked, looking up.

"Semens. I didn't name him. Anyhow, this guy—Jesse—had a converted bus parked out near that little RV spot by the state park. Hidden Springs Loop? They mostly get overlanders and retired hippies out there. Couple off-grid solar panels and a composting toilet and people think it's paradise."

Seth raised a brow. "He's gone?"

"Gone. Joe ran out there first thing this morning. Bus is gone. Neighbors said they saw them pack up early this morning."

Seth stared at the floor for a beat, jaw tight.

Peter continued, "I think they were—"

"Yeah," Seth cut in. "I figured."

He didn't say the rest. He didn't have to. Jesse had run. Left the girl behind. That was the part that sat wrong.

Back in San Francisco, this wouldn't have fazed him. You processed the arrest, filled out the paperwork, passed it along to the courts, and washed your hands. The names were interchangeable. The stories rarely unique. No one knew anyone. No one cared enough to feel.

But here he knew her. He remembered the brittle edge in Nettie's voice when she asked him if they could really bring her brother home. He remembered the way she stood apart from the others afterward, like she'd gotten what she wanted but somehow still ended up alone. Now she was sitting in the box while the boy who'd made her feel seen just enough to drag her down the wrong road was already halfway to Oregon.

Seth exhaled slowly, pinching the bridge of his nose again.

Peter clapped a hand lightly on the doorframe. "You want backup?"

Seth shook his head. "No. Let me talk to her first."

Peter stepped aside as Seth walked out of his office and approached one of the two interview rooms in their little police station. He rested his hand on the steel doorframe, which felt colder than it should. For a second, he lingered—just long enough to reset his face, steady his breath.

The room smelled faintly of pine-scented cleaner and the dusty tang of recycled air. Nettie sat with her hands folded in her lap, eyes fixed on a knot in the table's surface. She hadn't said much of anything. She knew she'd been recognized, somehow, when Noble's dad pulled up in his squad car and knocked on their front door. She should have known. Somehow, his recent appointment to the department had skipped her mind. Even on what she imagined was fleeting, grainy, black-and-white recordings, and obscured by masks, it likely hadn't been hard to identify her. He'd watched her grow up and she knew he'd been ex-military. And now she was here.

The door opened. Seth Wolfe stepped in quietly.

She looked up and her stomach twisted, because she owed him. Seth was part of the group that had brought her real brother home. He had been the one who looked her in the eye and explained the plan—not-George would be exchanged for her real brother, her George. For a while, it had felt like a miracle, like someone had finally believed her. But then George came home and it wasn't like before.

Seth closed the door behind him, no clipboard, no pen. Just a faint frown stitched across his brow and a bottle of water in his hand.

He set it in front of her. "You look thirsty."

Nettie didn't move.

Seth sat across from her, hands clasped on the table. "Nettie."

She blinked and finally looked at him, his hands folded calmly, and that old glimmer of gratitude burned in her chest like a coal. She didn't want to look at him. She didn't want to feel betrayed by someone who hadn't betrayed her.

"You know why you're here?"

A shrug.

"I'm not trying to trip you up," he said gently. "But we have three faces on camera, and only one of them I can name for sure. You want to make it easier on yourself, now would be the time."

Still, she said nothing.

Seth leaned forward, elbows on the table. "What were you trying to do, Nettie? Make a statement? Blow off steam? You didn't just tag a wall—you nearly got yourself and your friends killed. That excavator collapsed into something we haven't even been able to investigate yet. You're lucky no one was buried alive. If this had gone another way, we'd be having this talk with a coroner and I'd be knocking on your parents' door to deliver news of every parent's worst nightmare."

Her throat closed, and for a moment, the weight of what had happened pressed against her ribs like rising water. "I didn't know it would cave," she said.

"I believe that," Seth said.

Silence again.

"I know this last year hasn't been easy," he continued. "And I know you've been through a lot more than most people realize. But property destruction, endangering workers, trespassing on private property—those are real charges, Nettie."

"I thought he'd come back like he used to be," she said suddenly, voice cracking before she could brace it. "You said we'd be fixing it. Like we could reverse it all."

Seth blinked, caught off guard. "I realize nothing about that entire situation was optimal. We believed we were making the best decision for your brother, and for you, given the circumstances."

"Well, what if you were wrong." And in that moment, she wanted him to feel it—the weight of her grief, of her rage, of the nine months of pretending like the ending had been happy just because the good guys technically won. "I'm not mad that we got him back," she whispered. "I'm mad that I don't know what to do with who came home."

"I am sorry, Nettie. And if there's anything more I can help with in terms of George's treatment, I'll do everything I can. But we need to talk about you now."

Nettie gritted her teeth.

Seth leaned back. "Tell me what happened last night," he said. "Tell me why the excavator ended up in the pit."

Nettie swallowed hard. She could lie. Blame Jesse. Blame the machine. Blame gravity. But she said nothing.

Seth sighed. Not annoyed. More disappointed. He pushed back his chair. "Okay," he said, gently tapping the table. He hated to play games with her, but he needed her to talk. And he knew how to get people to talk. He slowly began to stand.

"You know why," Nettie mumbled.

"I have a pretty good idea. But I need you to tell me."

What was she going to say? Revenge? To hurt them? To stop those grotesque townhomes from being built? To stop the Orbriallis from killing trees and infecting their river with pollutants? It didn't matter. Nothing she said would change anything.

"Can you at least tell me anything about what happened? Were you hurt at all?"

Something flickered behind her eyes. She looked away. Down at her hands. Then out of nowhere, she whispered, "It wasn't empty."

Seth stilled, as gooseflesh sprouted on his forearms. "What?"

She shook her head.

Seth narrowed his eyes as he sat back down. "What wasn't empty?"

Nettie's right hand started to tremble. "It doesn't matter."

"Everything surrounding this scenario matters, Nettie. Everything. Did you see something?"

"No," she quietly replied, pulling her hands into her hoodie. "Not really."

Seth didn't like the look in Nettie's eyes. She had gone from defiant to afraid. There was nothing at the construction site this morning that would have evoked fear. What had she seen? "Nettie, you can tell me if you saw something."

Nettie's arms and shoulders started to shake as her eyes grew wider, her mind returning to the moment. "I'm not saying anything else," she muttered. "Because no one ever believes me anyway."

Seth leaned across the table. "Nettie, look at me."

She hesitantly looked up, part of her wanting to run away and curl up in a corner, the other part of her wanting to run into his arms for protection.

"Out of everyone here, I think you know that I'll believe you. The night we rescued your brother and Noble's sister, one of your friends controlled armed guards with his mind. My girlfriend is a witch."

Nettie couldn't hold back a chuckle.

"So, whatever it was you saw, you can tell me and I'll believe you."

"I don't know what I saw," she said, her eyes falling to the table. "But there were sounds from below. Wet, clicking sounds. They were terrible. They weren't right."

Seth swallowed, his heart rate ratcheting up.

"And then something...something big, something fast...it flew by."

"Flew?" Seth asked, perplexed.

"Flew, ran, moved. I don't know. And then it was gone. Like it was never there."

A sharp ringing began in Seth's brain. He didn't like this. No, he didn't like it one bit. A knock on the door caused both him and Nettie to jump in their seats.

"Be right there," Seth called out, locking eyes with Nettie.

"Do you know what it was?" she asked, panicked.

Seth shook his head. "I wish I did. Thank you for telling me what you could."

"Okay." Nettie nodded, tears filling her eyes. "I won't do it anymore. I promise."

Nettie's pained words stabbed Seth in the gut. "Look, I'll be back shortly. In the meantime, we'll call your parents. You're a legal adult now, so you'll likely be processed, but...we'll figure something out, Nettie. I'll do everything I can."

Seth stepped into the office and saw Nate and Sasha talking with Peter. He stepped quickly toward them. "Is he awake? What did he say?"

"Not a whole lot," Sasha said. "So, don't get your hopes up."

Seth squeezed his fists, his nerves on a fissured edge. "Well, you must have something if you're back here."

Sasha's eyes widened. "Are you okay, Seth?"

"It's been a rough day, Sasha," Peter jumped in. "There was destruction of property at the construction site this morning."

"Again?"

"And worse. An excavator was improperly driven and operated, causing it to collapse through the earth, into what we believe is a tunnel."

"There was another animal attack at the Bury farm," Seth added. "Cows. Killed in a very similar manner as Kevin Marlow."

"Shit," Nate remarked. "Poor Anya."

"And on that note," Peter said, looking to Seth.

"What?" Sasha and Nate asked simultaneously.

Seth sighed. "Look. Nate, I'm going to need you to be professional about this. There were three people we caught on camera at the site. The only one we could identify was Nettie."

"Fuck," Nate mumbled.

"She's in interview room one."

"I told her not to do anything stupid. I warned her."

"Why?" Seth asked. "Did you have any idea that she—"

"No, nothing like this. I just knew she was protesting and that she's still hella pissed at the Orbriallis. And all of us for that matter. She thinks we should all be as mad as she is. I told her she could protest peacefully but not to do anything stupid. Maybe I should have said something."

Seth patted Nate on the shoulder. "It's okay, Nate. Back to Clayton Meadows. Sasha, tell me what you know."

Sasha unlocked her phone screen and navigated to her notes. "Well, his toxicology report came back. The doctors said it was a miracle that he was able to say anything due to the 'historic' levels of psilocybin in his system. And, yes, that's the drug in mushrooms that fucks you up."

Seth forcefully ran his hand through his hair.

"Gotta stop doing that, Seth," Peter said. "I told you, your hair is far too nice to start pulling out."

Seth ignored him. "What else?"

"They've got him on constant fluids to help cleanse his system. He's been in and out of it all day."

"Mostly out of it," Nate added.

"Yes," Sasha agreed. "But what we were able to get out of him was that he was taken. At least that's what it's coming across like."

Seth's brow furrowed. *Taken?* "Taken? By who?"

"That's what we kept asking him. And he just kept saying—"

"'Not who. What,'" Nate said. "Or some variation of that."

"Not who. What," Seth mused. "What does that mean?"

"Joe told me about this cult that apparently lives in the Cursed Woods," Nate started. "They've apparently been there—"

"Cult?" Peter asked.

"Oh my God," Sasha exclaimed. "Do not listen to Joe and his stupid theories."

Before Seth could retort, his cell phone rang. "Now fucking what?"

Sasha and Nate exchanged a worried look, and then Sasha looked at Peter. "He's really not in a good mood, is he?"

Peter shook his head.

Seth saw it was Wes calling and stepped away from the group before answering. "Wes, what have you got?… Okay, and?… Jesus Christ… Great, that's all we need is another mystery. What are the positive identifications?… A squirrel? Great. Let's run with that… And what the hell is that?… What? Please tell me you've got something other than this… So, are you telling me that… Okay, so what is the mystery? Because neither of those could be the answer… I don't even know what to do with that, Wes… Excellent. We're all stumped then… And how long will that take?… I was really hoping for something conclusive to bring to the family… Okay, look, I've got to run. Thanks for the call, anyway."

Seth hung up and turned back toward the group, which Joe and Eddie had now joined, who were all looking at him with eager eyes. "As you said earlier, Sasha, don't get your hopes up. The DNA results for Kevin Marlow were a mess. Results were animals that make no sense given the wounds and an unidentified species."

"What does that mean?" Peter asked.

"Good question. Wes said the guy at the lab claimed that one of the animals was either a very rare or new species, but no clue as to what it could be."

Nate looked at Joe. "What do you think about this?"

Joe lifted his eyebrows. "Well, it could—"

"No," Sasha cut him off. "Don't even start."

Seth opened his arms to his team. "I'm glad everyone's here. As I said earlier, we're going to need all hands on deck at the fair. With the animal attack at the Bury farm, Clayton's cryptic message about 'not who, what' took him, and the thought of a new species of animal…I don't even want to get into that, I have a very bad feeling with the fair being half surrounded by the woods."

"The Cursed Woods, too," Joe added.

Sasha punched Joe in the arm.

"Ow!"

"Yes, thank you for that, Joe," Seth said. "I want everyone in uniform. Keep your radios on with the volume up. When we get there, I'll decide where to station everyone, but my guess is it'll be staggered on the precipice of the woods. Stay alert and communicate at all times. Got it?"

Everyone agreed and dispersed to get their things.

Chapter Thirty-Three
Inside the Zone

Story's house smelled faintly of lemon balm, rosemary, beeswax candles, and the faint echo of yesterday's bread. Sunlight filtered through the lead windows, casting quiet shadows on the old hardwood. Mary stood near the front door, arms crossed, her chunky boots tapping a slow rhythm on the tile. Her dark hair was tied back with a scarf, but a few strands had slipped free, framing a face made for expressions too honest to hide. She was fidgeting with the strap of her bag, looking less and less confident about her decision to join Story at the fair this evening.

Story stepped into her mudroom to grab a light jacket, then returned to her kitchen and grabbed her canvas bag off the counter. Inside, she'd packed a jar of salt, a few iron nails, a length of protective thread, and a jar of ash she'd ground herself the night before. She met Mary in her foyer.

"You ready?" she asked, voice light, trying for casual.

"No," Mary said honestly. "What's that?" Mary asked, noticing the jar of black salt tipping halfway out of the bag.

Story grinned and opened her arms in a helpless little shrug. "With a teeny-tiny detour. Fifteen minutes. Tops."

Mary's brow rose. "Where?"

"The Bury farm." Story shrugged into her coat.

"Story," Mary whined, exasperated. "I was serious then and I'm serious now. We should leave these glyphs alone."

"It's just a warding circle and some salt. It'll hold until I can do something stronger. I need to check the tree line near the pasture."

Mary's arms folded tighter. "This doesn't strike me as the kind of thing you just 'swing by.'"

"I'm not scared," Story said, stepping into her boots and giving Mary a sideways look. "Especially not with my badass backup coming along."

"I'm serious."

"So am I." She squeezed Mary's hand. "Besides. If something tries to eat me, I've got you."

"Ha ha," Mary said, her stance relaxing but a smile didn't quite make it to her face.

That was when Story's phone buzzed. She pulled it from her back pocket and frowned at the screen. Dr. Elias Raines.

She answered immediately, pressing the speaker and setting it on the little entryway table. "Dr. Raines?"

"Story, hi. Sorry to call instead of waiting to meet in person, but I think you'd want to hear this sooner rather than later."

Mary glanced at her.

She moved to the door and looked out the panes of glass, heart thrumming. "That's fine. I'm here with Mary. We're getting ready to head to the fair, so I've got you on speaker."

"Hi, Mary."

"Hello," she squeaked.

"I'll try not to keep you, but I've had a moment to look at some of the data and pictures."

"It's no trouble," Story replied. "I'm eager to hear some news, actually. I think we all are."

"Well, I'm not sure the news is good."

Story bit the corner of her lip, sensing the shift in his tone, the careful weight of a theory not yet proven but burning to be spoken aloud.

"I've been thinking about the glyphs," he said. "About the fungus growing within them. I don't think what Hannah stumbled across was all she surmised them to be. I've been comparing the photos," Elias continued. "The ones Hannah took last year, the ones I took at Old Timber Spur, and now the ones from the Bury farm. There's a difference."

"Different how?" Story asked.

"Age. Clarity. Healing," he said. "The glyph at the Bury farm? The bark is still raw, the cambium tissue exposed. No scar tissue, no darkening. The glyph at Gulliver's Gully where the boy, Clayton, went missing—that one's partially healed. Less sharp. The fungus there is young, lacy, just beginning to form the bioluminescent threads. But the ones on Hannah's map? They're nearly smooth. The glyphs have sealed in places. And the fungus is denser, embedded in the grooves like a second skin. It's mature."

"That sounds like they were carved at different times," Mary said, stepping closer. "Like...intentionally?"

"Exactly," Elias said. "I ran a few samples under scope. The younger colonies still show white hyphae—thin and fast-growing. But the ones from the older sites have transitioned to a thicker, filamentous network with integrated biofilm. It's ecological succession. They've been there long enough to develop structural layers. That tells me one thing: These markings aren't static. I believe they may be ecological markers? A form of designed habitat intended to cultivate something?"

Story's brow furrowed. "To cultivate the fungus?"

"Yes. The carvings expose raw tree flesh. They invite colonization. The fungus—*Mycena lux-grovis*, what I believe to be a mutated offshoot of a bioluminescent species, Mycena lux-coeli—is not just surviving in these wounds. It's thriving. Accelerated growth rates, biochemical alterations. It's almost...domesticated."

Mary's eyes widened slightly.

"And that's not all. I reached out to Wiyot elders and tribal historians from the Yurok and Hupa. None of them recognize these symbols. Not as language. Not as art. The responses were...uneasy."

Story's brow furrowed. "Uneasy how?"

"One elder told me, 'Not our marks. Not our story.' Another simply said, 'Bad spirits make bad signs,' and refused to say more."

"That's...not great," Story muttered.

"It's not unusual for some symbols to fall outside oral tradition, especially with displacement, and the Wiyot were significantly displaced. That was why Hannah was so invested in trying to restore some of their culture with this research," Elias said gently. "But the silence here is deliberate."

"They're superstitious of them?" Mary asked.

"Yes, so it seems," he responded. There was silence among them. Elias hesitated to say more but knew he had to continue explaining his findings. "There's something else," he said.

"What?" Story asked.

"I found claw sheath fragments embedded in the wood."

"Claw fragments?" Mary said, blinking.

"Not metal. Not stone. Organic. Keratin-based material, like sloughed claw tips. The kind you see in felines after heavy scratching, but too thick for a bobcat. Too curved for a bear. I ran pressure pattern modeling—it looks like the glyphs were carved in swipes, not with a tool."

Story felt the blood drain from her face. "You're saying an animal did this?"

"I thought that at first," Elias admitted. "Until I checked the soil samples inside each glyph site. I found localized spore clouds, unnatural density, and fecal traces."

"Poop," Mary said faintly. "You're saying something scratched this into a tree, pooped nearby, and left glowing mushrooms behind?"

"Crude, but accurate," Elias said with a humorless chuckle. "But here's the issue. The spores in the fecal matter, as I've said, match no native strain. They're more like the Mycena found in Japan that I told you about."

"Right," Story said, nodding. "The glowing mushrooms."

"Yes. It's as if the fungus is being dispersed intentionally, in cooperation with the carving."

"That's...coordinated," Story whispered.

"Exactly. And that's not typical animal behavior. That's ecological scripting."

A beat.

"You mean like a language?" Story asked.

Elias exhaled. "Yes. A spatial language. Each glyph is a sentence. And the organism—whatever it is—uses the trees to write. Each glyph has a pattern, a purpose. There's one Hannah nicknamed Cross-Claw. It appears in clusters, resting zones, she thought. Safe spaces. The Spiral Eye shows up at the edge of territory zones. And Split-Talon, that's the one we need to worry about."

Mary tensed.

"In every instance Hannah mapped," Elias continued, "Split-Talon appeared near sites of active predation. Prey species—deer, raccoons, rabbits—showed signs of concentrated hunting activity."

Story's voice went tight. "And the one near the Bury farm?"

"Is a variation of the Split-Talon," Elias confirmed. "The fungus colony matches. The glyph's orientation matches. Based on everything I've compiled, it's an active hunting ground."

Mary swore under her breath.

"The cows," Story murmured, meeting Mary's eyes. "Seth was called to the Bury farm this morning. Ethan wanted to report mutilated cows," she explained. "The cows could be their prey."

"They aren't the only cows that have been slaughtered recently," Mary muttered.

"I'm sorry, I didn't hear that," Elias said.

Story took a deep breath. "We've had a few farmers with cow mutilations and deaths in the area lately."

"How many?" Elias asked. They could hear him flipping pages in the background, clicking a pen open.

"I don't know," Story responded. "You could call Seth and ask. He'd have a better number. Or Cal, he'd know."

"Right, I'll follow up with him."

"So, these marks mean a hunting ground, and the unknown animal using these glyphs has marked the Bury farm as a hunting ground," Story went on. "But what about the effects on people?"

"I don't know enough yet. Leith, her daughter—they're close enough to be exposed. This isn't just rot in the woods. It's something designed. The glyphs cultivate microclimates. The fungus emits light, yes, but it also releases chemical signals. It doesn't just warn. It manipulates."

"The hallucinations," Story said.

"Yes and no," Elias said. "If my theory is right, the thing they live in symbiosis with isn't affected the same way. They aren't suffering from hallucinations. And even then...it's not hallucinations, it's neurochemical alterations. Disorientation. Temporal shifts. Memory erosion. This isn't some passive fungal bloom. It's acting more like a delivery system."

Mary moved closer to the phone, her expression no longer skeptical, just scared.

"Story," Elias said. "This isn't just happening inside Devil's Cradle. It's moving. It's adapting. These organisms—whatever's marking the woods—they're getting closer to human spaces. Neighborhoods. Paths. The school perimeter. They're spreading."

Story's fingers clenched tight around the fabric of her satchel.

"If this is the case," Elias continued, "then these woods aren't just haunted. They're rigged. This town isn't standing outside the system anymore. It's inside it."

The words lingered like smoke in the air.

Finally, Story asked, "What comes next?"

"Next?" Elias exhaled, a static buzz in the background as he shifted. "I've sent a few samples to the colleague I mentioned. He'll try to identify the biochemical compounds at play. Especially the psychotropic effects. But more importantly, we need to figure out what the fungus is bonded with. Its...partner."

"And you have no idea what kind of animal or...?"

Elias paused. "I don't know. Historically, we've seen mutualism—symbiotic partnerships—between fungi and all kinds of species. Ants that cultivate fungus in underground farms. Trees and mycorrhizal networks that share nutrients across an entire forest. But this?" He hesitated, searching for the language to match the gravity. "This is communication. Not just exchange. These glyphs...they're structured. Symbolic. Someone, or something, is using the fungus to write. That's not survival behavior. That's intention."

Story's voice dropped. "So what do you think it is? The trees and the fungus? Some kind of insect?"

"I don't know," Elias admitted. "I've been over it a dozen ways. If it's an insect, it's more intelligent than any we've documented. If it's mammalian—avian, maybe—it's acting with precision and pattern. Either way, we're looking at an ecological language system. And that..." His voice trailed off. "That changes everything."

Story didn't answer immediately. When she spoke again, her voice was quiet. "I'm heading out to the Bury farm."

"What? Why?"

"The woman who lives at the farm, Leith, she's been acting strange. Sleepwalking. Detached. Her family is worried. So am I."

There was silence on the line, then a shift in Elias's tone. "That's... disconcerting. Why is she being drawn in that deeply?" he said, trailing off into his thoughts. His voice came back stronger as he continued. "I mean, I wore protective gear, I was cautious, but it wasn't a biohazard suit. I don't like that news."

"She's been living beside that glyph for weeks," Story said. "God only knows what that thing's been doing to her."

Elias grew quiet before speaking again. "Please be careful. Don't go near the woods. And if you must, wear a mask. Preferably one rated for spores. And keep your distance from anything that glows."

"I'll be careful," she said. "And Elias?"

"Yeah?"

"Could you please call Cal and loop him in. He needs to know and he'll know how to better help you with whatever you need to get this figured out. He'll know who to tell to keep it contained."

"I'll call him after we hang up," he said.

"Thanks, Elias."

"Be safe, please," he said before they hung up.

Mary, shifting from one foot to the next in her foyer looked up and met her friend's eyes. "You still want to go to the farm?"

"I have to," Story replied, already reaching for her boots. "If that mark is still there, the Bury family is sitting on top of a hornet's nest. We can't wait to see what hatches."

Mary opened her mouth, but the protest died before it reached her lips. Story's voice had shifted to a tone that was sharp, final. There would be no arguing.

Chapter Thirty-Four
The Quiet in the Barn

Evening light settled across the Bury farm like it had nowhere better to be. It clung to the hills in long, amber strokes, catching the edges of the pasture fence lines and painting the tops of the grass gold. The scent of warm earth, clover, and hay drifted through the open kitchen windows. But none of it reached Anya.

Inside, the farmhouse felt too still.

Leith had just gone upstairs, her footsteps barely audible on the old pine treads. She hadn't said much. Just drifted past the hallway in that distant way she'd been doing lately. Anya watched her mother go, the hair on her arms lifting with something she couldn't name.

The side screen door opened and closed. Noble's voice came from behind her, low and easy. "You ready?" he asked with lighthearted affection.

She turned, softening a little at the sight of him. "Not yet," she said. "I need to check something first."

He tilted his head. "Check what?"

Anya moved closer, lowering her voice. "Can you stay here and let me know if my mom comes down? Just text me if she leaves the house."

His brows drew together. "Sure. Why?"

"I just—" She hesitated. "She's been going to the barn a lot the past couple days. I need to see what's in there."

"Like what are you thinking?"

"I don't know. I just have a sense that something odd is going on."

Noble stepped toward her, frowning. "Then let me come with you."

"No," she said, quicker than she meant to. "Please. Just stay. Watch for her."

There was a beat but then he nodded, slowly. "Okay. I'll stay."

Anya stepped out the back door and into the late-day light.

The world outside was golden, humming with that soft orchestral buzz that only summer evenings in Lost Grove could manage. A symphony of insects, birds, and far-off dogs barking at nothing. The scent of warm alfalfa filled her lungs as she passed the new paddock. The shaggy highlands and the two mini cows had been brought inside already.

She followed the dirt path behind the coop, past the shed where old garden tools leaned like forgotten soldiers, toward the red barn that had been there longer than anyone alive. It stood quiet and shadowed like it had drawn all the warmth out of the sunlit air and swallowed it whole.

The moment she stepped into the barn, the temperature dropped.

The smells of old straw and rusted nails, dry wood thick with time, and the faint metallic sting of urine hit her first. She moved slowly, each step muffled against the dirt-packed floor. The interior stretched long and narrow, lit only by broken blades of evening sun cutting in through cracks and missing slats, casting the dust in illuminated ribbons.

The paddocks were empty. Anya moved from one to the next, her fingertips grazing the wood slats, leaving faint trails in the dust.

Her heart picked up, the kind of heartbeat that was loud and echoing in her ears.

Why are you coming in here? she thought. *Why now?* What could her mother possibly be doing out here? What had drawn her into the barn lately?

The sixth paddock was empty. So was the seventh. Then, from the far end of the corridor, came a sound, soft at first, almost imperceptible beneath the creak of wood and the distant rustle of wind. It was a sob. Or something trying to be. Wet and broken, the sound curled out of the shadows like a child crying alone in the dark. But it was off, in that subtle, skin-prickling way that the mind notices before it understands. The pitch wavered unnaturally, the rhythm just a breath too mechanical, like an echo of grief without the soul behind it.

Anya froze, the sound crawling over her skin like cold fingers. She stayed that way for what felt like an eternity but in reality was a matter of heartbeats, seconds only. A hum reverberated in her bones and behind her teeth. Her breath caught high in her throat. She took a step and then another toward the final stall.

A shape shifted in the far shadows. It was huddled and small like an animal.

There was a wet slick of sound, the humming continued so that Anya felt dizzy, her eyes felt heavy, and her vision danced.

Warmth trickled down her lip. Anya blinked, disoriented, the world warping slightly at the edges. She swiped at her nose in a lazy, slow movement and tasted it before she meant to. Blood, salty, and copper-rich.

The sob started again.

Anya's vision tunneled.

The shape moved. It stood about two feet tall and walked forward, shifting out of the shadows and into a stream of light like an awkward toddler.

That was enough.

Anya stumbled back, sandals catching in loose straw. Her shoulder slammed into the barn wall. She gasped, breath tearing from her throat. She burst out of the barn, stumbling into the sharp cut of sunlight. She skidded across the dry earth, and she nearly tripped—only to slam straight into a solid chest.

"Anya!" Noble's hands came up instantly, steadying her. "What—are you okay—your face—?"

She tried to speak, but the words caught on the heat in her throat. "I—I think I saw—"

"Is that blood?" he asked, already reaching to swipe beneath her nose.

"I went in, and I heard—" Her voice cracked.

"Your mom is—"

"I didn't know there'd actually be—Noble, it sobbed."

They both spoke at once, tripping over syllables, grabbing for understanding in the same breath, each trying to talk and listen at the same time.

"What do you mean it sobbed?"

"It was in the last stall—"

"You're bleeding, babe. Are you hurt? Did you see who—?"

"No. No, not a person—"

The barn door behind them groaned in the wind. Anya spun, backpedaling.

Noble caught her by the elbow and followed, casting a look over his shoulder at the old barn.

A crunch of gravel and heavy boots grabbed both their attention.

"Anya?" Her father's voice rang sharp and close.

"Dad—"

Ethan strode across the gravel yard, Bear trotting at his heels, fur bristling. His face, usually reserved even in irritation, was tight with fear. "What the hell's going on? Are you bleeding?" he asked as he took a hold of her chin and examined her face.

"I—"

"Did you hit your nose?" Ethan asked. His eyes flashed up to Noble.

"Dad," she said, voice urgent, hands clamping around his arms. Her eyes roamed past him to the barn. "There's something *in there*."

That gave him a half-second pause. A flicker of uncertainty. "In the barn?"

Anya nodded.

Ethan scowled, pulled a handkerchief from his pocket and pressed it into her hands, then spun and started forward.

"No, don't—!" she called after him, voice cracking in the heat. "Dad, please—don't go in."

Bear began to growl. It wasn't her usual warning growl, but deep and guttural, vibrating through her chest.

Noble's hand landed on Anya's shoulder. His other pointed, stiff. "What is that—"

There, etched into the sun-bleached wood of the barn's exterior, was a thin, sharp symbol, carved with intent. A glyph, not unlike the one from the woods. Twisted lines forming what looked like a three-pronged claw splitting a circle.

Before anyone could speak, a mass of darkness fell from the roof of the barn.

Chapter Thirty-Five
Fairgrounds

A cacophony of jubilant voices buzzed in the air. Screams from children of joy, of fear, and excitement rose above the rest. The low-frequency buzz of machinery merged with the sharp clang of metals from little weights hitting old-fashioned bells, from pellets hitting bullseyes, with the pop of a pistol signaling the start of a horse race, with the sizzling of fried food. Music coming from the merry go round, the Ferris wheel, train rides, and the flying swings weaved together, forming the soundtrack to the evening's festivities.

Nate had only experienced the annual county fair from within, riding the rides, throwing baseballs at unbreakable milk jugs, winning stuffed animals for his kid sister Cheshire, eating hot dogs, cotton candy, and snow cones. Not only was he on the outside looking in on the opening night of the biggest yearly event in Lost Grove, he was in uniform, working with the Lost Grove Police, stationed at the outskirts of the fairgrounds with the Cursed Woods behind him, hoping whatever murderous animal responsible for mutilating Anya's cows and mauling a seven-year old boy wouldn't come charging from behind, poised to knock him aside like a bull.

Obviously it wasn't a bull, but what was it? It was claimed that a grey wolf was responsible for tearing the Green Man, Raymond LaRange, to shreds, but the answer to what was responsible for the current attacks seemed to be a complete mystery. A very rare or new species? *What the hell was that?* Nate pondered.

Oh shit! Nate's eyes opened as if he was tasered. He had just learned that Anya was a mermaid, or whatever Zoe called it. "A naiad?" he voiced. Did naiads grow claws and possess a hunger for human and animal flesh? "No, come on, guy, we're talking about Anya here." Nate shook his head, throwing the notion out of his mind. He looked over his shoulder into the maze of trees. The sun was just beginning to set but it was already dark as night in the woods. "Better not be any fucking fungus floating in the air," he mumbled.

"You talking to yourself there, hotshot?"

Nate turned back around to see Stan staring at him with a shit-eating grin, some of the rest of the Hensley family twenty feet behind her yukking it up among themselves. "Whatever. I was talking into my walkie."

"The one attached to your belt," Stan said, pointing.

"Look, why don't you go play with the rest of the kids out there. Go get a funnel cake or something."

"I love funnel cakes. You want me to bring you one?"

Nate scoffed. "Clearly I'm on duty. And clearly I'm a man."

Stan rolled her eyes. "You can't even grow a beard. And you can't eat on duty?"

Nate pointed to his head and then pointed out to the crowd with his index and middle finger. "Need to be sharp. Alert."

"Do you have any idea how unbearable you're going to be when you become an actual police officer?"

"Not near as unbearable as you're being right now."

Stan pointed to her left at the continuing tree line surrounding the fairgrounds. "I saw Eddie around the corner in the same position you are. And your *partner* Sasha further on down. What the hell's going on? Why are you guys all standing on the periphery here?"

"*Periphery.* You just learn that word? We're just keeping an eye out."

"For what?"

"Trouble. Like you."

Stan looked back into the mass of people meandering through the grounds. "You know," she said, turning back to Nate, "I don't ever recall the whole police department standing around the fair like bouncers at a concert before. Tell me what's going on. And don't bullshit me."

Nate wedged his thumbs behind his belt. "Nothing specific, Hensley. Just a precaution."

She stepped closer to him. "For what?"

312

"You know," he said, lowering his voice, "there's been animal attacks and shit. The Kevin Marlow kid, all the cattle lately. Did you hear about the cows on Anya's farm?"

Stan winced. "No, what are you talking about?"

Nate sighed. "Look, don't tell her I told you, but Seth got called out there this morning. Apparently a few of their cows were slaughtered."

"Oh my God. What is going on lately?"

"I don't know, but we just want to be sure everyone's safe in case something happens."

Stan was hit with the earnestness of Nate's voice. She looked back down to his utility belt. "Not that you have a permit or a license or whatever, but you're not armed."

Nate pulled the taser from one of his sealed pouches. "Got this."

"A taser? What kind of animal is it? Do you guys know?"

Nate shook his head. "Unfortunately not. Look, Hensley, don't go spreading word about this. We don't want to spook everyone or cause a commotion. Things have been tense enough around town as it is."

Stan nodded. "Okay. Be careful, yeah?"

"It's honestly probably for nothing. Just be better that we're all here on the off chance." Nate saw the rare emotion of worry on his best friend's face. He grabbed Stan's hand and gave it a quick squeeze. "I'll be good. Promise."

Stan smiled, touched by Nate's wildly uncommon seriousness and warmth. "You better. I'm going to get back with the clan over there," she said, jutting her thumb over her shoulder.

"Have fun." Nate smiled and gave her a nod.

"Okay, Jenna, this is my last one. And don't go telling the rest of your friends where you got these, guys. I don't want to disappoint anyone." Eddie was crouched down, surrounded by five children, ages between five and eight, their parents standing behind them, always grateful for the eldest member of the department's graciousness with the children in Lost Grove.

Eddie brought a yellow balloon to his lips and started to blow, quickly inflating the long tube shape. He tied it off and did the same with two more. He grinned to himself as he swiftly and expertly twisted and tied the balloons together. He had a bag of five hundred at home for his grandchildren and great-nieces and -nephews. He finished his creation and handed it over to young Jenna Gilford. "Here you go, sweetie."

Jenna's eyes blossomed as she carefully grabbed the animal. "I love it! What is it?"

"What does it look like?"

"I don't know. A giraffe?"

Eddie grinned. "Not a giraffe. Erika, what do you think it is?" he asked one of the other children.

"It's a horse!" she beamed.

Eddie laughed. "Close enough. It's a donkey."

Jenna wrapped her arm around Eddie. "Thank you for my donkey, Officer Eddie."

Eddie patted her back. "Of course," he said and then stood to his feet. "Have fun at the fair, kids."

Robert Gilford, Jenna's father, picked his daughter up and said to the group, "What do you say, guys?"

"Thank you, Officer Eddie," all five kids said in unison.

Eddie waved at the families as they made their way back into the fray. He checked over his shoulder. The unfamiliar feeling of paranoia had been raging through him since he got to the fair and was sent to his post by Seth. So many catastrophes in a two-week span. The image of Kevin Marlow's body had haunted his waking and sleeping hours ever since the awful night he found him. Was the same animal responsible for the cows? For Raymond LaRange? It was a miracle Clayton Meadows was found unharmed, but that didn't quell Eddie's concern for all the children and parents at the fair tonight and for the next two weeks. He could only pray the animal was identified and located swiftly.

The static of Sasha's walkie sounded as she was making her way back through the woods to her post.

"Kingston, it's Abbott. Safety check one-two."

Sasha laughed as she brought the walkie to her mouth, stepping over a fallen branch. "All good here, Abbott." Sasha wasn't sure why she was playing along with Nate's games. The kid had been a pain in her ass this summer. A pain in her ass that had miraculously grown on her. Behind all his bravado and sarcasm was a genuinely decent young man. When he let his guard down, Nate was actually intelligent and thoughtful.

"Good to hear. Have you seen anything?"

"Haven't seen anything. I heard some rustling in the woods but didn't find anything."

"You left your post to go into the Cursed Woods?"

Sasha stepped past the tree line to reclaim her post. "Yes, genius. That's what we do as officers of the law. We investigate."

"The chief told us to stay put."

Sasha shook her head and spoke into the walkie. "He didn't need to elaborate on what we're to do if we see or hear something, Nate. I heard a potential threat and I checked it out."

"Are you still out there? Did you see any glyphs? Be careful out there."

"I'm back at my post, partner. No glyphs, and I don't feel high. Not yet, anyway."

"Don't joke about that."

"Says the guy who jokes about literally everything," Sasha retorted, awaiting his response. A few beats passed and she thought he had just abruptly ended the conversation.

"What do I do if I see something? I mean, what if a wild cougar or something comes sprinting at me? My taser would be as useful as my dick."

Sasha grimaced. "That's completely—"

"You say 'Dolores' as loud and clear as you can into your walkie, Nate," Seth's voice came through.

"Right, right," Nate responded.

"What do you think you heard, Sasha?" asked Seth.

She looked back into the woods, her nerves on edge ever since she got there. "I don't know. Could have been a fox or a coyote or something. It was a scamper. Definitely something on four legs."

"Okay. Everyone," Seth prompted, "be alert."

"Ten-four," Sasha responded.

"Ten-four," Nate said.

"You got it, Chief," Eddie chimed in.

"Ready as ever," Bill answered.

"Thanks again for volunteering to be out here, Bill," Seth said. "I know you could—"

"Quit with all of that. It'll always be my duty to protect this town."

Sasha's heart warmed as she holstered her walkie. She missed Bill's fatherly presence around the office. He had given her a real opportunity in bringing her on. That, and he taught her the power of patience, something her partner, Angel, was beyond thankful for.

A large branch cracked behind her from high up in one of the distant trees. She spun around, her heart racing. "What the fuck?" She turned on her Maglite and shined it into the woods, quickly checking all directions high and low. Nothing there. Sasha let out a long sigh and took up a position where she could constantly keep her eyes on the forest and the fair. Town drunks, teenage scuffles, and even kidnappers didn't scare her. Unidentified animals tearing apart flesh with seemingly no provocation were another matter.

Sasha pulled her walkie back out. "Joe, how you doing? You didn't respond to Seth."

"Hold on one sec," Joe said to Ember and Emory Graff, who had come over to talk with him. Earlier in the spring Emory had discovered that CaseyOnTheCase, a handle on Reddit, was in fact Officer Joe Casey with the Lost Grove Police Department. They were both members of the "Lost Grove Mysteries" subReddit and had engaged in some highly speculative and wild theories about bizarre cases throughout the history of the town.

One evening while Emory, his sister, and Stan were at Moonlight Creamery & Bistro debating the eternal question of cone or cup, Emory spotted a familiar figure in line ahead of them. The young officer stood easy at the counter, chatting with Raquel, who worked most nights and knew everyone's order before they said it.

She handed him a thick chocolate shake with a flourish. "Here you go, Officer Casey."

Emory's eyebrows shot up. He nudged Stan. "Order me an Oreo waffle cone," he said, already peeling away from the line.

He caught up to the officer just outside. "Hey, man—sorry to bother you, but…" He leaned in slightly, lowering his voice with the weight of a secret. "You're not CaseyOnTheCase, are you?"

The officer paused. Then his eyes lit up.

Emory grinned. "I'm YourMindIsMyMind."

From that moment on, their weird little internet-born bromance was cemented.

"Hey, I'm here," Joe replied to Sasha, stepping away from Ember and Emory. "Sorry, I was chatting with a couple friends."

"I hope you're still doing your job," she said.

"Aren't we supposed to blend in?"

Joe heard Sasha sigh on the other end, a typical reply. "Yes, we are," she said. "It's just…I've heard something in the woods a couple times

316

now and it's starting to freak me out. As Seth said, be alert."

A swell of fear mixed with excitement ran through Joe's body. He and his new friends had just been tossing around theories about what animal might have killed Kevin Marlow. Emory had started the conversation almost like he knew that's why they were stationed out at the edge of the woods there in the first place.

Emory's bet was on the same grey wolf responsible for Raymond LaRange. Joe had his money on a puma—less dramatic but more plausible. Either way, he hoped neither one showed up at the fairgrounds. They were both protected species and he would hate to have to put one down. But if a wolf, a puma, or whatever rare species Seth was referring to, really did decide to make an appearance mid funnel cake stand and the Ferris wheel…it could turn into a scene straight out of a horror movie.

"Okay, yeah, I will be," Joe replied and placed his walkie back on his belt. He stepped back toward Ember and Emory. "Sorry about that."

"All good, man," Emory said. "Everything okay?"

Joe waved his hand in the air. "Yeah, just a regular check-in."

Ember looked at Emory like he'd said something—only he hadn't—and then without a word they both looked past Joe into the Cursed Woods.

Joe looked over his shoulder and then back at the twins. "What is it? Did you guys see something?"

"Huh?" Emory returned his attention to Joe and let out what sounded like a forced laugh. "Oh, nah, man. Just, ya know, keeping an eye out for that grey wolf." Ember tugged at her brother's shirt. "Stop it," he said, brushing her hand away.

Joe looked back once again, now starting to get more nervous than excited. Something had clearly grabbed the twins' attention. Maybe the same thing Sasha had heard. Shadows twisted through the forest animated by the wind that had picked up earlier today. With all that restless darkness, spotting an animal would be near impossible.

"Yo, Casey?" Emory called to get his friend's attention.

Joe turned back. "Hey, yeah. Just looking out for that puma," he said and forced his own laugh.

"Okay, man, we're gonna head back in and hook up with Stan." Ember smiled up at her brother. "Yeah, yeah," he quietly said and smirked at her.

"Talk to you guys soon!" Joe called out as they moved rather quickly back into the fair. "Or at least you, Emory," he said to himself.

Joe flicked on his Maglite and stepped into the trees, sweeping the beam around the underbrush. The distorting shadows disappeared in the beam of light, taking off the edge of eeriness.

Woosh.

Joe flinched and jerked the light upward, scanning the high canopy. The hairs on the back of his neck stood on alert. He thought he saw a shadow, but there was nothing there, just swaying branches and flapping leaves.

Joe backed out into the grass and clicked off his Maglite, keeping it in hand. He surveyed the people and attractions in front of him. More lights had come on than he realized. The Ferris wheel spun in slow twinkling rhythm, strung with blinking colors. The food stands glowed with carnival charm, their old-fashioned bulbs buzzing.

A little girl rode on the back of a foal, led by one of the female workers he recognized from Ross Ranch. There was a dude on stilts in a long coat and top hat, his face painted with dramatic flourishes that thankfully didn't look too much like a clown. Joe's gaze slid right. A cluster of kids were screaming their heads off in the sky chairs, the chain-swing ride whipping them in dizzying circles. He grimaced. He always hated that ride. He'd ridden it once as a kid and spent the whole time imagining the chains snapping, hurling him into the air like a slingshot toward a cartoonishly tragic and early demise. Never rode it again.

His eyes drifted back down to the crowd and landed on Peter Andalusian with his daughter Zoe perched up on his shoulders, grinning like she owned the whole damn fair. She slapped a high five to the stilt-walker as he passed, giggling at the contact. Peter bent slightly, caught her under her armpits, and with a practiced swing, lowered her to the ground. She stuck the landing like a gymnast, ponytail bouncing.

Beside them, his wife Jolie walked with a casual sway, holding a lemonade and looking, as always, effortlessly stunning. Tight jeans, cowboy boots, and a loose flannel shirt that revealed just enough of a sun-kissed collarbone to make Joe's stomach knot up.

God, I hope he doesn't know, Joe worried.

On one of their morning shifts about a month ago, they had stopped off at Ross Ranch while they were on their regular patrol. Peter wanted to bring his wife lunch from the local Mexican joint on Main Street. Joe had seen Mrs. Andalusian around town over the years, but never at such close range. Never in low slung jeans and that damned loose flannel button-down shirt, revealing the top of her cleavage. He hadn't meant to stare. His eyes just kind of…caught. Then lingered. By the time he sheepishly pulled his eyes away, Peter had been looking straight at him. He'd given Joe a knowing smile before turning back to his wife. Peter had never said anything to him, but Joe always worried. He certainly wasn't about to leave his post to go talk with them.

Joe kept scanning right, past the children's train ride, the funnel cake stand, the funhouse with its warped, vaguely demonic mirrors, over to the last attraction on the outskirts before the grassland led to the woods. It was that old midway game where contestants fired high-powered water guns into clown mouths, racing their little plastic jockeys to the finish line.

Joe smiled. He was always quite good at that game. A figure just beyond the game stand caught his eye. A young girl had wandered a few steps away from her parents up to a…

Joe blinked and cocked his head to the side. "That's a bizarre costume," he mused.

Seth slowly made his way through the throng of townspeople and visitors from all over the county and beyond, smiling and waving at the kids who looked up to him with wide eyes, nodding at familiar faces. The sun was setting behind the curtain of the Cursed Woods in the distance. He checked his watch. They had been here for over four hours. Seth had circled and weaved throughout the fairgrounds at least thirty times by now, keeping a friendly face, but continuously aware and alert. The timing of the cow attack at the Bury farm, this close to civilization, had him supremely on edge. The town could not afford another fatality, an accident, or even a big scare at this point.

The county fair was the biggest revenue driver for Lost Grove each year, filling up Airbnbs, hotels, and local B&Bs for two weeks, flooding the local businesses and restaurants, all helping to further spread the word about the quaint charm of their small town to encourage more visitors throughout the year. Raymond LaRange's death might have flown under the radar, but the deaths of Sarah Elizabeth Grahams and Kevin Marlow certainly had not. And then there was the week-long search for Clayton Meadows. The boy was thankfully found, unharmed at that, but the building publicity over the past year wasn't great.

Seth was banking on, hoping, praying to anyone or anything, that the cars, the flashing lights, the abundance of people and cacophony of sounds would be enough to scare off any wild animals. In a normal world it would. But this was Lost Grove and they were dealing with an unknown, possibly "rare or new species," which left the proverbial door wide open. He thought of the idea too late, but Seth wished he had asked Story to come out to the grounds and lay a protective spell around the perimeter. As long as they could get through the rest of the night, that was precisely what he would have her do. Late tonight, early tomorrow morning, whenever would give her time to do her thing.

Seth grinned as he saw the Andalusian family approaching, sans Noble. Peter had radioed him and asked if he could step away from his post to spend some time with Jolie and Zoe. Seth was cautious about the festivities tonight, but not so much so that he would deny Peter spending some quality time with his family at the fair. If Story were here he would do the same. And where was she anyway? She said that she was going to drag Mary here. He wasn't so sure she'd be successful, but he was surprised not to have heard from her since lunchtime.

Seth raised a hand and waved as the family emerged from the crowd. Zoe spotted him first and took off at a light jog, holding a stuffed owl aloft like a trophy.

"Hey, Uncle Seth! Look what Dad won!" she called, grinning, the owl's stitched wings flapping with every step.

Seth crouched slightly to meet her halfway, and as she came to a stop, he chuckled, eyes glinting. "Well, would you look at that."

She beamed, cradling the plush in her arms.

He still remembered the first time she'd called him "Uncle Seth." They'd all looked around, curious—Peter with one eyebrow lifted, Jolie giving a soft, polite laugh. Jolie had eventually asked, "Sweetie, why'd you call him that?" Zoe had just shrugged and said, "He's like...my spirit uncle." That was that. She'd called him uncle ever since.

"How'd he win it?" Seth asked, rising back to full height.

"At the strongman game," she explained, pointing vaguely behind her.

"The one with the hammer," Peter said, catching up with Jolie.

"Hey, Seth," Jolie greeted, smiling warmly.

"Jolie," Seth said with a nod. "Good to see you."

Zoe held up the owl. "Her name's Sabrina."

Seth raised an eyebrow. "Sabrina?"

Jolie grinned. "The teenage witch."

Seth smiled, a corner of his mouth twitching upward in that particular way it did whenever he thought about things best left unsaid—like the little spell kits Story had been sneaking to Zoe in tote bags labeled "botany experiments," or the time he'd caught them in the backyard drawing sigils in chalk under the guise of "nature art." Jolie and Peter knew Story was a bit earthy, sure—but they hadn't quite realized yet that their daughter was learning the difference between kitchen herbs and ritual ones. "Is she going to be Merryweather's friend?"

"Her sister, obviously," Zoe said, rolling her eyes. "Magic's better with friends."

Seth nodded. "Speaking of which, where's your brother?"

Zoe shrugged. "With Anya somewhere."

"I was expecting him by now," Jolie said. "He was going to pick up Anya. But you know…"

Seth nodded, getting her drift. Seth took a slow step to the side, giving Peter a look just subtle enough to pass unnoticed by the young girl.

Jolie, however, did notice it. "Should we go get in line for frozen lemonades?"

"Yep!" Zoe agreed.

"I'll be right behind," Peter said, tugging lovingly on his daughter's bouncing ponytail as she passed.

"Have you heard from Paddy yet?" Seth asked once they were out of earshot.

"I haven't. He said he'd be here, but no sight or word from him as of yet. Is there something up?"

"No, no. Just being, you know…"

"Cautious? Yeah, I think you've got the whole team in the right mindset. I did a perimeter sweep to check in with everyone firsthand before meeting up with Jo and Zo. They're ready. Should there be anything to be ready for."

Seth patted Peter on the back. "Appreciate that."

"No problem. I bumped into Seamus over by the funhouse earlier on. He said you asked him and Lashley to be here as extra hands. Sparing no expense, leaving nothing to caution, huh?"

"More the better. Did you catch Seamus coming out of the funhouse? Seems like something he would enjoy."

Peter laughed. "He had a grin on his face like he had just walked out, but I didn't ask."

"Alright, well, get back to your family. I don't want to keep you."

"I'm going to play a few more games with Zo, take her on the Ferris wheel, get her something with loads of sugar, and then I'll be back in position."

Seth grinned. "I'm sure Jolie will appreciate the sugar boost."

Peter scoffed and rejoined his family.

Former Chief of Police Bill Richards was stationed at the east side of the fairgrounds, near the entrance, over by the massive slide that kids and parents alike rode down on burlap sacks. It was one of the oldest attractions in the park, along with the Ferris wheel and merry-go-round. Bill had fond memories of riding down what he called the wave slide when he was a kid. Climbing up the four flights of stairs back then felt like he was climbing to the top of a water tower. He recalled that feeling of awe and unbridled fear being at the top preparing to go down. It was so far down. What if he hit one of those waves and sailed into the air, did a flip and landed on his head? Looking at it now, his only fear would be pulling a muscle in his back or twisting his knee when he hit the bottom.

The plan was for him to spend most of his time by the slide, which was in the northeast corner, butt up against the woods. He periodically strode up to the entrance to greet and say goodbye to people coming and going. The out-of-towners all had the same look of wide-eyed innocence and excitement when they walked through the gates, enticed by the smells of fair food, eager to go on their favorite rides. But after thirty-five years as a member of the Lost Grove Police Department, now a retired reserve officer, Bill saw something different in the eyes of the locals coming into the fair, something behind the veneer of smiles. They were on edge, wary, tired, and afraid. He recognized the variant hidden emotions the same as he saw in the mirror the last two weeks.

There was a universal aura around town of waiting for the other shoe to drop. Or rather the third or fourth shoe. The county fair was on one hand a great distraction, a chance to step away from realities of day-to-day life, to forget about the tragedies and trauma of recent days. But being surrounded by hundreds of children was a grim reminder of Kevin Marlow, an out-of-town child of seven killed in their own state park, and Clayton Meadows, a teenage son of Lost Grove who disappeared in the same Cursed Woods that served as a barrier to half of the fairgrounds.

The fresh news of his return didn't nullify the fear that any one of these children here tonight could wander aimlessly into the woods and never be heard from again. And that's why they were here, to prevent that from happening.

Seth continued his winding path through the fairgrounds, trying to mix up his route to keep things interesting. He had just missed the fair when he returned home last summer. The last time he had been to the county fair was with his then-girlfriend, Jaime Goodacre. They were both seventeen, the summer between their junior and senior year of high school. As expected, everything seemed much smaller to him now. Seth revisited the Lost Grove maze near the circus tent closer to the entrance, just for old times' sake. He and Jamie made out there that summer. The design was unfamiliar to him. Had he forgotten it, too caught up in teenage love? Or was the entire maze redesigned at some point over the years?

Seth took the direct route through the center of the grounds, en route to meet up with each member of his team at the back perimeter, when he registered chatter on his radio. He brought his walkie to his ear and listened to Sasha talking to Nate about a sound she heard in the woods. Seth's insides began to tighten as he slowly spun in a circle, looking for anything suspicious.

Seth clicked his walkie to speak. "What do you think you heard, Sasha?"

"I don't know. Could have been a fox or a coyote or something. It was a scamper. Definitely something on four legs."

"Okay. Everyone," Seth prompted, "be alert."

"Ten-four," Sasha responded.

"Ten-four," Nate said.

"You got it, Chief," Eddie chimed in.

"Ready as ever," Bill answered.

"Thanks again for volunteering to be out here, Bill," Seth said. "I know you could—"

"Quit with all of that. It'll always be my duty to protect this town."

Seth clipped his walkie to his belt and continued on ahead, his boots feeling heavier, his scalp starting to tingle. *Please not here. Not tonight.* He should have called the CDFW after the incident at the Bury farm and asked them to send officers up to search the woods. The risk was just too high. He was so concerned about getting to the fair and having his team spread out and post up that he didn't consider the additional measures he should have taken. Story, the CDFW, more officers from the county.

Seth saw Old Tom King approaching and knew he wouldn't be able to avoid the gossipmonger. "Hey, Tom. Enjoying the fair?"

"Not so much," he said. "Not sure why I come here every year. Just seems like the right thing to do."

"I suppose there's something to that," Seth said absentmindedly as he surveyed the area. The last crescent of the sun was fading behind the Cursed Woods, the colorful lights shining brighter around him.

"I heard that Meadows boy was found last night."

Here we go, Seth thought. "Yep, safe and sound."

"That's not what I heard. Stew Henderson said he was taken by a cult, brainwashed him. Can't even remember his own name, they say."

Seth ran his hand through his hair, thinking he'd be used to this by now. "No cult, Tom," Seth claimed, though that thin possibility was still on the table. "And he remembers his name and his family just fine. I've been to see him twice."

"That's what they want you to think."

"Maybe so. Have a good night, Tom," Seth said and continued on. It was only a matter of time before Tom talked to everyone at the fair, who would then start to look at poor Clayton differently. Like an outsider. Like Mary. Where were Story and Mary? He checked his cell, still no messages.

Seth moved ahead, his eyes drawn to the classic merry-go-round up on his left. His steps slowed with no conscious choice, the sound of the fair fading away, drowned out by a deafening silence encompassing his eardrums. His fingertips began to numb, like they were turning into rubber. He stopped in place as gooseflesh sprouted across his body. Was he about to time travel again? Had he been here before? Transported from within the cave? Before that? A faint piercing sound began to ring in his right ear, drawing his eyes in that direction, as if being pulled by a puppeteer.

Seth saw the funhouse in the distance, in focus, while everything else around it started to blur. He semi-consciously looked for Seamus, but didn't see the red-headed monster of a man. His eyes drifted to the right, a water gun game of some sorts. There was a man and a woman, standing behind a young boy playing the game. An even younger girl with curly brown hair lingered behind the man, her dad most likely. Seth saw something move on the periphery of his vision, something that caught the girl's attention. Her eyes grew wide in wonder as she approached the…

"What kind of costume…?" Seth wondered.

Someone dressed in a large owl costume stood still on the edge of the grass, the ever-darkening woods a short distance behind them. Seth's brain tried to file it away as someone getting overly creative. The figure didn't move. Not even a shift of weight or the subtle bob of breath. It was perfectly still, its robust, feathered form rendered in a hauntingly beautiful palette—browns and blacks and whites mottled together like bark and ash and bone. The wings were tucked against its sides, draping down the back like a cloak, but they flexed slightly with a tension that betrayed real muscle just beneath. It stood close to seven feet tall, imposing, looming. The head… The head was all sorts of wrong. The beak was wide, too wide, hooked but slanted, the skin around it jaundiced and stretched tight, like old parchment left in the sun. No feathers covered its face— just the sickly suggestion of human skin trying to imitate a bird's shape. Their eyes, glassy and black, reflected specs of light from the game sign. They didn't blink. They didn't look away. They weren't costume-grade lenses or clever glass. They were wet. Reflective. Watching.

Seth's eyes dropped instinctively to the legs, hoping for boots, stilts, costume seams. "Mother of God."

Marina Daniels stood behind her mother and father while her stupid brother, Beau, played his dumb shooting game. He always got to play more games than her. Her mother said it was because she refused to play the games when they offered, but what did that matter? Beau also got to go on more rides than her. Her father said it was because she wasn't tall enough, but who made those rules? Her parents? They thought the cotton candy and caramel apple somehow made up for it, which it kind of did, but still.

"I wanna go in the fun house," Marina proclaimed. No reaction from her parents. Typical. Beau was more important. Marina looked around, bored from waiting. Bored from being ignored. "Oh…"

A gigantic owl walked out from the woods, tottering back and forth. *What a cool costume,* Marina thought. Maybe there was a ride or a tent with more animal costumes. The owl stopped before stepping onto the concrete pathway and stared out into the fairgrounds. *How did they make those cool eyes,* she wondered. Marina, amazed at the detail and design of the costume, approached the person wearing it. "Hey, what's your name? I'm Marina. What ride do you work on?"

The owl's eyes darted toward Marina, and that's when she knew something was wrong. Very wrong. She froze in place as her bladder released, the warm wetness running down her inner thighs.

Raaaaaaak!

The owl's screech shattered Seth's temporary mind paralysis. He burst into a sprint. "GET AWAY!"

Every eye in the vicinity turned toward Seth and then in the direction he was running.

"Everyone! Get away!"

The young girl screamed at the top of her lungs.

The owl, reacting, scared, angry, defensive, spread its wings, causing Seth's eyes to widen in horror. They stretched at least fifteen feet wide.

"Gary! Get Marina!" yelled the girl's mother.

The man swooped in and pulled his daughter to safety as people all around stood still in utter befuddlement.

"It's real!" Seth yelled. "It's not a costume!"

No one seemed to register what Seth was saying. People stared at the giant owl, wings spread out wide, as if it was a spectacular attraction about to perform a magic trick or stunt.

"Look at its legs!" Seth yelled, which was the spark needed to snap people out of their trances.

"Holy shit!" yelled a man holding his young son's hand.

"What is it, Daddy?"asked the panicked boy.

"Roger, help!" hollered a woman who had stumbled over her own feet, falling to the ground a mere three feet from the creature.

Seth was twenty feet away and spotted Joe running up from behind the owl, his gun drawn. Seth shook his head, helpless, his voice stuck in his throat as people bounced off him, running in a panic. Stay away, Joe, was his first thought. His instincts, muscle memory, kicked in. His fingers wrapped around his radio and he drew it to his mouth as he ran. "Joe, don't fire! I repeat do not fire! There are too many civilians in the line of fire."

Just as Joe slid to a stop and lowered his weapon, the owl flexed its wings and thrust itself off the ground. Its wings beat deep, silent arcs through the night air, lifting it high above the fairgrounds.

And it was at that moment that all hell broke loose. Screams filled the air, coming from all directions, as the owl circled above. For a breathless instant, its shadow swept across the Ferris wheel and funnel cake stand, giant and silent, blotting out the colorful lights in its passage. Seth looked up and felt like a bug about to be squashed at any moment. What even was he seeing? Clearly something prehistoric. *A new species.* The words came back to him. Along with the tragic mistake he had made by brushing off Wes's earlier positive DNA identification of a squirrel and an…owl. Was this creature what killed Kevin Marlow? It must have been. Where had it been living? How had no one seen it? The animal remains in the cave under the construction site. Was that where? Why underground? Was this owl creature what attacked Story, Mary, and Dr. Raines in the cave they were in? Seth shook off the assault of questions running through his mind as people ran for their lives around him.

His voice sharpened as he addressed the rest of his team. "All units, we have a very large airborne predator in motion. Contain the area. Do not engage. We are in a live threat environment. Treat it like a rogue predator. Proceed with extreme caution."

Seth followed the owl's path as it circled above like a vulture. Amid the chaos at his feet—the thundering boots, frantic shouts, and panicked screams—another layer rose above it all: a distant murmur of alarm, growing louder, more focused. His heart tightened.

Then it came through the radio, slicing through the static:

"Seth! There's another one!" Sasha's voice came clearly through the radio.

He lifted his eyes toward the far side of the fairgrounds and saw it: a second owl creature, smaller but still massive, gliding low in a wide arc. It banked sharply, choosing a trajectory toward the center of the crowd, wings catching the fair lights in brief, ghostly flashes. How many of them were there? How many different caves did they make their home? It was the only place that made sense for no one to have come across them in… how many years he didn't have time to ponder.

"Jesus Christ," he muttered. Seth's stomach dropped as his fingers tightened on his walkie. "All units—second target inbound, southwest quadrant! Evacuate civilians. Get eyes on Sasha's location—anomalous avian entity, repeat, multiple. No shots unless lethal force is absolutely warranted!"

He darted toward the direction the owl was heading, adrenaline sharpening every fiber of his being.

Chapter Thirty-Six
Ritual and Bone

The trees beyond the Bury farmhouse shifted with a wind that hadn't reached the ground. Story stopped just before the first porch step, adjusting the satchel on her shoulder. Mary hung back a pace, gaze flicking toward the barn in the distance.

Story knocked.

A few seconds later they heard footsteps and the door opened. Leith stood there. She wore a gauzy blouse that clung to her arms and a linen apron that was already stained. Her expression was soft, if distant. Her pupils were too wide for this hour. She smiled, but it didn't land properly.

"Story," she said. "Mary."

"Hi, Leith," Story answered gently. "Mind if we come in for just a minute?"

Leith nodded and stepped aside.

The moment they crossed the threshold, Mary stiffened.

The house reeked of the acrid tang of butchery, raw and warm, like a wild animal had just left the room. The air clung close, almost wet. Story watched as Mary's nostrils flared, her face shifting almost imperceptibly.

Her gums ached. Her teeth began to press out of her gums and a metallic flavor bloomed at the back of her tongue.

Leith had already moved down the hall into the kitchen, and they followed. The clatter of a knife hitting wood started up in an uneven rhythm.

On the counter, a mound of offal was already half processed—livers, kidneys, a pale coil of intestine she hadn't quite gotten to yet. A bowl of dark meat sat waiting, slick and cold, while Leith's hands worked with mechanical speed at the cutting board.

Mary stopped dead in the doorway. Her voice, when it came, was low. "I need a minute."

Story didn't turn. "Go ahead."

Mary vanished back through the hall and out the porch door.

Leith never looked up.

The sound of her knife striking wood was steady. Over and over again. The meat beneath her blade had long since been rendered to pulp, but her arm kept moving, faster with every strike.

Story stepped to the side, watching her. "Leith, what are you making?"

There was a pause. A breath caught in the wrong part of the lungs.

Leith blinked. Her voice came quiet. "It's for the…" She tilted her head. Her mouth opened as if to finish the thought, but nothing came. Her brow furrowed.

Story stepped carefully to the edge of the kitchen. Her eyes scanned the room, and that's when she noticed the bowls.

Seven of them were arranged under every windowsill, on the counters, at the doorway leading into the back mudroom and the open screen door. Each one was filled with water.

The surfaces trembled gently, at first. Every time the blade hit the board, the bowls rippled like struck bells. A low hum began to build beneath the rhythm, vibrating up from the floorboards like a whisper in her spine.

"Leith." Story's voice was sharper now. "Look at me."

But Leith didn't. Her arm moved faster.

Thwack. Thwack. Thwack-thwack-thwack.

Her head tilted again. A little too far. Her neck strained as if listening for a noise behind her—something only she could hear. Her lips moved, but no sound came out. The smell of iron filled the kitchen. The air turned thick.

Story took a breath and stepped forward, one palm rising, open toward the ceiling.

"Leith, ma douce amie," she murmured. Her voice was low, almost musical. She pulled a length of blue woolen thread from her pocket and wound it once around her index finger. She pulled the other end taut, ready to pull the thread in two. "Il est temps de revenir maintenant," she said and snapped the thread.

329

The French spilled easily from her tongue, warm, comforting, ancient. A dispersal spell, woven from tradition and intuition. Meant to cut through confusion. To clear mal de l'esprit—the sickness of spirit.

As the last syllable left her lips, the knife stopped.

Leith froze. The bowls stilled. The humming ceased.

Story stood, waiting.

Leith finally lifted her eyes and blinked, her pupils shrinking. Her gaze found the butchered meat, the ruined cutting board, her blood-wet hands. "I... I don't remember..." she whispered.

Before Story could respond, a scream cut through the pastoral calm. Both women's heads snapped to the window, looking out the back toward the farm.

Leith set down the knife with a metallic clang and went to the window, leaning over the sink and gazing outside.

They both heard muffled noises, words and sounds too far off to understand.

"What was that?" Mary asked, coming back into the house. She held a hand to her mouth and nose, her voice muffled.

"I don't know," Story said and they all stopped to listen.

The thing hurtling through the air like a shadow given form at Anya, Noble, and Ethan was taller than any man. The creature, which could only passively be described as an owl, hit the ground in a crouch, dirt puffing up beneath it, feathers shaking loose like blackened leaves in a storm. Its wings draped like cloaks at its side, twitching with tension. Where the sunlight struck its feathers, nothing reflected, resembling nothing but a void, as if light refused to touch it.

Anya screamed.

Noble grabbed her and stumbled backward.

Bear snapped, charging forward, barking with violent fury.

Ethan didn't hesitate. He moved between his daughter and the thing.

The creature rose to seven feet tall. Its face caught in partial shadow, feathers falling away from one side to reveal the glint of pale, too-human flesh. Eyes set wide and deep, gleaming like the eyes of an old, sad dog. Then it moved, launching at them in a gait that felt like it was a stop-motion creature come to life.

Ethan tackled Anya sideways, slamming her to the dirt. Noble shuffled out of the way, trying to grab Bear and haul her back with him.

A whirr of feathers passed overhead like a hurricane of razors. The owl creature missed Ethan and Anya by inches and slammed into the side of the barn with a splintering crunch.

Bear snapped loose of Noble's grasp and was on it before the creature could recover, throwing herself at its side, teeth clamping into the thin, rubbery flesh at its exposed leg.

The thing shrieked with a voice that wasn't human and wasn't animal. It turned and slashed through the air with sickle-like talons.

"No!" Anya screamed.

Bear yelped and hopped aside in time to avoid the blow.

Ethan scrambled to his feet just as it came at them again, beak open, wings snapping wide. He shoved Anya behind him and brought his arm up.

The talon struck.

Blood sprayed across the dirt.

Ethan stumbled back, clutching his ribs. A massive gash curved from beneath his shoulder to his hip, deep, and bleeding too fast. His breath caught like it couldn't decide whether to leave him or not.

"Dad—!"

"*Run,*" Ethan rasped. He shoved her toward Noble with the last of his strength. "Take her. Go!"

"I'm not—" Anya started, panicked.

Noble grabbed her arm. "Anya, now."

She looked back and saw her father standing upright, blood running down his shirt, one hand clenched around a fallen post like a bat, the other pressed to his side.

"NOW!" he shouted.

Anya let Noble drag her, legs stumbling into motion as her ears filled with the terrible rustle of wings.

"Bear!" she screamed. "*Come!*"

Behind them, the creature lunged. Ethan swung. Wood cracked against feathered muscle. A pained, furious screech followed.

They ran.

Feet pounding the dry earth. The house rising ahead like a promise. Blood on Anya's lip. Blood on her hands. The sharp sting of her lungs working too hard.

She didn't look back again.

Not even when the wind shifted and brought with it that awful tang of fresh blood.

Chapter Thirty-Seven
Carnival Static

Peter's head jerked skyward at the sound of a collective gasp. The massive bird was still circling above, casting sweeping shadows over the fairgrounds. But then a smaller shape banked into view, gliding with unnatural precision through the warm night air.

Jolie's hand gripped his arm. "Peter..."

Peter stepped forward instinctively, one arm across Zoe's shoulders as he stared upward. The smaller one was agile, its path tighter, more focused. It wasn't just flying, it looked curious, it looked like it might be hunting.

"Everyone stay calm!" Peter barked into the chaos swelling around them. "Move to the exits. Orderly, now! Don't run!"

But it was like yelling at a tide. People scattered, cries rising like a wave. The smaller bird veered low, a blur of motion and feathers slicing the fairground lights.

Zoe clutched his waist. "Daddy—"

Peter didn't wait. He scooped her up, grabbed Jolie's hand, and pushed through the fleeing crowd.

His radio crackled.

"All units—second target inbound, southwest quadrant..." Seth's voice was taut and low.

"In here!" He headed into the Odds and Curiosities museum, a wood structure close to the entrance he prayed would protect them. About fifteen more people were already huddled inside, faces ashen with fear. He set Zoe down and brought his daughter and wife together to ensure they were holding one another. "Stay in here. Do not move." Peter looked up to the rest of the people. "All of you stay in here! Do not risk running to your cars or going to find someone."

"What is that out there?" a woman's crying voice asked.

Peter shook his head. "I don't know, but we're here to protect you. The whole department."

"Dad, no!" Zoe screamed, pulled free from Jolie to wrap her arms around Peter's leg.

"Zo, Zo." Peter squatted down. "I'll be okay—"

A sharp scream pierced the building, cutting off Peter's words. Zoe jumped, her fingers wrapping around her dad's arms as the people in the room went silent. Just outside the entrance into the museum, between the bodies of people running to get away, one of the giant birds stood like an overly excited juvenile, interested and annoyed and panicked. It moved forward, beak snapping, like a predator irritated by the noise of its prey scurrying away. The wings fluttered briefly.

"Daddy," Zoe whispered.

Peter pressed his daughter backward into his wife and stood in front of them. The weird thing was how interested the massive bird creature looked. It stalked forward again, pupils fixed on the panic beyond, snapping its beak at yet another person trying to get past it.

"It's an owl," Zoe whispered, so low Peter almost didn't hear it.

A child screamed. A pair of teenagers bumped into the owl, running past it with wild eyes. The owl clenched its wings closer and stomped its foot like an irritated creature startled from its domain. The bigger owl landed nearby, talons sweeping the air, daring anyone to get in its way. It moved to the smaller bird, wings flapping in annoyance. The smaller one flapped its wings back, lifted its head like it wanted to be fed as it chirruped. The bigger one nudged it and it hopped away then hopped into the air. The bigger one followed.

Peter turned to his wife, then looked down at his daughter. "Stay here with your mother. Promise me."

Zoe nodded with tears rolling down her face.

Peter met his wife's eyes. "Call Noble. Tell him to stay where he's at. Hopefully he's still at the Burys'."

Jolie nodded. "Okay. I love you."

Peter kissed his wife and ran back out into the fray, his weapon pulled. People sprinted by him, screaming, as he looked up to see three giant owls now circling the center of the fair. The smaller one was being shooed off toward the woods by the bigger one.

"What in God's name?" Peter jogged toward the danger area, dodging people and yelling, "Get to a safe shelter, people! Sturdy structures! No tents!" He grabbed his walkie. "Seth, I'm by the entrance now but heading back toward the center."

"Peter, stay put and protect your family!" Seth yelled back over the walkie.

"I've got them to safety. Where are you?"

Peter heard screaming on the other end before Seth came back. "Heading your way, by the swing. They're just hovering. I wish I knew anything about birds."

"Listen, the smaller one that landed, it wasn't attacking at first. It looked curious. Like it didn't know what to do with the chaos. I think it's a juvenile."

"Look, not sure if you've put this together yet or not, but the cave at the construction site, the bones..." Seth said.

"It crossed my mind. Especially with it being so close to here."

"The earth caves in around their dwelling. All this commotion so close to their nesting area. Could be."

"No clue, but it might explain why they're just hovering. Maybe they just want to chase us off."

"God, I hope so," replied Seth.

Peter picked up his pace.

Sasha led a group of terrified people into a large circus tent. She looked up and saw all the metal braces holding up the structure. "Okay, everyone! Stay in here. Get under the bleachers over there. The structure should hold, but stay under there just to be safe until we come back to get you."

The group of twelve people, seven of them children, all scurried toward the bleachers.

Sasha headed back out and started to sprint toward the center of the fair before a gunshot stopped her in her tracks. "Was that one of you?" she asked into the walkie.

"Who's firing?" Seth's voice was sharp over the radio.

"Negative."

"Not me."

"No."

A group of screams in the distance drew her attention. She looked up and saw one of the giant birdlike creatures dive toward the ground, to the source of the gunshot. "Oh no." It disappeared from view, but quickly shot back up into the sky. Sasha clasped a hand over her mouth as she noticed a person in the grips of the creature's feet. The bird of prey soared even higher and then released the person. "No!" Sasha sank to her knees as she watched the person plummet fifty feet toward the ground below.

Paddy and Cal sprinted through the woods toward the fairgrounds, the echoing screams leading their way. Earlier that afternoon, they had planned to be at the fair—along with others—at Seth's request, to help keep the peace and ensure everyone's safety. Cal had picked Paddy up at Devil's Cradle State Park, where Paddy was finishing up for the day, locking the gates and closing off the trails. As they drove north along Wildcat Highway in Cal's reservation vehicle, Paddy filled him in on the latest: There'd been an animal attack at the Bury farm. They were roughly three miles away from the fair when Paddy spotted the top of a tree in the woods shake as if a twenty-foot giant hand had shaken the base of the tree. "Holy shit, pull over, Cal," Paddy had said.

Grabbing their hunting rifles, the two ventured into the Cursed Woods. They hadn't expected to find much, but with the fair so close, they couldn't risk ignoring the signs. They meticulously covered the grounds, crisscrossing each other's paths, searching for tracks, claw marks, strange glyphs, any clues they could find. About a mile in, Cal felt a gust of wind hit him from above. He looked up to see a vast shadow slipping through the canopy. Something massive. They followed it for over a mile, eyes locked on the darkening sky as the sun dipped low behind the trees.

When the lights of the fair broke through the underbrush ahead, both men quickened their pace, urgency pounding in their chests. They burst through the tree line in unison like they were on the set of an action film, guns drawn. Cal's sweat-soaked V-neck clung to his chest, Paddy shirtless now, his own damp T-shirt knotted around his belt. Their chiseled frames gleamed under the fairground lights as they lifted their eyes skyward.

Cal's jaw slowly fell open. "Tah-tah-kle'-ah."

Paddy looked over at Cal. "What?"

"It's a myth. Or I always thought it was. Owl women. Giant owl women who feast on children."

Paddy looked back up into the air and then back at Cal. "Um, I don't think those are women."

Cal shook his head. "No. It's a myth. Fiction pulled from fact, from fear, from old tales."

"Whatever the case." Paddy cocked his rifle. "Looks like it's owl season."

Paddy tore off running into the fairgrounds. Wes sprinted after him. "Don't shoot them, Paddy!"

"Why not?"

"It will just draw their attention!"

"Isn't that what we want?"

"If they feel threatened they will attack!"

"You're the expert!" Paddy yelled as they encroached on the hot zone. People were running around like their hair was on fire. "Take cover! Get out of the open!"

Cal was jumbling his cell phone. He found Seth's contact and pressed his number.

"Cal, where are you?" Seth answered.

"We just got here. Paddy spotted one of these…owls from the road. We followed through the woods to try to track them down before they got here. Seth, tell your team not to fire their weapons."

"I already have. Any other advice?"

"Just get people into sheltered areas. And start a fire. Fire will likely deter them." Cal pocketed his phone and tried to catch up to Paddy, who was ushering scared people into covered structures. His pulse hammered as he looked up, still in complete shock, his mind not fully comprehending that he was seeing a manifestation of Yakama folklore his mother told them as children. The marvel that had befallen him vanished as he watched one of the giant owls descend from the heavens, heading straight for the Ferris wheel. A smaller shape had settled atop the highest Ferris wheel carriage. Its downy wings fluttered in panic, and it chirped like a desperate chick. A man inside a nearby bucket lobbed a souvenir at it, something weak, hopeless, but flung with frantic purpose.

"No, no, no," Cal moaned as he helplessly ran toward a structure a hundred yards away from him.

Above, the larger owl wheeled fast and low. When it struck the wheel, it felt less like a beast crashing and more like a mountain landing on a fragile toy. The wheel jolted, flooring passengers into each other, the entire structure swaying violently like a bearing had snapped.

The air filled with screams, metal shrieks, and the hum of electronics gone haywire. Cal's stomach cinched.

One of the buckled carts at the top tilted backward. A woman climbed out blind with dread, and then she jumped, insanely plunging clear of the wheel's drift.

"Stay with me!" Seamus bellowed, carrying three children in his arms. A small rabble of parents and more children followed in a chaotic line behind him. He slid inside the funhouse doorway and gently set the little ones on the ground. "You lads stay here, yeah?"

The adults pulled all the children further into the fun house.

"My boy's still out here!" cried a woman, trembling.

Seamus moved some people out of the way and approached her. "Hey there, what's your name?"

"Melissa."

"Melissa, what's your boy's name?"

"Robbie."

"Robbie, great. What's he look like? What's he wearin'?"

"Um, he…"

"Take a deep breath there," Seamus said, inhaling deeply with her. "Think. You helped him get dressed, yeah?"

The woman nodded. "Spider-Man. He wore his Spider-Man shirt and a red cape. Please," she said, grabbing Seamus's thick forearms.

"I'll get him, Melissa. You stay here now and watch over these kids here, yeah?"

Melissa nodded. "Okay. Please, find my boy."

Seamus gave her a quick salute and dashed onto the midway. The lights and screams mixed into a swirling maelstrom of panic and fear. "Robbie!" he called, voice so loud it rang in his ears. He turned in all directions yelling the boy's name. "Robbie, son! Your ma Melissa needs you!"

He made his way through the scampering crowd, continuing to call out for Robbie. "Anyone seen a boy in a Spider-Man outfit? A red cape?"

Bodies surged around him. People looked at him with eyes of fear and madness, like they didn't understand English, or maybe it was just his accent, as they ran for shelter. Some appeared to be running in circles. Kids sprinted by, and couples clutched arms as if letting go would lose everything.

Seamus continued forward, twisting, spinning, searching for a flash of red. "Robbie! I'm looking for a boy in a Spider-Man outfit!"

A voice rang out. "Over here!"

Seamus turned toward the cry. "Oye, Joe!"

The young officer was in the distance, crouched under the awning of a corn dog stand, his arms around who must have been Robbie, along with two more kids. Four adults had also taken shelter near the metal food stand.

Seamus felt his skin prickle and he spun around. A cloud of dark whooshed passed him, soundless, amazingly large. He turned and watched the giant bird scrape its massive talons along the roof of the food truck. The children shrieked, as did the adults.

"We got to get to someplace safer," Seamus bellowed, already building up steam as he started to jog over to the stranded group.

One of the male adults removed something from his back.

"No," Seamus immediately thought and said aloud, though not loud enough for the man to hear. He started sprinting when the man aimed at the sky and let off a round.

"Mate! Don't fire the gun!" Seamus yelled, knowing a gunshot would just draw one of the foul creatures in.

"Sir, do not shoot at them!" Joe instructed, trying to manage the screaming kids and the panicked adults.

"Shite," Seamus mumbled as he picked up his pace. "Don't shoot, pal!"

"Sir!" Joe tried again. "Lower your weapon."

The man spun around in circles, following the beast above. The pistol went off again. The owl creature dove: wings angled, talons outstretched.

"You bleedin' ejit!" Seamus yelled. He ran for a nearby park bench, jumped on top, and then vaulted into the air.

With every ounce of muscle he'd used in rugby, he intercepted the bird mid-dive, shoulder into its belly, knocking it off its path. The beast released a shrill sound of surprise and staggered, and for a breathless second, Seamus and the owl were locked in a savage grapple—wings whipping dirt and feathers, taloned claws scraping his jacket, beak snapping inches from his face.

Seamus shoved hard with both hands and stood back up from a defensive position. The bird got its legs under it too, only not so steady, and Seamus heard people shriek and scurry out of the way as one of the wings caught him in the shoulder. Both he and the owl toppled into the food stand. Metal squealed, the creature thrashed, and feathers flew like sparks in a campfire. Seamus pinned its shoulder for a moment, chest heaving, adrenaline roaring.

Then, with a savage flap, it kicked free and lurched forward. Seamus stumbled back, breathing hard and blood pounding in his temples. The owl staggered, shook itself, then threw open its wings and launched back into the sky, leaving the melee.

"You're a superhero!" young Robbie yelled.

Seamus blinked and grinned, catching the boy by the shoulders. "Right you are, lad. Right you are."

Joe had the man on his stomach, cuffs around his wrists. The gun sat discarded in the trampled grass. Seamus blinked into the darkening sky. He stooped, picked up the gun, and put it in his belt, then he helped Joe get the man back to standing. "We need to get everyone under cover," he said.

Joe nodded, blinking, mind working a hundred miles a minute.

"Right." Seamus waited only long enough to catch his breath before stepping forward—still a hero, battered but unbowed, determined to shepherd them to safety. He scooped Robbie up—his little cape trailing—and turned to the shaken group. "Come on! Shelter's this way—keep close!"

Chapter Thirty-Eight
You Brought Claws to a Corn Dog Fight

Seth pocketed his cell phone and turned to Peter. "We've got to start a fire."

"For what?"

Seth pointed up to the circling owls. "Cal said that fire could drive them off."

"It's going to have to be a big fire." Peter looked around for inspiration, quickly spotting one of the big tops. "What about that?"

Seth considered the option. "I don't think the fire would hold long enough." Seth kept looking and then it hit him. "The stables. The horse stables." A solid wood structure, filled with hay and haystacks, Seth knew it would go up quickly.

Peter looked across the fairground toward the stables. "We better get moving."

Seth took off, leading the way. He grabbed his walkie mid-stride, and before he brought it to his mouth to warn his team, a gunshot echoed through the night. "Goddammit!" He clicked on his walkie. "Everyone! Do not fire your weapons! I repeat, do not fire your weapons. You'll only draw them in. Peter and I are headed to the barn to start a fire in hopes to scare them off. We could use help if anyone's close. Otherwise, keep everyone under cover."

Bill came over the radio. "I've been ushering everyone into the big barn, Seth."

Seth cursed under his breath. It made sense for Bill to have organized everyone to head into the largest structure. "We'll have to try one of the smaller barns at the other end of the grounds," he said over the radio. Then to Peter he said, "Or at the very least, drag a big-ass pile of hay into the open."

Cal crouched beside a male carnival worker next to the young woman sprawled in the gravel after jumping from the Ferris wheel. Her legs and back were twisted at unnatural angles. Eyes vacant, unseeing, pulse faint, and breath short. "We can't move her," he said.

Paddy scanned the crowd.

"Stay with me," Cal murmured, pressing the carnival worker's rainbow jacket over her, careful not to move her. "Let's keep her covered."

"That's it?" asked the man.

"That's all we can do for her right now," Paddy responded. He pointed to the wobbling Ferris wheel. "We need to get those still on it to safety. We can't have any other jumpers."

They edged away, stepping over dropped food, beverages, and abandoned plush toys. Cal muttered softly under his breath as Paddy ducked beneath the nearest car, helping a white-knuckled teen out. Others followed, some with tears, some in shock. They shepherded them down the ladder, away from the loose wiring.

One by one they descended, blank faces staring ahead. Paddy dropped the last, a young boy, down to Cal. Once grounded, the boy bolted into a cluster of families under the carousel. Cal watched him go, his eyes darting between the sky and the boy. The owls didn't seem to notice. They were drawn by two pops of gunfire coming from the north.

Cal shook his head and surveyed the disaster. Under the carnival slide, several families huddled, covering children with arms. Others pressed in along the carousel's painted ponies and pastel hippos—eyes wide, motionless.

Paddy approached and nudged him to look somewhere else. "There's a group of people near the ring toss looking like they're getting ideas."

Cal saw them, a cluster of indecisive men. "What are they doing?" he asked as they fumbled around like chickens with their heads cut off.

"They're clearly trying to fashion weapons," Paddy said.

One already had a pipe in hand, another had the hook used to grab down the larger stuffed prizes from the rafters of the game tent.

Cal sighed. "They're going to get themselves killed," he said, both men already sprinting across the green toward the group.

"What are you all doing?" Cal yelled. "Get off the walkway and find cover!"

"We need to fight them off," bellowed the one holding the large metal pipe.

"If we all hide like cowards they're just going to pick us off one at a time," said another man with a stake in hand.

"Let us handle this," Cal pleaded. "You're not helping anyone being out here."

"What are you doing?" said a third man, holding a trash can lid in one hand and a sledgehammer in the other. "Why don't you put those guns to use?"

"We said, get to shelter," Paddy repeated, pressing closer to the men to physically usher them along if need be. "Under that ride, or inside the big barn—now!"

One of the men grabbed for Paddy's gun and received a swift elbow to the face. "What the fuck, man!" he said, grabbing his bloody mouth.

"One's coming!" a man shouted, panic splitting his voice.

Paddy's and Cal's heads snapped toward the sound. Across the green, Officer Eddie Cabrera was herding children into the open hatch of the Chicken Shack food truck. It was already packed—workers crammed shoulder to shoulder with frightened families.

Then a boy broke free, tearing across the grass in blind terror.

"Get those others inside. Stay here!" Eddie barked, sprinting after the kid.

Paddy bolted without hesitation. "Get him in the shack, Eddie!" he bellowed as he ran, feet pounding turf.

Cal held up a hand to the men behind them. "Stay put! Don't draw attention!"

Paddy was already halfway there.

Above them, the owl began its descent, gliding in a wide arc, massive wings slicing the air like blades.

Eddie caught the boy, hauling him into his arms just as the child pointed skyward and screamed, "He's coming!"

Eddie turned, shielded the boy with his body, and drew his sidearm.

"Don't shoot!" Paddy shouted, the words shredded by wind and adrenaline. "Eddie, no!"

The gunshot cracked through the night. Balloons tore free of carts. Flags whipped in the gust the owl carried with it.

It came down in a blink of speed and shadows and hunger. The owl struck with terrifying precision. Its beak drove down like a war hammer into the top of Eddie's skull, and the sound of bone splintering beneath it rang out.

Eddie stiffened. His arms locked around the child, even as blood exploded from his mouth and nose.

The creature's talons raked toward the boy, shredding cloth and skin as it tried to snatch him free, but Eddie's dying grip held fast.

The owl gave a frustrated shriek, wings flapping as it jerked away empty-handed.

Eddie sagged and fell like a rag doll, his head grotesquely slack, his face frozen in a look of defiance and pain. The boy in his arms cried at the fullest volume his little lungs could muster.

"NO!" Paddy's scream tore out of him as he reached the final stretch. He dropped to his knees, sliding along the gravel and grass beside Eddie. He heard Seth's voice coming from his walkie, but didn't have the presence of mind to process what he was saying. He flinched back, seeing the remnants of Eddie's skull scattered across the ground. "My God." He rolled Eddie's body off the child, relieved to see that the boy had been saved. "Don't look, don't look," he instructed, covering the boy's eyes as he turned him around.

Cal was already running to meet them, eyes scanning the skies. He swung his rifle back over his body and grabbed the boy. He had lacerations on his back and shoulder, but he was alive. "I've got you. I've got you, kid." His eyes flicked to Eddie's body. "Christ."

Paddy quickly grabbed his T-shirt from his belt. His hands shook as he lowered it over Eddie's head.

The smallest barn on the fairgrounds was empty of animals and easily emptied of the few scattered people. They'd ushered them into the neighboring barn, then started the assembly line. Seth was at the back of it, hefting another bale of hay to Sasha, who handed it off to Nate, then to Bill, who was standing on the first level of hay bales, and finally up to Peter, who was building a pyramid of hay to get close enough to the roof to catch fire.

"How many more do we need?" Seth called out.

"I think we've got enough," Peter replied. "Let's start this up and if we need to add more, we can."

Sasha wiped the dripping sweat from her brow. "What are we going to use to start this?"

Seth looked around, not seeing anything usable. He ran over to the barn entrance.

Peter started to unbutton his shirt. "Does anyone have a lighter?"

"Not me," said Nate.

"My cigars are at home," Bill added.

Seth spotted a food shack about fifty yards away. He looked up to the sky. The owl creatures were still circling. Two more gunshots echoed in the distance. "Son of a bitch." He turned back into the barn. "We've got to get this fire going. Bill, Nate, there's a burger shack right across the walkway out here. Go grab anything you can that you think is flammable. If they've got a fire-burning stove, try to fashion a torch that will last long enough to get it back here."

Bill walked up to Nate, who looked shell-shocked but trying his best to hide it, and patted him on the back. "Let's go, son."

Seth walked back inside and looked to the storeroom. "Sasha, why don't you check in there to see if you can find something. Peter, let's head out back," he said, pointing toward the rear opening. "I'm guessing there's a tractor or truck out there. Maybe we can siphon some gas."

"On it," Sasha said, already leaping off the hay bales.

Peter and Seth sprinted toward the back.

Bill crouched down just outside the stable entrance. He had his arm around Nate's back, who was squatting down next to him. "Christ in Heaven, what are they?" Bill said, looking up.

Nate's eyes were glued to the sky, trying to make sense of what he was seeing and everything that had transpired over the last twenty minutes. "They're the size of fucking Pterodactylus."

"Where'd they come from?"

"A time portal?"

Bill looked over at Nate. "Your guess is as good as mine. Let's get over to that food cart," he said, pointing to the nearest one.

Nate nodded. "I'm ready."

"You're going to make a fine officer, son." Bill led the way, running at an easy pace, trying not to draw their attention. They reached the food stand and Bill peered over the window opening. "No one in here."

"The door over here is open," Nate said and headed in.

Bill looked up and saw "Funnel Cakes" painted across the top in bubblegum pink and sunshine yellow. He jogged around and followed Nate in. They looked for anything that made sense. "Not a goddamn stovetop to be had," Bill said, motioning to the stainless steel surfaces and buckets of batter.

"Fryers are filled with grease," Nate said. "Can you light grease on fire?"

"I don't think it ignites like gas, but when it goes, it goes. We could try it. See if you can find something to make a torch out of. I'm going to look through these drawers and cabinets."

"On it," Nate said and paced around, looking for anything that would serve as a stake of sorts. "Don't they have any brooms or mops in here?" he said to himself. Not finding anything long enough, Nate exited the shack and looked around back to see if there were any tools. Garbage cans, a recycling bin, four plastic buckets. "What the hell?"

Nate spun around and saw a wooden fence behind a bench across the walkway. "There we go." He looked up for signs of any prehistoric creatures nearby before running across to the fence. He grabbed a hold of the top piece of wood and yanked back, trying to break it free. It creaked and cracked but was too sturdy to snap off. A group of high-pitched screams in the far distance caused him to spin around. The largest creature of the bunch was diving on the lighthouse structure that served as the fairground entrance. It stood above all else in Nate's view. The beast dove headfirst into the glass structure, causing a boom of destruction.

Nate swallowed hard. He had been trying to put it out of his mind, but a swell of fear ravaged his insides as he thought of his friends, Stan, Emory, and Ember. He was just grateful his parents and sister weren't planning to come here until Saturday. Probably not at all now.

Feeling time ticking away, Nate knew he needed to act quickly. He turned back to the fence and began to kick the top rung over and over. "Break, you fucker!" Finally, after a fifth angry kick, the wooden beam snapped, a loud crack echoing around him.

"There we go." Nate pried the beam loose and squatted down with it on his lap. He hastily took off his shirt and wrapped it around the end of the slat. He tried to tie it into a knot, but the material was shit for that purpose. "I know." He set the wood and shirt down and undid the lace on his right boot. He pulled it out and started to tie his shirt on the beam.

"Nate! Look out!"

Nate turned just in time to see Bill barreling toward him, his presence

345

bewildering, but primal terror flooded Nate's veins: a giant shadow swooped low, wings cutting air like obsidian blades. He caught sight of the beast before impact, a hulking silhouette with matte-black plumage and eyes so deep they swallowed light, their surface barely catching the fairground glow.

Just then, Bill tackled Nate, flattening him to the concrete, both of them rolling on impact. A massive wing slammed down where he'd been standing with a deafening crack and the heat of displaced air. It skidded across the concrete to the gravel and grass, overcorrecting since missing its prey. Stones sprayed outward from the impact.

Nate gasped, heart slamming in his ribs as he rolled over and watched the creature for its next move. "Holy shit."

Bill sat up. "You okay?"

It beat its wings once, unleashing a low, resonant thrum, and folded the limb-like appendages back to its sides. For a charged heartbeat, Nate stared straight into those unblinking black eyes, cold and merciless, and knew something ancient and alien observed him. Nate's chest heaved.

Bill turned around, getting his feet under him as the bird stalked toward them, walking like a creature trying to mimic human legs with backward-bending knees.

Whoo aye, it said to them, sounding like a human mimicking an owl, mimicking a human.

Nate's whole body trembled with an uncontrollable shiver. "What the...?" he whispered.

Whoo aye, it called again, head tilting, eyes black and wet and unblinking. Its beak snapped three times in a row. It dipped and bobbed its head, then crouched, wings spreading.

"Shit," Nate scurried to get into a defensive position, but Bill was already standing.

He pushed Nate back to the ground as the bird leapt and grabbed at them with wicked talons. It knocked Bill onto his backside, and with a rough flap, the creature took flight again, ascending into the dark sky.

Nate scrambled over. "You're bleeding."

Bill dabbed at the small cut on his forehead. "Nothing serious," he said as he reached out to the makeshift torch. "Good job. This will work. I've got this." Bill pulled a long Bic lighter from his back pocket. "Let's get to the stables."

Seth stood atop of the pyramid of hay bales dousing gasoline all over, while Peter had his own can, pouring it around the base.

"I'm good over here!" Sasha called out from the other side of the pile.

"Okay, get down from there then and go see if you can see what Bill and Nate are doing," Seth replied.

"We're right here," Nate shouted, entering the stable with the torch held high. "Check it out!"

Peter looked over his shoulder. "Great work. Bring that over here."

"Did you find something to light it with?" Seth asked. "All we found was—"

"We got this," Bill said, holding out the Bic lighter. "Enough to get the job done."

Seth leapt down each flight of bales until he reached the ground. "Okay, everyone else out of here except me and Peter. Nate, you get as far back as you can. Bill and Sasha, go do a quick perimeter check to make sure no one is camped out around the edges."

Nate handed Peter the torch and retreated out of the stables.

Bill handed Seth the lighter and met up with Sasha to plot their routes around the stables, and exited.

Seth grabbed his walkie and spoke. "Eddie, Joe, we're about to light this stable up. If this works, tell everyone to wait until the skies are clear, and then tell them to get to their homes or hotel rooms and stay there." Not getting an immediate response, Seth switched the channel on his walkie. "Dispatch, this is Chief Wolfe. We're setting a controlled fire at the county fairground stables as a deterrent. I need the county department on alert. Call in backup. Our local team won't be enough if this spreads."

A burst of static, then a voice said, "Copy that, Chief. County crews are en route."

Seth exhaled, then turned back toward Peter. "You ready?"

Peter backed away from the pyramid and looked down to the ground, at their feet. "You got gas on your boots there, Chief."

Seth looked down. "Guess I better stay away from the flames then."

"Give me that lighter. Go make sure Bill and Sasha are clear. I'll handle this."

Seth nodded, handed over the lighter, and sprinted out of the stables. He spotted Nate about thirty feet back, crouched down, looking up at the sky. Seth followed his gaze and watched the five beasts circling. What sort of nightmare had befallen them? How would they clean this up? Was there even a way?

"We're clear," Sasha called out as she rounded the corner of the stables.

"Good on my end," Bill replied, coming out on the other end.

"Okay, great, get back with Nate," Seth said, pointing. He stuck his head back in the stables and gave Peter the thumbs-up. "Light it up!"

Seth, Bill, Sasha, Peter, and Nate stood huddled together, eyes fixed on the sky as the giant owl creatures wheeled away from the billowing smoke, gliding toward the Cursed Woods until they vanished from sight.

"Now what?" Sasha asked.

Seth had been pondering that question for the last fifteen minutes. "Call the National Guard?"

"CDFW?" Bill suggested.

"The Orbriallis?" Peter said.

All eyes turned toward him.

"Sorry," he said, feeling their glares. "A little gallows humor."

"Joe!" Sasha yelled, spotting her longtime partner round the corner of the food pagoda. He was followed by Cal Hensley and Paddy Kipp. She ran up and wrapped her arms around Joe. "I was so worried when you didn't answer." She pulled back and saw the tears in his eyes, wetness coloring his cheeks. "Oh no. What? What is it?"

Joe looked from Sasha to the rest of the team. "It's Eddie."

"Oh my God." Sasha covered her mouth.

Peter grabbed his forehead.

Bill's bottom lip started to tremble.

Nate dropped his head.

Seth stepped forward. "What happened?"

"It's not good," Paddy stated.

"Shit." Seth ground his jaw and turned to his youngest full-time deputy. "Were you there?"

Joe shook his head.

"We were," Paddy said.

"Yeah," Cal mumbled.

Sasha walked over and gave Bill a hug. "I'm so sorry."

Tears fell down Bill's cheeks. He had spent the past thirty years working side by side with Eddie. He was a dear and close friend. Family. "Where is he? I want to see him."

Paddy shook his head. "I think it's best you don't, Bill."

Bill squatted down to the ground and wept into his hands.

"Know that it was quick."

Peter went to comfort Joe, putting an arm around his shoulder.

"This is so fucked," Sasha said.

"You guys okay?" Seth asked Paddy and Cal.

"Not good, man. Not good," Cal replied.

Paddy stepped closer to Seth. "I've seen some dark shit. Darker than this. But nothing like it." He looked back at Cal. "Tell Seth what you told me."

Now all eyes were on Cal.

Cal took a step forward. "Take this for what it's worth, but there's an old Yakama folktale we were told as kids by our mom. The Tah-tah-kle'-ah. Owl women. Or owl witches to some. They were big. Bigger than normal humans."

Nate and Sasha exchanged a haunting look.

"They were said to be cave dwelling."

Peter shot Seth a pointed look, his eyes wide.

"What?" Paddy asked Seth.

Seth shook his head. "Later. Go on, Cal."

"They ate frogs, lizards, snakes, things of that nature. Bad things. But they were also said to have feasted on children."

"Fuck this," Nate uttered.

"Lore has it they existed up in the Washington and Oregon regions. But the last ones, sisters they say, were seen in the early 1900s in Northern California."

"Well, that's just fucking rich," Peter said. "What the hell are we supposed to do with this information?"

"The autopsy," Seth said, looking at Cal. "You and Wes mentioned owls. You were theorizing. But you said—"

"Impossible. We never believed the myths to be true. I mean, how could they be?"

"Well," Sasha said, pointing up to the sky.

Cal looked down. "Right, but..."

"It's no one's fault, Cal," Seth assured him.

"But it kind of is. Just a few nights back we were having our weekly family dinner. Stan wanted to talk about the glyphs in the woods, the psychedelic fungus. She was worried about one of her friends."

"Anya," Nate said, stepping forward. The reminder of his friends renewed his worry.

Seth looked over to Nate, pieces starting to fall together haphazardly in his brain.

"I didn't want her to keep on about it. I didn't want panic to spread. And then Grandma Hensley, my mom, said it. Tah-tah-kle'ah. Stan asked what she was talking about, but Wes and I shut it down."

"I mean, Cal," Peter said, "if you had told us a story about owl witches, what would we have even done? It's not like there's a playbook for old Indigenous myths." He was reaching into the cargo pocket of his pants for his cell phone. He wanted to call Jolie and let her know he was safe and see if she'd gotten a hold of Noble.

Seth's brows were pinched tight. "You said Grandma Hensley reacted to Stan talking about the glyphs. So, are you saying there's a connection?"

Cal shrugged. "Clearly our mother thought so."

"So, what, the owls scratch glyphs into trees?" Nate asked.

Seth's cell phone rang, breaking up the train of thought. He answered it without looking at who was calling. "Wolfe." After a moment, Seth's eyes went wide. "Story! What are... Where... Fuck!" Seth dropped the phone from his ear and looked at Peter, who was scowling at his phone and the multiple missed calls from his son. He sensed the gaze and lifted his eyes.

"What is it?" Paddy asked.

"She's at the Bury farm." Seth stared right at Peter and he stared right back. "She said the glyphs are real and that they're there. In the house."

"Noble," Peter said, looking back at his phone. "We have to go. Now!"

Chapter Thirty-Nine
Predators Don't Knock

The Bury kitchen had fallen unnaturally still. Leith stood beside the sink, one hand braced against the counter, her blood-slick fingers leaving faint prints on the porcelain. Story lingered near the island, watching her, ears straining to hear anything more of the commotion that had startled them all. Mary, pale, her posture rigid as she stood just inside the threshold, bit the inside of her mouth against the acrid scent of raw organ meat that clung to the walls, made heavier by the stagnant stillness.

Leith saw them first. She blinked, and they came into view. Anya, stumbling over the uneven yard, Noble hauling her by the wrist, half dragging, half guiding her. Behind them, Bear charged, her white-and-grey coat streaked with a slash of darkness.

Leith shoved off the counter, panic blotting out whatever lingering fog still clung to her mind. A bowl of water crashed from the island as she moved. She barely noticed. She flung open the back screen door just as Anya and Noble hit the porch.

Anya barreled into her arms. "Bear!" she shouted again, twisting, trying to pull back toward the yard. "Come here, Bear!"

Noble jogged back to grab Bear, but she pulled away, slipping out of her collar.

"Bear, come!" Leith ordered, but the dog kept spinning and barking back in the direction they'd come. Then she noticed her daughter's face, her hands, the splatter across her shirt. "God, Anya, you're bleeding—" Leith said, gripping her daughter's face, her voice jagged with fear.

"It's not mine," Anya cried, shoving her mother's hands away. "It's Dad's! He's hurt bad, Mom. We have to help him!"

That stilled them all for a single, fragile beat.

Then Bear's growling shifted pitch into a low, guttural, defensive warning, telling whatever was nearby to back off.

A scrabbling noise hit the porch roof above them, sharp and sudden. A shadow passed over the kitchen, dimming the late light. All three of them ducked, instinct overriding comprehension. Bear yelped, a short, piercing sound that echoed straight through Anya's bones, then took off running.

"No—" She tried to bolt again, but Noble caught her, arms wrapping around her waist like a cage. "No, let me go!"

"She's gone!" he shouted. "She ran—"

"I can't leave her out here!"

A massive shadow dropped from the porch roof to the pea gravel with a crunch. It rose to full height, head tilting, and it's all-too-human eyes locked on the three humans remaining on the porch.

Story stood half out the open back door, one hand gripping the frame, holding it wide. Mary was pressed close behind her, still inside, standing in the doorway with one hand braced on the jamb.

"What the hell?" Mary whispered, her voice tight with hunger and horror. Her hand dropped from her mouth. Her fangs, still half extended, caught the light. Her hand flicked out and grabbed Story's wrist, then pulled her back to within the doorframe.

The creature walked upright, each step an uncanny parody of human movement. Its knees bent at the wrong angle. Its gait stuttered, studied. Like something mimicking people without truly understanding how they fit in their skin.

It mounted the steps with slow certainty. *See…rah*, it croaked, voice hollow and wet, a burbled echo rising from the base of its throat.

Mary flinched.

See…reeaa…seee…raa, it tried again, this time with a lilting rise in pitch. It dragged the syllables out like it was trying them on, stretching the vowels the way a child might parrot a word it had only ever heard through a closed door.

Story felt her heart thud once, hard and deep, like a warning bell sounding under her ribs.

Anya shivered, her heart pounding as the creature before them attempted to sound…human.

Noble stared at it, brows drawn tight, mouth slack, unable to move. "What the f…?"

See raa, it said louder, clearer. Then again, sharper. *See RAA!* The last word cracked the air like a branch snapping. It sounded almost human.

Then it charged.

Mary dragged Story inside.

Leith grabbed Noble's arm—who still had his arm around Anya—and yanked them through the kitchen threshold just as the creature lunged.

Its talons scraped the deck boards. Its hooked mouth opened in preparation to disarm its prey.

Leith slammed the back door shut with a sharp crack and fumbled for the bolt with trembling hands. She threw it just as the creature hit the door with a bone-jarring slam. She yelped and stumbled backward, landing hard.

Outside, the creature screamed, but it wasn't just a screech. It was Leith's voice, echoed back in a warped, strangled gasp. A breathless, high-pitched *haAAHH!* The same terrified sound she'd made when the creature first appeared. It mimicked her panic. Played it back like a question it didn't understand. Claws raked through the screening, *screeech-shhhht,* gouging lines down the door's back.

Then came another sound. Lower, more deliberate. *Ooo…eeeer,* it said, syllables dragging like wet fabric. *Ooo…eeere.* It repeated the phrase again, louder, closer to human but too exact, too measured. Like it had no idea what the words meant.

Claws raked through the screen, peeling away strips like wet paper. Wood groaned and splintered beneath the weight of its grip. Chips and splinters pattered to the porch floorboards like hail.

Then came the voice again—Leith's voice, fractured and broken: *HAAAHH!*—then silence.

Story stepped around the island, closer to Mary. Mary leaned, trying to peer out the window without drawing its attention.

"Dad—" Noble had his phone out. His thumb trembled as he hit redial. "Come on, come on—"

Voicemail. He cursed, trying again and again. Still nothing.

A soft *tap-tap-tap* rhythm disturbed the silence. It came again, *tap-tap-tap.* Over and over, increasing in pace and pressure until it was no longer a polite knock but an irritated pounding. The door rattled, thumping against its frame.

Overhead, a thump silenced and stilled them all. Their heads snapped upward. Footsteps on the roof echoed down to the first floor. The old house creaked with each one moving heavier and slow, creeping across the shingles as if searching for something specific. Not just skittering, not like a squirrel or raccoon. Heavy. Deliberate. Bipedal.

Leith stared up at the ceiling, her mouth open, her breath shallow.

The door behind them rattled again before that one fell silent. They heard its talons *click-click* on the wooden planks, and a nearly silent susurration of feathers.

Noble whispered a curse and said, "There's more than one—"

Leith turned to her daughter, brushing sweat-matted hair from her blood-streaked brow. "What happened out there? Where is your father?"

Anya couldn't stop the sob that clawed up her throat. "It—Dad tried to hold it off. He told us to run. There was so much blood—" Her voice splintered. She looked at her shirt and bare legs, splattered with blood. "There was so much blood."

Her knees buckled and Noble caught her, arms wrapping tight around her waist. Leith rushed in. She grabbed a dish towel from the sink, wet it under the tap, and gently began wiping away her daughter's flushed, blood-streaked face. Her touch was tender, but her eyes were wild, scanning every inch of her daughter like she expected something more to surface. Another wound, another secret.

From the other side of the kitchen, Mary's voice cut in, low and urgent. "It attacked him?"

Story shook her head slowly, eyes distant. "Is he—" She couldn't finish the sentence. The words snagged in her throat like barbs.

"Mom..." Anya whispered. "What's in the old barn?"

Leith's hands froze mid-wipe.

Story, hovering just behind them, turned sharply. "The barn?" she asked. No one answered. "What's in the barn?" she asked again.

Anya shrugged, eyes darting from her mother to Story and back. "I don't know what it was, I only saw it once. It was...small. But not like a baby animal. It moved weird, and it looked at me like... Then my nose started bleeding, and I felt like I was going to throw up. Then...all this started."

Leith swallowed, her voice soft, as if the words cost something. "I didn't know what it was. I just found it out there one night. Hurt. Cold.

I didn't mean to keep it. But every time I thought about letting it go, I'd just… I'd forget why I was trying."

"You think it's one of theirs?" Story asked quietly.

Leith nodded. "I think it's a baby. One of theirs."

Mary blinked. "You have one of their *babies*?"

The silence that followed was ruptured by a sharp *thump* above them, followed by a dragging, clawed scrape across the ceiling.

They all looked up.

Another heavier thump this time. One of the creatures was up there, moving, pausing, then shifting again. It didn't sound panicked, more like it was searching.

A rattle at the back door drew their attention in another direction. Then the handle twisted with sudden, violent pressure.

Story spun around. "It's trying to get in!"

The door jolted in its frame. A low, wet growl filtered through the old wood.

Mary rushed forward, planting her shoulder against it, heels scraping for leverage. "Help me—!"

Noble appeared beside her, bracing the frame with his back and planting one boot against the wall for leverage.

"Can we board it?" he barked.

Leith bolted into the pantry, returned with an old chair, and shoved it under the knob, jamming it tight. They could hear claws raking down the outside paneling.

Above them, another thud. It moved toward the far side of the roof, then doubled back.

"How many are there?" Noble asked, his voice quiet, back pressed to the door.

Mary's face had gone pale. "It's circling. It's looking for a way in."

"Upstairs windows," Leith whispered, wondering what would happen if it broke the glass and came inside.

They all gasped in unison as a faint scraping at the kitchen window shot through their nerves.

Story turned as a shadow darkened the glass. Something peered in, its wide, reflective eyes and the grotesque outline of a beak pressed too close to the pane. Then it reared back and slammed into the window.

Cracks spiderwebbed across the glass.

Story looked around and found a stool. She lifted it like a shield and ran at the window as the creature broke through.

"Story!" Mary yelled, wanting to move to help her dearest friend but stuck as the door rattled behind them. The chair wasn't making a good blockade compared to the power of these animals.

Leith went to help push the creature back out of the window. Blood from its claw streaked along the broken shards of glass, dripping inside and down the wall. Anya darted forward, grabbing the knife from the cutting board.

The creature pushed again, its clawed hand working at the edges of the window frame, prying, testing.

Anya drove the knife forward in a quick, desperate jab as the creature's talons breached the sill.

A shriek burst from its throat. The sound knocked the breath from the room, everyone grabbing their heads or pressing their palms into their eyes. The creature pulled back, leaving long, wet smears across the glass.

Mary recovered first, looking to her companions. Story had a trickle of blood coming from her nose, as did Anya. Leith rushed to the sink, blood gushing down the lower half of her face.

"Shit," Noble said, drawing her attention.

He wasn't bleeding. Not from his nose, eyes, or ears, but he squinted as if he had a headache that pained him.

"What the fuck was that?" he asked her.

Mary shook her head. A tickle on her lip made her tongue flick out and she tasted her own blood. Before she knew it, her senses were overwhelmed with the scents of iron, sweat, fear, panic. She swallowed, but her throat was dry. The taste of her own blood was precious on her tongue. Savory, warm, a delicious appetizer to the bouquet around her. She felt the pain in her gums and jaw, the crack of her knuckles as her fingers and nails changed.

Noble stared with wide eyes at her transformation. "Mary?" he whispered.

Story shoved the stool in place as if it was any kind of deterrent, but it was better than nothing. She spun and saw her friend shaking.

Mary started swinging her head back and forth.

"Mary." Story was beside her within seconds, her hands reaching out gently. "Mary, you're okay. I'm here."

Mary's breath hitched, her shoulders tight, jaw clenched so hard it looked like it might crack. "I can smell it," she whispered. "It's too much."

"It is not," Story said firmly, gripping Mary's cheeks, her palms cool but steady. She forced her to meet her gaze. "Look at me. Right here. Stay with me."

Mary's pupils had blown wide, almost eclipsing the hazel of her irises. Her hands trembled at her sides, curled in half-made fists. Her breath came in shallow gulps like someone drowning in the scent of iron.

"Tu es plus forte que ça," Story said softly. "Tu n'es pas seule. Respire avec moi."

Mary blinked. The words rippled through her, ancient and grounding. The cadence of them wove around her like warm hands drawing her out of a storm.

"Mary," Story said again, this time with deliberate softness. "I *believe* in you. You are not a monster. You're a *good* person. I know that. You know that. This is just a wave—you can ride it."

Mary shook her head once, then again, lips trembling. "It hurts," she gasped. "It hurts, Story. It's like hunger but it's in my bones. I don't want to—"

"I know you don't," Story interrupted, eyes shining now, voice fierce and steady. "Because you're still you. And you're not going to hurt anyone. You are not alone in this."

A sob escaped Mary's lips, bubbling up from her hot throat. Her body shook with restraint.

Noble reached out and gripped her hand, lacing his fingers through hers and giving it a solid squeeze. Mary gasped and turned to look at him. She looked down to their intertwined hands, then back up to his face. They sat with their backs against the door, a fragile barricade of flesh and willpower. She took a deep breath.

The door exploded inward with a deafening *crack*. A massive shoulder rammed through, wood splintering. Screws popped loose and shot across the kitchen like shrapnel. Mary and Noble were thrown from the door, toppling over Story into the kitchen.

The creature burst inside. It stood taller than the doorway, bent unnaturally to fit, its claws gouging into the floor for balance. It screeched, a sound like metal scraped over broken bone.

"Get out!" Mary roared, charging forward. She collided with the creature at the threshold, jaws wide. She bit down hard on the exposed flesh of its shoulder. A tearing snap made the thing writhe and howl in a pitch that wasn't animal or human.

Everyone scrambled. Leith fell again, caught under Story as they tried to clear the kitchen and stumbled into the dining room.

The creature pushed, trying to follow, jaws snapping with sickening claps, dragging Mary with it. Her legs kicked, trying to gain balance, a foothold to drive the creature back, but it spun and slammed her into the wall, its foot kicking her off with a sickening crunch.

Mary hit the floor, dazed, blood pouring from her face.

It struck again with a sweeping talon and Mary's cheek split open, one deep line of red flashing across her skin. She flew backward into the doorframe. Her skull cracked loud against the wood.

"Mary!" Story screamed.

Noble lunged. He grabbed the heavy iron candelabra from the sideboard and brought it down with a grunt, catching the creature square across the side of the head.

It reeled. Shrieked.

Story and Leith grabbed Mary's unconscious form and dragged her away.

Noble swung again. "Go! GO!"

The others cleared the kitchen. Noble backed through the doorway, swinging wildly, and slammed the door shut just as the creature righted itself and threw its full weight against it.

The frame groaned. Noble leaned against it, one hand on the handle.

Story dropped to her knees with Mary, checking her pulse, her breath, her eyes. "She's alive."

Leith stood above them, shaking, and then she was off, heading toward the front door.

Anya called out, "Mom?"

Story stood. "Leith, you can't go out there right now," she said.

"My husband is out there," she growled at Story. "I'm going to go get him."

They all jumped as wood crunched and Noble grunted. He fell backward ever so slightly, immediately wheeling his arms and slamming back into the door as the creature made another attempt to break through.

Story rummaged through her skirt pocket and found her phone. Her hands trembled, blood smeared across the screen.

The front of the house shook. The second creature hurled itself against the front door with a sound like a car crash. The old house groaned in protest.

Story hit speed dial.

It rang.

Once.

Twice.

Then:

"Wolfe."

"Seth!" she shouted, barely breathing. "We're under attack—the glyphs were real—Elias was right—they're in the house—"

BOOM.

The front door shattered inward.

Her phone hit the floor, skidding under the kitchen table.

Everything else was screams and feathers and teeth.

Chapter Forty
Claw Marks and Country Living

"It's coming inside," Noble said with a matter-of-fact tone belying their predicament. He ducked to lift Mary off the floor.

Her eyes were half lidded and unfocused, a red smear on her temple where her head met the doorframe, but she made an effort to stand.

Story dropped her phone, moving to support Mary.

"Upstairs. Now," Leith hissed. Story led the way with Mary, Leith gripped Anya's wrist, pushing her up the stairs, and Noble used his momentum to swing himself around on the newel post just as the crunch of the front door collapsing inward shuddered through the house.

He looked over his shoulder. This second owl creature was tall, malformed, its wings half open like a robe dragging behind it.

"Shit," he cursed. "Let's go! Move!" he hollered.

Story led the way, her shoulder supporting Mary as best she could, her other hand white-knuckled on the banister. Leith's movements were sharp, calculated, but her face was knotted in panic as she shoved her daughter ahead of her.

They hit the second-floor landing just as the owl on the roof found its way inside via an open window. It crashed through, pulling curtains down with it, and ran toward them. Noble reached in and tried to swing the door shut, but the owl was already there. The door bounced off the owl's body as the beak snapped. Noble pulled his hand away in the nick of time.

"Up here," Leith instructed, ushering them to the third story suite, Anya's bedroom.

"Go, go, go!" Anya urged them.

Noble turned back just as the owl creature reared to follow them through the door. With a grunt, he kicked it hard in the chest.

The thing stumbled backward, wings flailing, and slammed against the banister with the sound of splintering wood.

He slammed the door shut, twisting the lock with a breathless reminder to himself, "Move."

Then he was up the remaining steps, taking them two at a time, as behind him the knob began to jostle.

"Is it coming?" Leith asked him.

He shook his head. "Even these sturdy solid wood doors don't seem to keep them out though."

"Mom," Anya said, eyes wide and wet. "Mom, we have to get to Dad."

"I know, sweetheart," Leith said, already thinking.

The door below rattled.

"He was bleeding a lot, Mom," Anya continued.

Leith moved to her and clasped her face. "I know, baby. I know. Let me think."

Scratching, deep gouging sounds came from the other side of the door.

Noble, pale and wild-eyed, moved to the window and lifted the curtain. The warm air smelled of clover and summer.

"I'll go," he said quietly. "I'll get to a car. I'll find him."

"No, Noble," Story protested.

He turned to her. "I'm state champ in track and cross country. I can outrun them."

"That's foolish to assume," Mary murmured, gripping her head in her hands. She blinked multiple times, trying to recover.

Noble leapt out of his skin as his phone buzzed in his pocket. He answered immediately. "Dad!"

"Hey, kiddo. We're on our way. Where are you?" Peter said from the other end of the line.

"In Anya's room."

"Third floor," Story said, loud enough to be heard.

"Yeah, the third floor."

"Okay. Stay put—"

"Dad," Noble tried interrupting.

"Barricade the door to the room you're in. Stay low when you hear my order—"

"Dad!" Noble barked. "You have to get to Mr. Bury."

"What? He's not with you?"

"He's...he was at the old barn." Noble turned aside, dropping his voice, as if Anya didn't already know, hadn't already seen the blood. "He's bleeding bad. Like, he's bleeding out."

Noble listened as Peter muffled the phone and conversed with someone. His dad came back on. "Keep your phone handy. We're almost there. Do as I said, okay?"

"Okay," Noble said.

"Hey, I love you, okay?"

"I know," Noble said.

"Just be ready, okay?"

"I'll tell them." Noble heard the phone go dead and looked at the screen like it had betrayed him. "They're close."

This was met with a wall-shuddering thud from the door and a worrying crack.

"He said to bar the door," Noble added, looking around.

"With what?" Story asked, also surveying the room.

"Can we tip this dresser down the stairs?" Noble moved to it, pulling it from the wall.

Anya moved to help.

"It's an antique," Leith said, as if it mattered. She followed her comment by moving to help them.

They got it to the edge of the stairs and shoved. It tipped, paused, and then fell, rolling awkwardly and hitting the door with a crack that made them all wince.

Claws scrabbled and clawed at the window, screeching like nails on a chalkboard. Story jumped, Anya shrieked. Mary narrowed her eyes at the creature attempting to get inside.

"That window doesn't open," Leith said.

"Doesn't mean it won't break it," Mary added.

Wood splintered at the door. They all swiveled their attention.

"Crap. Maybe throwing the dresser down there was a bad idea," Noble said, as they watched a talon grip hold of a small crevice and rip.

Story moved intentionally into the bathroom and began looking for weapons. She found a pair of sharp-looking scissors. She charged back into the room and scrambled down the stairs, positioning herself in front of the door, one knee on the dresser, the other standing tiptoe on a stair.

The taloned foot made a second appearance, ripping more wood away. She stabbed but missed.

"Dammit," she cursed.

"Story, that might only anger it." Mary's head was clearing with each passing second, adrenaline shoving her body into fight mode. All the pheromones in the room had put her senses in overdrive. Her teeth were fully extended. She couldn't have hidden them even if she wanted to try, and she didn't. Everyone here already knew what she was.

"Or it might stop it," she countered.

The foot made another appearance. This time Story slammed the scissor points home. The owl creature screamed, a sound like a bird and a human, a mockery of its current prey.

The window cracked.

Leith turned to her daughter. "You need to go."

"Go where?" Anya asked, eyes wide with terror.

Leith grabbed Noble and Anya and dragged them to the far window. "We'll distract them. You crawl out—"

"Mom," Anya protested.

"Drop onto the porch roof. Then get to the car. Do you have your keys?" Leith asked Noble.

Noble nodded.

Glass shattered on the floor.

Mary rushed down the stairs and grabbed Story, dragging her back as the owl outside the door renewed its endeavor tenfold. "Well, now we know—"

"It only pissed it off," Story finished her friend's sentence.

"Go." Leith shoved open the window at the opposite side of the room even wider and began pushing Noble out.

"Mom, we can't go. Noble's dad is going to be here any min—"

"Anya, get your butt out that window, now!" Leith shoved her.

Noble fell, then clawed his way back to standing. The roof on the third floor had a wicked pitch, but if they carefully maneuvered down, he could lower onto the porch roof, which was much more level. He took a hold of Anya's waist. As she climbed through, they heard the door give and the dresser creak. A creature squawked in protest.

Story and Mary watched as the owl at the door clawed inside. It was determined to get in, even as the splintered wood dug into its talons and pulled feathers from its hide.

Mary pushed Story back to the bathroom. "Stay in here," she said. "Mary, I—"

Mary shut the bathroom door and went to Leith. "Get under the bed."

"What?" Leith looked at her like she'd just asked for a refreshing beverage at the most inconvenient time possible.

"Get under the bed. When you can, if you can, grab a hold of it and don't let go."

"What…what are you going to do?" Leith asked, already moving, falling to her knees, pushing herself under.

"I'm going to try and kill it," Mary said.

The owl outside the window at the other side of the room kept trying to break in, but it was too small. Mary thanked whoever might be listening for small favors. She moved quickly to the closet, leaving it partially ajar so she could see a sliver of the room, and waited.

Hinges groaned, wood creaked, and the creature unfolded into the room like a nightmare dragged from a child's wickedest dream. It shook, unfurling wings that scraped the ceiling, then fell like a cloak. Its taloned feet clacked across the hardwood floors. When it got to the rug that sat around the bed, it cocked its head. Talons tested the new material.

Under the bed, Leith's nostrils flared. She waited.

The creature bent, lowering its head, cocking its eyes, nails scritch-scratching on the rug. Its legs bent backward, seemingly going the wrong way.

Leith bit her lip, stopped her breath as she saw the creature's head come into view.

Mary considered pouncing now, considered leaping out of the closet and onto its back. But just as she was about to, the thing rose once more and made a strange, humanlike titter, as if the rug amused it. It stepped closer to the bed. Its head snapped out and pecked curiously at the duvet.

Closer.

Leith found it peculiar that the creatures didn't really have a distinctive smell.

Closer.

Leith grabbed the leg with both hands and sank her teeth into the bare skin beneath the molting feathers. The owl creature let out a jagged shriek. It reared back, knocking Leith's head against the underside of the bed, but she didn't let go. It dragged her out from under the bed, and Leith wondered how long she could hold on for, as blood seeped into her mouth and the hardwood floor banged against her elbows and knees.

Then Mary was on its back. Launched from the closet, her fangs plunged into its shoulder from behind. Leith let go, spinning away as the creature thrashed. She crawled away toward the bathroom, cutting her hands on shards of glass.

The creature crashed into the bed, knocking it sideways.

Mary took the blows from the powerful wings as she sucked, drawing the sweet, warm iron taste into her mouth, but the creature didn't fall. She would have expected it to weaken by now, to still, like any normal animal would, but it kept fighting. Mary wasn't sure she would be able to kill it.

The headlights cut like swords through the mist-silvered dusk. Dust kicked up in the gravel drive and curled around the tires like smoke. Seth's Lost Grove Police Bronco and Peter's truck slid to a halt on the far side of the circular driveway outside the Bury farmhouse.

Peter was out first, sidearm already drawn. Paddy stepped out, motion fluid, his military instincts honed to sharpness. From the Bronco, Cal cautiously exited with his rifle, eyes scanning the tree line with silent efficiency. Seth climbed out last, less experienced in tactical maneuvers but more than willing to defer to the men who knew war by muscle memory.

Seth checked his gun. It was a weapon he tried not to use often. "No response from Story. I tried twice."

"Noble rarely gets great reception when he's out here," Peter muttered. "It's a miracle he got through to me when he did."

They crouched behind Seth's Bronco, its engine still clicking with heat.

"So we don't know how many of them we have out here," Seth said.

"Or where they are," Cal added, sweeping the fields with a practiced eye.

"The fuckers could be hanging out in the trees just over there," Paddy said, pointing to a copse of oaks not too far in the distance.

"Leith and the kids are in the house," Peter said. "Ethan was last seen near the old barn and bleeding out. We need to get to him first."

"That's our split then," Seth said, jaw tight. "Paddy and Cal take the old barn. Peter and I clear the garage and house."

"No heroics," Paddy said. "Radio if anything smells off. Move clean. Move fast."

Peter clapped a hand on Seth's shoulder. "Stick close. Watch your corners."

Paddy tipped his head once in silent agreement to Peter, then the men split.

Paddy and Cal moved in tandem, one a silent weapon, the other quiet as a hunter, their weapons raised, feet barely making noise across the earth. As they neared the old barn, the quiet was broken only by the soft rush of wind and an eerie series of muffled cow calls in the distance.

The barn came into view, its silhouette gnarled by age and the heavy gathering dark.

"Movement," Paddy whispered, sensing, feeling movement just beyond.

The small figure bolted upright and barked.

Paddy approached cautiously. The dog wagged its tail but farm dogs could be lethal like that. "Hey, buddy," he said nice and low.

The dog whimpered and spun around another shape on the ground. There, slumped in the dirt just outside the barn doors, was Ethan. Blood pooled beneath him, soaking into the soil like wine spilled at a sacrament.

"Jesus," Paddy breathed, already running.

They crouched around him. His face was white as wax, eyes barely open. His shirt was soaked and clinging to him, the wound still bleeding from beneath a torn piece of flannel someone, likely Ethan, had tried tying down.

"Ethan," Paddy said, voice calm. "Stay with me."

Ethan blinked. "The barn..."

"I know. We'll handle it. But first—Cal, shirt."

He tore off his shirt. Paddy pressed it firmly to the wound and braced Ethan's head with his knee. His hands moved quickly, dressing the gash with practiced calm.

Cal took the police radio Seth had given him off his belt. "Ambulance to the Bury farm. Male victim, lacerations across the torso, conscious and breathing."

Ethan groaned and murmured something unintelligible.

"Stay with us," Paddy ordered.

"Where's Anya?" Ethan said, more distinct.

"Peter and Seth are getting her, making sure she's safe," Paddy said, continuing to address the wound.

"Ah...shit," Ethan said, looking down at his torso, then dropping his head back to breathe.

Paddy pulled the bindings tight. Ethan hissed.

"Do you know where it is?" Cal asked.

The dog came over and licked Ethan's face. "It's okay, Bear," he said, voice low. His throat bobbed. "No idea," he replied. "But Anya said there was something in the barn."

Bear moved on to Paddy, licking his face as if to say thank you. Or maybe she was saying *hurry up and get my dad somewhere safe and stop this damn bleeding.*

Cal stood, put his rifle into his shoulder, and pushed into the barn. His eyes took a moment to adjust and he felt Paddy enter behind him.

"On you," Paddy said.

The space smelled sweet and fungal with the sharp tang of urine. Dust swirled in lazy spirals through shafts of pale light. Cal swept his rifle across the stalls, corners, and rafters, but nothing moved. No shadows lunged.

A warbled chirrup, soft and broken, followed by a clicking noise, almost like teeth chattering, came from the back.

Holding his rifle steady with one hand, Paddy reached into his utility pocket and pulled out a flashlight, He clicked it on and took the lead. Tucked into what looked like a makeshift nest of tattered feed sacks and old cloth was a creature about the size of a toddler. Its downy feathers were uneven, still growing in. Its eyes, impossibly large, blinked slowly in the beam of their lights.

Paddy exhaled. "What the hell…"

The creature tilted its head, blinked once, then mimicked the clicking sound again almost as if it was talking.

Both eased their grip on their weapons.

"Weird little guy," Cal muttered.

Paddy shifted closer, crouched just slightly, watching it without getting too close. "You feel that?"

Cal nodded. "Like pressure in your head."

The creature warbled again, this time a soft *hmm-mmnnn*, like a child fussing in its sleep.

"Shit," Paddy whispered. "I think it's scared."

Cal slowly backed away. "Let's not spook it. It might call the parents."

Paddy looked back at him. "Don't you think he's already done that?"

They stepped out into the night, leaving the barn door open to see if the creature might make its own way out.

Ethan was still lying on the ground, Bear posted beside him like a loyal guard. "You find anything?" he asked.

Paddy exchanged a glance with Cal. "Whatever they were protecting, I think it's still in there. It's small. Not like the ones that attacked."

"A baby?" Ethan asked.

Before either could respond, a low sound rippled through the air. The deep, uneasy lowing of cattle. Each man paused. Bear lifted her ears, nose scenting the air. A low, ominous growl rumbled from deep inside her chest.

The sound was low and mournful and it wasn't coming from Ethan.

"The cows." Ethan pushed up. Paddy eased him not to move with a steady hand on his chest. They listened more as the lowing increased.

Dozens of them, in a rising chorus. Not moos of hunger or normal conversation, but of panic.

All three men turned their heads toward the new barn.

"You hear that?" Cal asked, voice sharp now.

Ethan nodded weakly. "They...they're scared. That's not right. They've been moved inside for the night. They shouldn't be making such a ruckus."

"I'll go," Cal volunteered.

"Like hell," Paddy responded.

Ethan coughed. "ATV...feed shed...shotgun."

Paddy looked at the man who refused to stay down, then helped drag him to the side of the old barn and rested him against it. He knelt in front of him. "Where?"

Ethan lifted a trembling finger toward the small structure near the gravel path. "On the quad. In the case."

Cal was already moving.

Paddy hauled Ethan into a better sitting position. Ethan grunted, hissing pain between gritted teeth. "You hold on," Paddy muttered.

Ethan let out a grunt that might've been a laugh—or pain.

Cal returned quickly with the shotgun and a small box of shells. He tossed them to Paddy, who caught them and began loading in practiced rhythm.

"You've got two in the barrel," he told Ethan, setting the gun beside him. He shook the remaining shells in the box. "Setting this right here beside your leg."

Ethan nodded.

Paddy hesitated.

"Go," Ethan snorted. "I'm not stupid enough to shoot unless I have to."

Paddy stood. He slung down his rifle and checked the barrel. "Let's go," he said. "Whatever's got them cows rattled—"

"It's not just them," Cal finished, eyes squinted into the darkness beyond, toward the cursed woods. "We're not alone out here."

Side by side, they stepped off toward the new barn, past the open pasture where the cows' bellows were rising.

Chapter Forty-One
Wings in the Dark

The shingles were sharp with heat and grit. Noble braced his sneakers, lowering Anya first, her palms scraping against the sharp edges of the gutters. She dropped onto the wraparound porch roof with a soft thud, knees bending instinctively. Her fingers clutched the side of the house, jaw tight with fear.

"Okay," she whispered up to him, glancing around. "Come on."

Noble followed, easing himself down with more strength than grace. The roof groaned beneath them—old wood, old nails. They crouched low and started to move, keeping their heads down as they crept toward the corner where the porch turned, leading out front.

They paused at the edge.

"Let me lower you down," Noble said.

Anya looked. "That's farther than up there. You go first."

"Anya, let me lower you. You catch your foot on the railing, just there, and run for the car," he said, pointing. "Then I'll come down and follow you." He pulled his keys from his pocket and hit the unlock button, just to be sure it was open and ready for her to jump inside.

The car beeped and a shadow dropped onto the roof of his car with the sound of warped metal. The windshield cracked with a spidering snap beneath its weight.

Anya gasped.

Another thud landed behind and above them. They both turned, and froze. Wings flaring like a curtain of shadows, another owl creature surveyed the lawn. It settled on the peak of the farmhouse roof above, silent and immense.

Noble's hand shot out, grabbing Anya close and clasping a hand over her mouth. He pulled her into the narrow slant of shadow beneath the upper eave, motioning for her to tuck herself beneath the awning. Her breath caught as they squeezed into the narrow nook, backs pressed to the wall.

The owl above shifted its weight.

The one on the roof made a sound that sliced through their ears and burrowed behind their eyes, vibrating the bone like a tuning fork struck too hard.

Anya winced and gritted her teeth, pressing a hand to her head. Noble's face was pale, his jaw twitching. He pointed back toward the house, then pantomimed a window and made a slithering motion with his hand.

Go back inside, he was saying.

Anya nodded, heart hammering. She moved as silently as she could toward the closest window—the round one above the second-story landing. Her fingers hooked the lip of the old sill, and she began to twist the frame open. The hinges gave a protesting groan. She slipped through feet first and vanished into the darkened interior like smoke.

Noble followed, headfirst, fingers locked on the outside molding so he could lift and swing himself in. As he swung his torso through, the rooftop owl shrieked. It sprang, wings slamming down in a deafening buffet of air.

Noble yanked himself inside just as talons struck the sill. The beak snapped shut inches from his heel. Wood splintered. He hit the floor hard.

Anya screamed.

The owl creature rammed against the glass, pushing its face in. Feathers and flesh smeared the sill. It tried to climb in, one talon groping wildly through the small opening.

"Go, go, go!" Noble shouted, grabbing Anya.

He pulled her up and sprinted for the nearest door. A hallway bedroom. He shoved it open, pulled her in, and kicked it shut behind them.

The owl's cry echoed through the hall, an almost human howl of outrage.

Noble grabbed a dresser and jammed it in front of the door. The legs shrieked against the wood floor as he braced his shoulder into it, panting.

Anya's back was to the far wall, shaking.

"Are you okay?" he gasped.

She nodded, but her eyes were wide, wild. "They're… It's like they're hunting."

"I know." He looked at the door.

"It's because of the baby bird, isn't it?"

Noble moved across to hug her. "I don't know," he said, his breath whispering across the top of her head.

A shadow passed outside the shuttered window. The floorboards above them groaned, followed by the clapping of feet running across the third-story bedroom.

Glass shattered, voices screamed incoherently, and a thud shuddered through the old bones of the house.

The night was heavy with sound. Seth and Peter could hear the far-off sirens of the county arriving at the fairgrounds. If they were at the top of the country lane, they could probably see the procession of lights coming over the bridge into town. There was a strange hissing wind, and the unsettled low of cows drifted through the dark. Peter kept his voice low, almost beneath breath. "We clear the garage first. No surprises at our backs."

He indicated it as a priority with the lift of his chin, pointing out that the double doors were already ajar, and anything could be inside. Hell, maybe even Ethan, if he hauled himself across the yard and driveway.

Seth gave a curt nod, his jaw set. "Right."

The gravel crunched under their boots as they moved in tandem toward the detached garage—a large white structure with faux barn trim, built recently but styled to match the house's Victorian charm.

Inside, the garage was surprising in its cleanliness. Metal-paneled walls, a sealed concrete floor that gleamed faintly beneath fluorescent bulbs. It smelled faintly of hay, grease, and lemon cleaner.

Seth surveyed the massive garage, if it could be called that. A place like this had to have a different name. Warehouse came to mind. There was a classic utility tub in stainless steel and then another area, like a walk-in shower, deep enough to clean a small calf, with the drain shining clean at the bottom. Past that, an orderly row of two ATVs sat beneath charging ports, one of the ports missing a vehicle. The gleam of a polished dusk-blue truck, another vintage truck with pink detailing Seth knew to be Anya's restored Ford, and a corner workbench lined with tools in shadowed rows.

"Jesus," Peter murmured. "Cleaner than my damn kitchen."

Seth moved to the gun safe in the corner, checked the keypad. Locked. "Nothing out of place."

Peter's ears caught it first.

A human scream knifed through the night air.

They were already moving, weapons raised, boots thudding as they burst from the garage onto the gravel lot. The scream echoed once, then was swallowed by silence and the hum of insects gone suddenly still.

That's when the air dropped, a sudden vacuum of space.

Peter's gut twisted. "Down!"

A beat too late.

The owl creature launched from the crumpled top of Noble's car, a blur of black wings and eyes like firelit glass, striking from above with terrifying grace. They didn't hear it coming, just felt the wind parting, then the impact.

Seth caught the glancing blow, talons raking across his shoulder as he twisted to fall away, a searing pain that felt like fire had kissed bone. He hit the gravel hard, rolled, and tasted blood.

Peter threw himself sideways beneath the towering oak in the center of the turnaround, branches whispering overhead. From his vantage, he caught the creature's wingspan against the moonlight, fifteen feet of absolute nightmare, feathers frayed like torn paper, its back slick with molting.

Seth ducked behind his Bronco, pressing a hand to his bleeding shoulder. "Shit! Shoulder's hit."

"You okay?"

"I'm good."

The creature wheeled midair, rising above the tree, circling once as if to choose which man it would finish.

The scent of manure and churned-up earth hit Paddy and Cal the moment they opened the heavy sliding door to the milking barn. The cows were shifting restlessly, great flanks jostling, hooves clattering on concrete. The air was taut, humid with sweat and sour with fear.

"They know something's wrong," Cal muttered, keeping his rifle low, noticing each worried face looking back at him.

"Yeah," Paddy said, scanning the upper beams. "They feel it."

A blur passed across the upper vent windows, darker black against the fading sky. Then another from the other side. They didn't make a sound. Just shapes skimming the edges of the barn, barely catching the light. Cows lowed and stomped harder. One let out a plaintive moan, tail twitching wildly.

Paddy moved to the left aisle. "I'll take the feed corridor."

Cal nodded, disappearing down the opposite side.

Paddy kept the butt of his rifle tight to his shoulder, finger along the guard. Every stall he passed was filled with muscle and breath—panicked eyes rolling, shifting weight, twitching flanks.

A low vibrating hum began in his chest more than in his ears. "What the hell is that now?" He reached the end of the corridor and then everything exploded.

A massive crash came from behind him. Cows bawled, wood cracked, a wild chorus of hoofbeats like a freight train slammed through the barn.

"Shit!" Paddy turned just in time to see a dark form hurtle through the upper opening. An owl creature, massive and angular, folded its wings just enough to slide between the rafters and land with a thunk inside the barn.

On the far side, Cal turned, eyes going wide just as the cows broke.

A support post cracked and split under the weight of a panicked mother cow. She surged forward, hooves flying. Another followed her. The chute narrowed as the herd shoved, panicked, and Cal had no time.

One cow clipped him and sent him sprawling sideways into the iron rails of a feeding stall. He shouted, rolled, and tucked himself between two stalls just in time as the bulk of the herd thundered past, eyes wild and white-rimmed, eager to get away from the predator in their midst.

Paddy raised his rifle, but a massive brown cow slammed into his shoulder. He staggered back, the rifle knocked from his hands, and just as he turned to recover, the owl hit him.

It came from the side, talons out, the full weight of its seven-foot form slamming him against the barn wall. Feathers like rotting velvet, pale flesh beneath. Paddy grunted, drove his forearm up under the beak, shoving its head back. Its breath was hot and damp and smelled of old blood.

He wrapped an arm around its neck, trying to get leverage. They tumbled into a pile of old straw.

"Cal!" Paddy roared.

Cal, pinned in place behind the wooden slats as the panicking cows trampled awkwardly around, tried to kick loose the latch. "I'm working on it!"

The owl slashed with a talon, catching Paddy across the thigh. He gritted his teeth, kicked the creature's stomach, and used the moment of recoil to scramble on top of it. He went for his belt, his knife... The creature bucked and rolled, wings flaring.

A second owl dropped from the rafters behind them.

Paddy was still struggling with the first.

"Cal!" he yelled again, eyes locked on the second beast as it flared its wings, ready to pounce.

The bedroom had become a whirlwind of motion and violence. Mary had her arms locked around the owl's torso, her fangs sunk deep into the soft flesh where the neck met the shoulder. She'd braced her legs under its flailing wings like a jockey on some mad, nightmarish mount.

It released a jagged, ragged sound that rattled the windows and made Leith flinch, then thrashed wildly. One wing swung out, smashing into the bookshelf beside the bed. Books rained down in a sudden, papery avalanche. A framed picture shattered as it fell from the wall, glass spraying across the floor. Anya's desk caught the edge of a wing, and papers, pens, and notebooks exploded across the room like frightened birds.

"Hold it!" Story shouted, dodging a flying lamp as she grabbed a child's riding crop from beside the closet door and swung it. The keeper and shaft thunked against feather and flesh, but the creature barely flinched.

Leith found her daughter's old riding helmet had rolled from the closet. She grabbed it, ducking under the massive wing as it swept through the room, then slammed the helmet into its skull. The impact did nothing but incense the animal.

Mary gritted her teeth, blood smeared across her mouth. Her sharp fingers dug into the creature's molting feathers and soft skin as it bucked beneath her.

"Dammit," she hissed, "why won't you drop?"

Leith lunged from behind, wielding a splintered chair leg like a spear, jabbing toward its exposed flank with a wild swing. The owl creature shrieked again and reared up violently.

Mary lost her grip.

One monstrous leg caught the windowsill and crashed through it in a burst, cracking the wooden frame. Mary screamed as the force dragged her with it. For a horrifying second, they were tangled, airborne.

WHAM.

Mary's back struck the roof shingles with a bone-jarring slam. The creature twisted, wings snapping out, and tumbled down onto the lower porch roof with a skidding thud before dropping with a sickening, heavy crash onto the ground below.

"Mary!" Story screamed, leaping for the window, already half out, reaching with her hand. Her eyes were wide with horror.

Mary groaned, fingers scraping against the edge of the roof. She caught the gutter just in time, her nails digging in.

"I'm—okay—" she ground out, barely above a whisper. Dried blood was caked on her temple, one front tooth chipped, though her fangs glistened. Her arms shook with effort as she tried to haul herself up.

"Leith, help me!" Story shouted.

Leith was already moving. They scooted on their butts down the roof and grabbed Mary's arms, pulling with every ounce of strength.

The house groaned beneath them.

From somewhere downstairs, a roar answered, a communication from the other creature still present. It was still hunting.

"Get her in, now!" Leith barked.

Mary's boots scraped against the shingles as they yanked her body through the window, just as something down below slammed into the porch posts, shaking the whole structure.

They all tumbled onto the floor of the attic bedroom, breathing hard, blood mixing with sweat and fear. Outside, the owl below screeched again.

Story turned Mary's face toward her, her hands cupping her friend's cheeks. "Are you okay? Mary—hey, hey, look at me."

Mary blinked slowly, smiling through bloodied lips. "That bird's as tough as it looks."

Talons and the rustle of wings approached, clicking up the stairs once more. Leith pulled herself upright, grabbing the broken chair leg again. "It's not over," she said grimly.

The echo of shattering glass ripped through the summer dusk. Seth froze against the frame of the Bronco, breath held. He heard the scream, thin and sharp, rising from inside the house.

"Mary!" Story's voice cracked with fear.

Peter remained crouched low behind the trunk of the oak tree, eyes sweeping the windows above.

"That came from the third floor," Seth muttered across the distance between them. His heart hammered against the tight bruising where the creature had clipped his shoulder.

Peter nodded once, his mind already ticking through possibilities. "Okay. Listen. I'll move to the Bronco, then you run for the porch while I cover you."

Seth opened his mouth to protest.

Peter cut him off with a look. "You're bleeding. You don't argue."

Seth clenched his jaw, nodded.

Peter bolted.

The gravel popped underfoot as he sprinted across the driveway, sliding the last step behind the Bronco. The massive bird-thing was still somewhere nearby. Seth could feel it in the tension of the air, in the hush that fell like a held breath.

Peter ducked down and surveyed Seth's injury. The blood had seeped into his shirt, painting it with a splotch of dark red, but it wasn't life threatening, and Seth still had color in his lips and face. He slapped the back bumper. "You good, Chief?"

Seth slid up to a crouch, gun between his knees, taking steadying breaths. "Peachy."

Peter lifted his pistol, finger set near the trigger. "On your go, Wolfe."

Seth looked up at the darkening sky, wondering where it was. "Okay. On three."

"You sure?" Peter asked.

"No," Seth muttered. "But what else are we gonna do?"

Peter nodded.

"One, two, three." Seth didn't wait. He dashed across the space, boots slipping slightly on the gravel. The porch rose before him like a battered lifeboat. As he reached the stairs, he ducked low, scanning the roofline, the tree branches, the car still dented from the owl's landing.

He didn't see it, but he could feel it. Watching. He slid into position and took some calming breaths. It had been years since his tactical training in school. He was glad to at least remembered some of it.

He readied his sidearm. "Go!" he yelled, waving Peter forward.

Peter didn't hesitate. He darted out, crossing behind the Bronco, covering the same zigzag path.

Seth crouched at the top step, weapon drawn, ready to fire at the first flutter of feathers.

Peter vaulted the stairs, and together they spilled into the house through the gaping hole where the front door had been.

The wood beneath their boots creaked. Feathers lay scattered across the floor like the aftermath of some unnatural pillow fight. Blood streaked one wall.

"Jesus," Peter whispered, surveying the damage.

Seth raised his weapon. "Upstairs."

They went in tandem, guns raised, dread pooling behind their ribs.

The crash came overhead like thunder, a hard scrape, followed by a heavy thump on the roof just above them. Dust fluttered from the ceiling. Then came the shadow, lurching past the window like a dying thought given form, and something hit the earth below with a solid, sickening smack.

"Mary!" They heard from above.

Anya turned to the window but was afraid to approach it. "Was that…?"

"Something just fell," Noble said, breath shallow, feeling sick. "Or someone."

They crept to the window. Outside, the approaching moonlight silvered the landscape into an eerie calm after chaos. Down below, floodlights from the garage threw streaks of pale light across the gravel turnaround and the grass beyond, casting every movement into high relief.

Noble patted his jeans, wondering where his father was and why he hadn't called back. "Shit. My phone. It's gone."

Anya turned to him, the whites of her eyes stark against the darkness. "We have to get out of here. Maybe they're in the barn. Maybe they found my dad."

He was already shaking his head. "Not we. Just me. I'll go. I can drop down, try to find them. You stay here, stay safe."

"I'm not staying," she said, voice sharp.

But Noble was moving toward the window. "Just let me—"

A sound stopped him cold.

Click. Clack.

Like claws on hardwood. Like bone tapping the floor. It came from inside the house.

They froze, listening. There had been a moment of stillness after the crash. Now there was movement again, heavy and cautious. The one that had nearly taken Noble's head off at the window was back.

Anya's breath caught. "It's in here."

Noble glanced around the room as if looking for another way out, but the window was the only option. He gritted his teeth and started toward it again.

"You can't go out there alone," she whispered.

"I'm not letting anything happen to you."

He pushed the window up, then froze again.

From outside came a furious sound, a familiar bark punching the silence. Bear was back.

Anya darted to the window, leaning out. "Bear!"

The dog barked harder, standing near the corner of the house, her body taut, her head pointed directly at something in the yard.

An owl limped forward, dragging one wing, feathers ragged and bent at an unnatural angle. It lifted its head, glaring at the dog with an expression too intelligent.

Bear didn't back down.

"Bear, no!" Anya shouted. "Go! Run!"

The creature lowered its body and hopped. Despite the wing, it moved fast, feet slapping the dirt, that sickening gait like a man who forgot how to walk. It launched forward.

Bear twisted away and bolted toward the old barn. The owl gave chase.

"Shit—" Noble was out the window before Anya could say another word. He dropped down, hit the grass with a grunt, then was off running toward Bear.

"Noble!" Anya screamed after him, her heart skidding sideways in her chest.

Below, Noble sprinted across the gravel, legs pumping, every nerve screaming at him to be faster. The adrenaline hit differently than it ever had at a starting line—less like fuel, more like fire. At meets, it sharpened him. Here, it flooded him, wild and raw, making his limbs feel both electric and too light, as though his muscles were burning through calcium and oxygen faster than his body could keep up. It wasn't power, it was more like panic barely tethered.

Where the hell are you, Dad? he wondered, heart pounding, a terrible ache rising in his chest, not from running but from the idea that maybe he'd be too late.

Peter's boot hit the next step, his eyes tracking instinctively upward. A glint on the old wood floor caught the corner of his vision.

Noble's phone. Lying face up on the stair tread like a dropped clue. He barely had time to register it before a shadow detached from the ceiling and hurtled toward them.

"Down!" Peter barked, but it was already too late.

The impact was a freight train. Feathers and claws and raw, brutal mass slammed into them, knocking both men back. Seth tumbled first, crashing against the banister, then bouncing down the stairs like a rag doll. Peter followed, grunting as the side of his head cracked against the rail. Something warm spilled down the side of his face.

A wing whooshed past. Talons scraped plaster from the walls. A hooked beak snapped just shy of Peter's ear, so close he could hear the wet clack of its mouth close over empty air.

Seth scrambled upright in the foyer, but the owl, all momentum and animal speed, crashed into him and knocked him sideways, sending them both skidding across the floor into the dining room. A chair cracked beneath them.

Peter rose on instinct, staggering just long enough to gain his bearings. He raised his gun, lining up a shot, but the damn thing was tangled with Seth.

Then, a second staccato of sound: nails. Claws. *Click-clack* on hardwood. The owl that clipped Seth's shoulder hopped up onto the porch and was lurching toward the open door, head jerking side to side like a bird clocking prey.

Peter pivoted, sharp and precise, and fired.

The doorjamb exploded. Splinters of white-painted wood shredded in all directions. The owl shrieked, pulling back, wings flaring wide.

Peter didn't even acknowledge the blood now freely dripping down from his temple. He spun back, stepped over the busted remains of the stair rail, and moved like a shadow into the dining room. The second owl had its wings up now, bracing for another strike.

Peter didn't hesitate.

He fired again.

Ethan's head lolled sideways. The evening air had cooled, dusk sliding like a velvet shroud over the old barn. Somewhere distant, a cicada droned. Somewhere closer, Bear was barking.

She wouldn't stop barking.

It rattled through his head like a broken bell. Rhythmic. Fierce. Loyal. God, she had such a bark when she meant it.

Ethan blinked.

His eyes stuttered open and the scene came back into focus. Blood sticky at his side, the barn looming behind, and a figure moving toward him out of the deep blue haze of twilight.

It stepped from the gathering dusk like a ghost on stilts. Seven feet tall, those unnatural, black feathers refusing to catch the light, its wide eyes shimmering like twin pools of sorrow. It tilted its head, talons flexing against the dirt, its beak hung slightly open in a grotesque mimic of speech, or a smile.

Ethan's breath hitched. He reached blindly, fingers closing on the cold metal of the shotgun at his side. He jerked it into place, hissing as pain flared through his ribs. The whole left side of his torso screamed in protest, but he raised the weapon anyway and pulled the trigger.

The shot rang out, echoing across the pasture, but it went wide, tearing up a swath of dust to the creature's right. He shot again. It went high, zipping past the creature, who remained undeterred.

Bear didn't flinch. She stood like a sentinel between him and the owl, barking so violently her whole body shook with it. Her growls turned guttural, hackles raised so high she looked double her size.

"Bear," Ethan croaked. "Move. Move, girl."

She didn't budge. The owl kept coming. Its wings fluttered open, a silent cloak of death like it was trying to intimidate Bear.

Ethan reloaded. Another shell in, another round chambered, another agonizing lift of the barrel. The third shot missed again.

Bear darted forward, barking straight into the thing's face, snapping her jaws with clacks so ferocious it was like she'd break all her teeth. Ethan swore and fumbled the gun as pain seared his whole body, his muscles weak, his eyesight blurry. "Bear, get back! Goddammit, move!"

The owl creature flinched. A rock thwacked off its skull with a hard, satisfying crack. It snapped its head sideways, momentarily confused.

"GET AWAY!" a voice shouted.

Ethan turned his head, blinking the haze away.

Noble stood on the edge of the field, arm already cocked back. Another rock spun through the air and struck the owl in the shoulder. He was making himself large, waving his arms over his head.

"GET BACK! I'm here!" Noble shouted. He knew all the things to do when confronted by a predatory animal. His father had taught him on all their hiking expeditions. Get large, flail your hands, yell and speak, so they know you're human. Throw things. Don't back down, don't turn your back and run. That was prey behavior. And yet this creature wasn't backing off. It calculated. "I'm not prey! I'm not prey!" he continued, picking up another rock, hurling it at the creature's head.

"Noble, don't!"

The owl lunged toward its new prey, but Noble had already turned. He knew better than to stand his ground with this one—not a bear, not a cougar. This thing didn't bluff.

He ran. His legs pistoned like a machine, gravel flying beneath his sneakers. Each stride ate up the earth, momentum born of training and terror. He was fast—state-champion fast—but even as he ran, he could hear the thunder of wingbeats and taloned feet closing the distance.

Behind him, the owl tore across the grass on two legs, like a monstrous marionette learning to sprint, and it was learning fast.

Noble's breath came in bursts, but he didn't slow down. He couldn't. He just ran harder, jaw clenched, eyes scanning for anything—a tree, a car, a shadow—anything he could use.

Back at the barn, Bear paced, a low whine in her throat. She looked at her owner, then decided to book it in the direction of the threat. "Bear," Ethan called, his voice thick with exhaustion. He fumbled the final shell into place and whispered, "Don't you die, kid," he said, grimacing, and used the shotgun to try to stand.

Chapter Forty-Two
The Cradle Comes Home

The air inside the barn was hot with panic. Thick, damp, and pungent with the musk of cow sweat and fear. The big-bellied beasts bellowed as they shoved and jostled to escape, hooves clattering against concrete and iron. One gave a frantic moo that pitched into something like a scream as it bolted past Paddy, nearly knocking him off his feet.

He didn't have time to dodge the next. A wide-eyed heifer clipped his hip, sending him careening against a wooden post. Pain bloomed across his ribs, but he kept his feet. His rifle had been knocked aside, lost somewhere in the storm of hooves and heaving flanks, and the owl was coming again.

It came low, its body like a thrown shadow, wings tucked as it leapt. Paddy barely raised his arms before it slammed into him. They went down hard. Paddy grunted, twisting to keep the creature's beak away from his throat.

Claws scraped against the concrete. He searched his belt and got his hand around the hilt of his knife.

"Come on, you bastard," he growled through clenched teeth.

Meanwhile, Cal was moving. He'd hoisted himself up onto the low concrete ledge that ran along the side of the barn, where the feeders used to sit. Cows were still stampeding out through the open doors, some trying to turn and double back, confused by the madness. Cal hugged the wall and made his way along the edge, heart pounding as hooves stampeded beneath him.

At the far end of the barn, the chaos lessened. Most of the cows had made it out, and the space opened up. He spotted Paddy's rifle half buried in hay and grit.

"Hold on, Paddy," he muttered, and dropped down.

The first owl screeched an ugly, sharp, tearing sound and Paddy answered with a bellow of effort. He twisted violently and drove the knife upward. Feathers exploded in a dull puff. The owl's body jerked, shriek cut short.

Blood spilled, black and shining, onto Paddy's arms.

The creature twitched once, then went still.

Paddy shoved it off with a grunt, chest heaving. His shirt was torn, his knuckles scraped, but he was alive. "Jesus," he muttered.

A movement—sharp and sudden—made him spin.

The second owl dove from the rafters, wings scraping beams as it shot downward, straight toward Cal.

"Cal!"

But Cal had already rolled. He came up with the Winchester in hand, brought it to his shoulder with practiced speed, and fired.

The owl let out a garbled cry and veered hard to the left. It careened through the open barn doors and vanished into the night sky, wings wobbling as it rose.

Cal exhaled, slow and shaking.

"You hit it?" Paddy called, already limping toward him.

"Maybe," Cal replied, staring after the dark blotch receding over the pasture. "It won't forget me if I didn't."

BOOM.

A shotgun blast echoed from the direction of the old barn.

Paddy and Cal exchanged a look. Without a word, they both ran.

Peter's boots crunched over broken wood and glass as he scanned the room. "You good?"

Seth pressed a hand to his shoulder, wincing as his fingers came away sticky with blood. "Yeah," he said, jaw clenched.

They turned in unison toward the grotesque mass of feather and limb sprawled halfway into the dining room. The owl creature twitched before falling still, blood pooling beneath its twisted torso.

Then came the sound of movement, of quick footsteps on wood.

Peter spun, his weapon still in hand, until the shape resolved at the top of the stairs. A girl. Anya.

She carried an iron fireplace poker gripped in both hands like a weapon. It was old and ugly, its handle forged into a grimacing lion's head. She descended slowly, her wild eyes sweeping the wreckage below.

When she saw it was Noble's dad, she couldn't think of what to say, nor express the relief washing over her. She caught his eyes glancing off the poker. "It's from the set my mom hides in the spare room closet. She says it's ugly," she offered breathlessly. "But it's heavy."

Peter moved toward her. "Are you okay?" he asked, voice suddenly softer, hand reaching to touch her arm.

She tumbled down the rest of the stairs, running into him like he was a surrogate father figure she needed comfort from. "Yeah," she said, blinking at him. "But are you?" She nodded toward his forehead.

Blood had trailed down past his temple and into the curve of his cheek. Peter reached up, finally registering the warm wetness, and grunted.

"Head wounds always bleed worse than they are," he muttered. "Where's Noble?"

"He ran after Bear," Anya said, voice cracking. "Bear went toward my dad, and Noble...he went to help."

Peter's head snapped to Seth. "We need to move." He was already turning toward the door.

Seth stepped forward. "Peter—"

But Peter was already out the broken frame, gun raised, boots pounding on the porch.

Seth cursed under his breath, sparing only the quickest glance back toward the stairs where the rest of the women were now appearing.

Leith nearly tripped in her rush, catching the banister with one hand. "Anya!"

Anya turned and collided with her mother's arms, the poker still clutched awkwardly in her hand.

Seth looked at Mary, bloody mouthed and wild-eyed. Her arm was around Story as if they were holding each other up. He locked eyes with Story for a heartbeat—hers wide with fear and relief, lips parted, as if she had something to say but couldn't find the words. She gave the subtlest nod, then he turned and bolted after Peter.

Anya broke free of Leith's arms and chased them both into the dark.

Paddy and Cal crested the rise toward the old barn, legs pumping, rifles ready and eyes on the sky. Dust and feathers still hung faintly in the air.

Ethan was upright—but only just. He leaned against the wall of the barn, shotgun drooping in one blood-soaked hand, his face drawn, hollow-eyed. Sweat streaked with blood clung to his brow, and one leg trembled with every breath.

Paddy didn't waste time. "Jesus, Bury, you're standing?"

Ethan gave a pained half smile. "Don't ask me how. But you gotta go. Noble ran off that way—" He gestured with the shotgun's barrel, just past the driveway curve toward the garage and the house. "He distracted one of those things. Led it off...away from me."

"Dammit," Paddy muttered. "He's just a kid."

"He might've just saved my life," Ethan said, voice cracked and raw.

Paddy turned to Cal, already backing away. "Stay with him. Get the ATV. Bring him to the house. Fast as you can."

Cal didn't argue. He crossed to Ethan's side, looping an arm under his shoulder. "Come on, big guy. We're not done yet."

Paddy was already moving, rifle raised, legs pumping hard across the grass and gravel, following the path the creature and the boy had vanished into, chasing the echo of Noble's footprints across the darkening land.

Noble tore across the lawn, legs pumping like pistons. His sneakers skidded over the edge of the gravel drive as he passed the garage—doors wide open, nothing to barricade them. No time. He'd never get them closed before the creature caught him.

Keep moving. That was the only plan. Make it all the way around the garage. Create distance, then the porch. If he could hit the porch, even if the doors were off their hinges and the owl thing crashed in after him, at least inside he might find something to fight back with. A bat. A knife. Anything.

He slammed on the brakes and rounded the corner.

The pasture stretched out before him, the sky an ink-blue dome streaked with the last burn of sunset.

He darted past the firewood pile, and *goddammit*, his eye caught the glint of an axe leaning against the stack too late. He was already past, gravel loose beneath his feet.

He stumbled. His ankle twisted for half a second, and he pitched forward hard. Gravel bit into his palms. He gritted his teeth. Behind him, a rush of wings and scrambling feet drew near. He rolled over, preparing to deflect the ambush—

—and Bear exploded from the side yard in a streak of muscle and fur.

With a savage snarl, she launched herself straight into the owl's flank, jaws catching its wing in a brutal grip. The impact was enough to stagger the creature sideways, claws scraping violently against the ground as it tried to hold its balance. Feathers scattered in the air, and Bear shook her head violently, growling deep from her chest, ragging the beast with every ounce of her strength.

The owl reeled, shrieking, barely staying upright. One talon struck out blindly, raking the air.

"Bear!" Noble shouted, scrambling to his feet, eyes wide with horror. "Bear, come!"

The dog hesitated—growl still rolling through her throat—but at the sound of his voice, she let go, panting hard, tongue lolling, still coiled tight with adrenaline. She turned, bounding toward Noble without a second's hesitation.

Noble didn't wait. He grabbed Bear's scruff mid-stride and ran, the two of them tearing toward the distant pastures, every breath slicing his lungs like glass.

Nate gripped the steering wheel tight as he tore up Hollow Pine Road, the dark trees rushing past like walls closing in. He'd been at the fairgrounds, feeling stunned, vacant, uncertain, when Bill came up and told him to go home. But as Nate reached his car, a strange tightness had bloomed in his chest, restless and cold. By the time he hit the streets to head home or turn toward the country roads leading out to the farms, his finger was already moving, signaling into the country. Foot on the gas, ignition hot, he took the open road like a dragstrip.

The country road unspooled beneath his tires, bouncing him hard enough in the seat to jar his teeth. He caught air over a low ridge, headlights flaring off gravel. The potholes were craters—bone-rattling— but he didn't slow. All he could think about was his friends.

He pulled into the Bury driveway with a spray of dust and brake lights. Before he could even register what he was supposed to do next— what could be done—he saw a blur of movement. Noble sprinting full-bore past the garage, arms pumping, hair wild.

Nate elbowed open his door and was halfway out, air built in his lungs to call to his friend, when he realized why Noble was running.

One of the owls, a big one, was right behind. The way it moved was uncanny and fast. It sprinted like an ostrich, its cloak of wings spread out, billowing behind, like a creature from a Guillermo del Toro nightmare.

Close behind it came the farm dog. Bear. That was her name. Nate remembered now, just in time to see her hot on the owl's heels, barking with a fury that sent chills down his spine. Nate didn't think, he flung the door open and followed. Gravel underfoot, legs pounding, adrenaline surged like a race gun had gone off in his chest.

He had no plan and no weapon, just a refusal to let his people face whatever this was alone.

Noble and Bear ran hard, their shadows flaring long under the moonlight. The gravel path twisted through the side yard like a snare laid in stone.

Bear darted ahead, then circled back, unwilling to leave him, teeth bared, lips pulled in a silent snarl. Noble risked a glance behind. It was far too close. The owl bounded after them, its limbs snapping between flight and lurch, half glide, half crawl.

They rounded a distant shed. Noble tried to pivot, but the turn came too tight, too fast. His boot skidded out. He crashed to his knees with a cry, Bear barking furiously at his side.

He scrambled back up, heart hammering, and turned just in time to see the creature unfurl to its full, towering height. Its shoulders rolled, talons clenching like the hinge of a trap.

Thinking fast, Noble grabbed a rusted-out bucket and flung it. The thing recoiled. Bear lunged again, snapping at its legs, giving Noble the split second he needed to sprint toward the cow barn.

But it leapt with astonishing speed. Its shadow rose above them like a falling star. Noble spun, ready to throw his arm over Bear…

Crunch.

The sound hit like a punctuation mark in the dark.

The owl creature went stock-still. Its shoulders hunched and stiffened. Its head cocked at an unnatural angle. Another sound followed, wet and sloppy like a soaked towel slapping pavement.

The thing let out a choked, almost human gurgle, then collapsed forward, wings twitching, claws splaying out uselessly.

Behind it, axe gripped in both hands, was Nate.

His chest heaved. His face was bloodless. His wide, wild eyes were locked on the thing he'd just put down.

Noble blinked up at him, chest still rising and falling in panic, unable to speak.

Nate stared at the creature's twitching body, then down at the blood-slick blade of the axe.

"Holy shit," he whispered. "I didn't—I didn't mean to swing that hard."

Noble pushed himself up on shaking elbows, voice hoarse. "No, dude. You meant to." *And thank God he did.*

There was a pause. A breathless, stunned sort of silence between them. Then Nate's knees buckled and he stumbled forward, the axe slipping from his hands with a dull *thunk*. He dropped to his knees beside Noble, eyes glassy, chest still hitching with adrenaline and disbelief.

They stared at each other for a beat.

Then Nate reached out, awkward and hesitant, and grabbed a fistful of Noble's shirt, pulling him into a clumsy hug.

It wasn't graceful. It wasn't even comfortable. Just limbs and dirt and the thud of their hearts against ribs as they sat in the gravel with the dead thing cooling beside them.

Noble let out something between a laugh and a sob feeling like they were just two guys celebrating another victory at a track meet.

"Okay," Nate muttered, voice shaking as he sat back on his butt. "Okay. That just happened."

"Yeah," Noble said, nodding. "It really did."

For a long second they didn't move. Just two boys trying to catch their breath in a night that no longer felt real.

Peter leapt the final porch step in a single bound, boots hitting gravel hard enough to sting his knees. His eyes caught a figure moving across the far end of the driveway, a teenage blur.

"Nate?" he called out, already moving.

The boy didn't stop. Just disappeared behind the far edge of the garage. Peter's legs lengthened their stride.

Behind him, Seth caught up, breath rasping in his throat. "What is it?"

"I swear I just saw Abbott take off behind the garage."

Seth felt it then—that pit in the center of his chest. That breathless space where dread curled like a vine. *Please, not another kid. Not another goddamn kid.*

They ran. Boots scattering gravel, hearts pounding with a rhythm that had nothing to do with effort and everything to do with fear. They rounded the corner past the woodpile. The smell of fresh-cut pine met the sour tang of fear, mixing with the adrenaline in their bloodstreams. They continued toward the fields, following the dark shape of a teenage boy as it turned behind another outbuilding. Peter kicked up his pace. Seth followed suit. His shoulder burned. Blood slicked the grip on his gun.

Both officers rounded the corner filled with dread and there they were, two boys on the ground—Noble with dirt streaked up his cheek and blood on his knees and elbows, and Nate pale as paper, shaking, the haft of an axe resting beside him. At their feet, an owl creature lay twisted and motionless, its ruined wing spread wide like some broken ceremonial fan.

Peter didn't think, he just moved. Noble sprang up to meet him. They collided with a thud, arms locking. Peter crushed his son against him, one hand fisted in Noble's hair, the other curled around the boy's shoulders like he could shield him from the very memory of tonight.

"I got you," he muttered, voice thick. "I've got you."

Seth crossed to Nate, crouched low, and offered a steady hand. Nate looked up, dazed, then stumbled into him, wrapping his arms tight around his chief like he might fall apart if he didn't. Seth blinked, wrapped his arms around the kid, and held him.

"You did good," he said quietly. "You're alright now. You're safe."

Paddy rounded the other side of the garage and saw the huddled group. He'd backtracked, hoping to cut off the kid and the owl, but was happy to discover everyone was safe and in a blissful reunion. He dropped his rifle and sighed, shoulders slumping with relief.

The distant sound of an engine interrupted them, an ATV roaring over gravel from the direction of the barns. Tires squealed as it skidded to a stop out front.

"Dad!" Anya's voice, bright and high and terrified, echoed over the farm.

Peter released his son partially, one arm still around Noble. Seth turned toward the noise, jaw set.

A siren began to wail in the distance, thin at first, then growing louder, echoing over the hills of Lost Grove like a weary sigh.

Seth exhaled hard. "Let's finish this night from hell," he muttered.

But they all knew the truth. The night might be done, but this day, the wounds it left, the questions it raised, was far from over.

Chapter Forty-Three
Of Owls and Offspring

The sound of gravel shifting under tires carried across the quiet field, breaking the hush that had settled over the Bury farm since the ambulance had gone. Story watched Peter and Seth shuttle the kids into Nate's car and force them to head back to the Andalusian house so Jolie could see her son and they could all be comforted and safe. The porch steps creaked as Story sat down beside Mary, both of them wrapped in thick emergency blankets, their clothes rumpled and streaked with dirt and soot. Mary had one boot off, her socked foot propped on the next step down, a bloody gash visible along the top of her arch.

"You really did a number on yourself," Story said. She reached out and squeezed her friend's hand.

"You should see the other guy," Mary teased. Her fangs had finally retracted, but her broken tooth—cracked at a slant—still caught the moonlight when she grinned.

"You've got a real pirate smile going on there," Seth said to Mary as he approached, voice gravelly, worn.

Mary barked a laugh. "What, this?" She tapped the tooth with her fingernail. "Rugged charm. Some girls pay good money for imperfections."

"You're positively radiant," he said, deadpan.

She snorted, then winced. Her ribs were likely bruised.

Story hadn't spoken to Seth since the paramedics loaded Ethan into the ambulance. She'd just watched, holding herself still like one wrong move would shatter her.

When Seth finally turned his attention on her, she crossed the porch in three strides and threw her arms around him. Seth breathed into her hair, grounding himself there for a second he wanted to last much longer than it could.

He pulled back just enough to look her over. "You okay?" he asked.

"We're fine," Story whispered. "Bruised. Rattled. But fine."

Seth looked into her eyes and felt calmed by the subtle, abnormal flicker reflecting back at him. Story lifted onto her toes and he met her lips with a kiss, his hand sweeping into her hair to cup the back of her head. Only now did his body shake with the terror of the notion that he could have lost her. He'd been a professional, with a job to do, people to rescue, up to the moment her soft lips touched his. He gave into it for a moment before regaining his composure, telling himself there was still more to do.

He pulled away. "You should go home. Both of you. We'll sort everything out later."

Tires popping on the gravel drive drew their attention. A silver Subaru pulled in, dust rising like a ghost behind it. Dr. Elias Raines stepped out before the engine had fully cut off. He took one look at the porch, the torn screen door, the blood-dark trail smeared near the barn, and froze.

Seth frowned. "Did you call him?" he asked Story.

"No, not..." she said, squinting toward the car. "He called before we came out here. He sounded unsettled but I didn't think he'd actually—" Story raised her hand and waved when she saw Dr. Raines look their way. He offered her a confused wave back. "We'll get out of your hair," Story said, reaching for Seth's hand. She kissed his bruised knuckles and scowled at the field dressing on his shoulder. "Please make sure you get that properly looked at," she remarked.

Mary rose, putting pressure carefully on her injured foot.

"Dr. Raines!" They heard Cal call out, already heading for the perplexed, astonished-looking paleoethnobotanist.

"Don't die before the epilogue, cowboy," Story remarked as she patted Seth on the chest. He glanced down at her devilish grin as she moved away, keys jangling in her hand.

Mary smirked as she limped after her. "Real fairy tale shit," she muttered, tossing a wink at Seth over her shoulder.

Their teasing remarks aimed to lift Seth's mood, and he had to admit, in a way, they did. Story and Mary were safe, the kids were safe, and that was one less trouble he didn't need to worry over. By the time he crossed the gravel, Elias was mid-conversation with Cal, his brows drawn into deep, analytical lines.

"I was already on my way," Elias said to Cal as Seth approached. "After our call... I don't know. I felt the need to investigate this further. Maybe speak with the Burys. Try to get a clearer understanding of the glyph patterns. Their context."

Paddy and Peter approached.

"CDFW is on the way," Peter explained, sliding his phone back into a Velcro pocket. "Might be a while, but they're rallying a whole squad to come handle this."

"Perfect, thanks." Seth nodded to his friend, his sergeant.

Elias gestured toward the barn and the house, the mention of the CFDW not lost on him. "What exactly happened here?"

"We can give you the short version," Peter said.

Elias waited, eyebrows raised.

"Owls," Seth said.

"I beg pardon?" Elias swung his gaze on the four men standing before him, each one looking equally exhausted and gobsmacked.

"Big fucking owls," Cal added.

Elias's eyebrows shot up. "An owl did this?"

"They're no ordinary owls, Doc," Paddy remarked.

Elias blinked, still processing. "You're telling me that an owl species of a previously undocumented scale and aggression level...attacked this property?"

"Come on. Let's have you take a look. It might make more sense once you see one," Seth remarked, already heading toward the nearest one, the one behind the garage.

Everyone followed.

"I supposed—to Story, that is—the glyphs could have been made by an avian species," Elias said. "But I wasn't thinking...I don't know what I was thinking to be honest." After a pause Elias continued, "No, that's not true. I was thinking insects. A boring kind of insect that might eat away the bark and tree flesh, then transport the spores of the fungus to the location. Perhaps nesting beneath it... Jesus, I don't know."

"But you did suspect it was living in symbiosis with another creature?" Cal asked.

Elias nodded, shrugging. "How the hell else would you explain them? Unless we consider the fungus itself was eating away the bark, etcetera.

But why make repeating marks? They mean things. This isn't just graffiti or tribal marking. These glyphs are part of a living system. The fungus, the markings, the psychic effects, they're all intertwined. Symbiotic, maybe even cooperative. I think the…well, the owls I guess did this. It's not just territorial, it's communicative. It's how they organize, maybe how they hunt, or even how they pass memory."

Seth darted a glance at Peter, then returned his stare to the professor. "You're saying they're writing. Like, *language?*"

"At its most basic, yes," Elias said. "A biological one. Living glyphs. Imagine if your blood could leave behind a message. Imagine if instinct and intent could grow out of the bark of a tree." He shook his head slowly. "Whatever was carved near this property…it wasn't random. It meant something distinct. I came here to figure out what."

Seth's shoulders squared. "Then you came to the right place."

"Jesus." Peter ran a hand down his face, feeling the stubble scratch his palm. He locked eyes with his chief. "So not only are they massive predators, they can communicate too?"

Elias stopped dead in his tracks, eyes locked on the lifeless form on the ground no more than fifteen paces ahead of them. "Am I looking at…" He continued forward, eyes locked on the creature in both intrigue and horror.

"You on social media?" Seth asked.

Elias shook his head as much to understand what was being told to him as to Seth's question. "I mean, yes, but I've not been on it."

"I'm sure it's all over by now," Peter commented offhandedly.

"The owls didn't just attack this farm and its occupants," Seth explained as the professor stared down at the massive owl. "They hit the fairgrounds as well. Stirred everyone into a full-scale panic. People were trampled, others made irrational choices, some folks didn't make it."

Elias looked ill. "Jesus Christ. I didn't expect…" His voice faltered.

Seth shook his head. "Neither did we."

"Nobody did," Peter added.

Cal's eyebrows lifted slightly. *I might have*, he thought. If he'd paid any attention to what his niece was saying to him, he may have been able to figure it out. After all, his mother had pretty quickly surmised what it could have been. The Tah-tah-kle'ah may have been a myth, but facts were often buried in myths. Instead, his fears of losing Constance to the woods had won out and he'd let that fear still him into inaction.

Elias squatted near the owl, though he didn't touch it. The toes of his boots crunched in the gravel as he turned his body, looking around at the distant pastures, the massive barn in the distance. "What were they after?"

That question hung a little too long.

"A baby," Paddy finally said. "Or...something like one. Smaller, lighter colored. Still in the barn last we checked."

Seth's posture tightened. "There's a baby one of these in the—in what barn?"

"The old barn," Cal said. "We went in to clear it after the attack. Just me and Paddy. And...there was something in there. Not like the others. This one was smaller and younger."

"You think one of them left it behind?" Peter asked.

"No," Paddy said. "We think someone was keeping it."

"Keeping it?" Seth asked.

"A baby?" Elias half whispered, his mind running rampant with theories.

"That's our guess," Cal replied. "Makes sense, right? You cage one of theirs, they come back angry."

Paddy added, "And what we saw at the fair—it lines up. Big ones swooped in, drove off the others, pulled the smaller ones out. Protective behavior. We thought maybe that was just nesting instinct, but..."

Seth and Peter exchanged a look, equal parts confusion and dread.

"You're saying someone around here found one and decided to keep it?" Seth asked. He recalled Leith walking off toward the old barn with something in her arms, the tidbits Story had told him about her actions, and was starting to wonder if the effects of the glyphs had warped Leith's actions.

"Looks like," Paddy said, already turning toward the barn. "Come see for yourself."

The group moved across the gravel drive, boots crunching rhythmically, shadows stretching ahead of them beneath the waning porch light. The night was still heavy, thick with mist. The moon behind the clouds cast a silver sheen over the barn's roofline.

Bear trotted alongside them, tongue lolling, tail low but wagging slightly. She darted forward, then back to Seth's side, as if leading them on some instinctual route she alone understood. Seth absently patted her head each time she returned.

Paddy ran a hand along the open doorframe. "We didn't disturb anything. Just took a look, backed off and left the door open in case it wanted to make its way out."

"Be warned," Cal added. "There was something in the air. Not quite right."

"A pressure in the head," Paddy said. "Mild. Not hostile. But…not nothing."

Elias's face had gone pale. "Show me. I want to see where it was kept. And I want to see any glyphs."

Seth's jaw flexed. He looked back toward the house, toward the place Story and Mary had just left, the ambulance tracks still fresh in the dirt.

The door groaned as they pushed it open, the smell of hay and damp wood spilling into the night air.

The stall where the creature had been was empty.

"Could've slipped out," Peter said, scanning the corners.

"Or was retrieved," Elias murmured. "Hard to say."

Cal offered to sweep the grounds, see if he could find any trail. He was already halfway back toward the main house by the time Seth and Peter told him to be cautious.

Inside, the others stood near what was clearly a nest—blankets, a pile of old straw, and an overturned milk crate lined with fabric. Someone had cared for it. Someone had fed it.

Seth exhaled slowly. "Leith might have been keeping it. She wasn't acting in her right mind though. Story told me she'd been sleepwalking… could this be from the psilocybin in the fungus?" he asked the professor.

Elias crouched to examine the straw, fingers ghosting over the fabric. "I can't say. Not yet. From the communication of how Leith was behaving, to the notes from Hannah, they are markedly different, and I just don't know why."

"But they both noticed changes to themselves?" Peter inquired.

Elias nodded. "Oh yes. I believe the fungus may be highly volatile. You say there are glyphs nearby? Do you know where?"

"The side," Paddy explained, thumb tossed over his shoulder.

They stepped outside, the side of the barn etched with markings that shimmered faintly in the moonlight. Elias adjusted his glasses, pulled out a small flashlight, and swept the beam across the siding. The glyphs pulsed back subtly, their fungal edges just developing.

"This one." He pointed to a jagged spiral. "This denotes danger. And this"—he indicated a second, more elaborate symbol—"is what Hannah noted as a hunting zone. Combined, they may have marked this barn as a target. Not by accident. As if they read it like a signpost."

Seth rubbed the back of his neck. "So what do we do?"

"Erase it," Elias said simply. "Cut it out, burn it, chip it away—just get it off the barn. I'd recommend the same for any tree within a mile. If these things use glyphs as communication, we change the message."

Seth said, "Dr. Raines—"

"Elias, please."

"You're going to have to coordinate your knowledge with that of the CDFW team."

Elias nodded, distracted. "I imagine I will."

"We could try that in the park too. Erasing the marks," Paddy clarified, looking off into the woods. "Maybe clear a corridor, redirect them deeper into the forest. Not sure how the CDFW would feel, but I'll raise it."

"You're the expert there," Elias said. "But I insist we start here."

Peter took a step back and looked at the barn wall. "Then let's get rid of them."

Elias stayed behind to photograph each glyph with care, cataloguing the fungi's luminescence and collecting samples, while Seth and Peter walked toward the garage. Bear trailed behind, her tail wagging in big, lazy arcs.

Inside, Seth grabbed a hammer and crowbar from a wall hook. Peter found the chainsaw resting against a sack of feed. He checked the fuel level, then the primer.

Seth leaned against the tool bench. "This is all a little unbelievable, isn't it?"

Peter chuckled, low and humorless. "I keep waiting to wake up. Glyphs that cause hallucinations. Owl things that can mark their territory with fungus? If you pitched this to me a month ago, I'd have laughed you off the property."

Seth nodded toward the chainsaw. "Take Elias with you into the woods. That tree glyph started all this—make sure it's gone."

Peter slung the chainsaw over one shoulder. "I'm gonna take one of these," he said, gesturing to the parked ATV.

"Please do," Seth said. "Faster that way."

Peter gave a short nod, then turned and walked toward the ATV. The engine rumble echoed into the trees as he disappeared into the night.

Seth headed back toward the barn, crowbar in hand, the weight of the night finally beginning to settle across his shoulders.

He watched the red lights of the ATV head into the bleeding darkness of the woods in the distance. The wind rustled through the trees and he hoped that all the owls had cleared out, scared back into the wild depths of the state park.

Nate pulled up to the Andalusian house and shut off his car. They all paused, breathing, before forcing their bodies into the next movement. Noble was out first, the front door already opening, his mother charging out to greet them.

Jolie swept him into her arms. "Oh, my baby. Are you hurt? Are you bleeding?"

"I'm okay, Mom," Noble muttered into her shoulder, voice thick.

Jolie's eyes fell on Anya. She released Noble only to throw her arms around Anya next. "You too, sweetheart. Jesus." She pulled away, holding Anya by the arms, before one hand darted to her face. It was smeared in dried blood. Her clothes splattered with it. "Let's get you clean, and Nate—oh, honey, thank God."

Nate took Jolie's embrace, thankful she promptly returned to fretting over Anya.

Zoe was crying as she rushed outside to her brother's arm. Noble picked her up, though she was far too old and too big to be held like a little monkey anymore, and let her hang off his neck, squeezing the life out of him. He set her down inside the door, shutting it carefully behind as Nate took off his shoes. He watched his mom lead Anya upstairs to help her wash her face and find something clean to wear.

"What happened? Was it the owls? Mom said it was the owls," Zoe worried, her voice soft in the hush of the warm, quiet home.

"It…yeah," Noble said, brushing the top of her head. He moved into the kitchen, kicking his shoes off into the hallway as he went. He went to the sink and turned on the hot water. Nate joined him, both of them washing their hands, not speaking but standing shoulder to shoulder in silent companionship.

Zoe climbed up on a stool and stared at the back of her brother's head. She kept pulling her bottom lip into her mouth and raking her upper teeth across it. "Noble?" she whispered.

He smiled over his shoulder and turned to wipe his hands on some paper towels. "I'm okay, Zo," he said, dabbing the small scrape wounds carefully.

The water upstairs shut off, and they heard Jolie and Anya move into Noble's bedroom. She was likely finding one of his shirts or sweatshirts to wear.

Jolie came downstairs shortly after, a first aid kit in hand. She set it on the counter. "You need any…"

"They're just scrapes, Mom. Nothing worse than falling off a bike," Noble reassured her, and gave her another hug.

Car doors slammed outside.

"That'll be them," Nate said.

Jolie nodded, smoothed her son's shirt sleeves. "Go change," she instructed.

Noble nodded, met Anya on the stairs as Nate opened the door to Emory, Ember, and Stan. Stan wrapped Nate in an unexpected hug. Stan saw Anya and leapt away, her veil of dark hair falling over Anya as she practically swallowed her whole, wrapping her arms around her.

"Oh my god, Anya, is your dad okay?"

"They think he'll be fine," she said, voice muffled by Stan's shoulder.

Noble washed his face and changed into sweats and a shirt. He found the others in the kitchen and nearly lost his breath when Stan finally got her arms around him. She hugged them like she was reassuring herself they were real.

Jolie shepherded them all in like strays in a storm, fussing and scanning for injuries. Once she was sure they weren't actively bleeding or in shock, she clapped her hands once and pointed to the stairs. "Basement. Couch. Go."

Then she turned, grabbed Zoe by the elbow, and hauled her toward the kitchen. "You're not eavesdropping this time. Go drink your chocolate milk and then you're going to bed."

"I can't go to bed now," Zoe complained.

"You can watch something in our bed then," Jolie explained as the teens headed down into the basement.

Downstairs, the six of them collapsed into a heap across the big sectional and scattered beanbags, legs tangled, shoulders brushing. The space smelled like laundry and faint candle smoke, dimly lit by the low sconces Jolie always left on for ambiance. No one turned on the TV. No one touched their phones.

They just sat there, shell-shocked.

"I don't know what was more surreal," Stan finally said, rubbing her temple. "The owls or the panic. All those lights, the screaming. The Ferris wheel…" She trailed off.

"Feels like it didn't even happen," Ember murmured. "But I've got blisters on my feet, so I know it did."

Everyone treated her words with a shocked silence, as if they had space to still be shocked. But hearing her voice was strange, a different kind of wonder, a nice one among today's nightmare.

Stan met each of their looks with a shrug.

Her brother acknowledged it. "Yeah. She's kind of talking now."

"That's amazing," Anya said. She sat curled between Noble and the armrest, knees pulled to her chest, Noble's arm around her shoulders. She hadn't spoken much since the car ride.

They were all waiting for updates and explanations. For the adrenaline to wear off.

Nate cleared his throat. "Hey, uh…so, another thing to add to the insanity of tonight. Nettie's in custody."

Heads turned.

"What?" Stan said sharply. "She *what*?"

"She got into…" Nate started, voice low. "Apparently she and two others drove an excavator into the ground and it broke through into some kind of underground cave."

"Jesus," Noble muttered, pulling Anya closer.

"We told her not to do anything stupid," Stan hissed, running a hand through her hair.

"She didn't listen," Nate said. "But—here's the thing—your uncle told us something. At the fair, when everything started going to hell. He said, according to old stories, the Tah-tah-kle'ah—the owl women—they lived in caves."

Stan sat forward. "That's the word. The one my grandma said."

"Yeah, well…it's a weird fucking story," Nate huffed.

"*What* lived in caves?" Emory asked, brows drawing together.

Nate looked at him. "Them. The creatures from the park."

"The owls?" Noble asked.

"Yeah, whatever the hell they were. Your uncle, Cal, he told us about them. The story about these owl women things."

"Owl women things?" Stan scowled, shaking her head.

"Nate," Emory said. "Those things weren't women."

"I mean, obviously. They were big fucking owls. I'm just saying that's what they were called in this old folklore tale or whatever."

"And how does all this tie into Nettie?" Stan asked. "Is that what you're getting at?"

"Look." Nate raised his hands in surrender. "Don't get mad. I'm just saying—maybe Nettie stirring shit underground pissed them off. Maybe this wasn't random."

"She woke them up," Noble said quietly. "Or maybe scared them. The cave collapse. If that was their home, maybe they panicked. And then the fairgrounds, all the lights, the noise, it was too much."

"Yeah," Stan added, nodding. "The rides, the music, all the people. It probably felt like an invasion after their den got busted into."

Anya, who had been quiet until then, finally spoke. Her voice was barely above a whisper. "The caves…that's what it was."

"What? What was?" Nate asked.

Anya looked up at the expectant faces. "That time we went into the caves? To find the door to the Orbriallis Institute? You guys heard me—"

"You screamed Noble's name," Stan interrupted. "We came running."

"Because there was something in there," Anya continued. "I saw it. I thought it was a hand, with long fingernails, but no, it was a claw. It just happened to be the size of a hand."

"Jesus," Noble whispered.

"But what *are* they?" Ember asked. "Where did they come from?"

"And how the hell have they been living in Devil's Cradle this whole time and no one noticed?" Anya added.

Nate gestured to her, half defensive. "Okay, well—no one knows about you either, right?"

Anya blinked, caught off guard. "Excuse me?"

"Not like—ugh, not in a bad way!" Nate groaned. "I'm not trying to be a dick. I'm just saying…if *naiads* exist, then why's it so weird these owl things exist too? That's all I meant."

"Bro," Noble muttered, shaking his head.

"What? One, it's true. Two, she's a water spirit! That's a lot to process."

Stan sighed and rubbed at her face. "There were like ten owl creatures. There's only two naiads."

"That we know of," Nate shot back. "And—look—I'm just trying to understand. Like… Anya. What does it even mean that you're a naiad? Can you breathe underwater? Talk to fish? What are the rules?"

Anya exhaled slowly, then sat up a little straighter. "I can manipulate water. I can sense where it's been—what it remembers. I can raise tides and bend streams. My mom…she can do more."

Nate stared at her. "You're fucking with me, right? About raising tides and bending streams?"

Anya shrugged.

"Okay. That's…cool, I guess. Still don't totally get it. But cool."

That was the rhythm of the night. Shock. Questions. Reactions that came too fast or too blunt. Half-sincere jokes. Long silences.

At some point, Ember asked again if there'd been any updates on Ethan.

A few minutes later, Anya's phone buzzed.

She read the text. "He's stable. They're keeping him overnight."

The room collectively exhaled, and like puppets whose strings had finally gone slack, they all folded down into the cushions. Blankets were dragged over shoulders. Someone turned out the last light. Beanbags became pillows. Bodies huddled together like pups in a den, warm and worn and still trembling inside. And then they slept—deep and dreamless—the kind of sleep only terror, exhaustion, and teenage resilience can buy.

Chapter Forty-Four
Soft Hours, Hard Truths

The sun was daring to rise when Seth Wolfe leaned against the hood of his Bronco, the engine beneath him long since cooled down, leaving nothing to thaw the weariness in his bones. Beside him, Peter stared across the field where the CDFW crew were working under floodlights, the hazmat-suited team moving methodically as they tagged, bagged, and prepped the owl carcasses for transport. Each massive creature was tethered in place like the aftermath of a myth gone wrong.

"You should head home and see your family. Check on the kids," Seth said to his sergeant.

Peter nodded, quiet, reflective, his badge glinting in the dawn light as if it were ashamed to shine. "Jolie has been keeping me up to date. They're all in the basement, sleeping now."

"All of them?"

Peter nodded, smiling. "A regular sleepover."

"You should also grab a few hours of sleep if you can."

Peter dropped his crossed arm and stretched. "I'll get a few when we're wrapped here, then head in to start on reports."

Seth nodded and slapped him on the back. "Appreciate it."

Peter grabbed his hand in a firm shake, then moved in for a hug. It was brief, strong, but grounding. They both settled into leaning against the Bronco once more.

"Could use a coffee," Peter mumbled.

"A five-shot Americano would be nice," Seth agreed.

"I could check the house for a pot," Peter suggested but made no move.

As if reading their minds, Cal came striding down the porch steps, three steaming mugs in hand. His eyes scanned the activity as he approached. "Didn't know how you take it," he said, handing each a mug.

"Does it matter?" Peter said, blowing on the hot liquid before taking a healthy sip.

Seth did the same. "Thank you, Cal."

Cal nodded, his mug raised in a subtle acknowledgment before he gulped down a healthy amount of caffeine.

Seth looked around. Trucks lined the Bury farm like a surgical team surrounding a battlefield. The team of CDFW officers wandering around in white bio-suits, collecting samples, spoke in hushed tones like priests before a reckoning. The woman leading the charge, Director Marisol Reyes, finally arrived. She appeared poised and in field gear with a CDFW badge on her chest. She had a fierce demeanor and the athletic form of a professional basketball player.

She introduced herself with a handshake that nearly swallowed Seth's.

"We've never seen anything like this," she said. "The feather samples alone could take months to process. Are you sure there are only three?"

"At this site, yes," Seth answered. "But more were involved. We lost people at the fair. We're still assessing."

She nodded at that.

"I'm sure it's too early for anything concrete, but do you have any idea what these are? Besides the obvious vague determination of an owl?"

Something akin to a smile crept into Marisol's expression. "I mean, we're looking at, without question, a landmark discovery for both science and conservation. The only thing I've ever read about giant owls were of fossils found in Cuba that were prehistoric. I think they measured somewhere between three and four feet. But these were from well over 10,000 years ago. Maybe a hundred."

Seth exchanged a guilty look with Peter. "I can assure you that every death was solely in self-defense—"

Marisol held her hand up, stopping him. "I've seen the wounds and damage inflicted. We can only hope that the remaining owls find a safe harbor and we can locate them before crazed hunters go out looking for, what I can only describe as, a big game kill."

"We've already been strictly patrolling the woods to keep hunters out after we had the incident with the young boy."

"Yes, I heard about that. I…" Marisol paused, her brow wrinkling. "Did you determine yet what—"

Seth sighed. "We literally got results in earlier today. Or yesterday, I should say. Overall, the results were inconclusive. But what they did find was DNA from a squirrel, clearly not responsible, unidentified DNA which the guy at the lab said could be a new or rare species, and…an owl."

"Jesus."

"It didn't occur to me—"

"Or any of us," Peter interjected.

"That an owl could have possibly done what happened to Kevin Marlow, the boy, so I was leaning toward the 'unidentified.'"

"I'm sure I would have as well," Marisol added sympathetically. "As I said, prehistoric fossils. No one could have known."

"Have you ever seen anything like this before?" Peter asked. "I mean, a discovery of a prehistoric animal that was assumed to be extinct?"

Marisol nodded. "I've been thinking about one exact incident like this ever since I first laid eyes on one of the deceased owls."

Peter and Seth both crossed their arms and leaned in, as if it was a rehearsed reaction.

Marisol pulled out her cell phone and started to type while she spoke. "The Indonesian coelacanth, a rather massive prehistoric fish, often mistakenly described as a 'living fossil' or 'dinosaur fish,' was photographed for the first time just this past October by an underwater explorer and photographer. A group had been studying it for just over a decade before this. Back in the late 1930s, an Indonesian coelacanth was discovered somewhere in South Africa, I believe. Before that, it was believed to have been extinct for over seventy million years. Some fossils date back to seven hundred million years. Here's what she looks like." Marisol turned her phone around to display the image she pulled up on an oceanic website.

"Wow." Seth breathed out the word. It wasn't the size of the fish that brought about a feeling of awe, it was the coloring of the scales. Spotted all around brown and white, it had the effect of an aged brown-painted wall that had started to peel and flake through deterioration, revealing the white drywall beneath. Its eyes and mouth looked, in fact, like an old, grumpy man.

"Unbelievable," Peter uttered.

"I'm sure there was no shortage of photos and videos taken at the

405

fair," Marisol said. "But we need to locate them, study them, ensure their survival."

"We'll do everything we can to assist you in those efforts. I assure you," Seth promised.

Marisol nodded in appreciation. "Thank you, gentlemen."

"Well, unless you need anything else from us here, we'll get out of your way."

"I think we're good here, thank you. I'm assuming you'll want me at the press conference," she said.

"Right," Seth sighed. The press conference. Mayor Sumner was already on top of things, writing drafts of what to say, setting up a time with the press, weighing which location best suited them. "Yes, that would be incredibly helpful for everyone. If you have time, it would be great if you could swing by the station before heading to the town hall to fill us in on any further updates or discoveries. Then we can come up with a quick game plan of how we'd like to handle the conference."

"I'll do that." Marisol turned and headed back out into the field where her crew was still working to clean things up.

Seth looked at Peter and then nodded to his Bronco. "Can I give you a lift?"

Peter glanced over to where his truck was previously located. "Right. Noble." He made for the passenger side of Seth's vehicle.

Just as Seth grabbed his keys, his cell phone rang. He quickly grabbed it, seeing Bill's name. They had briefly spoken before the cavalry arrived, exchanging the quickest of updates. "Hold tight, Peter, it's Bill."

Peter circled back around to join Seth.

Seth answered and put his phone on speaker. "Hey, Bill, I've got you on speaker. I'm here with Peter."

"Hey, boys, how are you holding up over there?"

"Aside from exhaustion, we're okay. We got Ethan off to the hospital. Leith is with him. Paddy saved his life. He was bleeding out pretty badly."

"Thank God for that. We've had enough fatalities the past two weeks for the next decade as far as I'm concerned."

"Couldn't agree more," Seth said. "Have you got everyone cleared out of there now? Civilian-wise."

"Oh, yeah. Sheriff Hayes and his team came in here like a military operation. We all worked together, along with the paramedics, the fire department, and the CDFW to triage the wounded, take statements, and clear the fairgrounds. The majority of the fire department is still here. The fire at the barn has long been put out, but they're combing through the woods to make sure no floating embers made their way out there and started up something worse."

Peter groaned. "Yeah, let's try to avoid a full-blown wildfire if we can."

"I haven't seen any smoke. Not that that means anything. Hayes has rightfully already declared the fair closed for today and tomorrow. They've got crime scene tape around any conceivable entrance into the park. He said someone from his team would get the word out and that he'd talk to you and Mayor Sumner about what to do after this weekend."

"I can't fathom they would shut it down for the rest of the run," Peter said. "Too much revenue for the town."

"That was my thought as well," Bill agreed. "But we'll see. I can't say there's a precedent for something like this here. Probably not anywhere for that matter."

"What's the status with the rest of the team?" Seth asked.

"Well, Sasha's right next to me, but pretty much everyone else has left. Sasha sent Joe home a couple hours ago to get some sleep, figuring he'd be needed again soon enough. I sent Nate home hours ago. That poor kid had seen and experienced enough."

Seth raised an eyebrow in Peter's direction. "Yeah, about that. Nate actually showed up here, straight from the fair."

"He saved Noble's life," Peter added.

"How so?" Bill asked.

Seth laughed with no humor. "Well, something straight out of a horror film, Bill. The last remaining adult owl on the farm had Noble cornered just outside the house, and Nate came from behind and drove an axe through the back of its head."

"Mother of God."

"My sentiments exactly. We were quick to get the three kids out of here. Peter sent them back to his house and told them to stay there and get some rest."

"That kid's going to have more police experience going into his first year of college than anyone else, maybe ever."

"He's clearly got the fortitude for the job," Seth said. "Did you or anyone else happen to run into Seamus or Vince?"

"Sure did. They both stuck around and helped out until maybe an hour or so ago. Apparently during that whole foray, your buddy Seamus tackled one of those damn owls midair and fought it off, saved a bunch of kids."

Seth and Peter both laughed and shook their heads. "I can't say that surprises me to hear," Seth said.

"May want to think about making that man an offer to join the force," Bill offered, his tone sober.

Seth dropped his head. *Eddie.* He hadn't even had time to process the loss of their oldest deputy and friend.

"Bill, I'm so sorry about Eddie. He meant so much to the department and this entire town. I can make the house call if someone hasn't already—"

"No, no. It's gotta be me," Bill said. "Linda and I have been friends with the entire family since we were in our late twenties. Sasha already said she'll accompany me. We're heading over there after this call."

"I understand. What can you tell me about the other fatalities?"

"Let me put you on speaker. Sasha's got all that info," Bill said, as the audio coming from his end changed.

"Hey, Seth," Sasha said. "What do you need?"

"Hey, Sasha. You holding up okay?"

"I'm alive and uninjured. I'm grateful."

Seth raised his eyebrows. "That's an inspiring response."

"Are you fucking with me?"

"Have I ever? Of course not. It truly is."

"Well, thanks, I guess." Sasha laughed. "What info are you looking for?"

"Details on the deceased. Last I talked to Bill it was a total of three, including Eddie."

"It's four now. That's the final tally. Hold on a sec, let me grab my notebook."

Seth ran a hand through his hair, wondering if he would have any hair left by the end of the year, the way things were going.

"Okay," Sasha said. "The guy I saw get dropped from about a mile in the air, which may have taken over for the worst thing I've ever seen in my life, was Henry Mills. Forty-five years old and a contractor from Sacramento. Multiple witnesses say they saw him firing a gun at the owl that snatched him up."

"That's at least three people now, citizens, that had a firearm in the park," Peter said. "What's the point of the metal detectors we have there?"

"About that," Bill jumped in. "Clearly an issue with the junior staff at the gates. Sheriff Hayes already said that if the fair does in fact continue, he's going to have members of his own team at the entrance."

"Okay, noted," Seth said. "Who's next, Sasha?"

"Laura Chambers," Sasha responded. "She was the bright one who thought jumping from the top of the Ferris wheel was somehow a good idea. She was a tourist, in from Portland with her boyfriend, who astutely stayed inside the cart. She was thirty-eight, a hairdresser. Apparently well loved."

"Did you talk to the boyfriend? Any reason as to why she jumped?"

"I did speak with him. Todd Dawkins, thirty-two. He's a sous chef at the Happy Goat in Portland, in case you're interested. All he could say is that she was scared. He almost fell out of the cart himself trying to grab her, which was verified by a couple in the cart above him."

"That had to have been just horrific," Peter said.

"He was in legit shock," Sasha said. "He was fortunate though. One of the other people on the Ferris wheel, a woman named Bryce Reid, is a counselor for the county of San Francisco. She apparently came to his aid once everyone got off the ride and was still with him when I showed up."

"Well, at least that's something," Seth commented.

"The last one, the one we didn't know about right away, was George Tilly. He—"

"The teacher?" Seth asked, eyes wide.

"Um, yeah. I guess you would maybe know him."

"He was a helluva guy," Bill added.

"He was my history teacher in tenth grade," Seth said. "Fuck. What happened to him?"

"Heart attack," Sasha answered. "He died in his wife Betsy's arms. Fear, shock, all the chaos. Not sure. Suppose it really doesn't matter."

"Okay, thanks, Sasha."

"Seth," Bill started. "About Eddie. I know you're going to have your hands beyond full."

"Bill—"

"Now, listen to me goddammit. I've already made my decision, so don't even start to argue with me on this. Until you find a replacement, I'm coming back to help the team. We both know you don't have the staff to cover the shifts, especially under the current circumstances. My only request is that I work the evening shift. Linda and I have a nice morning routine now, golf, walks, canoeing—"

"Canoeing?"

"Yeah, what of it?"

"Nothing. I just didn't know you ever canoed."

"I didn't," Bill said. "Always wanted to. Anyhow, that's how it's going to be."

"Sasha, I hope you didn't encourage this incorrigible man."

"I don't know why you'd ever think I would do such a thing," she answered.

Seth rolled his eyes. "Yeah, alright. Well, thank you both. There's going to be a press conference at the town hall later on. I'm guessing late morning, early afternoon."

"I'll be there," Bill said.

"We'll be there," Sasha added.

Seth disconnected and let out a massive sigh.

Just after noon, under the shade of a borrowed tent set up near the fairgrounds, the press conference began. News crews huddled in clusters, cameras poised. The hum of drone blades buzzed faintly above them. Camera lights blinked. Phones recorded. Hashtags were already trending: #RedwoodOwls, #KillerOwls, #LostGroveAttack, #TitanOwls, #OwlTruthers.

Mayor Diane Sumner stepped to the podium, composed and polished despite the heaviness of the moment. She wore a navy blazer and a somber expression. Behind her stood Seth, Director Marisol Reyes of the CDFW, Chief Ranger Malcolm Yazzie of Devil's Cradle State Park, Patrick "Paddy" Kipp, and several others from the emergency response team.

"Good morning," Mayor Sumner began, voice steady. "Thank you all for coming. I want to begin by acknowledging the lives lost and the many shaken by the events of last night. Lost Grove is a close-knit community, and we grieve together." She inhaled, visibly collecting herself. "We are grateful to our law enforcement, fire services, park rangers, and federal partners for their swift and brave response. Now, I'd like to turn things over to our chief of police, Seth Wolfe."

Seth approached the mic slowly, the rustle of notepaper in his hands more for grounding than guidance.

"Thank you, Mayor Sumner," he said. "Last night, an unprecedented event unfolded in our town. Large avian creatures in the owl family, which we have yet to fully and properly identify, descended upon the county fairgrounds. At this time, we have confirmed multiple injuries and, regrettably, several fatalities. One of which was someone close not only to me and the rest of our department but to everyone in our town. Sergeant Eddie Cabrera lost his life protecting a child at the fair. Our tight-knit unit at the station mourns him deeply, as I'm sure the whole town will. Eddie leaves behind a devoted wife, three children, and six grandchildren."

A murmur passed through the gathered press, a susurration of whispers, scribbles on paper, and shutter clicks.

"We are not releasing the other names at this time out of respect for the families," Seth added quickly. "We ask that the media and the public be mindful of the grief many in our town are now facing." He continued, "I'm sure you all have many questions as to the hows and whys of what occurred. Our department is working closely with the California Department of Fish and Wildlife, and I'll let Director Marisol Reyes speak to those questions. She and her team have been on-site, collecting biological evidence, tracking flight paths, and evaluating the threat level moving forward."

Seth stepped back and motioned to Director Reyes.

She stepped up to the mic, her uniform pristine. "Thank you, Chief Wolfe. We have collected three carcasses from a nearby farm of the creatures in question that were killed in self-defense. While it may take weeks to months to properly identify the birds, I can conclusively state they are from the order Strigiformes. There are over two hundred known species of owls. Whether or not these creatures fall into one of the known species or is a new species altogether is of the utmost interest to us."

"Why did they attack?" someone from the crowd shouted.

Mayor Sumner stepped up. "Please keep all questions until the end of the press conference, and I promise we will answer each and every one of them to the best of our abilities."

Director Reyes continued on. "Why did they attack? It's a fair and obvious question, one to which I will elucidate based on our early findings. And for simplicity's sake, I will refer to the yet-to-be-identified species simply as owls. Based on numerous witness testimonies, both from the local police force to residents and visitors at the fair, I believe the owls were acting on purely animalistic and maternal instinct to protect their young or themselves. In each incident at the fairground, before the

411

attack occurred, either gunshots were taken at the owls or objects were thrown in their direction. At the farm I previously mentioned, there was a baby owl being held by humans, we believe for protective and nurturing reasons, that prompted the adult owls to encroach upon the property in an aggressive manner.

"As to the next obvious question of 'where did they come from?' we have confirmed that earlier in the morning, yesterday, before the fair began, a construction site was vandalized. More specifically, an excavator was commandeered and mishandled, causing it to collapse into the earth, which revealed a nesting area in a caving system for the owls. Samples of the owl feathers and droppings from this cave system confirmed they belonged to the giant species of owl seen later that very night.

"The fact that the owls were nesting in an underground caving system is of keen scientific fascination that will be a part of our expansive research, and also points to one of the assumed reasons why these creatures have not been seen before. We believe the remaining, surviving owls have fled in fear and are in search of a new nesting area. Chief Ranger Malcolm Yazzie will elaborate on this, but we implore you, all of you, not to go in search of these endangered creatures. The situation is being well handled by a sizable team of CDFW agents, local and county police officers, park rangers, and scientists." Marisol looked back to the team gathered on the stage. "Chief Yazzie?"

Malcolm Yazzie nodded and stepped forward. "Effective immediately, Devil's Cradle and surrounding woodlands are closed to the public. Our rangers will be assisting CDFW in locating any potential nests, tracking movements, and ensuring the safety of the perimeter. And to emphasize Director Reyes's point, we are dealing with a potentially unknown and most definitely endangered species here. Anyone caught hunting or even discussing hunting these creatures will be punished to the highest extent of the law. If there is anything you reporters might want to lead with, it's that."

Malcolm turned and motioned for Paddy to join him at the podium.

"I'd also like to announce an important promotion. Patrick Kipp, or, as most of you likely know him, Paddy, has been a distinguished member of the rangers for nearly twenty years. In addition to a select few others, which I'll let Chief Wolfe laud, Paddy went above and beyond the call of duty last night in volunteering his time to assist the police at the county fair. When the attack transpired, turning the fairground into chaos,

Paddy put his life at risk multiple times to save others. From there, he accompanied Chief Wolfe and members of his team to the nearby farm experiencing a separate attack, and continued his heroics in saving lives."

Chief Yazzie placed a hand on Paddy's shoulder. "Effective immediately, Patrick Kipp will take on the role of superintendent at Devil's Cradle State Park and will lead the local investigation."

A light round of applause greeted them as Malcolm shook Paddy's hand. Paddy gave a humble wave and nod of the head before turning back to join the rest of the team on stage. Malcolm leaned back into the mic. "I'll turn it back over to Chief Wolfe."

Seth returned to the podium and motioned to an area just off stage for three men to join him. Walking onto the stage were Seamus, Vince, and Cal, followed shortly thereafter by Joe. "In addition to the heroics displayed by my good friend Paddy Kipp, I'd like to take this opportunity to honor three men who displayed valor of the highest order."

Seth grabbed the mic off the stand and walked over to the first in line, Seamus. "If you've visited the Orbriallis Institute at any point in the last decade, you've likely been awestruck at the size and appearance of Seamus Owens."

"What do you mean by appearance, mate?" Seamus asked. "You referring to me good looks?"

Seth laughed. "That's right, I'm referring to your good looks." Seth turned to the audience. "Seamus Owens volunteered his time yesterday as an extra set of hands, giant hands at that, for security at the fair. When the attack happened, Seamus took it upon himself to usher many people to safety, reuniting children with their parents, and saving a group of children being led to safety by Officer Joe Casey over here," Seth said, motioning to Joe, "by literally tackling an owl midair believed to be approximately seven feet tall, weighing well over two hundred pounds."

Seamus shrugged. "Weren't nothing, mate."

Seth stepped next to Vince. "New head of security at the Orbriallis Institute, Vincent Lashley, also volunteered his time at the fair yesterday. Vince, who has an honored history in the Army as a field medic, put those skills to use by attending to every injured person at the fair before the paramedics arrived."

Seth moved onto Cal. "Many of you in the community might already know Cal Hensley, brother of our chief medical examiner, Wes Hensley. Cal is a former agent of the CDFW and is now a reservation officer. Cal has been assisting us in local investigations into wildlife attacks the past few weeks and also volunteered his time last night, not only at the fair but with us at the farm where further attacks transpired."

Seth walked back toward the podium and ushered Joe forward. "Myself, Mayor Sumner, and every member of the Lost Grove Police Department would like to present each of these men with the Civilian Medal of Appreciation for their acts of valor."

The crowd applauded, locals in the audience adding some whooping and hollering, as Joe presented each man with a medal.

After Seamus, Vince, Cal, and Joe exited the stage, Seth turned back to the audience. "We appreciate the public's patience and understanding. Please continue to follow updates from verified sources. If you see anything unusual, report it immediately. And we literally cannot stress enough times, stay out of the state park, stay out of the forest, and do not even attempt to hunt these creatures."

Then the questions came.

A reporter raised a hand. "Will the fair continue?"

Mayor Sumner answered, "Yes. The county fair will resume. We believe it's important to maintain normalcy. But extra precautions will be in place."

"So how do you know it won't happen again?"

"Based on the information provided by Director Reyes, we believe the immediate threat has passed. We're not taking this lightly."

"Do these animals have any connection to the recent events at the Orbriallis Institute?"

Seth's jaw tensed.

"There is no connection," Mayor Sumner interjected firmly.

Another shouted, "People online are saying this is just a hoax. A publicity stunt?"

"This is not a hoax," Mayor Sumner said calmly. "Again, we ask that the media be responsible and the public remain considerate. Lives were lost. This is a serious matter."

The flashing of cameras punctuated the air. More voices, more questions.

Somewhere on a Reddit thread, people were comparing the creatures to a species of prehistoric owls long since thought extinct. Social media was awash with footage of the night's events. Theories included portals, cryptids, and genetic experiments. Many were posting links to the news and leaked documents of Dr. Neil Owens and the Orbriallis Institute. Seth wondered if Lina and Jane were already working on a press release.

God, he wanted another cup of coffee and twelve hours of sleep. He wanted a quiet room. He wanted to wrap Story in his arms and hibernate. But instead, he braced himself for what came next. The news cycle would explode. The scientists would dig in. The town would never be the same.

Seth caught a glimpse of his reflection in a lens—drawn, exhausted, and still full of fight. Somewhere in the back of his mind, he knew the next wave wouldn't be wings in the night. It would be scrutiny, politics, and unraveling truth from speculation.

Chapter Forty-Five
What Remains

A halo of mist still lingered over Devil's Cradle State Park as reporters arranged their tripods and camera operators adjusted angles. The air was crisp with pine and memory. It was just shy of a month since the creatures took to the skies of Lost Grove, but the town had aged in the shadow of that night.

Seth made his way through the gathering outside the visitor center to rejoin Story, Peter, and Jolie, threading between news vans and curious tourists. He had just finished a call with Dr. Jane Bajorek, the final piece in a puzzle that still refused to form a full picture. The not-children, she said, had skin identical to the synthetic dermis the Orbriallis Institute had once developed for burn victims. So did the not-man, dubbed Teddy by Jane for documentation. Liam, once not-George, was also made of the same material.

While Dr. Bajorek didn't have any conclusive evidence as to where the not-children came from or why, she had a strong working theory that they were failed experiments by Dr. Owens and his private team set out to achieve what Geiger Orbriallis's ultimate goal had always been, creating a perfect child. Jane believed after hitting a brick wall, Owens pivoted to having women carry genetically modified fetuses for the same purpose, carefully choosing the candidates to carry them by their special gifts. Seth learned that it wasn't just Sarah Elizabeth who had these special gifts, but that Daisy Sutherland and Kelly Fulson were previously chosen for the same reason.

Seth was grateful for the sharing of information and findings, but he knew there was more he was not being told and likely never would be. For the time being, he was willing to live with that, because he had information that he was not sharing with her. In the week after the harrows at the county fair, Story and Mary had gone to the Institute to gauge what they could using their unique experience and abilities from the bodies of the not-children and Teddy. While Mary shared what she could with Jane about her observations of the not-children's skin and how it aged, Story had told her that she was unable to glean anything using her witchy powers, as Seth called them.

That information was for Seth and for anyone on his team he felt that it would be useful for. Because Story had seen. She saw from Teddy's eyes a vast desert landscape, men in suits, people in white head-to-toe coveralls, black cars with no license plates. She was unable to decipher the muffled dialogue being spoken around Teddy, but Story said, if she had to guess, he was once located in New Mexico. Seth was at the station when Story fed him this information and he immediately grabbed a burning-hot red pin and placed it on his map of the United States as a potential location for Dr. Neil Owens.

That was a pipedream for a different day. For now, his focus remained on the living—on the vacant badge Eddie Cabrera once wore and the growing demands of a police force that might soon double in size if Goldenvale was officially annexed. The mood was leaning toward a positive vote. He was already making calls, vetting new hires.

Seth reached out to County Sheriff Bernard Hayes for potential referrals, as well as Joe and Sasha for anyone they may have been close to in training. Seth's first call had been to Seamus, who respectfully declined, saying he "had it pretty good" at the Orbriallis, exactly as Seth expected. Cal Hensley, on the other hand, said he would seriously consider the offer.

Seth snuck up behind Story and wrapped his arms around her waist.

"I sensed you coming from thirty feet back," she said, kissing his cheek.

"Of course you did."

"You learn anything?"

"I'll fill you in later."

The platform ahead was draped in garlands of wildflowers and pine, a woven altar to survival and mystery. Mayor Diane Sumner stepped forward, dressed in a slate-grey suit, the weight of weeks behind her eyes.

The murmuring crowd came to a hush.

417

"Thank you all for being here," she began, her voice lifted clear above the hush of pine boughs. "Today, we reflect. We mourn. And we honor. The events of last month revealed more than just a hidden species. They revealed our fragility and our interdependence with the land. Devil's Cradle is not just a park. It is an ancient forest, alive and wild, and we must tread with respect."

She paused, letting her gaze sweep over the gathered crowd—locals, rangers in crisp uniforms, reporters with pens half lowered. Children shifted close to their parents. The wind moved gently through the trees, as if listening.

"There are things in this world older than our roads and fences. The land sometimes reminds us—abruptly, fiercely—that we are not its masters. We are its guests." She stepped away from the podium, hands now lightly gripping either side of it, her tone more intimate. "We grieve for those we lost. We celebrate those who stepped forward in courage. And we recognize that what we thought was wilderness is, in truth, a kind of shared home. One we must protect. One we must learn from, again, and again, if necessary." She gave a brief, reverent nod to the rows of tribal elders seated beneath a garland-draped canopy. "I want to thank the tribal councils who came forward to offer wisdom and help restore harmony. And I want to acknowledge the scientists and conservationists who have dedicated themselves to understanding the truth of what happened here—not to exploit it but to preserve it."

Then she straightened slightly, her voice rising with formal clarity.

"Which is why I'm honored to introduce someone whose work has long stood at the crossroads of science, ecology, and stewardship. Please welcome California Department of Fish and Wildlife Director Marisol Reyes."

Mayor Sumner stepped back as Marisol in a forest-green blazer approached the podium—tall, composed, and sun-browned from long hours spent in the field. She extended a hand as she climbed the platform.

Mayor Sumner took it without hesitation, and the two women shook.

"Thank you, Director," Diane said quietly.

"Thank you, Mayor," Marisol replied just as softly, then turned to face the waiting crowd as Diane stepped aside.

Marisol rested her hands on either side of the podium and leaned forward slightly. "Thank you all for coming here today," she began, her voice rich with clarity, measured but warm. "It means something—something real—that so many of you have shown up not just to witness, but to listen. What we experienced here was not merely an incident. Not merely a discovery. It was a collision—of ecosystems and towns, of old stories and new science, of mystery and fact. We do not often get the opportunity to witness the birth of a new chapter in natural history…but we are living it." She glanced toward the line of tribal elders, then back to the crowd. "It is rare that such a moment demands more than categorization or conservation. This one demands understanding. This discovery is of an unprecedented new avian order, never before documented. We have formally classified the species as *Strigaformes tah-tah-kle'ah*, a name given with permission from our tribal partners.

"We are entering a chapter where myth and science converge. It is our duty to protect these animals and the ecosystem that birthed them. We will continue research under strict ethical oversight and with partnership from the communities most affected. With that, I welcome Elder Mead of the Wiyot Nation."

They nodded to one another, as Marisol stepped aside.

"Welcome, friends. My name is Leo Mead, of the Wiyot people. It is good that you have come." His voice was clear and deeply resonant. "I stand here today not only as a witness to change but as one who remembers that this land has always been alive. The creature discovered in the deep hollows of the Cradle is not new to these forests, not to the wind or the trees or the stone. But it is new to your eyes. And so, we welcome it with caution, with respect, and with the knowledge that every step we take forward must be done gently." He let that breath carry through the gathered crowd before continuing. "There was another discovery made in the weeks following the long night. A place hidden within a cave and painted on the stone walls were our stories, long forgotten by most, even among my own people. The symbols found in the earth were once part of teachings long buried. But they rise again. We have begun work to preserve what was lost, to teach the stories that were nearly silenced.

"I wish to honor the spirit of the young woman who helped lead your eyes to these truths. Hannah Albrecht." He paused, looking out over the crowd with eyes heavy and kind. "She was not of our people, but she carried the old blood. She walked with respect. She listened to the land. She followed paths most would overlook, and for that, she gave her life. Let her name be remembered, not only in loss but in what was found.

We thank her. We thank her spirit. May she find peace among the trees she loved."

As Elder Mead stepped back from the podium, the hush he left behind lingered like incense. A few bowed heads remained still as a new figure approached. He nodded to Leo Mead in quiet respect before taking the podium.

"Hello and thank you for coming. My name is Samuel Tomkin, of the Yurok." His voice was softer than Mead's, but no less potent. "I thank you for holding silence with us. That silence honors more than the dead—it prepares the spirit for what comes next. We are not meant to control the land. We are meant to walk with it. But too often, we forget our place, and the land must remind us." He gestured gently toward the tree line, where the forest loomed like an old sentinel. "The ceremony we offer today is not for spectacle. It is for balance and healing. We dance for the wounded ground. For the disturbed spirits. For those who could not leave the dark without carrying it with them. And for those who gave their lives so the rest of us could stand here in peace." He stepped away from the microphone, and as he did, the first low drumbeat rang out deep and round as a heartbeat buried under soil.

Smoke rose from sweetgrass bundles, curling skyward in sinuous prayer. Dancers moved in slow rhythm, footsteps echoing with memory.

Noble kept Anya close, his arm around her shoulders. Anxiety pooled in his stomach on a daily basis. He was leaving soon. His classes had been chosen and he'd be flying to Tennessee in a matter of days, not weeks. The idea was thrilling, terrifying, and sad. Beside them, Nate, Stan, Ember, and Emory stood quietly. Stan and Ember's clasped hands went unmentioned, but not unnoticed.

Nate nodded at Anya. "Have you actually spoken to Nettie yet?"

Ever since Nettie had been arrested, she hadn't left her house or talked to anyone besides Anya, despite everyone else reaching out to see how she was doing. She had only exchanged curt text exchanges with Anya, revealing little. A court date was set, but there were still many unknowns as to what she'd officially be charged with and if she'd serve jail time.

"I did, actually," she said.

Everyone's eyes darted to hers.

"Really?" Stan said.

Anya nodded.

"What did she have to say for herself? Did she explain why she has ghosted the rest of us?" Nate asked.

"She's embarrassed. And she's ashamed. That guy she was with who was recently arrested, they were, I guess you could say, dating."

"Dating?" Stan asked, eyes wide.

"I wouldn't tell you this, but she told me she'd rather have me tell you than have to tell everyone individually, but he took her virginity and then obviously bailed on her."

"I'll fucking kill that dude," Nate exclaimed.

"Easy, tiger," Noble said. "You're an officer of the law."

"No, you're right, Nate. Fuck that guy," Stan said.

"I'll go find this guy with you," Emory said to Nate.

"Vigilante justice," Nate said, holding a fist in the air.

"Anyhow," Anya said, rolling her eyes, but secretly hoping they did, "just give her time, I think she's definitely past her rebellious phase. I told her that everyone is worried about her and cares for her. She promised she would reach out."

"Even to me?" Emory asked.

Anya shrugged. "I hope so."

"I feel like she hates me now that I work at the Orbriallis."

"I really don't think so."

"I still think we should just go crash her house and make her let us in," Stan suggested.

"How do you think she would react to that?" Noble asked his girlfriend.

"I guess we could find out," Anya said, wincing.

"That's it! We're going after the ceremony," Nate said and then pointed at Noble. "This dude is leaving, like next week. We can't have this aura hanging around us."

"Aura?" Stan said, raising an eyebrow.

"Yeah, you know, it's like the feeling that encompasses someone. Like awesomeness does me."

"Okay then," Stan sighed.

From across the parking lot, Cal Hensley moved through the crowd, approaching his niece and her group of friends. "Hey, kiddo," he said, wrapping her in a hug.

"Hey, old man," she said, her voice muffled by his shoulder.

His eyes roamed over each of her friends, all of them soon to be parted as their college adventures and times for departure grew dangerously close. "It's good of you all to come."

The kids nodded.

"I'll see you later for dinner?" he asked, already moving off.

"Yep!" Stan said, waving as he slipped into the crowd.

Cal found his way over toward Paddy, looking smart in his pressed uniform.

"Tonight, after eleven we can meet by the east trail, marker 46," Paddy said, his voice low.

Cal nodded. His mother got it stuck in her head that the darkness of the land needed to be cleansed, and while she didn't originate from these lands, Cal learned to listen to her gut. Especially considering the Tah-Tah-Kle'ah myth originated from her Yakama bloodline. So they planned on having another ceremony, different from the one they were presenting now for the cameras and the public eye. This ceremony might be for the cameras, but the land needed something deeper. Paddy moved on, spotting Noble in the crowd with one arm around his girlfriend and the other around his sister. He gave the boy a mock salute.

Noble smiled and turned back to Nate. "What did they say?"

"Focus, dude. They said the Orbriallis Institute was testing cryptid DNA. You believe that?" Nate asked the group.

"Bigfoot confirmed," Emory added, laughing. A thousand Reddit forums had popped up, all the footage was being scrutinized on YouTube, it had conspiracists coming out of the woodwork, which was part of why they were here now, making this public spectacle and reminding people to stay home.

"Stop reading those forums," Noble said. "All the weird shit they make up."

"I don't believe all of it," Nate defended. He gestured toward Anya. "But… I mean, she's proof of some of it, right?"

Stan punched his arm. "Dumbass."

Anya giggled. Her friends had been so supportive and understanding of what she was that she had started loosening up about it, sharing more and more details about her and her mother.

"Hollywood already bought the story rights," Emory said. "Documentary incoming."

"That's true," Nate said. "I think it was either HBO or Netflix."

"Of our town?" Zoe asked. "Of the fair and all?"

"I don't know, Zo." Nobel shrugged. "It probably won't happen."

"Or not for a while at least," Emory added.

"They'll definitely want to interview me," Nate said.

Zoe squeezed her hands tight and jumped up and down. "I'm gonna go tell Mom," she said, skipping back through the crowd to her mother's side.

"Grateful it didn't get worse," Peter muttered. "Fair ended without more surprises. That alone's a miracle."

Seth nodded but said nothing. Only Story knew he had brought her out in the dead of night to bless the fairgrounds with protective spells. She reached for his hand.

"Mom! Noble's friends said they're gonna make a documentary of our town," Zoe enthused.

"Is that so?" Jolie remarked.

Peter grinned. "And who told them that?"

"Reddit?" she said, one shoulder lifted.

"Don't listen to your brother's rumors," Jolie said, pulling her daughter's hair over one shoulder.

"It was Emory, not Noble," Zoe said offhandedly. "Can we get a soda?"

"Sure," Jolie said, taking her daughter's hand.

"I'll come with," Story said, but paused when she saw Mary stepping through the crowd. "Actually, I'll catch up," she said to Jolie as she waved at Mary and moved to join her.

"You look nice," Story said.

Mary fussed with her shirt and brushed invisible fluff from her skirt. "Too much?"

"Not if you're looking for someone," Story teased.

Mary flushed. "I'm not—this is because of Dr. Jane's instructions. And you pestering me all the time to follow them."

"Alright," she said. "Do you want to say hi to some people?"

"No." Mary's eyes went wide as Story dragged her through the throng of people.

They passed Peter and Seth.

"New dress?" Peter asked, grinning.

Seth just smiled, letting the moment pass. A flicker of her youngest sister Asterin's romantic dramatics glimmered in Story's eyes now and again and it softened something in him.

Peter glanced away. "Eddie's funeral was packed," he said quietly. "Didn't expect that many people."

Seth's smile faded, replaced with something closer to solemn pride.

"They came from every county. Some of them didn't even know him personally, just wanted to pay respects. Guess the idea of a man going down fighting monsters struck a nerve."

Peter nodded. "Yeah. They turned him into a folk hero. 'The Cop Who Took On the Owls.'"

"Better than what could've happened," Seth murmured. "I was scared they'd turn it into something ugly."

"They still might," Peter said. His gaze flicked to the news vans lining the edge of the lot, reporters still packing up gear like vultures that hadn't decided if the feast was over. "They're already pitching segments to national outlets. True crime podcasts. Monster hunters. Some girl tried to sell owl-feather earrings from 'the' owls on Etsy last week. It's all a circus."

"Welcome to Lost Grove," Seth muttered, rubbing his jaw. "Off-season tourism was supposed to taper. But instead, it's doubled. Hikers, cryptid chasers, influencers in wide-brim hats pretending they found the 'cursed trees.' You can't swing a pine cone without hitting a YouTuber."

Peter barked a quiet laugh, then sobered. "We're stretched thin."

"I know," Seth said. "Hayes sent over two names. Joe vouched for one of them, so maybe we'll get lucky. But for now..." He exhaled slowly, watching a drone buzz low over the treetops. "For now, I'm just keeping the seams stitched."

Peter eyed him sideways. "You okay?"

Seth offered a half grin. "Ask me again when the cameras are gone and the people stop asking if they can take home owl pellets as souvenirs."

Peter laughed again. "It's not all that bad, Chief."

"One guy tried to buy the fence post the creature scratched. Offered a thousand in cash."

Peter shook his head, marveling at the absurdity. "You think we're out of the woods yet with the string of batshit crazy events falling in our lap?"

Seth was quiet for a beat. The wind pulled softly through the pines. Somewhere beyond the stage, drums still echoed faintly.

"Probably not," he said honestly. He looked over at his sergeant, catching his eye. "But I've got people I trust, both inside and outside of the station. And I don't want to lose another one of them. Eddie's death—"

Peter's hand clapped his shoulder, warm and solid. "That's not on you. I've told you that. Not on any of us. Eddie went out like a hero. All things being equal, I think we did pretty good, Chief. We saved a hell of a lot more lives than we lost, and you led the way."

"Maybe so."

"It's not debatable. Look around us. Good has come out of it, and the town is repairing itself like it always does."

Seth nodded, eyes narrowing against the golden light drifting through the trees. He didn't know what came next, but Peter was right, a fragile kind of peace had settled over Lost Grove.

If you enjoyed reading *Blood on the Trailhead*, please consider giving an honest review on Amazon, GoodReads, and/or anywhere else where reviews can be found by readers like you. Reviews are extraordinarily important to both readers and authors alike, and each and every one is appreciated. *Thank you!*

Acknowledgments

We would like to thank Ben Brown, Director of the Cultural Department for the Wiyot Tribe, for generously sharing his time and guidance with us as we worked to portray the Wiyot community with respect.

Many thanks to Chief Ron Sligh and Sergeant Robert Lindgren of the Ferndale, California Police Department for answering our questions and sharing stories that may (or may not) sneak their way into future novels. Any resemblance to characters is purely coincidental...or is it?

Huge thanks to our copyeditor, Lisa Gilliam, who is always a treat to work with and who never fails to remind us that we really do have to stop naming every other character Greg.

Our thanks to all artists—past, present, and future. Your music becomes our soundtracks, your films our muse, your television our guilty pleasures, and your writing our ongoing reminder not only of how to craft a novel, but how to break the mold.

And finally, a note: any errors, liberties, or outright fabrications are entirely ours. The generous professionals we sought counsel from should not be blamed (though they're welcome to roll their eyes at us).

About the Authors
Charlotte Zang

CHARLOTTE ZANG writes dark fantasy, horror, and paranormal mysteries full of shadowed forests, twisted folklore, and morally gray people doing questionable things. She was raised in a small Midwest town and now lives in the Pacific Northwest with her movie-savant husband and three basset hounds, who have the emotional range of Shakespearean actors and the density of small planets.

She believes in the healing power of carbs, walking barefoot, writes like a gremlin, and deeply enjoys moody movie scores, disturbing folklore, and the occasional existential baking session.

If you'd like to talk about tragic love stories, 1980s Bowie, or which dog is currently lying on her keyboard, come say hi on Instagram @charlottezang or sign up for her newsletter at charlottezang.com.

Alex J. Knudsen

ALEX J. KNUDSEN was born in Minneapolis, Minnesota, and attended the University of Southern California. He first started writing in the third grade when he created the short story, Mr. Raquetball. He went on to write numerous unpublished short stories and a bevy of screenplays. Knudsen is the founder of Gantry Productions and is the writer-director of numerous films, including the Independent award nominated feature film, Autopilot and the award nominated short horror film, Consuming Beauty, which was adapted from his wife's novel of the same name. Knudsen is a self-taught mixologist and devourer of horror films. Alex currently lives in Oregon with his wife and three Basset Hounds. The Nawie is his first novel.

You can follow him on Instagram @knutzauthor and visit his website www.alexjknudsen.com.